High praise for Lee Killough's Garreth Mikaelian vampire novels!

"Killough can be looked to for surprises in plot."
— *Library Journal*

"*BloodWalk* is a terrific blend of mystery, fantasy, and the supernatural!"—*The Bookwatch*

"Before *Forever Knight* hit the small screen, Lee Killough's vampire detective Garreth Mikaelian walked the streets of San Francisco, searching for his killer. So what's so special about *BloodWalk*? What kept this book from disappearing into the out-of-print chasm that has swallowed so many other worthwhile novels? The answer is so simple, is sounds ridiculous, but the books are **fun** to read."—Glenn R. Sixbury, *E-scape*

"A fine blend of mystery and the supernatural. Who says you can't do anything original with the vampire story?"
— *S.F. Chronicle*

"Let's hear it for Meisha Merlin Publishing! Thanks to this Georgia-based publisher, Lee Killough's excellent vampire detective stories, *Blood Hunt* and *Bloodlinks*, are back in print after a hiatus of some ten years, *BloodWalk* is strong in both police procedure and character development...BloodWalk's final resolution is a testament to Killough's skill as a writer."
— *The Vampire's Crypt*

"One of the pleasures of Killough's fiction is persuasive characterization. If you're looking for a different kind of novel, this is it."—*Fantasy Review*

"Fantasy readers should appreciate Killough's variations on the standard form."—*Locus*

"Vampirism plays a strong motivation and plotting in *BloodWalk* but at its heart, this is a detective story—a police story worthy of McBain or Wambaugh."—*Baryon Magazine*

"Lee Killough's *BloodWalk* is a dark duet of previously unavailable vampire novels that have been resurrected for the enjoyment of readers of this genre or anyone seeking a vampire story with a different slant. Killough's writing blends supernatural elements with fantasy and mystery to create an alluring story with intriguing characters."—*Explorations*

"The police procedural segments of the tale are well written and the supernatural elements seem so real. However, it remains Garreth's internal struggle between entrance into one world while keeping a foot in the other that turns Lee Killough's vampiric story into a great book that will please the fans of vampire and police procedural novels."—Amazon.com

BLOOD GAMES

BY

LEE KILLOUGH

Meisha Merlin Publishing, Inc
Atlanta, GA

BLOOD GAMES

An MM Publishing Book
Published by Meisha Merlin Publishing, Inc.
PO Box 7
Decatur, GA 30031

Editing & interior layout by Stephen Pagel
Copyediting & proofreading by Teddi Stransky
Cover art by Kevin Murphy
Cover design by Neil Seltzer

ISBN: 1-892065-41-X

http://www.MeishaMerlin.com

First MM Publishing edition: May 2001

Printed in the United States of America
 0 9 8 7 6 5 4 3 2 1

For Denny...
who makes life special
and fills it with rainbows.

A special thanks to Officer Ryan Runyan for technical assistance and valuable input. Thanks, also, to Sergeant Stanley Conkwright and the other instructors of the Riley County Citizens Police Academy for twelve weeks of informative fun.

BLOOD
GAMES

1.

Later, Garreth Mikaelian wondered if he should have seen
the pain coming. Ingrained police habits in him insisted that
memory might just be revising itself in accordance with sub-
sequent events, but having grown up around his Grandma
Doyle and her Feelings, those uncanny visions of the future,
should he have sensed that his life was about to be ripped
apart once again?

The evening certainly began inauspiciously, with a cold
front permeating the Baumen Police Department headquarters. That despite the temperature outside remaining a stifling
ninety-five degrees. Voice flat, never once looking up from
her computer screen as she completed her final reports, Sergeant Maggie Lebekov briefed Garreth on current warrants
and the activity occurring on her shift.

Then she disappeared into the locker room with her duty
belt, reappeared a minute later carrying her shoulder bag, called,
"Good night, Sue Ann," to the Swing shift clerk/dispatcher,
and disappeared into the short hallway between the locker room
and Chief Danzig's office leading to the back entrance.

Pointedly excluding fellow officer and sometime lover
Garreth Mikaelian...though who could say he did not deserve it. Grimacing, he adjusted his own duty belt more com-
fortably on his hips and reached down for his briefcase sitting beside the desk.

"The thaw is later than usual this time 'round."

Garreth eyed Sue Ann Pfeifer over the top of his mirror-
lensed glasses. "You're keeping track?" A rhetorical question,
of course. In towns the size of Baumen everyone minded
everyone else's business.

Her plump face crinkled in a shameless grin. "What other office romance do we have to watch? And yours and Maggie's is like a soap opera." The telephone rang. "Police department. Oh, no...again?...Of course. Baumen Four," she said into her headset. "You go together, fight, break up, date other people— You're needed at Hammond's Greenhouses. Della Stott's locked herself out of her car again. Then you two break up with *them* and get back together. Seven times in sixteen years."

He stared at her. Sixteen years? A current of dismay trickled through him. That long? Somehow he had never counted the actual number of years he'd lived here.

She logged the call on her computer. "I asked Maggie why you keep doing this on/off, hot/cold, love/hate thing and she said that—Go ahead, Seven. Sorry, I can't run any DL's right now. The DMV files are down." She scribbled on a note pad. "I'll run it as soon as we're up again. She said that while nobody understands her the way you do, why she wants to be a police officer even more than having a family—though you know, she could have the kids, too, if you two got married."

He grimaced. "I've been married twice already. That's enough."

"Did you ever think the third time might be a charm? But anyway, Maggie says that what always ends up driving her crazy is you're always so guarded and never give her more than a hint of what you're feeling and thinking."

Hearing the words he saw Maggie's face, the hurt and anger in her eyes. He sighed. *Maggie...if only I could tell you everything.*

"I told her that from what I've seen you never have a whole lot to say and can't she just accept that you're the Gary Cooper type? Why would she even *want* you to talk about painful stuff like your second wife dying, and waking up in the morgue after that psycho woman in San Francisco attacked you, and being responsible for your partner out there almost dying? She said it isn't the past stuff that bothers her but the now stuff, like why you're always going out to the cemetery to the grave of that guy who used you and Ed Duncan for archery practice when you first came here and why you've never taken her out to California to meet your family." The phone rang. "Police department. Just a moment, please. Maybe she has a point. Why *haven't* you ever taken her to meet your parents?"

"I'd better hit the street." Carrying the briefcase, he headed for the rear entrance. "See you on the radio."

Outside he slogged across the parking lot to his patrol car. Even this near sunset, daylight remained crushing. He opened the briefcase on the passenger seat and belted it in place, then started the car and turned on the radio. To the accompaniment of Sue Ann's voice and traffic from Sheriff Offices in Bellamy and surrounding counties, he punched the row of rocker switches on the console between the seats and walked around the car checking his light bar and flashers, buzzed the siren, then made sure the shotgun was locked and loaded in its overhead rack.

But he ran the check automatically, his thoughts lingering on the conversation with Sue Ann. Why had he not let her meet his family? He grimaced, cold knotting his gut. Because that would reveal the lie he had been living here. That he came on false pretenses. He had claimed to be hunting his grandmother, Madelaine Bieber, who had been born here but after leaving had had his father out of wedlock and then abandoned the baby with her landlady. In reality he wanted Mada because living under the name Lane Barber, she had been the woman who attacked him in San Francisco. Dressed in men's clothing, she had also been the archer who attacked him here, but after he killed her in self-defense, he tampered with the evidence to conceal her identity. How could he tell Maggie that, and more, how could he reveal the real nightmare, that Lane had not merely tried to kill him in San Francisco but *had* done so. He re-lived the red glow of her eyes in the darkness of that alley, the pain of her teeth tearing out his throat, his terror as he lay in his blood listening to his heart and breathing stumble to a halt.

A tilt of the rearview mirror reflected sandy hair and a thin face, a face that in sixteen years had not changed, that in fact looked even younger than the twenty-eight years he had been when he came here. He pulled his glasses down his nose. Above the mirror lenses, his gray eyes caught the reflected rays from the setting sun coming in through the rear window. The eyes flared red.

Most of all, how in the world could he tell Maggie that Mada/Lane had made him a vampire?

He shoved the glasses back in place and readjusted the mirror. A few people knew about him...his ex-partner Harry Takananda, and Harry's wife Lien, who had accepted him without hesitation. His Grandma Doyle knew, too—a Feeling told her when he died—but that first visit home afterward she had run from him. *Dearg-dul* she called him, bloodsucker, and demanded to know why he still walked. That memory still stung. But when she learned not to fear him, she embraced him with a boundless love that time and again had been all that made his existence bearable. Could Maggie be like Grandma? Down-to-earth Maggie, skeptical of ESP and UFOs and the existence of things not quantifiable by weights and measures...He just could not bring himself to risk finding out.

Putting the car in gear he pulled out of the parking lot and east toward Kansas Avenue, Baumen's main street. An easing of pressure signaled coming night. Clouds overhead glowed in a spectrum of reds, bright copper in the west darkening eastward to blood red.

He grimaced. *My color.* Even if Maggie accepted that vampires existed, would she believe that he had never sucked anyone dry, that his blood came in the opaque plastic bottles in his refrigerator labeled as liquid protein health food, shipped to him by the carton from the Philos Foundation, a vampire-friendly blood bank chain?

He turned south on Kansas, into the thick of Friday night traffic. If he had not changed in sixteen years, neither had

Baumen. The local teenagers wore different faces, drove different cars, but those in town on Friday and Saturday night still spent the evening cruising Kansas Avenue...south to the Pizza Hut, across the railroad tracks running down the middle of Kansas, north to the Sonic Drive-In, then back across the tracks and south again, honking horns at each other and calling back and forth between cars, and passengers sometimes jumping out at the two traffic lights to change cars.

He burped the siren in warning at a pair of vehicles ahead running abreast with a girl hanging out the passenger window of the car in the inside lane toward the pickup in the outside lane. "Back in the car...and buckle up!"

The girl rolled her eyes but pulled back into her seat.

At the Pizza Hut corner he crossed the tracks along with everyone else and headed back up the other side of Kansas, one ear listening for his number on the radio. Leland Nancy, the newest addition to the department and one of the two officers working the Swing shift, requested car registration information. Sue Ann sent Ed Duncan, the other Swing officer, to take a car burglary complaint. A Bellamy County deputy called an open pasture gate in to his office.

The sun slid below the horizon, but even with that release and his deep breath of relief, a sense of pressure lingered, disquiet prickling in his gut and along his spine. About Maggie? About time? Well, he would sort it out later.

Past the Sonic, the northbound lanes ended. But instead of crossing the tracks with the cruise traffic, he turned off, passed the railroad station, and swung into the sale barn parking lot.

The sale barn sat idle this time of night, but not its parking lot. The ritual here, too, remained untouched by time. Summer evenings it filled with pickups and horse trailers and riders warming up horses as they waited their turn to practice in the rodeo arena. They had just four more weeks before the county fair and rodeo down in Bellamy at the end of August. A calf scrambled for the far end of the arena with a horse and rider in pursuit, while in the field beyond several girls took turns barrel racing. Near the bleachers, a barrel suspended between four posts served as a practice bull, with four grinning cowboys making it buck by hauling on the attaching ropes. Laughter and groans reached Garreth from the group at the barrel as the boy on it lost his grip and nose-dived into the surrounding mattresses.

A horse halted outside Garreth's window…too close for him to see more than a bay shoulder and the rider's leg, but he recognized the leg. "Evening, Nat."

"How's it going?"

Sweat darkened the hair around the leading edge of the saddle. Its acid scent and that of the horse drifted in through the window, strong enough to almost mask the blood scents of horse and rider.

Garreth's disquiet sharpened. Lieutenant Nathan Toews had been Sergeant Toews when Garreth first came. The department had probably changed more than the rest of Baumen: personnel retiring, others promoted, new faces joining, blue uniforms replacing the old tan ones.

Another rider landed on the mattresses.

Garreth shook his head. "Those guys are crazy."

"And you're *not*?" Nat said. "*Inviting* the bulls to chase you?"

"Call it just more serving and protecting." The increased speed and faster reflexes that came with being a vampire kept him well out of danger. Capering around in his comic sheriff's costume, though, big plastic star on his chest, while he drew bulls away from fallen riders, gave him a chance to let loose, his physical prowess applauded rather than arousing envy or speculation. And it gave him a way to join a community activity, to feel, almost, that he belonged.

"Which only confirms that you're crazy. Have a safe tour." Nat legged the bay into a jog and off across the parking lot.

Sue Ann's voice came over the radio. *"Baumen Five, we have a domestic at 230 South 3rd."*

Garreth groaned. The Snyders again! Give him a charging bull any time over that crazy old couple. But he sighed, "Ten-four," and put the car in gear.

For a change no screams or breaking crockery greeted his approach to the house. A neighbor hovered near a tree in the front yard...probably the reporting party. She rushed to meet him. "Thank goodness you're here! He's got a knife and he's threatening to use it!"

Turnabout. Last time *she* had been waving the knife at *him*. "But Mrs. Snyder is all right so far?"

"Oh, he isn't threatening Marilyn. I heard him yell that he's going to kill *himself* and make a mess of the living room! That's when I called you people."

A change of venue, too. Usually they squared off in the kitchen.

Inside Mrs. Snyder's voice sneered. "Go ahead and try to kill yourself. You won't. You know very well you can't stand pain." Garreth pictured her with arms crossed over the generous bosom that together with her rosy-cheeked plumpness and white hair made her look, incongruously, like a Mrs. Santa Claus.

He peered through the front window. Mr. Snyder stood in the middle of the all-white living room with the point of a butcher knife against his throat. Bent with age but still near six feet tall, he glared through the strands of hair falling down his face. "I can take it if it'll hurt *you!*"

Garreth tried the door. Unlocked. Gingerly, he pushed it open. In this situation he had legal entry and even as a vampire he had long ago secured free access to the house, but he still never touched a house door without remembering the searing agony barring him from entering any dwelling uninvited the first time...and how Harry Takananda almost died because of it.

As he stepped into the hall the blood scents of the couple enveloped him, warm, salty, Snyder's edged with the acid tang of emotion-produced adrenalin. "Good evening, Mrs. Snyder. What seems to be the problem tonight?"

She stood in the archway between the hall and living room, arms folded. "Hello, Officer Mikaelian. Do come in out of the heat."

Mr. Snyder shouted, "Go away!"

"Don't pay any attention to him." Mrs. Snyder smirked. "Now there's two of us to watch this peckerwood make an even bigger fool of himself than usual!"

Garreth hung his glasses on his pocket. Having stepped on the land mine of this domestic situation, he needed every tool available to step off without detonating it.

Mrs. Snyder said, "But three is even better. You come in, too, Alice."

Garreth swore silently as the neighbor followed him inside. An audience might make it impossible for Snyder to back down.

Already Garreth smelled a new charge of adrenalin in the blood scent from the old man. Through the archway he saw Snyder's grip tighten on the knife handle. "I'll show you, you damned harpy!"

In one flash Garreth envisioned the point breaking the old man's skin, followed by his yelp of pain and dropping the knife. Smearing blood on the carpet. At which Mrs. Snyder would explode...but probably at Officer Garreth Mikaelian, blaming *him* for the damage to her carpet.

He stepped into the living room...positioning himself where he could watch both of the couple. "Mr. Snyder!" As Snyder focused down at him, Garreth stared into Snyder's eyes. "Wait. We don't want anyone hurt here." The fixing of Snyder's gaze told him he had control of the old man. "Listen to me. Put...down...the...knife."

Snyder's grip on the knife eased. He reached toward a table.

So far so good. But he could not relax. There remained Mrs. Snyder to neutralize, and strong-willed, she never yielded easily and never without hard eye contact.

Even as he turned toward her, though, she snorted in the laugh that preceded one of the barbs Leland Nancy had dubbed her *coup de taunts*. "That's right...use any excuse that comes along to give up. Rather than be a man, you let this kid—"

"Mrs. Snyder!" Damn her! He caught her eyes. "Be...quiet! And stay right where you are!"

"You can't talk to my wife—"

"*Freeze, Snyder!*" The motion in his peripheral vision halted. Adrenalin blasting icy hot through him, Garreth snapped his gaze back to Snyder...to the fury twisting the old man's face, the foot sliding along the carpet in a step his direction...the hand frozen in the act of swinging forward with the knife. Garreth stared into Snyder's eyes until he hoped the old man felt impaled. "*Don't...you...move...one...muscle!*"

Snyder petrified until even his breathing seemed to stop.

Garreth wrenched the knife away. "What the f—" He caught himself...took control of his anger. "That was really really stupid! I might have shot you!" And been fully justified in doing so, but cold washed him just thinking of it...Snyder bleeding out on the carpet, the white room splattered with blood, Alice Brede screaming. The vision edged his voice in steel. "Put your hands behind your back!"

Moving mechanically, Snyder obeyed.

While Garreth slapped on the cuffs, he caught Mrs. Snyder's eyes again. "Both of you listen to me! Mr. Snyder is going to jail, and it's *your fault*, Mrs. Snyder. If you hadn't opened your mouth this could have been resolved quietly. You think about that when your husband is in court charged with assaulting a law officer. I'm taking him out to the car now and you *will not* interfere, Mrs. Snyder. You will stand right there with Mrs. Brede and not move until I drive away. Okay, let's go."

Every nerve alert, Garreth caught Snyder's arm and propelled him out of the living room past Mrs. Snyder and the gaping neighbor. Mrs. Snyder did not move.

He left the front door open so he could keep watching behind him. But Mrs. Snyder remained motionless, and when he had Snyder secured in the back seat and his key in the ignition of the patrol car, Garreth finally started breathing again.

With Snyder downtown locked down for the night, the rest of the evening passed with routine calls, with brief amusement rescuing Duncan from a Rottweiler that had come over the fence from its own yard to tree him while he investigated a prowler complaint at the neighbor's house. For Garreth the dog quit trying to scramble into the tree after Duncan and flung itself on its back at his feet, tail stub a frantic metronome. Then it meekly followed him back to its own yard.

Duncan slid to the ground and brushed bark from his trousers. "Damn dog was jumping around so much I couldn't hit it with the pepper spray. Cody is lucky, my cousin or not, I didn't just shoot it. I don't know why you won't show the rest of us your trick for making animals and people roll over for you. Well, I'm off to check doors and gates along 282. Chances are the Donnelly boy and Pfannenstiel girl are parking behind the Co-op just about now." He wiggled his eyebrows. "She is *so* hot. You don't know what you're missing by running your light bar and giving these couples time to dress before approaching them."

Staring after Duncan, Garreth remembered Sue Ann once saying in exasperation, "*What a jerk. Sometimes I'd like to deck him.*"

"*Don't,*" he had told her. "*Besides the paperwork that would make, he does have this birth defect.*"

She had blinked. "*Birth defect?*"

"*Being born with an asshole where his brain should be.*"

Her remembered laughter followed Garreth back on patrol.

Duncan and Nancy went off at midnight, leaving Garreth alone for his last four hours. The cruise traffic had petered out when the fast food places closed. The few cars still parked along Kansas belonged to youthful offenders pushing curfew and hard-core drinkers determined to close down the bars, the only businesses still open.

An office light still shone at Duerfeldt Chevrolet, how-ever. Garreth pulled into the lot and tugged on the show room door. Locked. The light might have been left on accidentally. But just in case he walked around the building checking each door and playing the beam of his flashlight across the cars in the rear lot. All seemed in order.

Back around in front, Garreth found John Duerfeldt, the dealership owner, peering out of the show room. He unlocked the door, forehead smoothing. "I hoped from the car there it was you I heard walking around back."

"You're working late tonight."

Duerfeldt grimaced. "Employer wage reports to the state. I need to move to a planet with, oh, a forty hour day."

Garreth nodded in sympathy. "Do you know your car isn't anywhere outside?"

"Today I'm driving a 'Vette we got in trade and I pulled it inside the garage." He frowned. "While we have pretty good kids around here, I'm not so sure about the ones who come up from Bellamy and I hate to tempt them." He cocked a brow at Garreth. "You ought to take this car for a test drive. You'd love it...a '78 T-top Indy Pace Car replica. One of only 6500 built."

Only one car in the area fit that description. But what would make Hal Landreth ever sell his beloved 'Vette, symbol of recapturing his youth? "Does it have an engine anymore?"

Duerfeldt raised a brow. "As a matter of fact, it has a brand new one, aluminum V-8, 375 horsepower. Mr. Landreth remarried and I guess started feeling more responsible. Any-way, he traded for a minivan."

The 'Vette for a *minivan*? That had to qualify as some class of blasphemy.

"I know it's older than your 280 ZX," Duerfeldt said, "but as long as you have Helen Schoning for a landlady, she might as well help you keep a hotter car running. Every time I see her driving that old Rolls I think what a waste to have all that mechanical talent clerking for the Municipal Court. She should have been born either a boy or a generation later. We can make you a good deal on the ZX."

Except, as much as the 'Vette tempted him, how could he ever give up the car he and Marti bought together? While he kept it, he still held a piece of her...and the last time in his life he could call himself truly happy. "I'll think about it. Good night, Mr. Duerfeldt."

The next time he passed that end of Kansas, the office light had gone out.

After the bars shut down at one, followed by the inevitable handful of discussions with citizens about walking home rather than driving, nothing moved downtown but him and a couple of cats prowling along the tracks. When Garreth walked both sides of Kansas and the alleys behind at about two, checking doors, the disquiet he had managed to ignore through most of the evening returned in force, raising goose bumps on his arms and neck, and he found himself repeatedly glancing over his shoulder. When the cats clashed, squalling, over some mouse or cricket, he started, heart pounding. Why? He always enjoyed this time of night. Only the occasional barking dog or distant yipping of coyotes broke the silence. A breeze coming in from the prairie swept away the lingering reek of exhaust fumes, replacing it with the scents of grass and dust. Little but static came over his radio, often going ten and fifteen minutes between calls, and those just Sheriff Office traffic or time checks from Doris Dreiling, his Graveyard dispatcher. So what spooked him so much tonight?

"Garreth."

He whipped around at the familiar voice. About eight feet away stood Grandma Doyle. But that was impossible! She lived with his parents in California. She could not possibly be here, and certainly not dressed in just a nightgown. Could he be experiencing something like one of her Feelings? Except none had ever happened to him before. "Grandma? What—"

"I couldn't leave without saying goodbye to me favorite grandson and warning you."

Then he understood. She was doing this, not him. Her vision must be a terrible one for her to come to him like this. She had never done anything like it before. "What do you see?"

"A man...evil...pale as Death with eyes of blood. He brings death and pain. And he can destroy you!"

Garreth went icy. "Do you know—" Then the question died as her first words hit him. Say goodbye? Panic blasted him. "Grandma! No! Don't!"

She smiled. "I must."

He started toward her, feeling as though a knife ripped upward through him. "No! Don't leave me! Let me come out there and—"

A shake of her head cut him off. "No. I know you mean well, but...the price of forever's too high. Besides, I've never stopped missing me darlin' Jamie, and he's calling me. When you're weary of forever, no matter how long that tis, remember it'll be just a moment of Eternity and we'll both be waiting to welcome you."

He wanted to plead with her, to beg for more time, but his throat had closed tight, strangling all speech. He could only shake his head desperately.

She seemed to know his thoughts, however. She sighed. "I'm sorry for the pain I'm causing. But I leave you me love, me dear poor *dearg-dul*, and a gift to protect you." She blew him a kiss.

And then only he and the cats stood on the street.

Garreth raced for the patrol car, to find a phone and call home.

2.

The wake filled his parent's house in Davis and overflowed into the front and back yards. Grandma Doyle had left instructions on her bedside table to throw an Irish wake for her, even including money and a guest list for it. She wanted her life celebrated, she wrote, not mourned. And judging by the noise level, Garreth reflected, everyone had taken her wish to heart. Everyone but him. He felt...adrift, lost. And along with daylight dragging at him, the noise and smells knotted his stomach and made his head pound—a flood of blood scents, two groaning tables of food, two with beer kegs and cases of Irish whiskey. Would anyone notice if he sneaked off?

"Garreth?"

He forced a smile at the pouter-pigeon woman bearing down on him. Iris something. One of his mother's cousins.

She enveloped him in pillowy arms and blood scent. "It's so good to see you again after all this time, though I thought you must be Brian until your mother corrected me."

Obviously she had not seen his son in a long time, either. Brian had three inches and seventy pounds on him.

Iris Something kept chattering. "You're certainly looking good. Is there a fountain of youth in—wherever it is you're working now?"

He grimaced inwardly. How many variations on *that* remark he had heard the past week? "Just plenty of clean air. You haven't changed either."

But of course she had. They all had. Though when had it happened...his parents aging, his brother Shane losing hair? And when had Harry Takananda acquired iron-grey hair and jowls?

Peering around, he spotted his old partner at the bar and shouldered through the crowd that direction. "What do you think of all this, Harry-san?" He raised his voice to be heard.

Harry grinned. "I thought *cops* have loud parties. I'm surprised the neighbors aren't complaining."

"That's because everyone in a two block radius is probably *here*. You can see why even though she died last Friday, we waited until this Saturday for the wake. Everyone she wanted to attend are here and tomorrow everyone can sleep in or go to church and ask forgiveness for their drunken excesses. What say we go outside and find some place we can carry on a conversation in a normal tone of voice?" He would take even daylight over being in here. Now someone had started singing, too, and even if the singer had been sober enough to actually carry a tune, Garreth could not bear another rendition of "My Wild Irish Rose", or "Rose of Tralee," or, god knew, "Danny Boy."

"Well, actually..." Harry topped off his glass and set down the bottle of Tullamore Dew. "...I just came over for a refill and was figuring on going back to the cop corner there. I'm surprised you're not there, too."

With his father interspersing the war story exchange with announcements about how well Shane's college coaching was going and how Brian made all A's his first year in law school and was interning in the San Francisco DA's office this summer, but his only son to become a cop kept turning down promotion to sergeant because it would mean giving up working nights? Garreth's stomach knotted. No, he had heard enough of that this past week. *It's really all about not being willing to take on responsibility, isn't it? You divorced Judith; you let her second husband adopt Brian and raise him; you quit the force in San Francisco before they could discipline you for getting Harry shot; and you've buried yourself in a nothing department in the middle of nowhere and even there you refuse to try to make rank. I just don't understand. I never thought a son of mine would be a quitter.*

Garreth made himself smile at Harry. "Maybe later. I'm going to circulate some more."

He thought about looking for Lien. She, at least, had hardly changed. The smile in her eyes remained undimmed, her skin still smooth, her helmet of black hair just shot through with grey. But along with many of the other women here, she probably hovered over Judith's mid-life surprise twins.

"Man, what a blowout," said a voice at his shoulder. Garreth looked up to find a grinning Brian beside him. "I don't even know most of these people."

"Me either," Garreth said. Brian had changed the most of all, of course. Grown up. And Garreth liked what saw. Judith and Dennis did a good job raising him.

"How did Grandma Doyle even meet some of them? Have you see that Russian girl? What a babe!" Brian's voice went conspiratorial. "I heard she's staying in San Francisco with the Takanandas. I wonder for how long. And if she'd go out with me."

The skin prickled on Garreth's neck. Brian's relaxed familiarity thrilled Garreth after all the years of stiff formality during their brief visits. He wanted nothing to spoil the camaraderie. Somehow, though, he had to caution Brian about Irina. Not that he feared harm to Brian, but she had, after all, brought Lane Barber across to the vampire life and despite helping found the Philos Foundation so vampires could live without hunting, she might still enjoy taking some of her blood warm. "If so, you'll find her very interesting. I do. She's been places and seen things and people we've only read about in books." Five hundred years of history. "But...some things you ought to know about her first—and please don't think I'm trying to go paternal."

Brian laughed. "Are you kidding? It's weird but I have a hard time keeping in mind that you're my father. I mean, I look at you and it's more like we're...cousins or something."

The goose bumps sharpened. Did that explain the change toward him? "Okay, consider this a cousinly FYI, then. She's been on her own since fourteen and sometimes had to live by prostitution, and she told me that she ran away from home because she engineered the death of a man who raped her." The vampire who forcibly brought *her* over.

Brian's eyes widened. "Whoa! Did Grandma Doyle know?"

"Yes." Garreth raised a brow. "Grandma never let a person's past stand in the way of friendship. You shouldn't either. Just...don't forget that past. And now if you'll excuse me; I have to get out of here for a while."

The back yard brought instant relief. Fewer people over-flowed here, so the noise level dropped and the smells thinned. Long shadows and a red sky promised imminent sunset, too. The ground at the foot of the big oak called to him...cool, shaded. But sitting there invited people to talk to him. So he climbed the dangling rope ladder to the platform high in the oak's branches...and pulled the ladder up after him.

Some of the planks looked new, as did the guardrail around the edge. Garreth ran his hand along the rail...admiring the satiny perfection of the sanding, enjoying the scent of wood preservative. For forty years his father had meticulously main-tained the tree house, keeping it safe for children and grand-children, and soon probably great-grandchildren. He stretched out on the planks and lay staring up into the thick canopy of leaves overhead. Warm contentment seeped through him. How many hours had he and Shane spent up here...on pirate ships and space ships, destroyers, castle towers, and indian forts. Later Garreth read and studied here. Shane sneaked girlfriends up. The one time Garreth tried he had been caught because the girl's bra fell over the side. And his grandmother found it. No waiting until his father came off duty for that lecture. Grandma Doyle had delivered it herself as soon as she sent the girl packing, and he still cringed before her remembered fury.

The memory blasted away his contentment, bringing back the flood of grief. Here in solitude he could give himself up to it. Pressure on him vanished, signaling sunset, but he still felt crushed by a blackness even darker and deeper than the one when Marti died. Then, at least, he had been numbed by shock. Nothing blocked the raw pain this time. How could she die? She knew how much he needed her, to know she was there for comfort and encouragement. *Her* mother had lived to almost a hundred. Grandma Doyle should have, too.

The anger in that thought, the sense of betrayal, startled him. But how could she abandon him with only some un-named "gift" and that warning!

Apprehension trickled into his misery. As pale as death with eyes like blood? A real person? Or something symbolic of death?

And then a sense of another presence interrupted the specu-lation. He looked around to see Irina sliding under the guard-rail onto the platform.

At his glance toward the pile of rope ladder she sighed. "No, I do not defy gravity and fly like movie vampire. I have, of course, learned to free climb. A most useful skill on occasion. You should learn." Sitting down cross-legged on a corner of the platform, framed by the branches behind her, she seemed more elfin than ever, and every bit fourteen rather than the twenty her clothes and cosmetics aimed for. The ears half-seen though her artful tousle of sable hair looked almost pointed, and violet eyes dominated the delicately Slavic face. She glanced around, frowning. "You should not be here."

He sat up. "Why not!" Her disapproval sharpened the anger he had discovered in his grief. "How did you find me?"

She shrugged. "Blood calls to blood. You sensed my pres-ence also, I think." Without waiting for him to confirm or deny she said, "This is childhood place, yes?"

"What's wrong with that?"

If his anger disturbed her, she showed no sign. She scooted closer, frowning, choosing her words. "This is past. You can-not cling to past. You must move on."

Cold seeped through him. "I don't know what you're talking about."

"I think you do. Listen, child." She leaned toward him. "I understand your pain. I have experienced it, too. Not only did you love her and she you, but she knew you for what you are and accepted you wholly anyway. Losing such persons is hardest."

The words reverberated in him. Yes. She had nailed the reason he hurt so much. One of the few people with whom he could be open and he had lost her. Tears started to choke him. "I begged her to let—" He sucked in a breath, fighting the constriction in his throat. "She said the price of forever is too high."

Irina took a deep breath. "Grania was very wise. If there are truly old souls reborn over and over, she must be one because with her I felt almost like sisters." To his surprise, a tear spilled down her cheek. "I will miss her greatly, too. But...I will also let her go. Because we will never look in mirror and see we have grown old, is hard for us to accept aging and death. But you must. She has died. They will all die. Your handsome son who looks like your brother today will one day look like your father. You will become contemporary with your grandchildren. Grania understood one price of our existence is standing rooted while time carries away all we know and love."

He turned to ice, though ice shot through with unbearable pain.

It must have shown in his face. Irina reached out to grab his hands. "Child, hear me. To survive we must accept and go on. Love can come again...though always loss again, too."

He thought of Lane, attacking but letting him live to come across, then offering him the world. "What about a vampire companion?"

"As Mada intended you to be?" She jerked her hands back. "No! Think. Do you really wish to bring another to this life? You and I were forced to it, and we have both hated our rapists...and destroyed them."

No, of course he would not dream of forcing this life on someone else. The recorded suicide note of one Christopher Stroda, brought across after a car crash by a travel companion who wanted to save his life, still sometimes haunted his dreams. "But what if someone fully informed consents...or asks..."

The violet eyes flashed. "Mada asked. And innocent people paid for my acquiescence with their lives. No, do not repeat my mistake."

She was right of course. He nodded.

"Now, other reason I came up. Why do you remain in Baumen? You planned to stay only while Mada's mother still lived, I believe. Well...she has died four years ago, yes?"

Cold ran through him again. "Well, yes, but—"

"But now you are settled in?" Her tone chided. "You have friends, comfortable routines that let you pretend you are like everyone else but for unusual dietary needs? Child, leaving is difficult, I know, but you must. You know in time your perpetual youth will be noticed and arouse dangerous curiosity. Perhaps is true already, you have remained so long."

He frowned. "I don't know that I can afford to move on a small town cop's salary."

She clucked her tongue. "You will go to Hell for lying. What of Mada's two hundred thousand her mother willed you?"

He started. How the hell did she know about that? "It's wrong to use that. I shouldn't even have it."

Irina frowned. "Of course you should. Consider it reparations for destroying your life. And as her blood son, is natural that all her estate comes to you."

One word reverberated in his head. "What do you mean, all?"

Irina grinned. "However naive, he observes well. My innocent, do you think Mada kept only one account? Financial security comes of diversity. Mada made herself very secure. I have located everything and transferred it to you."

He stiffened. "What! No! I don't want it."

The violet eyes flashed. A knuckle thumped him on the head as Grandma Doyle used to do. "Don't be foolish. You will need it. Is too late to refuse anyway. Everything is already in your name."

He stared at her. "That's impossible."

She sighed. "Why do children never believe their elders? Listen...I am expert forger—a skill you need to learn also. When next they check signature cards, they will find yours on them. Not accounts in your name, but each alias signed in your handwriting. And changing names on accounts requires only clever hacking. Learning this skill is why you have taken my suggestion to become computer literate, true?"

"You shouldn't have done it." But his protest sounded weak in his ears. He felt trapped.

She rolled her eyes. "So you say now. In fifty years, hundred years, tell me so. Now—" She stood in a smooth motion. "—we will rejoin the wake and toast Grania Megan Mary O'Hare Doyle, old, dear soul. I have with me a vintage we can enjoy. Is disrespectful to her memory to wallow in misery. She wished, deserved, to be celebrated. I'll bring financial records to you in Baumen. But—" She stared hard down at him. "—you must plan for leaving there."

"I'll think about it," he said.

3.

The wake seemed a lifetime away, not just the day before. Maybe because it felt so comfortable coming back on duty after the torture of a week at home ducking meals and his father. He certainly liked the unreserved warmth of Sue Ann's smile.

"Welcome back, Garreth."

Nice. On the other hand, he had never heard quite that lilt in her voice before. What gave? He checked his locker with care before opening it. She did not generally play practical jokes, and setting up someone coming back from a funeral seemed more Duncan's style, but...it paid not to take chances. The padlock appeared untampered with. No fire extinguisher foam showed through the louvers in the door. The catch slid up without obstruction. He eased the door open. Nothing gross fell out. No one had stuck cotton balls to the hook side of the Velcro fastener on his duty belt. In fact, the locker appeared just as he left it.

Wrapping the duty belt around him, he returned to the office. "Sue Ann, not that you aren't always cheerful, but...what's up?"

She turned from her communications console and winked. "I think it's spring."

He blinked. "What?"

Maggie banged in through the rear entrance. "Sue Ann, that key pad on the door still isn't working right. I had to punch the combination twice before—Garreth!" He found himself wrapped in leanly muscular arms and the sweet scents of her skin and blood. "I'm so sorry about your grandmother. And I'm sorry I didn't have the chance to see you and say anything before you left for California. And—" She shoved him backward into the locker room and turned the lock behind her. "—I'm so glad you're back."

Apparently. Her kiss knocked his glasses sideways. Recovering from his surprise, he pulled them off so he could participate without interference. No matter that in wrapping his arms around her he felt mostly the body armor under her shirt, the feel and taste of her brought a warm flood of pleasure...followed by a surge of desire as he responded to the urgency of her mouth. Only when his arms banged into the lockers and the cases on her duty belt ground into his torso did he realize he had lifted her off her feet and she had wrapped her legs around him.

Moving his mouth back far enough to talk he said, "Sergeant Lebekov, is it your intention to incite me into having you right here up against the lockers?"

She sighed deep in her throat and tightened her arms and legs. "I'd like nothing better. We're such fools—well, I'm a fool. Life is too short to waste wanting more than you can give me. But...I suppose I better wait until you're off duty." She unwrapped her legs. "What say I have the bed at your place warmed up and waiting?"

"That'll be—" No word he could think of sounded superlative enough. "It's a date." With a last hard kiss, he made himself release her, then taking a deep breath to clear his head, headed for the door

"Just one more thing."

He glanced back.

She grinned. "Better carry your briefcase in front of you on the way to the car."

As he left the locker room, Sue Ann eyed him with satisfaction. "I was right. Winter's over."

4.

Warmed up and waiting? Any warmer and the bed would catch fire. She met him naked at the door of his apartment over Helen Schoning's garage, pulled him inside and across the room by his uniform shirt, hauling it off him in a rip of Velcro, followed by the Velcro on his belt ripping open. Her mouth fastened on his. By the time they reached the bed his zipper had also yielded to her urgency. He peeled out of trousers and boxers faster than he could ever remember before, giving thanks that his boots zipped, too...and that he had drained his thermos before coming upstairs. Even with his hunger satisfied, the pulse pounding in her throat brought a surge of appetite that made his teeth ache, while the rest of him ached at the scents of skin and blood rising from her like steam. He fell onto the bed with her, letting the steam envelop him.

Later, lying in contented lassitude against her back in the tangle of sweat-soaked sheets, he re-lived the tumultuous session. That had to be the reconciliation of all time. His back stung where she scratched him and even *his* muscles might feel the strain tomorrow. Forget his promise to Irina; he could not think of leaving now. He refused to hurt Maggie.

True, he needed to be careful. She had given him a terrible moment when she started to bite his shoulder. He had quickly turned her head and kissed her, but he still went cold at the possibility of her touching his blood.

According to Lane, vampires carried a retrovirus. The small amount present in saliva rendered a single bite harmless to a healthy human, but give that human vampire *blood* with its high concentration of virus, as Garreth had received by biting Lane in defense during her attack, and that person became incurably infected, the retrovirus waiting in every cell for death to let it assume power. If Maggie continued this intensity of passion, he needed to watch out for her teeth.

One thing he could not help wondering, however much he welcomed this gift horse: Why did the death of his grandmother give Maggie this acute sense of mortality? It seemed too distant to affect her. Had she lost someone close and just not told him yet?

He buried his nose in the nape of her neck and ran a hand down her side over the curve of her hip, admiring how well she had maintained physical condition. Only grey in her hair and lines in her face hinted at her age. He breathed in the scents of her skin and blood, savoring them.

And then fear socked him in the gut. Free from the heady distraction of sex, now he registered the actual substance of those scents. Another breath, long and slow and analytical, confirmed his suspicion. Her blood smelled different than it had in the past...wrong...tainted. By what he had no idea, but presumably Maggie knew, and feared it. He thought of Grandma Doyle's vision. Could the pale man be Death itself...coming for Maggie? He gathered her tighter against him until dawn, smelling the taint of whatever and feeling chilly darkness swirl around them.

Maggie woke with sunrise as usual, as he once had, but this time did not dress and slip away before the neighbors woke up, leaving him free to escape daylight in sleep, settling into his micro fiber pallet with diamond-shaped quiltings containing not magnets, like the mattress pad it resembled, but earth. Instead, she rolled over and pressed against him. "In this weather I wish I had your low body temperature. But sleeping with you is next best...like tucking against a body length cool-pack." Her lips worked their way up his neck and along his jaw while her hand slid to his groin. "How about an eye-opener?"

But this time he clearly smelled the fear in her. He stopped her hand and pulled back enough to see her face, though without looking her in the eyes. Let her choose to talk, if she would. "Suppose you tell me what's wrong."

"There's something wrong with wanting to make love to you?" Maybe she intended to sound sarcastic, but the words emerged as defensive.

He ticked his tongue. "Come on, Maggie, you know that isn't it." Fortunately he had a ready way to explain his knowledge. "I've been a cop too long not to recognize the body language of fear. What is it you want to use sex to deny?"

She jolted as if slapped, then with a shudder, buried her head against his chest. "I found...a lump...in my breast..."

Which explained everything. Her mother had died of breast cancer at about this same age.

"I have an appointment in Hays this morning for a mammogram and needle biopsy. And I'm scared to death what they'll find."

He wrapped his arms tight around her, feeling her terror. His own gut knotted. "I know."

She pulled back to look up at him. "Garreth...I don't think I can face this by myself and I haven't had the courage to tell Dad yet. I know it's asking a lot when you haven't had much sleep and aren't a morning person, but...will you come with me? Please?"

As if he could sleep now. "Of course."

"And will you drive? I can't concentrate enough."

He hesitated only a moment. "Sure."

5.

The drive back to Baumen had so far been silent. Daylight made him feel even more leaden than usual and despite his trooper glasses, the sun glaring through his windshield set his head pounding. He had tinted the ZX's side windows nearly opaque and the rear one as dark as allowed by law. If only the windshield could be smoked, too.

Beside him Maggie sat rigid and pale, hands clenched together in her lap. When he laid his own hand over them, they felt icy.

He squeezed her hands. "Well, we could have guessed you wouldn't have any results today. But they said they'll let your doctor know in a few days."

"I don't know how I'm going to stand the wait!"

"The first thing is to tell your father and family. It'll be easier with them to support you. And you have me, too. Let's be optimistic." He poured all the soothing persuasion possible into his voice. "If it isn't benign, you'll be catching it early." He had smelled nothing wrong in December, the last time they were together. "No matter what happens, I'll always be here for you."

Irina could be wrong. Depending on what happened, there might very well be a time to offer what he had to give. He knew nothing about the retrovirus's effect on a healthy person. Maybe it would bring her half over...cure her without taking away her humanity. Then they could decide what to do at her death—like a living will—let her come on across or give her true death.

"What if I end up flat-chested, and hairless from chemo?" Bitterness and fear mixed equally in her voice.

"I'll go right on loving you."

He spoke without thinking and realized it was true. All these years, despite being lovers, he had thought of them as just intimate friends. He saw now he had been fooling himself, maybe from some notion of "faithfulness" to Marti, still thinking of her as his wife. But though he would love Marti forever, that other half of his soul, he saw he loved Maggie, too. Differently, but still loved her.

He felt her eyeing him, and then at the edge of his vision saw her smile faintly. "Garreth, as much as you've infuriated and frustrated me, shut me out, evaded, and refused to trust me with a look into the dark corners of your life, you don't out and out lie to me." She took a deep breath. "Okay. I'll talk to Dad and probably Aunt Susan. I'll try to relax and not—Garreth! That van!"

He blinked. "What?"

She pointed to a conversion van ahead of them. "The Colby police have an alert bulletin out for a van like that. Maybe you haven't read it yet since it came in while you were gone. Suspect is a tall, thin male in his twenties, very pale skin, black hair, driving a late model Dodge Ram, tan with dark brown striping, Colorado tags."

"Let's have a closer look."

Garreth stepped on the accelerator and swung into the left lane. Nearing the van, though, a sense of menace shot through him, and an image flashed in his head...young man, pale skinned, white-haired, with eyes glowing red.

"Garreth!"

He straightened the car just in time to keep from running into the van's rear quarter.

"Are you all right? You look like you've seen a ghost."

He felt like it. That had to be Grandma Doyle's vision! And he looked like a real person, nothing symbolic. But...why had *he* seen it, too?

I leave you me love and a gift to protect you, Grandma Doyle had said. Did she mean this? Her Feelings?

"What's this guy wanted for?"

"He forged a stolen check to pay his motel bill, and apparently they also found bloodstains and a bloody cup in the motel room. Are you sure you're all right?"

He gripped the wheel harder to keep his hands from shaking. Bloody cup! The vision's eyes glowed in memory. Was the suspect in the van the man in the vision? And a vampire?

A minute later they pulled even with the van. Garreth had braced himself to see that pale face behind the wheel but a girl drove...about fifteen or sixteen years old, a mane of dark hair. Beyond her in the passenger seat, he just glimpsed the head of an even younger, blonde girl. "Any mention of female companions in the bulletin?"

"No."

But they had the right van. He knew that in his bones. "She looks pretty young to be driving without an accompanying adult. The male might be in back." Though it was impossible to tell with the huge side windows tinted almost opaque. "Call it in." He slowed to let the van pull ahead, then slid in behind it.

The department let them keep their high-band portable radios off duty. Often he turned his on to keep track of area activity, but today had forgotten it until now. Maggie picked it up from between the bucket seats and switched it on. "Ellis or Bellamy SO."

After a moment the radio crackled. *"Ellis County. Go ahead."*

"We're off-duty Baumen PD officers Mikaelian and Lebekov, following a suspect vehicle proceeding east on I-70, approaching the Victoria exit." She gave the van's description and tag number.

Another voice came on. *"This is Bellamy County. Continue to follow and keep us informed. We'll intercept at the Trubel exit."*

Garreth kept tucked in behind the van. They passed Victoria. Maggie reported their position. His radio picked up the Highway Patrol band, too, but Garreth heard no indication of an area trooper being close enough to assist. He found himself running up on the van's rear bumper and slowed to keep his distance, but then presently found himself closing on the van again.

Two cars sped past them, then a semi. He glanced down at his speedometer. "Shit!" It read sixty miles per hour.

Maggie glanced at him. "What's the matter?"

"I think we've been made." Rather than him being lead-footed, the van had been gradually slowing! And in his concentration on keeping behind it, he let himself be tricked into slowing, too. With almost everyone else going not just the seventy mph speed limit but seventy-five, nothing indicated better that he was deliberately following the van. "I'm going to pass and hope they think I was just an inattentive driver."

As he accelerated around the van, the sense of menace shot through him again, but even stronger, and this time looking sideways he found the face in the vision. A male in his twenties, bone thin, albino pale, eyes hidden behind wrap-around sunglasses.

Maggie grinned. "Yes! He's changed his hair color, but that's got to be our suspect!"

Who had indeed made them. The driver's face turned toward them. His left hand lifted in a familiar one-finger gesture. Using the extended middle finger he pushed up his nose into a pig snout, then drew the finger across his throat. The van surged forward.

"He's booking!" Garreth stamped his accelerator. He intended only to keep up and drive the van into the waiting arms of the Bellamy deputies, but just as he had felt certain of the van's identity, he suddenly knew the driver had other plans. "Maggie, he's going off at Walker. Call it in." The exit lay just ahead.

"How can you—"

But even as she started the question, the van swerved right, rode the shoulder around a recreational vehicle and shot onto the exit ramp. It blew past the stop sign and slewed left in a scream of tires, narrowly missing a southbound pickup. Garreth followed, with Maggie shouting the change of direction into his radio.

Excitement colored her cheeks. "You think Walker has time to put up a road block?"

But the van did not follow the highway into Walker. It turned off onto a county road, continuing straight north, then several miles later swerved onto an eastbound county road. Garreth could have sworn the turn was too sharp for a vehicle like the van, but while it swayed and fishtailed, the tires kicking up clouds of dust, it remained upright. Garreth hit the turn with a death grip on his wheel, alternating brake and accelerator. The ZX pivoted on its front wheels, loose gravel scattering beneath the tires like shrapnel.

"There's the Bellamy County line!" Maggie thumbed the switch on the radio mike again.

Ahead, brake lights flared.

"He's turning north on 12!"

Garreth gritted his teeth and fishtailed through the turn. Ahead the van had accelerated still more. It shot past a tractor hauling a huge round hay bail. And though they climbed a hill, Garreth swung out to pass, too.

And faced a truck and stock trailer coming over the crest.

"Garreth!"

He floored the accelerator. The car leaped ahead. Giving thanks for letting Helen Schoning talk him into dropping a Chevy small block V-8 engine into the ZX, he squeezed right with what seemed like bare inches of clearance from both tractor and truck.

Maggie whooped. "I think those farmers just damned your soul to hell."

"Some would say they're a few years after the fact."

She hissed. "Garreth Doyle Mikaelian, I'll swear, one of these days I'm going to string you up by the balls until you explain these cryptic cracks of yours!"

Maybe he would tell her without torture. If he loved her, maybe the time had come to trust her. "Find out if there's anyone in a position yet to head this turkey off."

She asked, but it appeared Bellamy had no deputy in that end of the county right now. Garreth silently cursed the way the wide-open spaces spread law enforcement officers so thin.

A voice announced itself as a Rooks County deputy. *"We can be waiting with road spikes if he stays on 12."*

If the van stayed on 12. But the way this turkey had been zig-zagging... "We have, what, two roads intersecting 12 between here and the county line?" he asked Maggie.

"Ten-four...with the first one not long after we cross the river."

"Then we better not give him a chance to turn."

The suspect handled his vehicle with professional skill, and daylight and the sun's glare beat at Garreth, but thanks to the ZX's power and a low center of gravity, he kept gaining on the van. And each time he did, the van speeded up enough to keep ahead. They could use that against the albino. If he kept pushing the albino to drive faster, at some point it would become impossible to turn without losing control. Then whether the albino stayed on 12, or rolled trying to turn, they had him.

Garreth kept the accelerator down...pushing.

The road dipped, following the side of a hill down from prairie plateau toward bottomland and the Saline River. As the curve tightened Garreth maintained speed, but hugged the center of the road.

Then the van's brake lights flared. Its rear end slewed sideways.

Garreth smiled in grim satisfaction. Speed had finally caught up with the suspect, though hopefully the van would not roll here. On the outside edge of the curve the hill dropped away steeply from its thread of shoulder. He wanted the suspects captured, not killed. A forged check was hardly worth dying over.

For a moment, as the van continued sliding, Garreth feared it might go over, but despite spinning a hundred eighty degrees, the van, incredibly, remained on the road.

Far from losing control, clearly the driver had intended to spin the vehicle, executing a bootlegger turn as slickly as any movie stunt driver. In spite of himself, Garreth had to admire the albino's nerve and skill.

Then the van leaped forward...straight toward them!

"Garreth!"

"Fuck!"

Through the van's windshield he could see the death-pale face of the albino, grinning at him, and the two girls clinging to each other on the passenger side.

Heart thundering, Garreth eyed the space on each side of the van. There appeared to be just room enough to squeeze by on the outside. He steered for the edge of the road.

As his front wheel passed the van's, the other vehicle suddenly swerved into him. In a scream of meeting metal, the car wrenched sideways. Garreth fought to keep hold of the wheel, to keep control, but even as he did so, the steering went spongy as the right tires lost ground contact. In a flash of comprehension, of fear, of disgust at his lack of perceptiveness, he saw that the suspect had laid another trap. *He brings death and pain. And he can destroy you.*

The car heeled over. Maggie screamed. Ground, river, and sky cartwheeled to the accompaniment of shrieking metal and the crunch of collapsing roof and shattering glass. His glasses went flying. Sunlight slammed into his eyes and daylight crushed him. Then everything went black.

6.

He became aware of smells and sounds and sensations first...alcohol, antiseptic, soft beeps, a metallic/salty smell he could not identify, a bed that elevated his head, and the feeling of a great weight pressing down on him. He savored the sensations, even the last one, with relief. *I'm still alive.*

Opening his eyes Garreth peered up at monitors over his bed tracking heartbeat and respiration, and tubes running from his arms up to an IV drip, blood, and a blood pressure monitor. Alive but in an ICU. Deservedly, he decided. Bandages wrapped his chest, where each breath brought a sharp pain in his left side. Bandages covered his forehead and left forearm, though oddly enough, not this throat. How could that be? He had felt that psycho singer's teeth tear flesh open, had watched his blood flowing onto the pavement of that alley. Then what had she done to him? Not content with savaging this throat, had she used him for a trampoline? His body throbbed in one massive ache.

Beside the bed a uniformed figure sat reading a paperback. An officer waiting for him to regain consciousness of course.

"How long have I been out?" Long enough to have used at least one unit of blood. The bag overhead was almost empty.

The officer closed her book. "About eight hours I think."

Did blood loss do that to a brain? It certainly left one hell of a headache. "Well, tell Harry Takananda and Lieutenant Serruto I'm ready to give a statement."

And what a hell of a statement. Especially the part about the dream? hallucination? he had somewhere between the attack and regaining consciousness...that Lane Barber was a vampire and made him one, too, and that—

The officer came over to the bed. Her nametag read: *Vogrin.* "Who are Harry Takananda and Lieutenant Serruto?"

Garreth stared at her uniform and six-pointed star. Bellamy County Deputy Sheriff? Where the hell was Bellamy County? Then he saw the state seal of Kansas in the middle of her star, and in a sickening jolt, memory caught up with him. And despair. He had hallucinated nothing. It all really happened.

With that understanding came a frantic thought: "How is Maggie...Sergeant Lebekov? The other officer in the car with me."

Deputy Vogrin shrugged. "Sorry...I don't know anything about her condition. I just came on at four and I've only been sitting here with you. I saw someone go out on a stretcher as I came in. Do you feel up to talking to Sheriff Reichert about what happened?"

Despite the knots in his gut Garreth nodded. The sooner they had information to broadcast, the better the chance of catching the albino...who already had an eight-hour head start.

"I'll call in." Vogrin left the room.

A nurse in scrubs printed with blue and lavender hearts passed her in the doorway. The nurse leaned over the bed, smiling. "Welcome back among us. I'm Trina Lucas. Joanne Brewer and I will be your nurses all night." She shined a penlight into each of his eyes. "How do you—Oh!" Her eyes widened. "They were right."

He winced inwardly. Damn. "Who? About what?" As if he had to ask.

She smiled. "Oh...the nurses on the day shift said your eyes reflect red. I've never seen a person's do that before except in flash photos."

All the years of experience countering these incidents still never prevented the spurt of panic that came with someone stumbling over one of his oddities, the fear that someone would realize the significance and decide to become the next Van Helsing. He made himself smile back and shrug. "It's a familial thing. The same happens with both my mother and grandmother. I think we must have a werewolf in our ancestry somewhere."

The nurse's brows rose. "If you're able to joke, I'd say that answers the question of how you feel."

And he should feel even better soon, thanks to the blood and perceptibly nearing sunset. "Now I have a question. How is Maggie Lebekov?"

Lucas gave the blood bag one last squeeze that continued on down the tubing. Then she disconnected the empty bag, capped the IV catheter in his arm, and injected the catheter with a few cc's from a syringe on the bed table labeled: *Hep Saline*. "We're still assessing her condition, as we are yours."

Still assessing meant Maggie was at least alive. "In eight hours you must have some preliminary diagnosis. When they took Maggie out this afternoon—" He gambled that had been she on the stretcher. "—where were they taking her?"

"To x-ray for routine recheck chest films."

How many times had he fed that hoary "routine" line to cover situations sometimes anything but? "*Four hours* of x-rays doesn't sound routine."

She eyed him. "We don't know what they found that might necessitate additional radiographs." She laid a hand over his. "Look, I can understand your concern for Miss Lebekov, but please let us worry about her. Right now you need to concentrate on taking care of yourself. Okay?"

"Okay." But only because right now he saw little other choice.

After she left, Garreth closed his eyes. Not that he expected to rest. He remembered vividly his last hospital stay and the futile struggle to find a comfortable position. Oh for his pallet!

"Don't wear him out," Lucas's voice said.

Garreth opened his eyes to see Sheriff Nicholas Reichert striding into the room. Back in his trooper days Reichert's barrel chest and the starched armpit arch of his shoulders must have made him look wide as a semi in the side mirror of speeders he pulled over. Garreth pictured him in a uniform with knife-sharp creases, though these days he went tieless and wore permanent press...except today his khaki shirt and trousers, wilted by heat and sweat, looked anything but.

"Did you get them?" Garreth asked.

Reichert hung his Stetson on the IV stand. "Not yet. They slipped by us somewhere. We have one lead we're following. The tags come back as belonging on a 1997 Lexus, but the tags haven't been reported stolen. The Denver police are trying to contact the Lexus owner." He leaned on the side rail and eyed Garreth. "Your Chief Danzig is right; you have more lives than a cat. We swore you were dead when we cut you two out of that car...stone cold, no detectable pulse or breathing, and you weren't bleeding from those gashes on your forehead and arm. We declared you DOA and issued an ATL on the suspects for murder of a police officer. Then near town in the ambulance you startled the hell out of the paramedic and me when the body bag heaved, and we opened it to find you'd turned over on your side inside it.

"Which has sent our esteemed county attorney into a tizzy deciding how to charge these bastards. Seitz must have paced around the men's room at the courthouse for half an hour, agonizing. 'Nobody's dead after all. But maybe one or both of them will end up that way. How do we know they were deliberately run off the road?'"

"Oh, it was deliberate all right." But another statement Reichert attributed to Eldon Seitz concerned him more. Both might end up dead? "How badly hurt is Maggie?"

The sheriff shrugged. "I'm no doctor. She has head injuries and some broken bones, probably some internal injuries the paramedic said. But she was conscious when we found you and in and out during the ambulance ride. She also said this guy deliberately ran you off the road, though not exactly how."

Garreth described the maneuver. "He has to be a professional driver of some kind." And there, finally, went the sun.

Garreth sucked in his first breath free of daylight pressure. "I think he hoped we'd die. He made us as law officers...gave us this little parting gesture on I-70 before he booked." Garreth demonstrated, complete with the pig snout and throat cutting.

Reichert grimaced. "I doubt we can take that to court. Any two-bit defense attorney will argue that you weren't identified—unmarked car, no visible badges—at least up to taking Lebekov's purse, and if he'd wanted you dead, he'd have used that knife to stab you, not just cut your and Lebekov's arms."

"Cut..." Garreth glanced at the bandage on his arm. Then the significance of Reichert's words smacked him. "You mean after we crashed he came down to the car?"

"I don't know. 'They,' came down, Lebekov said. She didn't specify how many, though it was the females she described to Dan Seward, who was first on the scene. She was doing pretty well to be coherent when I talked to her." A crease appeared between Reichert's brows. "She said they took her weapon. What does Lebekov carry off-duty?"

Garreth cursed himself for not thinking of that before. He must be brain damaged after all. "A Desert Eagle .44 magnum." Which meant the pursuit now involved suspects with one hell of a firearm. Cold ran through him thinking of it.

Reichert's eyes widened. "Holy shit! What kind of monsters does she expect to run into? You don't carry a cannon, too, I hope, since they got your weapon as well."

"I wasn't carrying anything." He had not even owned an off-duty weapon for years. When so little could threaten him, why bother?

Reichert grunted. "That's something at least." His mouth tightened into a grim line. "These are real sickos. They come down, find you apparently dead or dying, and—this freaked Lebekov—decide to have a little more fun by drinking your blood. Mikaelian!"

Garreth realized he had sat bolt upright. Above him, the monitors shrilled as his heart and respiration went turbocharged. Though their frantic beeping came nowhere near the chaos in his head...thoughts crashing into one another around the image of the albino's red-glowing eyes and terror for Maggie.

Somewhere in the tumult he was aware of Lucas tearing into the room and laying into Reichert as she pushed Garreth back flat...*What did you do to him? I don't know...nothing. Well, whatever, that's enough; you'll have to leave for now.*

Garreth focused on them. "Wait!" He had to know! "Sheriff, do you mean 'your blood' as in *my* blood, or collectively? Did they bite Maggie, too?"

Reichert turned from the nurse to stare at him. "No one *bit* anybody. We're not talking vampires here...though maybe that's what they're playing at. That's why they cut the two of you, according to Lebekov. They talked about drinking it while they caught the blood in a couple of cups."

The sheriff could be very wrong about vampires. But vampires or not, use of a knife protected Maggie from infection. Garreth relaxed. The monitors dropped back to their previous leisured rhythm.

Still, Lucas handed Reichert his Stetson and firmly ushered him out the door.

Garreth closed his eyes and made himself breathe slowly, forced himself to think calmly. With Maggie safe, he had to consider a second horror, the consequences of drinking *his* blood. But it also raised questions. *Why* drink it, if the albino were vampire, which the vision suggested? Vampire blood was useless to another vampire, and no vampire wanting the master/Renfield relationship the albino appeared to have with these juvie females would want his servants drinking it, either. And if the albino were vampire, why use a knife rather than bite Maggie?

Unless the albino had, like himself, come across with no one to explain things, such as the bonds blood forged. Or unless the albino stayed in the protection of the van and just the girls came down.

But whether or not the albino was a vampire, or if the three just played at it or satanic rituals, the fact remained that one or more of them appeared to have drunk his blood. And any vampire games would stop being just games.

The hiss of the ICU door opening broke into his thoughts. Rubber wheels whispered on tile. A moment later two aides in scrubs pushed a gurney past his observation window. It had to be Maggie. Her father followed in his motorized wheelchair.

The nurses stood up behind the desk of their station across the corridor. Lucas said, "Give us a minute to put her in bed, Mr. Lebekov, then you can stay in with her as long as you want."

Unlimited visiting hours in an ICU? An icy hand squeezed Garreth's chest. "Martin!"

Martin Lebekov wheeled around. Thumbing the joystick on his controls, he ran the wheelchair into Garreth's room and up to the bed. "This is a relief. From the way everyone talked, I thought you were in a coma."

Garreth grimaced. "I'm harder to kill than that. But how's Maggie?"

The rugged face went grey beneath the weathering from years of working Ellis and Russell County oil fields. "I don't know all the medical mumbo-jumbo, but the gist is that she has broken ribs and a broken arm and leg, and this Dr. Woodard who's treating her had to drill a hole in her head because her brain is bleeding, and then open up her chest to plug some leak in—"

"Had to drill—" Garreth interrupted, then broke off for fear of upsetting Martin more than he already was. But what the hell was this Dr. Woodard doing treating serious head and chest injuries himself instead of transferring Maggie to the trauma center at Hadley in Hays?

"I know. It sounds barbaric, doesn't it." The stumps of Martin's legs twitched. "I don't mind admitting I'm scared, Garreth. I'm so afraid I'm going to lose her."

"No!" Garreth could not bear the thought of it. "I won't let that happen."

Martin raised a brow. "I've always liked you. You're a queer duck but you've always been good to Maggie...and good for her if only she'd forget this obsession with 'sharing'. But some things aren't in the power of even a good man." He reached through the side rail to squeeze Garreth's hand, then thumbed his joystick and wheeled out.

Garreth listened to the whine of the motor fade, then tuned in on voices at the nurse's station, and through the blinds made out a short, stocky man in scrubs who stood at the desk writing in a chart.

Garreth pushed the call button. When Lucas hurried in he said, "If that's Dr. Woodard out there I'd like to talk to him."

"Actually," said a voice from the doorway, "I'm already on my way in to see *you*." He strolled to the bed and peered at Garreth over half glasses. "You're certainly looking much better. How do you feel?"

"Very concerned that Maggie Lebekov hasn't been transferred to Hays when she obviously has severe head and chest trauma. Shouldn't she be having an MR to see what's going on with her brain?"

Dr. Woodard's face froze. "And where did you earn your medical degree, Doctor Mikaelian?"

Garreth tried not to bristle in return. "By osmosis in twenty-five years of hanging around ERs with victims of traffic accidents, shootings, stabbings, beatings, rapes, domestic violence, and attempted suicide."

Lucas looked undecided whether to smile or frown. The doctor's eyes narrowed, then he shrugged. "Fair enough. I agree, she should be in a Level I trauma center, and she should have had an MR hours ago, but I wasn't sure she'd make it to Hays. That either of you would. Sometimes it's a hard call. So I'm treating what I can the best I can while trying to stabilize her enough to ensure she survives the transfer. If that meets with your approval?"

Garreth felt heat climb his face. He deserved that sarcasm. "I'm sorry. I'm just worried about her."

"So are we all."

"I want to see her." With her condition that precarious, he had no time to lose if he wanted to save her.

Lucas stared at him in disbelief. Dr. Woodard dropped into the measured tone of one speaking to the intellectually challenged. "Officer Mikaelian, while I sympathize with your concern for your partner, surely someone with your knowledge of medicine grasps the concept of Intensive Care. Your presence here indicates we consider your condition serious. You've regained consciousness but you remain severely bradycardic, hypothermic, and hypotensive. Or do I need to explain that means you have an abnormally slow heart rate and low body temperature and blood pressure? And during unconsciousness your breathing was virtually undetectable. We almost put you on a respirator and oxygen until we discovered that, incredibly, your blood contained a normal O_2 level. And the latter is only one aspect of a puzzling blood picture. All these are conditions which we need to explore before you're in any condition to go visiting."

How many more times would panic attack him tonight? Now adrenalin pumped at the idea of his blood being drawn. Why had he not thought about it before when the transfusion indicated they must have run at least a cross match? His blood posed no danger to the hospital personnel, thanks to AIDS making everyone paranoid about contact with others' body fluids, but...what would a detailed examination of his blood reveal? Just how different *was* his blood from normal? When the medical examiner in San Francisco, who over the years had unknowingly handled the bodies of a few truly dead vampires, told Garreth about the anatomical anomalies of the group he affectionately called his "Martians," he never mentioned oddities in their blood. But was that due to minimal differences, or because he judged the differences of no interest to Garreth? How dangerously curious could Garreth's blood make Dr. Woodard? "I know my vital signs seem pathological, but they're normal for me.

I've had them all my life." *This* life. "So my blood profile is probably normal, too."

The minute the words left his mouth Garreth winced at how incredibly lame they sounded. And Dr. Woodard's expression as he peered over the top of his half glasses left no doubt about *his* opinion. "I'm glad you're so confident but I think I'd like to have a look at you anyway."

Garreth submitted to the peering, probing, listening, tapping, a tongue depressor dragged up his soles, a light shined in his eyes and commands to follow the doctor's finger movement. And he answered the endless string of questions. Did this hurt? Could he feel that? With eyes closed could he touch index fingers to each other? Touch finger to nose? Could he solve this math problem? Recite his social security number and phone number? How had he acquired this scar, and that one?

When he finished, Dr. Woodard stepped back with arms folded. "Well, if I hadn't admitted you myself, I wouldn't believe you came into the ER this morning more dead than alive. Maybe you're right about what's normal for you. I want to keep you here for a full twenty-four hours anyway. So, get a good night's sleep...and in the morning if all goes well we'll see about taking you in to see Miss Lebekov. Trina, as soon as this Ringers runs out, discontinue the IV drips."

He breezed out and toward Maggie's room with Lucas in his wake. Garreth lay with mind churning. Wait until morning? Could he afford that? Besides, though what he needed to do needed only a few moments, how could he manage that with a nurse watching? But going now and pulling loose from the monitors would certainly have the nurses all over him.

Shortly, Dr. Woodard came back into the corridor, giving instructions as he walked. "...holding steady in the morning we'll transfer her to Hays, but if there's any drop in her blood pressure or sign of more hemothorax, call me *immediately*. I'm going to make rounds, then I'll be sleeping on the couch in the physicians' lounge."

Garreth chilled at the tension in his voice. If Woodard was that worried, morning was definitely too long to wait to see Maggie. But if he went now, he needed move fast.

Careful of the IV tubing, he reached out through the side rail and picked up the syringe on the bed table. A press of the plunger emptied the contents onto the floor. Then he pushed the needle through the cap on the catheter that had been used for the transfusion and drew back the plunger. The syringe filled with blood. Now all he needed was a few seconds to inject the blood into one of Maggie's IV's. After recapping the needle, he slid the syringe under his pillow.

Not a moment too soon. Lucas came in to disconnect the IV and pull the catheter. While she put pressure on the insertion site, she said, "Miss Lebekov seems to be holding her own. Her blood pressure is up almost to normal and she's beginning to respond to touch, so there's every hope she'll regain consciousness." She moved a finger to check his arm and her brows rose. "You clot fast." She moved around the bed and pulled the other catheter.

The other nurse, who looked like a Wagnerian soprano, leaned in the door. "Are you about done there? I need to run down to my locker for a minute."

"Go on. I'll be right out."

Brewer moved out of sight up the corridor.

Now! "Trina." When she looked at him he stared into her eyes. "Go back to the desk. Don't look up from it or pay any attention to my monitors."

As soon as she turned her back he snatched off his leads, grabbed the syringe from under the pillow, and vaulted the side rail. Bruised muscles protested but he had no trouble standing or walking. Night and blood had worked their restorative magic. He grimaced more at the rush of air up his back as he sprinted for Maggie's room. Hospital gowns!

Martin glanced around as he entered, and started in a double take that almost made him drop Maggie's hand. "Garreth? Good god! How—what—"

Garreth waved him silent and circled to the far side of the bed. "I had to see her." He hardly recognized her, though, with her face swollen and bruised and her body festooned like some science fiction cyborg in bandages, tubing, and wiring. The room swam in blood scent from the blood running into her. "The nurse says she's holding her own and maybe starting to come around?"

Martin looked down at hand he held. His grip tightened. "When I call her name, sometimes she moves. But her hands are ice cold. Her feet, too." His voice trembled. "Her mother and my mother were like that as they went...like they died from the edges in. Maggie!" He raised his voice. "Maggie, it's Dad. Can you hear me?"

Did her hand move? Garreth could not be sure. He hovered in an agony of indecision. Should he give her his blood or not? Did she need it?

But even as he asked himself, the answer slid down his spine and crawled through his gut. Before his eyes her color changed, going not so much pale as translucent, transmitting light from some unseen source. He Felt death coming.

Do it now, man. Once the other nurse came back and they found him out of bed, his chance disappeared. But even with the syringe in hand and Martin oblivious to anything beyond Maggie's hand and face, Garreth could not make himself reach for the IV tubing mere inches away. Voices chorused in his head. His grandmother's on the price of forever, Irina's pointing out how she and he hated their rapists, and loudest of all the tormented cry belonging to Christopher Stroda, suicide number whatever off the Golden Gate Bridge, who was brought across under exactly these same circumstances, without consent, and could not bear to live with what he became. No, it would be wrong to bring her over by force. She must agree.

Surely she would. He felt sure she wanted to live.

"Maggie." He added his voice to her father's, putting all possible persuasive power into his words. "Maggie, wake up!

Open your eyes and let me talk to you. I've lost Grandma Doyle. Don't you dare let me lose you, too!"

Incredibly, it seemed to work. She stirred, rolling her head, sighing. Her eyelids fluttered.

Joy lighted Martin's face. "That's it, Maggie girl! That's it! Come back to us!"

Garreth felt himself grinning, too. Contrary to his Feeling, maybe she was going to be all right without his blood.

Then he noticed the blood pressure monitor. It read lower than when he came in. And as he watched, the reading dipped some more...and more yet. Blood trickled out her chest tube. Through the voices in his head came his own inner one, screaming. *Now! Screw consent. You can help her adjust. So do it* now *you stupid flatfoot or you're going to* lose *her!* But even while the inner voice urged action, his physical one shouted, "*Nurse!*"

Unnecessarily. Both were already pounding into room, followed in seeming seconds by other nurses and aides. Garreth dropped the syringe in the wastebasket and backed into the corner. Brewer reached for the joystick on Martin's wheelchair to back the wheelchair away from the bed. "We need you out of the way."

Fear twisted Martin's face. "What's happening?"

No one had time to answer in the scramble to administer drugs and more blood. The trickle of blood became a stream. Woodard arrived panting, but still with breath enough to rattle off orders while he grabbed one of the blood bags and squeezed, trying to push blood into her faster. Then, suddenly, the stream out the chest tube became a gush. The smell of blood flooded over Garreth. Maggie's pressure plummeted to zero. And in seconds the cardiac line on the monitor fluttered, hiccupped, and went flat. Its single high, monotonous tone overrode every other sound in the room.

The nurses and doctor stared at the monitors, then each other, faces grey with defeat. Then Dr. Woodard set down the half-emptied blood bag and in a voice as flat as the cardiac line, said, "Time of death is ten-oh-four p.m."

Guilt ripped through Garreth. Why did all the big decisions in his life come down to lose-lose? Damned if he dragged her across to a life that might freak her out, and certainly damned for standing with life in his hands and just letting her die.

"No!" Martin stared at the bed in disbelief. "*No!* I don't understand. *What happened?*"

Dr. Woodard leaned down to the wheelchair. "We need an autopsy to tell us exactly but possibly the aorta had more damage than the tear I sutured, an area not torn clear through but weakened enough that without the other leak to relieve the strain, bringing her blood pressure back up caused it to rupture. I'm so very sorry."

The stricken expression on Martin's face wrenched at Garreth. He came out of his corner around the bed. "Martin."

Everyone stared, noticing him for the first time.

Dr. Woodard recovered first and his sigh echoed of bone deep weariness. "I won't ask how you manage to be in here. You appear to be not only part Lazarus but part Houdini. I won't even suggest you return to bed since you clearly value your own medical opinions over mine and the bed can be put to better use occupied by a patient who wants help." Pulling the half glasses from his scrub shirt pocket, he headed for the nurse's station.

Leaving Garreth feeling like a dog accident on the carpet. He cringed inwardly under the stares, some curious, some exasperated, of the departing crash team. He pulled the gown together behind him.

Lucas and Brewer began disconnecting their equipment from Maggie...pulling off leads and removing catheters.

Martin watched, stone-faced. "I wish to God I still had legs so I could help you hunt down those cop killing bastards!"

Anger flared in Garreth. Bitterly he reflected that the county attorney should have no question now how to charge the three.

As the nurses finished, they smoothed the sheets and drew them up to Maggie's chin. Lucas turned to Martin. "Can I get you anything? Call someone for you?"

He shook his head. "I just want to stay here with her for a while."

"As long as you like. But you—" She stabbed a finger at Garreth. "—back to bed. No arguments!" she said as he opened his mouth. "People accomplish astounding feats when they're pumped up, but I think your adrenalin is running out. Look how you're shaking. Let me help you back before you collapse."

He *was* trembling, he realized, but from emotion...grief and guilt, anger and fear. Martin's word reverberated through him. Maggie's death did make the trio cop killers. Cop killers who had stolen from him life he could not give someone who deserved it infinitely more! But Maggie's death would also ratchet the manhunt up to a whole new level of intensity. As outraged as it made him to think of a vampire albino jeering at their efforts to catch him, he feared the alternative more...three humans without conscience carrying a vampire time bomb in their blood.

"Officer Mikaelian...please?"

He nodded. Anger and vengeance cried for him to start hunting *now*, but emotion would only cloud his judgment. He needed to sit back and think, to plan. And he needed to stage a suitable "recovery" period anyway.

Martin clamped a hand around his wrist. "You catch them for me, Garreth! You make them pay for what they've done to my little girl!"

His anger fed into Garreth through the touch. He gripped the back of the hand on his wrist. "You've got my word!" He had to catch them! He had the only chance at tracking a vampire, and if they turned out to be merely human, he needed to find them first, to capture them alive so they remained human.

7.

They discharged him from ICU to the medical ward the next morning. But his resolution to play sick quickly faltered. Beginning when a lab tech came in to draw blood from him.

She looked shocked at his refusal to let her. "But it's for tests your doctor's ordered."

"Which I decline to have."

Of course he had to repeat the refusal to the floor nurse, and then Woodard...who eyed him in utter disgust and stalked away, telling the nurse: "Don't bother arguing; just log his refusal in the chart."

Garreth tried to sleep, but could not find a comfortable place or position in the bed. Every inch of the sheets felt hot and sticky, and wrinkled in creases sharp as edged weapons. The two times he did start to doze he faced the albino, grinning at him through the van's windshield, and heard Maggie's scream, then spun off into a blackness filled with mocking laughter. He started awake with his head throbbing from anger and the glare coming through the blinds the old man sharing the room insisted be kept wide open.

The old man also complained loudly to the aide picking up their lunch trays, "He didn't eat at all, not a bite...just messed everything up with his fork! Young people don't know how to appreciate food anymore. They wouldn't have to worry about gaining weight if they'd get out and do some work in the world, not just sit around on their backsides watching TV and playing computer games!"

Seeing the aide eyeing the amount left on his tray, Garreth cursed silently. Just what he needed for a roommate, a stoolie!

The deputy who appeared at mid-morning with the Identikit to help Garreth put together composite sketches of the suspects provided the one bright spot in the morning.

"As soon as I photocopy these we'll start distributing them," the deputy said.

Reflecting back as he lay fighting the sheets and contemplated raiding the old man's flowers for moss and soil to dump under the bottom sheet, Garreth realized that his restlessness came not from being unable to sleep but resentment at being idle while the albino and his bobbsey bitches roamed free. Instead of wasting time here he should be out tracking them down! He phoned the Sheriff's Office to see if they had been spotted yet.

To his frustration, no one had seen them or the van.

Late in the afternoon Reichert dropped by, sitting down in a chair he dragged over to the bed. "I want you to know I understand how you feel about finding these turkeys—we all want them—but can I ask you to quit bugging my dispatchers asking if we've heard anything? I give you my word we'll let you know the minute we have anything."

Garreth frowned in protest. "I haven't been—"

Reichert interrupted with a cluck of his tongue. "One or two calls an hour, according to them. Even Emma's protesting and you know she feels you can do no wrong."

Because fifteen years ago when she was kidnapped during an attempted jailbreak, Garreth had been the officer who slipped in through the rear of the barn where the kidnapper held her and rescued her. He winced in chagrin at leaving her in the position of being annoyed but reluctant to tell him so. "I'm sorry. But all I can do is lie here thinking about—"

"I know," Reichert said. "I understand, but from now on please wait for us to call you. We will as soon as there's any new development. There've been sightings of similar vans, but none had left front fender damage." Reichert grimaced. "The vehicle description didn't give us any hits from NCIC, so apparently it isn't stolen, and the suspect descriptors don't give us anything that looks useful. We've photocopied and faxed out the sketches you put together this morning. Maybe they'll produce something. One thing we have accomplished...processing your car."

His pleased tone brought Garreth sitting up and leaning toward him. "You found some good prints?"

"Yep." Reichert drew the word out into two syllables. "Before I forget, I have a carton of the personal stuff we salvaged sitting down at the office for you, except for your radio, which I returned it to your office. Here's what we took off you in the ER." He handed Garreth a manila envelope.

Garreth emptied the envelope into his lap. Along with the contents of his pockets, out fell his glasses. Scratches marred the mirror lenses and the frame had bent, but straightening the frame the best he could, Garreth longed to slip them on. "Tell me about the prints."

Reichert nodded. "A recent wash and wax—thank you for that—made a near clean surface to start with, then the crash damage and the coat of road dust gave us the perfect device for identifying post-crash prints."

For a moment Garreth heard nothing beyond "crash damage." His stomach lurched. Though he had heard the windows breaking and the top crumpling, until this moment he never considered what that meant in terms of the car's physical condition. "How much crash damage?"

Reichert grunted. "You heard me say 'salvage', didn't you? The car landed upright, but the suspension didn't take at all kindly to that, and we had to cut the top off with a torch and pry the doors open to pull you out. You've worked enough accidents to imagine its condition now. Let your insurance company total it, then buy a new car." Reichert cocked a brow. "Are you still interested in the fingerprints?"

"Yes, of course. Go on." But while he listened, he stared into a gaping hole torn inside him, watching Marti disappear down it...now truly lost to him, their last physical link gone. With anger at the albino smoldering hotter inside him, he focused on Reichert's voice.

"Once we eliminated everyone in the rescue group, we had prints from two individuals, both female judging by the size, so either the male didn't come down or he was careful not to touch the car."

Did not come down to the car, Garreth guessed, because why would he have stood back and let the girls have all the fun cutting up dying cops?

"The females didn't take much care, though. We lifted some very nice prints from the roof above each door—good thing we cut off the roof instead of prying it up or we'd have damaged them like the ones on the doors—and we have two complete handprints just behind the driver's door. It looks like when they came down the hill one of them stopped by catching herself against the car. Pushing away she smudged the fingerprints but the palm prints are perfect. Now all we have to do is catch these freaks so we have someone match prints *to*." He grimaced. "Too bad the male didn't touch the car. I'll lay bets we'd get a hit on his prints."

Garreth would not. Staying in the van suggested the albino wanted to avoid the sun, and that in turn favored the albino being a vampire. Cold settled into his gut. And if that were indeed the case, the question became: how old, how powerful a vampire was he up against? *He can destroy you*, Grandma Doyle had said. "Are we doing anything to backtrack this creep and put a name to him...like calling Colby to learn more about what happened there and the name of the victim he stole the check from?"

Reichert leaned back in the chair and propped a boot on the opposite knee. "As a matter of fact, yes. We're still trying to reach the owner of the Lexus the tags belong on. Since she hasn't reported the tags stolen, I'm hoping she's involved with the suspect and can tell us his name. In the meantime I called Colby. The story is, a housekeeper at the Ramada Inn found blood in a cup in a room registered to a Gerald Greenstreet of Cheyenne, Wyoming. She also found wet towels in the bathroom that someone had tried to wash bloodstains out of and a wet discoloration on the carpet where it looked like someone tried to clean up blood there. She called the manager, who called the police. It was blood, but turned out to be animal blood, probably from the dog they found with its throat cut in one of the motel dumpsters. But before they learned it was animal blood, Colby ran Greenstreet's DL and his tag number from the registration through the Wyoming DMV. The tag came back on a burgundy 1998 Lincoln Continental, and Greenstreet's driver's license describes him as forty-five years old, five-eleven, a hundred ninety pounds, brown hair, brown eyes."

"Obviously not the albino." Garreth pursed his lips. "If Colby faxes us copies of the check and registration form, we'll have a sample of the suspect's handwriting."

Reichert nodded. "Good thought. I'll have them do that. Colby called this Greenstreet, who said yes, he had checks stolen, but it happened about a year ago and he has no idea who stole them or how. The suspect's description didn't ring any bells. We've faxed the albino's sketch to the Cheyenne PD and asked if they'll show it to Greenstreet. I'm hoping a picture will jog his memory."

Just the albino's picture? "What about the bobbsey bitches? He—"

"Bobbsey bitches?" Reichert's brows hopped. "That's cute."

Garreth grimaced. "Cute like scorpions. Look, if this Greenstreet doesn't recognize the albino, maybe the albino used one of the females to steal the checks." As he used them to collect blood from Maggie and him.

Reichert shook his head. "There's no indication they were with him until after Colby. He didn't register them at the motel and no one interviewed there saw them, not even the guest who watched the suspect leave."

"Watched him leave?"

Reichert nodded. "That's how they knew what tags were on the van." Reichert tugged at an ear. "We're checking for runaways from towns along I-70 from Colby to Hays but so far we've come up empty." He stood. "I'll keep you up to date on any developments. So you take it easy and rest. Don't worry. We'll nail these turkeys."

But Garreth found himself brooding over whether the albino had been alone at the motel. He doubted that, and he doubted it because of the dog. A vampire by himself had no need to cut the poor beast's throat, or even to kill it. He could suck the little blood he needed. Nor did killing it make sense for someone alone playing at vampirism. But a vampire would have to cut the dog to let his bitches share the blood, and the theatricality of draining the dog's blood fit a vampire charade perfectly.

Even aside from the dog, however...if the albino had picked up the females in the last few hundred miles, would he be willing to turn driving over to one of them, and trust the pair to go down alone to collect blood from two dying police officers? Even a vampire capable of exerting powerful control over humans would surely be more cautious than that with new human flunkies. Garreth frowned. No, seen or not, the females had to have been at the motel.

He slid out of bed and pulled the curtain around his bed—*Spy on me now, old man*—then he put on a second hospital gown backward so he wore it like a robe, picked up some of the pocket change Reichert had returned to him, and snagged his boots out of the closet. After a quick check of the hall to be sure no nurse or aide saw him, he hurried to the stairs and down to and out the fire exit at the bottom. Daylight felt so heavy it almost drove him to his knees, but he forced himself to stay upright and stride around the building to the pay phone out front. He made no attempt to hide, despite his makeshift robe...counting on the fact that people generally assume a person appearing confident and purposeful has a right to be where he is.

First he called Directory Assistance, then used his calling card number to reach Colby's Ramada Inn. There he asked for the manager and introduced himself. "Your forged check there has become linked to the murder of a police officer here in Bellamy County. We need the name and phone number of the housekeeper who cleaned the check forger's room so we can contact her for some more questions."

The manager hesitated a moment before answering. "Our police department has that information already. I'm sure if you're who you claim, they'll be happy to give it to you."

But this was faster...or he had hoped it would be. Garreth pushed persuasion into his voice. "Listen to me. Listen." And crossed his fingers. Here in daylight and over the phone, he might have no power. "Are you listening? Tell me if you're listening."

In a faintly puzzled tone—confused by this sudden compulsion?—she said, "I'm listening."

This time when he asked for the housekeeper's name and number, she gave it. Though she acted under compulsion, he thanked her, but made sure that before he hung up, he asked her to forget the call.

Then he called the housekeeper. Once past introductions, he had basically just one question. "Mrs. Muñez, do you think Greenstreet slept alone in that room?" Maids could always tell.

Mrs. Muñez did not disappoint him. "No, he had someone else there, too. But it was strange," the shy voice said. "I think they just slept and did not have sex."

Garreth felt his neck prickle. "How do you know that?"

"The bed did not smell like sex." She paused. "I guess they were busy killing that poor dog and drinking its blood?"

The observation sent the chill from his neck down into his gut. If the albino were playing vampire, Garreth would have expected him to use the charade as a turn-on. So if sex did not figure in...

Garreth felt again that blast of menace he had experienced on I-70...and it lingered with him as he walked back into the hospital and up toward his room. Whether or not the menace and the preference for blood over sex meant the albino was vampire, it reinforced the urgency of finding him. *He brings death and pain.* Had the sketch jogged the memory of the check victim in Cheyenne? What more could he be doing to find the bastard?

In his room he found the curtain pushed back and the supper tray sitting on his bed table. The old man smirked at him. "You're in trouble, young man. The nurse says you're not supposed to be out of bed."

Screw you, old man. Garreth jerked the curtain around his bed again and slumped back against the pillow. Impossible as it was to sleep in, the bed at least gave him a place to quit fighting the crush of daylight while he thought. And a few minutes later he thought of "something more" and swore at himself for not remembering it earlier.

Reaching for the phone, he dialed the Sheriff's Office. At the dispatcher's sigh when he announced himself, he said quickly, "Don't worry, Cheryl, I won't ask you if the van or suspects have been located. Cheryl *is* what I've heard the deputies call you, isn't it?"

"Yes." Wariness cooled her normally perky voice. "Then...how can I help you?"

"It's how I hope I can help *you*. Earlier the sheriff updated me on what he's doing to put a name to the suspects and I just thought of a suggestion for him."

"Do you want me to have him call you?" she asked.

"Not necessarily, because anyone there at the office can do this, a deputy if one's free for a few minutes, or you if you have time."

"What's the suggestion and I can tell you if I have time."

"It's to phone NCIC and ask for an off-line search, sorting for items in which the suspect descriptors match our male suspect. They need a stated time period, so I'd say make it from April of this year to January two years ago. And of course we tell NCIC our query is relevant to a police officer's death. If

I'm repeating what you already know perfectly well, please forgive me. From what I've heard in your dispatches you probably know as much about contacting the data banks as any of the deputies."

"You wouldn't being trying to butter me up with flattery, would you?" But her voice had warmed back to perky. "I'll make the call. The results go to Sheriff Reichert, of course."

"Of course. Although...I'd like to know them, too, please, if that's no trouble."

She hesitated a moment. "It's not much trouble."

"Oh...just one more thing."

Her voice went wary again. "You're not going to be like that Columbo character are you?"

He grinned. "I promise no. The other thing is, I know Reichert faxed the male suspect's sketch to Cheyenne. Could you send them the two females' sketches, too? That check theft victim might as well have a look at all our—" He glanced up at the singing of curtain rings to see the floor nurse jerking aside his the curtain, her lips so thin they had almost disappeared. "—our suspects. Call me at..." He gave her the phone number fast. "Gotta go. Thanks."

Another time he would have slunk down, regretting being so much trouble, but having this Nurse Ratched rail at him about some stupid *doctor's orders* while Maggie's killers escaped enraged him. He stared into the eye of the storm. "I walked down to the sun room. I don't know how you missed seeing me there. No, I don't remember Dr. Woodard telling me I couldn't. Whatever I look like, I feel fine. Go ahead and report it to Dr. Woodard."

After she left he stared at his reflection in the bed table mirror. He did look terrible...his skin almost as white as the bandage on his forehead, cheeks sunken, and eyes like bruises. Worse, he felt like hell and it seemed like more than the usual daylight misery. Obviously the crash still affected him. Did he need more blood, even though he felt no hunger yet? Or maybe he really did need to dump the old man's plants into the bed so he could sleep.

"Garreth, how are you?"

He looked up to see his landlady Helen Schoning in the doorway. He hit the controls to raise the head of the bed and lay back against the pillow. "Better than I look. It's good to see you."

She smiled. "And it's certainly good to see you. At first we heard you were dead. Shouldn't you be eating?" She pointed at the supper tray.

"Hospital food?" He shuddered. "No thank you."

She laid a hand over his. "I'm so sorry about Maggie."

Pain lanced through him. "Thanks."

"I called Martin to offer condolences and when I mentioned I'd be coming down to see you he asked me to give you a message. He says don't worry about not being able to make it to the memorial service tomorrow because—"

"Tomorrow!" Garreth frowned up at her. Impossible. How could it be that soon in a homicide case? "The coroner can't have released her body already."

"It's a *memorial* service. Martin said that since Maggie hated funerals he won't make her attend one. He's having her cremated and his message is that burying her ashes will be a private ceremony at the cemetery and it won't be until you can be there." She bent down and picked up a carry-on bag Garreth recognized as his. "I brought you a robe and slippers, your toothbrush and electric razor, and some clothes for when they let you go home, since I'm sure the ones you wore yesterday aren't fit to wear again."

Garreth grimaced. "No, since I'm sure they were cut off me in the ER. Thank you very much." Clothes! Yes! His ticket to freedom so he could really *do* something. He started planning his moves. "What time is that memorial service?"

She blinked. "One o'clock, but—you're not thinking you'll be able to come, are you?"

He made himself meet her eyes and give her a candid smile. "I just want to know so I can be there in spirit."

She stayed about half an hour giving him everyone's best wishes and reporting how shocked and angry everyone was at what happened. The story had occupied the entire front page of the *Telegraph* last night and again today. It had been thirty years since Baumen had an officer killed in the line of duty.

An aide picking up the supper trays interrupted, frowning at Garreth's tray. "You didn't eat anything."

He shrugged her off. "No I didn't. Go on, Helen."

"That's about it. Oh, a girl with a foreign accent telephoned you last night. I saw the light blinking on your answering machine when I went up to your apartment to pack your things so I played back the message. I called the number she left and told her what happened to you. When I mentioned how at first we thought you'd been killed, she said someone ought to call your parents and your friends Lien and Harry before they hear the wrong information, too, then she said to tell you that she'll see you sometime in the next couple of days, depending on how long business keeps her in Chicago. She must be older than she sounds."

Garreth sat upright. Call his parents and Harry? God, yes! He crossed his fingers that some law enforcement friend of his father working for an agency in the Great Plains had not already seen the ATL and called offering condolences.

As soon as Helen left, he reached for the phone.

Fortunately word had not reached his parents. "Just ignore any rumors of my death," he told them. "I don't know why people keep making this mistake. I'm fine except for cuts and bruises. I'm in the hospital right now for observation, but I'll be out by tomorrow at the latest."

"Will you come home for a while?" his mother asked. "Surely they'll have you on sick leave."

"I have to help hunt down the bastard who did this to Maggie."

"Now that's the attitude I like to hear in a son of mine," his father said. "Just be careful. And don't do anything that will dishonor you or that badge!"

"No, sir!" His father held that nothing on the job mattered more than personal honor and professional integrity.

Word *had* reached Harry via another old partner, Vanessa Girimonte, who had gone on to law school and was now an assistant district attorney in Denver. "But Lien didn't believe it. She seemed surprised I would and wouldn't let me call your parents. She said—" Harry's voice went apologetic. "You know how she's always been into this mystic stuff, like with *I Ching*. Well now she's—well, she said if you were dead your Grandma Doyle would tell her." He paused. "I can see how we got excited and made a mistake when we found you in that alley with your throat mutilated, but why did they think you were dead this time?"

"Because it was daylight, I got knocked unconscious."

After a moment of silence, Harry said, "What difference would daylight make?"

Garreth sighed. Harry seemed to deal with what Garreth had become mostly by denial. "Never mind. Give my love to Lien."

Once he hung up, he carried his overnight bag into the bathroom. For clothes Helen had brought him jeans and both a polo shirt and long-sleeved henley. He chose the henley. Dressing took just minutes. While pulling on his boots he felt the sun go down and grinned as some energy finally seeped into him. At last! He picked up his bag and headed down the hall.

As he passed the desk the nurses started. "Just what do you think you're doing, Mr. Mikaelian?"

"Signing myself out." And they should be glad to see him go. He saluted them.

The one he had named Nurse Ratched hurried around the end of the desk to block his path. "Mr. Mikaelian, you can't—"

"I'm going by or over you. Your choice," he said. Then when, after a moment, she stepped aside, he added, "There's no point in wasting any more of your time. I'm sorry to have been such a pain. Am I headed the right way for the office?"

In the office he signed a waiver absolving Emma Dorn Hospital of all responsibility for his health once he crossed their threshold, then walked out into the night.

8.

In the Law Enforcement Center behind the county courthouse, laminated glass stretched to the ceiling above the front counter the SO and Bellamy PD shared. A clerk stood on the far side, talking through the one low opening to a citizen filling out a form on the counter. Garreth held his badge case up to the window. "Buzz me in, please?"

She gave the ID a cursory glance and reached below the counter. By the time he reached the end of the counter, the lock on the door in the adjoining wall had clicked open.

Beyond, a corridor divided the wing, with the PD offices on the left, the SO's on the right. In the SO main office Garreth headed for Dispatch, moving down the room between a couple of computer work stations and a counter with office machines and a tall rack of forms. Above the photocopier, his suspects' sketches had been tacked to the cork facing on the partition. A faint odor of blood and hazelnut cinnamon coffee drifted over the glass topping the partition separating the office from Dispatch. He rapped on the glass.

When the thirtyish woman inside—on this shift it had to be Cheryl—swiveled her wheelchair from her computer screens, he held up his identification. Her eyes widened in disbelief. "*Mikaelian?* But you're—"

He tried not to stretch the truth too far. "I *was* in the hospital, but they released me. Fate's a bitch, isn't she? My partner dies but I pretty much just walk away from that wreck." No lie there at all! "I came in hoping that since Dan Seward lives in Baumen, I can catch a ride with him after the shift." And no lie there, as far as it went.

Cheryl said, "I'll see." She swiveled back to her monitors. Moments later her voice broadcast from the scanner set on a shelf above the workstations. "Bellamy County Fifteen. Please public service 10-19."

Garreth set his bag on a desk by the partition, then sat on the edge of the desk. Waiting gave him a good opportunity for the main reason he had come down. "Do you have any results back from the off-line search?"

She replied without looking around. "Not yet."

Searching those data banks for inactive information took time, he knew. Still, he grimaced in disappointment. "The sheriff said we had some hits from NCIC on the suspect description. Any idea where that printout is?"

This time she glanced around. "Probably on his desk. Sorry."

Because Reichert's office, located up on the second floor along with the PD administrative offices, would be locked. Not a problem for him, however.

Garreth pushed off the desk. "I need to visit the restroom. If Seward calls in while I'm gone, will you just ask him if it's convenient to give me a ride? If it isn't, I'm sorry I've bothered him."

In the corridor, a PD officer came up the stairs at the far end. Garreth nodded a greeting and crossed the corridor toward the restrooms. But as soon as the officer turned in at the Patrol Division office, Garreth sprinted for and up the stairs. No lights showed in the offices along the corridor upstairs. Garreth stopped at the sheriff's door, took a quick glance around to be sure he was alone, then leaned into the door.

Wrench!

He sagged against the inside of the door, grimacing. Lord he hated that sensation...as if everything in him jerked all directions at once. Though it and the twinge of guilt for trespassing were probably a small enough price to pay for access.

With a deep breath to clear his head, he crossed to Reichert's desk and began searching through the papers on it.

Which did not take long. The NCIC printout he wanted sat in the first section of a file sorter. Glad he could read without the risk of turning on a light, Garreth sat down in Reichert's oak swivel chair and read through the printout.

Oddball as he looked, the albino did not possess a unique description. Tall, thin, pale males had been involved in auto theft in Georgia and North Carolina and some armed robberies in Chicago and LA. Garreth could see why Reichert dismissed their suspect's involvement, however. The most recent auto theft took place on Saturday, the same day the albino checked into the motel in Colby; the suspect in Chicago escaped on a bicycle after robbing ATM patrons; and the suspect in LA stuck up convenience stores with a black partner. Yet, while not involved in these crimes, the albino must have a record somewhere. Garreth could not see the stolen checks as his first offense. Hopefully the off-line search would turn up something useful.

He returned the printout to the sorter and headed back downstairs to the office.

Wheeling her chair from her screens, Cheryl gave him a thumbs up. "Seward says he'll pick you up here at the end of the shift. And the off-line results came in." She rolled across to open her door and hand out the printout. "I called Sheriff Reichert and he's on his way in."

Garreth nodded and sat down to read. The search gave them three hits. Credit card theft in Spokane two years ago. Person last seen with the victim of a suspicious death in Billings a year and a half ago. Bad checks in Albuquerque six months ago. All three looked worth checking out based on geographical location alone. The albino could easily have come north to Denver from New Mexico or better yet, south from Montana and Washington, passing through Cheyenne on the way. It bothered him, though, that except for this involvement in the suspicious death, the crimes seemed so petty for someone with vampire powers. Did that argue against the albino being vampire? On the other hand, Garreth had met

vampires hustling on the streets in San Francisco and the albino had definitely stolen checks and license plates, also nothing if not petty crimes.

He tapped on the glass.

The dispatcher held up her hand, gesturing for him to wait
while she finished a dispatch. "...a hitchhiker about three
miles north of Bellamy, reportedly making inappropriate gestures at passing motorists who don't stop to help him."

On the scanner, the designated deputy's voice drawled,
"Then I think I'll head that way and see what inappropriate
gestures he makes at me."

Garreth could not help but smile.

The dispatcher turned, smiling, too. "Yes?"

He held up the printout. "These all look worth requesting
more details from the agencies involved."

Her brows arched. "Then I'm sure Sheriff Reichert will
do so."

Which puts me in my place, Garreth reflected wryly.

Behind him he heard a doorknob turn. Reichert paused
for a moment in the doorway, then strolled up the room.
"Mikaelian. So you really aren't hallucinating, Cheryl. Where's
this printout from NCIC?"

Garreth handed it to him.

Reading, Reichert said, "I understand this was your idea,
Mikaelian?"

Garreth tried to read the emotion in Reichert's voice, but
the tone came across as merely rhetorical. At least he did not
sound hostile. "I didn't mean to step on any toes, Sheriff. But
after you left I thought about off-line searches so...I called in
to suggest it."

"Good suggestion." Reichert kept reading. "Do you have
any others?"

Garreth peered at him. The sheriff sounded genuinely
interested. "Request more details from these three agencies, and maybe fax them our sketches for their witnesses
to look at. Speaking of which...have you heard back from

Cheyenne about whether the check victim recognizes any of our suspects?"

Reichert looked up. "Any? But I sent them just—" He turned to eye the dispatcher. "Did you send the females' sketches, too?"

She nodded. "Sure. He suggested it and it sounded reasonable."

Why did that make him feel guilty? Garreth wondered. When Reichert turned back to face him, he tried not to sound that way. "Sir, even though no one saw them in Colby, I have this gut feeling the bobbsey bitches have been with the albino for a while."

Reichert arched a brow. "Do you want to ramrod this manhunt?"

Now Garreth heard a dry edge in the sheriff's voice. In response he felt heat climb his neck. "No, sir! I'm sorry if I've acted like it. But...I do want to help."

Reichert nodded. "Of course you do. But I don't let my deputies investigate their own crimes and I expect your department has the same policy."

That had the sound of refusal. Cold trickled into Garreth's gut. He forced his voice to remain reasonable. "I can't sit around doing nothing."

Reichert sighed. "I understand, and sympathize, but you've been in law enforcement long enough to understand my position, too."

Garreth swore silently and caught Reichert's eyes. He hated doing this to the sheriff, but by hook or crook he needed an official role in the hunt. Hopefully Reichert's sympathies leaned toward him and persuasion just pushed Reichert the way he wanted to go anyway. "Sheriff, listen. Let me help." He leaned toward Reichert and lowered his voice to keep Cheryl from hearing. "Think what an asset my investigative experience can be, and a wounded officer on sick leave is perfect for a desk job, manning a phone. And if I'm part of the team, you'll always know where I am and what I'm doing." He had played lone wolf in hunting Lane...no badge, no authority, all alone outside in the cold. Forget ever doing that again!

Reichert stared back at him, blank-faced for a few moments, then frowned and tugged at an ear. "On the other hand, you do have investigative experience that can be useful." He cocked a brow. "Will you be satisfied with just manning a telephone at a desk?"

"Yes, sir!" Garreth put all possible sincerity into the words.

"All right." While Reichert did not rub his hands together, his voice carried the tone of someone doing so. "Let's request the details of these three cases and then for god's sake you go home and sleep. It may be your last chance until we nail these bastards."

9.

Dan Seward picked Garreth up in the garage under the Law
Enforcement Center. Grinning, the lanky deputy loped around
the Cherokee to open the rear passenger door so Garreth could
toss his bag and the carton of effects from the ZX on the seat.
"Man, you're a fucking walking miracle, you know that? I
couldn't believe it when Missy Ironsides told me you'd already
been let out of the hospital. I was first on the scene out there,
you know." He raced back around to jump under the wheel
and head his patrol unit out of the garage. "I worked a double
shift yesterday because Clay Kinderman's wife went into la-
bor at 0600. They finally had a little girl about 2200." He
halted at the parking lot exit, but though the street lay empty,
he sat staring ahead. "That's about when Lebekov died, isn't
it? You know, I had this new age type I pulled over once try to
tell me the reason I'd really stopped her was left-over anger
from when we were married in another life...that we all live
over and over because there are just a certain number of souls
and as the body dies the soul goes to a new body. A lot of
bull, of course, but I let her go for being so creative." He
revved the motor and pulled out. "Now I kind of hope it isn't
bull. It'd be nice if Maggie Lebekov got another chance in
Clay's daughter, because if anyone deserves another go-round,
it's Lebekov."

She certainly did. Irina, too, had speculated about old souls.
Could it be true? If he ever met the Kinderman child, would
he see a spark of Maggie peering from her eyes?

Seward rattled on. "When I saw your car down there on
top of that fence looking like it'd lost a round with a trash
compactor and all I could see of you was a bloody arm

hanging out the slit that used to be your window, I thought, 'Fuck, they've bought it.' And I half fell, half slid down to the car and your arm is stone fucking cold and I can't find a pulse, so I'm screaming into my radio, 'He's 10-40! I think they're both 10-40!' And about that time Lebekov starts moaning something and I run around to her side and find her not only still alive but trying to talk. She's saying, 'They drank our blood, they drank our blood, they got my weapon,' and then she starts giving me the descriptors on the females, which I'm yelling into my radio as she gives them to me. There she is, had to be in a world of pain, head injury, chest injury, broken bones, bleeding, and probably thinking she's dying, but she's making sure we know what the bitches who did this to her look like. Now is that a hell of a cop or what?"

Not that Seward expected an answer, rattling on without pause, but Garreth nodded. It was all he could do to reply since the sudden tightening his throat made speech impossible. He blinked back tears. Maggie had acted exactly as he would have expected of her...one hell of a cop indeed.

I'm so sorry I never let you meet my father, Maggie. You were his kind of cop. He would have been crazy about you.

As they pulled into Baumen, Seward broke off his monologue to ask for Garreth's address.

Garreth said, "Can you run by Duerfeldt's first? I want to take a close look at Hal Landreth's Corvette." He did not intend to stay on a desk, of course, but he would be stuck unless he had wheels.

Duerfeldt displayed the 'Vette on the front corner of the Used Car side of the lot, facing the northbound lanes, where the lot lights would gleam on the silver panels of its T-top and the Limited Edition medallion on the side. Garreth and Seward circled it, Seward salivating. Black over silver, it seemed not so much to park as crouch poised for attack, like the Mako shark it had been styled to resemble. But even while imagining himself behind the wheel with the kick of

375 horses driving him into the bucket seat, Garreth had to wonder if the car would hold up to a chase like that last one after the albino.

A Baumen patrol unit drifted up the deserted street and pulled in behind Seward's. Nancy swung out. *"Mikaelian?"*

Garreth sighed at the tone of disbelief. "You're not hallucinating. Except for being knocked cold in the crash, I've pretty much just walked away from it, so I've also walked away from the hospital."

Nancy grinned. "That's cool." He sauntered over to join them by the 'Vette. "And now you're window shopping? If Duerfeldt's got you hooked by this baby, you'd better take a close look at the engine before you sign any papers."

Garreth nodded. "I will. Though he told me it has a brand new engine. He said Landreth traded it because he got married and wanted a minivan instead."

Seward blinked in disbelief. "A *minivan*? Now that's true love."

Nancy chuckled. "Sorry to dash your romantic notions, but I've met the new Mrs. Landreth—we go to the same church—and while her three children won't fit in a Corvette, I have to tell you that *whipped* best describes the dynamic in that relationship."

Seward and Garreth exchanged glances. Seward grimaced. But Garreth reflected that if the new wife made Landreth give up the 'Vette, it might be in good shape after all. He liked the idea of hunting the albino in a shark-shaped car. In the morning he would see what kind of deal he could cut with Duerfeldt.

10.

As soon as his hand touched the knob on his door, Garreth felt a presence waiting inside. For the first time in years he regretted owning no off-duty weapon. Then he remembered the folding shovel he had kept in the ZX. Taking care to make no sound, he set the carton and his bag down on the landing, and eased the shovel from the carton. Then crouching low, he pressed against the door.

Wrench!

He came through more doubled than crouched, clenching his teeth against the pain. Huddling behind the drum table beside the door, he reached out with his senses to locate the other presence. It seemed to be at the far end of the couch. Not until he started to peer around the table did the lack of blood scent and a familiarity in the feel of the presence register.

He laid down the shovel and pushed to his feet. "Irina."

She sat cross-legged on the couch, brows arched in amusement.

Opening the door, he pulled in the carton and bag, then flicked on the light even though he did not need it to see her.

"You felt my presence. Good. Better, though, if I found you in hospital." She frowned. "I flew into Bellamy to see you there. You should not reveal how quickly you heal."

Resentment flared in him at the chiding tone. He crossed to the little refrigerator and pulled out a pint bottle. "It's impossible to sleep in a hospital bed. Would you like half of this?"

She waved it away. The gesture seemed to also brush aside his excuse. "Nonsense! Surviving means doing whatever necessary. *Whatever* necessary. I endured Holy Water when I believed it could destroy vampires. This—" she tapped her head "—is key. Be determined. Be imaginative. Example. Bed sits on floor, true? Floor rests on joists, connected to sill, and sill rests on foundation and foundation on earth. All places, except flying aircraft, ultimately connect to earth. Feel such connections and you, too, touch earth. Is stopgap but sufficient...like drinking animal blood. But never mind. Is done. I'm sorry about your Maggie. Is doubly difficult I know so soon after losing Grania."

Guilt wrenched at him. He pulled the top off the bottle and gulped half of it. The salty metallic aroma filled his head and flowed sweet over his tongue. Even cold, the blood warmed him, sending heat and energy spreading out from mouth and throat and stomach. The last lingering pain from the door passage vanished in the heat. So did weariness. But bitterness remained. "I could have saved her."

"No!" Irina shook her head. "Prolonged her life, but not saved her."

His jaw tightened. "She deserved my blood more than that scumbag and his bagettes." While he finished off the pint, he told her about the albino.

Irina sucked in her breath. "This is bad. You must find them and guard them from harm...or see they die true deaths. We cannot afford such predators at large."

Amen to the latter. "My big question is the albino. Is he a vampire? Do you know him?"

She frowned. "No. But I have in no way met all of us in this world. You saw in San Francisco how it is...like illusion necklace, beads strung distantly on invisible thread, so each appears to float isolated...not like social club, nor even clan."

The sharp edge on the dismay in him told him how much he had been counting on her being able to settle the question about the albino. "Do you know any tricks that will help me hunt down the bastard?"

She raised a brow. "As you found Mada, you can also find these three. You are trained in detective skills, and though not your fault, these are of your blood and so your responsibility. If I hear anything useful I will communicate it. Now...to business as I am overdue already in Geneva."

Unfolding from the couch, she picked up a briefcase he had not noticed until now and carried to the kitchen table. She motioned him to sit down while she sat in the other chair and began removing papers and envelopes, bank books and check books from the case. Within minutes Garreth forgot all about the albino. He sat growing numb as Irina presented stock portfolios in half a dozen names, accompanied by bank accounts—four in off-shore banks, all with safe deposit boxes—bonds, real estate holdings, and a Swiss account. "You have credit cards I assume but I have acquired additional ones in these account names. Also forged various documents to verify identities."

He stared at the cards. Platinum? Titanium? He felt as if he were drowning. Lane had bragged about investment information she hypnotized from the men she bedded and bled, but he never imagined it resulting in *this*. "I don't know what to do with all this or how to manage it. The tax work has to be staggering."

She smiled. "Most would not complain so about acquiring a fortune." She patted his hand. "It will sort out in time. As Mada did, you may let stock brokers continue handling your portfolios and Trueblood Financial Management Associates in Chicago looking to all else, including taxes. Here are stock broker and Trueblood addresses and phone and fax numbers."

"They're like business managers?" He frowned. How many stories had he heard of business managers embezzling until they left the client dead broke. "They can be trusted?"

"Of course you should compare all bank statements to their reports, but...yes. I helped found Trueblood, and we hold a majority of board positions. We also comprise many of clientele. Unknown, of course, to all but selected human

Trueblood employees. Corporate records list you as six different clients. Acquiring multiple e-mail addresses will support this. And for unexpected expenses where credit cards or checks may be inconvenient, use this." She opened the back half of the briefcase to reveal packets of hundred dollar bills.

He gaped at them.

She returned everything to the briefcase and pushed it across the table to him. "I must go. I wish to be airborne and well on my way before dawn."

"Will you be able to take off from our airfield here?" He assumed she must be flying some corporate jet if she intended to reach Europe in it, and like a number of other air fields around Kansas, Baumen's was a decaying artifact from World War II. Crop duster pilots and the flying club kept a length of one runway in repair, but the remainder of it and both other runways had been left to weeds and frost heave.

"No problem." She grinned. "I learned flying in 1915, so have flown off far more fields and country roads than tarmac. Flying is valuable skill for you to learn also." She headed for the door. "Take care, child. But do find those three and neutralize them."

11.

He always bought clocks with the loudest, most obnoxious buzz possible. Even so, when Garreth pried an eye open, the time indicated it had sat blasting for a hour before it dragged him awake. Groaning, he pulled the pillow over his head. He had just gone to sleep for heaven's sake, so tired he slept soundly even while still dark and even with the albino's mocking laughter ringing through a weird dream about a baby with Maggie's eyes.

Maggie! Pain and anger jerked him upright. Memorial service!

He swung his legs over the edge of the bed and started to reach for yesterday's shirt and jeans. Shaving and showering could wait until he dressed for the memorial service. Then he discovered that he still *wore* yesterday's clothes. Stretching out for a minute on his pallet on the unfolded bed had turned into hours.

The briefcase Irina brought still sat on the kitchen table, standing open. Garreth reached out to close it, but could not make himself touch it. As he could not after Irina left. Yes, he needed money to track the albino and eventually set up a new life elsewhere, but...blood covered all this...blood both from Lane and her victims. And why had she accumulated so much? More than someone could spend in several lifetimes.

He heard his last thought and felt the kind of wrench he did passing through a door. A mocking laugh echoed in his head. *Lover,* Lane's voice said, *you are such a slow learner. How long will it take you to grasp that 'lifetime' has a whole new meaning here? Take the money. As long as you've murdered me you might as well enjoy the fruits of your crime. In your place, I would.*

He slapped the case closed. Dealing with this could wait until later. Right now he had things to do.

Foremost being the acquisition of wheels.

He fished his spare pair of mirror glasses from the top dresser drawer, settled his cowboy hat down over his forehead and the bandage there, and headed out the door.

Sales personnel had already opened the showroom when he arrived at Duerfeldt's. Garreth started for the Corvette, sure one of them would show up momentarily with the key, then he stopped short. Through the glass of the showroom he could see Duerfeldt pulling into the drive on the far side in a car Chevrolet never built...a black Porsche 911 Carrera.

That's a car! Lane's voice sang in his head.

It sucked him toward it like a magnet, and had barely stopped before he reached it.

"*Officer Mikaelian?*" Duerfeldt climbed out of the car, gaping at him in disbelief.

"I turn out to be much less seriously injured than first thought so they let me out of the hospital." Garreth ran his hand across the Porsche's hood. It felt almost alive in its warmth, with vibration from the engine coming through from the rear like the purr of some great cat.

"No offense, officer," Duerfeldt said in a concerned voice, "but you don't look like you should be out of the hospital. Come on inside and sit down."

Garreth shook his head. "Really, I'm fine. You can't tell me someone traded *this* for a minivan."

Duerfeldt laughed. "No. It's my brother's, or was. He's taking it away from my nephew for speeding and being DUI. He handed the keys to me when we were up visiting in Lincoln this week end and told me to sell it."

Sell? The word reverberated in Garreth. He took a breath, staring at his reflection in the paint. *German engineering*, Lane breathed. *Power*. And much newer than the 'Vette, Garreth reflected. "What are you asking for it?"

Duerfeldt stared at him. "Are you interested in it? I have to be frank...the price my brother wants is no bargain."

Probably something in the price range of a mid-sized house. He must be crazy to consider spending that for a car. But Lane's whisper goaded him: *Do it, lover, do it...for me! It's my money and you know how much I loved fast, expensive cars!* Then, slyly: *You need something like this to catch the albino if there's another chase.*

She was right. Garreth said, "Life is too short not to splurge once in a while."

The expression in Duerfeldt's eyes changed to: *Ah, yes, I understand.* Thinking, Garreth supposed, that the brush with death in the crash had brought Garreth a sudden sense of mortality and desire to make the most of fleeting time. Duerfeldt walked around to the passenger side. "Let's talk while you take it for a test drive."

12.

Parking in the rear parking lot of the country courthouse, Garreth checked his watch. Fifteen minutes to go before the county treasurer's office opened and he could register the car. No problem. He would use the time to drop into the SO.

Following the walk up from the lot to the LEC entrance he found himself humming. Not that he felt *good*—the light pressed down on him just as hard and the glare of the sky sneaked around the brim of his cowboy hat and rim of his glasses—but he felt…euphoric. No doubt a result of oxygen shortage to his brain from the shock of writing a check that size to Duerfeldt. And he had others yet to go. His personal property taxes had probably skyrocketed, and judging by his insurance agent's *Ah!* when he phoned from Duerfeldt's, his car insurance certainly had. But glancing back at the lot where the Porsche gleamed darkly in the sunlight, he regretted nothing.

Nothing except that Maggie would never ride in it. His throat tightened picturing her…eyes alight, cheeks flushed as he picked a stretch of empty country road and floored the accelerator. "But I'll use it *for* you, Maggie." Wherever the albino surfaced, the car would reach there in record time.

The clerk at the front counter studied the badge and ID he plastered against her glass and buzzed him on through. In the sheriff's main office, a female deputy Garreth had seen before but did not know sat at a work station talking on the phone. "No, ma'am, you *have* been officially served. We aren't required to *hand* you the papers." She put her hand over the mouthpiece. "Sir, may I—oh—" Her eyes widened. "You're Mikaelian! How can you be—Ma'am, glass cleans pretty easily and isn't a little tape better than a hole in your door from nailing—" Her voice went sugary. "You have a nice day, too, ma'am."

Above their heads the scanner said, "Bellamy County, Baumen Five."

Garreth started at his number and wheeled toward Dispatch to find Emma Carson beckoning to him. "Bellamy County clear," her voice murmured from the scanner, then shouted down the room, "Garreth Mikaelian, you get yourself in here and tell me why in heaven's name you're *here*!"

She had her door unlocked and open when he reached it. He pulled in the chair at the desk outside and while she went on working, gave her the public version of his activities and health status.

Her brows rose. "Then you'll be interested in knowing that the fax copies of that check and motel registration came this morning, and we have twixes from Denver, Spokane, Albuquerque, and Billings."

He straightened in the chair, satisfaction shooting through him. *Yes!* "Where?"

She pointed at the sorter standing between the teletype and fax machines. "You should have plenty of time to read them before Nick comes back from his press conference."

Press conference! Garreth froze in mid step toward the sorter and swore silently. In his focus on the albino and bobbsey bitches he had forgotten all about the media. It was probably too much to hope that the press considered the briefing a sufficient source of information and had no interest in him. "It's in some distant part of the court house, I hope."

She eyed him with amusement. "The county commissioner's meeting room."

The far side of the moon would have been better. He fought the urge to slink down in the chair while he read the printout. Denver had located the Lexus that the van's tags belonged on. Rather, the owner brought it to their attention by reporting the tags stolen. She had been parked in the long

term lot at the airport for the past two weeks and while checking the car's condition after her arrival on a red-eye flight this
morning, discovered her front tag missing and an unfamiliar
one on the rear. She had been shown sketches of the three
suspects but could not identify any of them.

Garreth had to give the albino credit...a long term parking
lot made a good source for tags. The theft might go undiscovered for days, especially when he covered the theft by moving
the front tag of some other car to the back of the Lexus.

The bad checks in Albuquerque had been passed over the
course of a week in March...written to clothing stores, an ap-
pliance store for CD/tape deck sound system, and a used car
dealer for a 1993 Miata.

Miata? Garreth frowned at the printout. If the paper hanger
were the albino, he had switched vehicles since then. Because,
like Hal Landreth, he had acquired 'family'? Though Garreth
could not see any vampire or serious vampire pretender ever
buying a vehicle open to the sun. And it appeared only the car
dealer remembered the check writer's description, and he estimated the suspect's age as early thirties.

The credit card theft in Spokane occurred two years ago,
three cards stolen over a one week period. A tall, thin, white-
haired male in his twenties had bought a number of items with
the cards. The perpetrator's description was unfamiliar to the
victims, who claimed to have no idea how the cards had been
stolen. None had lost either wallets or cash. None discovered
the thefts for two days to a week after the perpetrator started
using their cards.

The death in Billings occurred a year and a half ago...a
black female approximately seventeen years of age found
with slashed wrists in the suite at the Sheraton Billings Hotel
where she had been staying for two days with her alleged
uncle. Although hesitation cuts on her arms and her fingerprints on the new kitchen knife found by the body were all
consistent with the wounds being self-inflicted, champagne
bottles at the scene, the high alcohol content of her blood,

and evidence of having had sex about the time of her death, made the Billings PD wanted to talk to a male seen entering the suite a couple of hours before the estimated time of death—Caucasian, twenties, over six feet, thin, pale skin, white hair. White pubic hairs had been found on the body. Her alleged uncle—Caucasian, middle-aged, approximately six feet tall, heavy-set, glasses, mustache, greying hair—was also wanted. The investigation discovered that the credit card he used checking in had been stolen from a local businessman the day he checked in.

Along with the teletype information Billings had faxed a photo of the victim. She had been a pretty girl...wide eyes, exotic cheekbones, definite Negroid features though moderated, probably by the same genes that gave her light skin and delicate-looking bones. Hard lines around her mouth suggested that in life she had been sly and street-tough...but able to hide it enough to trade on her waif's appearance.

Garreth frowned. He would not rule out the albino in any of these cases, though Albuquerque looked least likely and in Billings, who was the other male and where did he fit in? "May I use the fax machine?"

Busy with a phone call, Emma nodded.

He stepped out into the office after the suspects' sketches. In taking them down, the photocopier caught his eye. He ran the sketches through, and the check, motel registration, and the teletype printout and faxed photo. Who could say when he might need personal copies of this information? Then he returned to Dispatch and faxed Albuquerque, Spokane, and Billings copies of the sketches.

As the last of the sketches fed back out of the fax machine, Emma said, "I'd have thought you were a bit young for their music."

What? He stared bewildered from the sketches to her. "Music?"

She laughed. "Not the suspects'...Cenotaph's."

"Cenotaph?" She still made no sense to him.

She raised her brows. "The singing group? Self-proclaimed Cassandras of social conscience? Very big at the end of the sixties?"

None of it rang any bells.

She rolled her eyes. "For heaven's sake...you've been humming their 'Shades of Midnight' ever since you came in."

In a quick check of memory he realized he had. "Shades of Midnight" sounded appropriate for the Porsche but Garreth did not recognize the tune in his head. "I don't remember the group, or hearing that song before."

"Well, you grew up in California with Berkeley and San Francisco and hippies practically next door. I was one of those hippies, did you know that? Until Vietnam. My brother was killed over there and that ended the Age of Aquarius for me." She shrugged. "Anyway, you probably heard it as a child and something triggered the memory of it today."

He could not imagine what. Then, abruptly, he did. His dream. Someone had been singing it to the baby with Maggie's eyes.

"I can still remember some of the words." Emma hummed the tune...broke off to answer a call from a deputy, then sang while typing the tag number into the computer. "*Among us there live shadow brothers/Disenfranchised from the light*, something something something something *Forced to live in shades of Midnight.*" She broke off to relay the car registration information to the deputy. "It ends with a warning that the disenfranchised just might reject light and choose to live in shades of Midnight. I think it's from the *Night Gardens* album." She eyed him in concern. "Are you all right?"

Garreth forced a smile. "I'm fine." Just suddenly feeling cold as hell. His jaw tightened. Hearing the words brought the same blast of menace as he had felt out there on I-70. If the albino were vampire, Garreth felt sure he had not been raped into the life but, like Lane, wanted it.

He heard the knob on the office door turn.

"Emma!" Reichert's voice boomed. Garreth glanced over the top of the partition to see the sheriff stalking up the office. "I hope someone made coffee this morning."

"It's in Records as always."

Reichert punched the combination on the Dispatch door keypad and let himself in. "Morning, Mikaelian." He breezed past and on through the half door connecting to the Records section both the SO and PD shared. Garreth heard him joking with the clerks, then he returned with a mug of coffee and leaned back against the half door. "God, I need this. You get the feeling the media, that obnoxious clothes horse from KAYS in particular, thinks if we're not out there racing up and down every road in pursuit of these killers then we're just twiddling our thumbs waiting for them to drop from the heavens." He eyed Garreth. "They found out you signed yourself out of the hospital and will be looking for you. I didn't tell them you're assisting in the investigation but they'll twig to it if they catch you hanging around here. Speaking of walking out of the hospital, this morning you look like you shouldn't have."

Garreth thought fast. He peered over his glasses at the sheriff. "Of course I don't look bright-eyed. For sixteen years this has been my bedtime. As far as the media is concerned, if they catch me here, my response is...why not? I'm on sick leave and anxious to keep track of the manhunt. Here. These came in while you were being grilled." He handed Reichert the faxes and printout off the teletype. "I took the liberty of faxing them the suspects' sketches."

Reading, Reichert nodded. "Albuquerque doesn't look much like our suspect, though, does he, and I wonder about Billings. But...it never hurts to see."

Garreth glanced at his watch and stood up. "And I need to see the county treasurer about registering a car and transferring my tags to it."

The sheriff did not look up. "You didn't waste any time buying a new one. Did you get a real one this time?"

Garreth opened the door of Dispatch. "That depends on whether you define 'real' as having four-wheel-drive or going *vroooom!*" He left Reichert shaking his head.

Beyond the front desk a door connected the Law Enforcement Center to the rest of the courthouse. Garreth kept watch for reporters as he stepped through but spotted none. And the treasurer's office seemed clear, too. He took a number and filled out a set of forms while he waited.

"Excuse me, you in the dark glasses," one of the clerks said.

Already? He carried his forms to the counter.

The clerk leaned across it toward him and lowered her voice. "Someone named Emma in the Sheriff's Office called and said I should get your attention, and without announcing it to everyone, tell you that you need to come back to the office right away for a call from Cheyenne."

It took all Garreth's control to make himself walk. In the office he found Reichert on the phone at a work station. The sheriff held up two fingers to identify the line number and pointed to the phone at the other work station.

As Garreth picked up, Reichert said, "We're being joined by another officer involved in our investigation. Let me repeat for him what you've told me. Mikaelian, Detective Dana Bradshaw showed our sketches to Mr. Greenstreet. Mr. Greenstreet said he's never seen any of the three suspects before."

"But..." Garreth prompted. Reichert's tone implied the word.

From Cheyenne came a whispery voice. "But...he was lying through his teeth."

Finally...a break!

Bradshaw went on, "Not about the male. He didn't turn a hair at that sketch. But he definitely recognized one of the females. The thing is...I talked to him at his business, which is a Christian book store, and he looked the sketches over while standing at the checkout counter. I'm thinking that since it's a juvie female he recognizes, it might be more productive to re-interview him in less…restraining surroundings. So I wondered if one of your deputies would like to sit in on the interview."

Reichert tugged at his free ear. "I appreciate the offer, but I'm a little tight on man—"

"Sheriff!" Garreth waved at him. "I'm free to go."

"Let me put you on hold for just a minute," Reichert told Bradshaw. He frowned at Garreth. "Mikaelian, you're riding a desk, remember…working the phone, letting your fingers do the walking?"

"This isn't much more." Garreth leaned toward Reichert. "I wouldn't be conducting the interview, just shadowing Bradshaw, and Greenstreet isn't a suspect, after all, but a victim. Where's the problem in me going?" He shoved his glasses up on his head, ready to persuade Reichert by whatever means necessary. Urgency pulsed in him. "Come on; we need to know all we can about these people." And whether they hunted a vampire or latent one. "Let me go."

Reichert would not meet his eyes, frowning somewhere past him instead, but after a long pause, the sheriff reconnected with Cheyenne and said, "I do have someone free. When did you have in mind to do the interview?"

"How soon can your officer be out here?"

Garreth answered for Reichert. "We have a memorial service this afternoon for the officer who was killed. How about tomorrow morning?"

"That's fine. Meet me at the Criminal Investigation Division at 9:00 o'clock."

As he hung up, Reichert still frowned. Garreth said, "It'll be all right. You won't be sorry."

Now Reichert focused on him. "It better be all right, because if in your zeal to find these turkeys you get carried away and step over the line, this department and I will be just as deep in doo-doo as you are."

The color of law. Garreth met his gaze, but with no attempt to trap it. "I'm well aware of that…and I won't forget it."

"Well, just so you don't..." He left the room, and presently returned carrying two magnetic signs. "Put these on your car to remind you that you're representing this department."

Garreth eyed the signs Reichert handed him: reproductions of the department emblems, a six-pointed gold star with the Kansas state seal in the center and lettered *Bellamy County Sheriff*. He grinned inwardly, visualizing them on the Porsche. That should raise some eyebrows.

But thought of the Porsche reminded him of unfinished business. He stood. "I'll put them on before I leave town. But right now I'd better finish registering the car and run some errands. I'll see you at Maggie's memorial service."

13.

Although not wall to wall law enforcement officers like police funerals Garreth had attended in San Francisco, Maggie's drew enough representatives from area agencies—dress uniforms spotless and knife-creased, leather gleaming—to widen the eyes of the family and friends who filled the remainder of St. Thomas More church.

The media had sent representatives, too, but only a handful...reporters from the papers in Baumen, Bellamy, Russell, and Hays and a pair from the TV station in Hays. And they were held to the fringes, blocked from the family by the seemingly accidental but persistent wall of uniforms. When Garreth appeared, widening eyes, too, then given a series of thumbs up from fellow officers, he received the same protection.

Martin Lebekov started, then beamed, seeing him, and had his sister Susan bring Garreth forward to the family pew instead of letting him join the Baumen PD contingent. "You're almost family. You should have been."

The words twisted in Garreth. *Maggie, both of us were such fools! Why did we waste all that time?*

He sank gratefully onto the pew beside Martin.

The way Chief Danzig's eyes narrowed at the sight of him, it seemed judicious to delay contact there in any case. At fifty-five and hair mostly grey Ken Danzig retained a physical presence no less intimidating than when Garreth joined the department.

Susan said, "I don't think you should be out of the hospital yet, Garreth. You look terrible."

Good. He *felt* terrible. To keep from looking too healthy, he had his glasses hung on his pocket and had come hungry, and the combination of daylight's pounding glare and the flood of blood scents left him cramping and dizzy. In addition to daylight, the fresh bandage on his forehead should also help the effect he wanted. Under the gauze pad and tape, of course, only a red line remained of the laceration, and in a few more days, all sign of the wounds would be gone. The only scars that ever remained were the ones on his neck from Lane's attack, faint silvery ridges webbing the skin to remind him where he came from and what he was. He had not bothered to rebandage his arm since his uniform shirt sleeve covered the area.

Martin glanced around, shaking his head. "I've never seen so many badges at one time, and the last time I was in a group of armed men this large I was shipping out for Korea. I'm overwhelmed."

Garreth smoothed his uniform trousers over his knees while he fought the knot in his throat. "It's no more than Maggie deserves. She died doing her job." And every officer here knew that another day this service could be for him or her.

And who was to say it should not *be* Garreth Mikaelian, Garreth reflected later while Chief Danzig delivered the eulogy. Fate continued to play cruel games with him, destroying Maggie, who wanted life, who deserved it, yet preserving him. A large portrait photograph of her stood on an easel before the altar in lieu of a coffin: Maggie in uniform, staring into the camera trying to look serious and professional and not grin down at her shiny new sergeant's badge. The photograph and recalling that photo session brought back memory of her with the force of a physical blow...her laughter, the feel of her skin, the smell of it and her blood. His throat squeezed shut. *I'm so sorry, Maggie. I'm sorry I couldn't...wouldn't save you. I hope you can forgive me and understand why. And I hope you finally know everything about me you wanted to.*

It occurred to him that now he was talking to her with a freedom he never did in life. The thought brought a stab of guilt.

At Martin's house afterward, the mourners quickly separated into civilian and law enforcement groups, with Garreth swept from the hugs of Sue Ann and Helen Schoning into the middle of the latter circle. Danzig did not join them, Garreth noticed, but huddled with Reichert in a private corner. Garreth took a deep breath. He did not need Grandma Doyle's Feelings to know that before the end of the day he could expect a chat with Danzig.

A number of the law enforcement group had participated in the pursuit, so after expressions of condolence and wisecracks about how good Garreth looked for someone DOA two days before, the conversation turned to the chase.

Dan Seward expressed the thought probably uppermost in all their minds: "I don't understand why the hell we haven't found that van."

Echoing him, other voices reflected their combined anger and frustration. The ATL had gone out statewide and to Nebraska, Missouri, and Colorado as soon as Garreth and Maggie were found. The information that the suspects were armed and dangerous and had killed a police officer guaranteed every similar vehicle would be stopped, every rock kicked over. Yet so far there had been no sign of either van or fugitives. The group speculated whether the suspects had gone into hiding, or abandoned the van and acquired other transportation. Stolen car reports in the area warranted double checking. Though someone looking like the albino should be easy to spot whatever he drove, and if they dumped the van, why had it still not been found?

"Maybe they hid it," Garreth said. "As long as we think they're driving the van, the vehicle is what we'll look at first. If we find the van abandoned, we start looking at every driver. Whatever else this albino is, he's a thinker. He plans his moves. He could have run me off the road anywhere, but he took the risk of waiting for a location where he could inflict maximum damage."

"You don't think he just got desperate when he saw you gaining on him?" an Osborne County deputy said.

Anger rose in Garreth. "Not him! We all learned one-eighties in the academy, right? But could you pull one off in a panic where he did? That took nerves of steel, perfect timing, and plenty of previous practice." Considering Irina's comment the other evening about when she learned to fly, for all he they knew this bastard could have learned one-eighties in a chariot. "He obviously knew exactly what he was doing. I saw his face before he sideswiped me, and he was enjoying every minute."

As he perhaps also enjoyed the blood pumping from that dog's slashed throat, and maybe from the wrists of the girl in Billings, Garreth speculated angrily. Anger and fear and impatience all spun together in Garreth. He felt Time whirling away from him. Where *was* this bastard? *What* was he? They needed a lead. *Grandma, help me out here!*

A hand caught Garreth's elbow. "Excuse me, officers, but I need to speak with Mikaelian."

Here came that chat.

Danzig pulled Garreth through the group and out onto the porch. Garreth tried not to wince, though out here daylight felt doubly oppressive. He put on his cap, pulling it down to his eyebrows, and sat on the swing.

Danzig kept his cap tucked under his left arm. Propping a hip on the porch railing, he sighed. "I wish I knew what the hell goes on in your head. I'd have expected you to show better sense. Walking out of the hospital doesn't surprise me, given how doctor-shy you've always been, but what the hell kind of voodoo have you pulled on Nick Reichert to make him let you work on his investigation? And then send you to Cheyenne!"

Why did he so often end up feeling like a truant child? Garreth found himself slinking down in the corner of the swing, but angry at himself for doing so. He had no time for this! The albino roamed out there perhaps about to kill someone else, or worse be stumbled over by officers who might kill, if not him, then the bobbsey bitches! "I can't sit doing nothing!"

He realized he had spoken too emphatically when Danzig's forehead creased in a wary frown. His chief leaned toward him. "Look, I understand how you feel, but...even aside from being the victim, which compromises your objectivity, no way are you fit for any kind of duty. Have you seen yourself in a mirror? You look like death warmed over." His expression and voice sharpened. "That's amusing, is it?"

Garreth hurriedly blanked his expression. "No, sir." Now what did he say to counter Danzig's arguments? Emotions pulled at him. Part of him wanted just to stand and walk away, to do what he had to do. But he would feel better if he had, if not a blessing, then at least his chief's acquiescence. Garreth moved over to sit on the porch rail beside Danzig. The sun hammered his back and he hunched his shoulders against the assault. "Sir, I'm just running around collecting background information. Doing that I'm not likely to ever come in contact with the suspects." He crossed mental fingers against the lie. "And even if by some chance I should, with all due respect, I think that over the years I've demonstrated an ability to remain professionally objective and employ the least force possible despite provocation. I want to see the suspects captured *alive*, with no more blood shed, either theirs or ours." No lie there!

Danzig shook his head. "I believe that, but will the general public...or jurors, if anything untoward happens? The media, the public, not to mention some defense attorney, will roast us."

"I'm not about to do anything to cause that."

Danzig eyed him sidelong and sighed. "You remind me of my youngest brother. Always well behaved, always polite and respectful, yes sir and no ma'am...but when he wanted something, he never gave up until he wore everyone down. So...all right." He spread his hands in surrender. "I totally disagree with this, and told Reichert so, but...it's his investigation and if he wants to gamble on you, you're his for the duration. Just keep it by the book and don't make him regret this, okay?"

Garreth tried not to grin in relief. "I'll make sure he doesn't, sir."

Danzig stood and put on his cap, sliding his fingers along the brim. "And if there's anything I can do to help, call. Good luck."

14.

Garreth had no mental image of Bradshaw, yet he found himself caught off-guard by the detective trotting down the corridor to meet him at the front counter of Cheyenne's Criminal Investigations Division. The round face, seraphic smile, and vestigial fringe of hair around Bradshaw's head looked more suitable for someone wearing a monk's habit than a Beretta 9mm in his armpit.

He shifted the suitcoat he carried to his other arm and extended a hand to Garreth. A clean smell of deodorant soap mixed with the blood scent drifting from him. "Dana Bradshaw. Glad to meet you." His whispery voice made every sentence sound like confidential information. Behind the round lenses of his glasses his eyes measured Garreth, taking in everything from Stetson and sportcoat to jeans and boots. "Long drive?"

Garreth found his own voice dropping to match Bradshaw's tone. "Not bad, and I caught a couple of hours of sleep at a rest stop along the way." After dawn, in the car, wrapped in his earth-filled pallet.

"Not bad" actually constituted an understatement, since he made the approximate six hundred miles in under six hours. After moving to Kansas, Garreth had quickly learned to enjoy prairie roads, long open stretches with few turns and, away from the main highways, little traffic. As he hoped, heading north on 282 after dark he met no one, and presently turned the Porsche loose. It leaped forward, engine snarling in exultation, driving him into the bucket seat. The wind blasting in through the open windows bought a rapid succession of scents: of late farm suppers, of pungent farmyards and the warm blood smells of livestock, of sun-baked grass and newmown alfalfa. As he continued being the only vehicle on the road, his dash lights and the headlights tunneling into the darkness seemed intrusive. With his night sight, what did he need with headlights? He switched them off.

He had done the same racing after Emma's kidnapper, he remembered. Maggie had been along, both excited and terrified by the chase. He could almost feel her riding with him now. "Is it as good for you as it is for me?"

With darkness came a rush of exhilaration, as though he had shed tight shoes. He and the Porsche became shadows, flying up the grey ribbon of highway beneath an infinite dome of sky. Running dark let him see the stars overhead. In the years of living with the night he had learned the constellations' names and he noticed that, fittingly, driving north pointed him toward Leo.

He had almost regretted reaching I-80. The Interstate might be a better road, but he had to switch on his headlights again, and slow to a speed more compatible with driving in traffic...and with traffic enforcement. At least until midnight, when he hoped the Nebraska State Patrol, like the Kansas Highway Patrol, went home to bed.

Bradshaw shrugged into his suitcoat. "You look pretty much like you've driven all night, though. I was going to suggest walking to the bookstore since it's only five or six blocks away, in the Historic District, but...let's drive."

Garreth resisted the impulse to thank Bradshaw. The morning sunlight seemed heavier and more glaring than ever at this altitude. "We can take my car."

"Lead on." As they left the building, Bradshaw exchanged his glasses for sun glasses. "My idea is to come on chummy...invite Greenstreet to have coffee, then give him the chance to tell us on his own that he recognizes one or more of the females. But—" He broke off as they reached the Porsche, staring at the Bellamy SO emblem on the driver's door, then he grinned. "Kansas rural law enforcement must be better off than I thought. What's the rest of your fleet like,

Beamers and Mercedes SUV's? You must have entertained the troopers on your way here."

"I didn't meet any." But if he had, they would not have seen the emblems. Garreth left them off until reaching Cheyenne. If he lost his gamble about when the troopers went to bed, he had wanted the speeding citation on his head alone. He unlocked the door. "What were you going to say about if Greenstreet doesn't talk on his own?"

"Oh, yeah. If I have to push him, how's your Andy Sipowicz impression?"

Garreth slid under the wheel. "I...don't have one."

Bradshaw stared at him. "What do you do when you have to play hardball?"

With amazement Garreth realized that it had been over sixteen years since he had to do so. "In Baumen everyone's always cooperated with me." Not that they had much choice.

Bradshaw eyed him...trying to determine of Garreth were putting him on? Finally he pulled the passenger door closed. "Maybe I should check out Kansas job openings. At the corner turn right and head south on Carey to 17th Street."

The New Wine Bookshop sat in the middle of its block, its door flanked by windows that each showed an amphora on its side with wine flowing out and down to form the letters of the store name. Through the windows Garreth could see a bright, airy interior with shelves holding not only books but statues of angels and cherubs—Caucasian and Black—cute animals, crucifixes, rosaries, chalices. Behind an open-tread stairway leading to a mezzanine second floor Garreth glimpsed some café tables and easy chairs.

Bradshaw switched back to his regular glasses. "I know there's nothing you can do about the scar on your forehead, but can you lose the Terminator shades while we're playing Officer Friendly?"

Reluctantly Garreth pulled off his glasses and tucked them in his breast pocket. "Anything for the cause...but we both know that if he's lying about recognizing a juvie female, odds are it's because they've had sex."

Bradshaw nodded. "Still, we'll give him his chance." He rapped on one of the windows.

A girl inside looked around, frowned, and came to the window. Her voice reached through faintly. "We don't open until 10:30."

Bradshaw held up his ID. "I need to speak with Mr. Greenstreet."

She headed for the door. At the same time they could see her call into the back of the store. After letting them in, she relocked the door behind them. "Mr. Greenstreet will be right with you."

The man coming around the staircase, wearing a tie but no suitcoat and a frozen smile, had to be Gerald Greenstreet. He matched the descriptors from the driver's license check Colby had run: forty-five years old, five-eleven, a hundred ninety pounds, brown hair, brown eyes. His clothes and grooming also made him look prosperous—Christian books had obviously done well for him, for him to be driving a Continental—and Garreth suspected that normally Greenstreet would radiate an air of moral superiority and righteous good will. But right now he looked nervous as hell, eyes shifting from Bradshaw to Garreth and back. The acrid odor of sweat almost overwhelmed his blood scent and an artery pulsed hard under the angle of his jaw. It lit a tickle of thirst in Garreth's throat.

"Detective Brady." His voice boomed in false heartiness. "To what do I owe the pleasure today?"

Bradshaw's Buddha smile went even more serene. "Detective *Bradshaw*, Mr. Greenstreet, and I'm so sorry to bother you again. This shouldn't take long, though; my superiors just want Officer Mikaelian and me to dot some i's and cross some t's. Let us buy you some coffee at Lexie's or the Java Joint and we can be comfortable while we talk."

The pulsing artery in Greenstreet's neck said he saw no way to be comfortable in their company, here or anywhere.

"I...have to be here to open the store." His voice had dropped to match Bradshaw's tone.

Bradshaw's smile never wavered. "Not for an hour yet. We should be finished well before then."

The frown deepened. "I'm not sure what details we have to talk about. All the checks are accounted for now and I'm not out anything except for the first two. Surely any questions you need to ask you can ask here."

"Well...no." Bradshaw reached into his coat and brought out papers he unfolded and held up before Greenstreet. Sketches of the bobbsey bitches.

Now Greenstreet reeked of fear. "I told you yesterday I don't recognize any of these people." But his voice lowered even more as he said it, and sent a quick glance toward the two women at the cash register.

Bradshaw's voice went silky. "Then perhaps I ought to show to them to your clerks. They might have seen one of the girls in here sometime."

Greenstreet paled. "No, no, I'm sure they haven't!" He called, "Ingrid, Tracy, I need to talk to Detective Bradshaw. I'll be back in a few minutes."

Officer Friendly or not, Garreth put back on his glasses as they left the store.

They walked down the street and turned up Capitol Avenue to the Java Joint with Garreth wishing he had brought his Stetson from the car. The sunlight felt crushing. He barely heard Bradshaw pointing out historic buildings along the way.

At the café Bradshaw secured them a semi-isolated table, then studied his menu. "It's one of the pleasanter places in Cheyenne to have breakfast. I highly recommend their pastries. Mr. Greenstreet? Mikaelian?"

But only he ordered a cheese danish. Pasty-faced, Greenstreet asked for just coffee.

Garreth sipped tea, concentrating on how soothing the hot liquid felt. He should have used that last stop for gas to drink one of the bottles in the electric cooler in the rear seat. Once

ignited by the pulsing artery in Greenstreet's throat, his thirst
had grown from a tickle to a smoldering fire. But the tea helped,
along with the food smells in the cafe—coffee, toast, bacon,
waffles—which drowned most of the blood scents around him.

Bradshaw handed Greenstreet the sketches. "Take your
time with these. It's possible that being preoccupied yesterday by running your business you didn't look at them as closely
as you should. With a day to reflect, maybe the sketches look
familiar after all."

Bradshaw had given Greenstreet wiggle room. Now if
only Greenstreet used it.

But with barely a glance at the sketches Greenstreet said,
"No, they still don't." Then, obviously realizing he had spoken too quickly, he added, "I've been thinking about them
since yesterday but even looking at them again, none ring a
bell. Sorry."

Anger flashed through Garreth. The jackass! This could
have been easy on him, but no, he thought he could stonewall
them.

If Bradshaw felt anger, it never showed. He cut his danish
into small bites with his fork. "Tracing these people is very
important to us. They murdered a police officer."

Greenstreet went pale. "*Murder*...But she wou—you
mean the guy killed the officer, right? These girls look like
just *kids*."

Bradshaw sighed. "Unfortunately these past few years
we've seen plenty of kids commit murder. But we won't know
the extent of their involvement until we talk to them. Which
one of them did you meet?"

Greenstreet barely hesitated. "I already told you. I've
never seen either of them."

Garreth's anger sharpened. Greenstreet had to realize that
they knew he was lying, and still he refused to level with them.
Enough of this crap! Every delay gave Maggie's killers more
time to escape. He peeled off his glasses and hung them on
his sportcoat's breast pocket. "Mr. Greenstreet."

Greenstreet jumped, then stared, as if he had forgotten Garreth's presence.

But Garreth used that to trap Greenstreet's gaze. He stared deep into Greenstreet's eyes, a variety of angry openings running through his head. *Did we mention that the murdered officer is a* woman...*and my partner*! *We all know why you're lying. Can you say: indecent liberties with a child?* But aloud he said, "Mr. Greenstreet, a man like you, solid citizen, religious, I can tell that you're being eaten up inside by what you aren't telling us. Don't let it destroy you. Talk to us. Tell us about the girls. Tell...us...about...the...girls."

Greenstreet trembled. "It was an accident," he whispered. "I don't know how it happened. She gave me a hug and kiss to thank me for buying her a bus ticket home and—"

Garreth said, "Which one was it and do you know her name?"

Greenstreet almost sobbed. "The dark-haired one. Her name's Valerie Daniels." Then his tone turned thoughtful. "At least, she said it was. But she probably lied, didn't she."

Well, well. When panic subsided, the man demonstrated intelligence. Garreth reached into his coat for his notebook.

Bradshaw pulled out a notebook, too, and started taking notes. "So where did you first meet her?"

"The first and only time I know of was in the lot where I park my car." He took a deep breath. "Mondays I work late going over accounts and sales receipts. That night I left about nine-thirty..."

Greenstreet checked the street around him as he locked the store behind him. Half past nine. The late hour did not really worry him, however. In all these Monday evenings, he never felt even threatened. He made his way to his car confident that the Lord protected him.

At the entrance to the lot, however, a muffled scream made his heart skip. He froze, trying to determine the direction of the sound. Then he saw them...a man and woman struggling near his car. The man had his hand over the woman's mouth and was dragging her behind the car.

Greenstreet reacted automatically "Hey!" He ran toward the pair. "What are you doing? Stop that!"

The man half turned. Greenstreet glimpsed a swarthy face under a shock of unkempt hair. Then the man dropped the woman and fled, bolting toward the rear fence and scrambling up over it.

Greenstreet hurried to the women, who huddled on the ground, sobbing. He reached down to touch her shoulder. "Are—"

She recoiled, flinging up an arm protectively across her face. "No, please, don't touch me again!" Then she stared up at him over her forearm, great dark eyes widening. "Mr. Greenstreet?" She sighed in relief. "Oh, thank god!" Her hand reached up to him. "Is he gone? You chased him away?"

"He's gone." He helped her to her feet. "Do I know you?"

He did not recognize her, and surely he would…a pretty little thing like her with those huge eyes and mane of dark hair. Her clothes gave no clue—cowboy boots, worn jeans, an oversized sweatshirt lettered: *Frontier Days, Cheyenne*—and the parking lot lights turned her makeup garish, making it difficult to judge her age, perhaps eighteen or nineteen?

"Don't you recognize me? I'm Valerie. I wait on you at Rusty's Cafe."

"Oh, of course." A lie, but he was ashamed to admit to her that he did not know the faces of his waitresses. "Do you know the man who attacked you?"

She shook her head. "He—he just jumped me." She clung to his hands, trembling. "How can I ever thank you? If you hadn't come along…I—I don't know what would have happened." She glanced around. "Do you see my purse? I know I held on to it while he dragged me here."

Greenstreet vaguely recalled something flapping from the mugger's hand. He grimaced. "I'm afraid I didn't save your purse."

Valerie stared at him in horror. "Oh! Oh, no!" Her grip tightened on his hands as her voice rose in despair. "All my tips for today were in there! And my paycheck! All the money I have in the world!" She burst into tears. "What am I going to do! What am I going to *do!*"

He squeezed her hands back. "The first thing, obviously, is to call the police. You can use the phone in my store."

She nodded and looking dazed, let him lead her back to the book store. There she sank into the chair he pushed up next to his desk and sat hugging herself, shivers wracking her.

Obviously in shock, poor child, Greenstreet reflected. If only he had a blanket to put around her and something hot for her to drink.

The nearest he could find was a cloth they used on the table for author signings and tea made with water as hot as it came from the tap in the restroom, but Valerie gave him a wan, grateful smile, and gulped the tea. "Thank you. I'm sorry to be such a baby."

He patted her shoulder. "Don't worry; it's a perfectly natural reaction." He picked up the phone to call the police, then put it down as she crumpled sobbing in the chair. Anxiety shot through him. Was she going to be hysterical? "What's wrong?"

"It's stupid." Her voice squeaked as she talked through the tears. "Suddenly you sounded just like my father and I—I—god, I miss him! I wish I could go home!"

Greenstreet stared. "Why can't you?"

"Because—" She lifted her head, wiping her eyes with the backs of her hands. The smeared mascara made her eyes look like a raccoon's. A rather touching effect, Greenstreet reflected, and suddenly realized that she was much younger than he first thought, fifteen, or even younger. A little lost waif. Eyes brimming, she said, "Can—can I talk to you?"

"Yes, of course, child." He pulled another chair over to face hers and sat down.

She drew a long, trembling breath. "My mother died when I was ten. I don't have any brothers or sisters so then it was just Daddy and me. Until last year, when he married...*Raegene.*" Valerie spat the name. "I'd been cooking and cleaning for Daddy but according to *Raegene* I didn't know anything about cleaning or cooking. And my clothes were too tomboy, not feminine. And—well, it doesn't matter what else. We fought all the time and she had him so pussywhipped that he always took her side. So I ran away, leaving a note saying that as long as he stayed married to her he'd never see me again. So now I can't go home again."

Greenstreet sighed. "Why? Because it would hurt your pride to back down?" How much unhappiness pride caused Humanity, and how like a child to think in black-and-white absolutes. "What's more important to you, your pride or your father?"

She hesitated, biting her lip. "Daddy, of course, but...after the way I acted he won't want anything to do with me. *She* probably won't allow it."

"If you really want to go home again, why don't you call your father and find out? I think you'll find he misses you, too, and you can work something out."

She stared at him, uncertainly at first, then with hope lighting her face. "You think so? Please, can I use your phone right now? I'll reverse the charges."

He handed her the phone. "Don't worry about the charges; just call."

"No, I'll reverse the charges." She straightened in the chair. "I won't impose on you. But..." Her eyes begged. "...do you mind stepping outside while I call?"

He left the room while she dialed, but as the door closed behind him he heard her say, "Daddy? Daddy, it's Valerie." Then a few minutes later she opened the door, face shining. "He wants to talk to you."

Greenstreet came in and picked up the receiver.

"Mr. Greenstreet?" The voice coming over the line sounded shaky but joyous. "This is Richard Daniels. I don't know how I can ever express my gratitude to you for talking Valerie into calling. I've been hunting her from the day she ran away and I was beginning to be afraid I'd never see my little girl again. Could I possibly ask you for a very large favor? If you buy her a bus ticket to Douglas—that's the closest the bus comes to Kaffley and I'll meet it there—and give me your address, I'll send you the money to reimburse you."

Greenstreet glanced back at the doorway, at the girl hovering there, holding her breath. So, it had worked out just as he thought it would. He winked at her. "Of course I'll buy her a ticket, but don't worry about reimbursing me."

"Praise the Lord there are still men like you in the world."

He drove her to the bus station and bought the ticket, but the departure time worried him, 2:00 am. "I hate to have you sitting down here until then."

"No, that's good," she said. "That gives me time to walk home to pick up my things and say goodbye to my roommate."

"Walk? At this time of night? I'll take you home and bring you back."

She bit her lip. "But you've already done so much."

"We don't want you mugged again...or worse. Where do you live?"

She gave him directions.

He had never heard of the Niobrara Hotel and seeing it, could understand why the guidebooks did not include it in the list of tourist accommodations. While not exactly sleazy, some art deco features placed its heyday in the thirties, and some very questionable-looking people occupied the sagging lobby chairs. One tall, rawboned woman with a thigh-high skirt and a mound of red hair that had to be a wig showed a decided adam's apple.

"Why are you living in a place like this?" Greenstreet asked.

She shrugged. "It's all Billie and I can afford. But it isn't so bad. The owners keep it pretty clean because they like to be able to kick everyone but the geriatric residents out during Frontier Days and rent to tourists, and the hookers—"

"*Hook—*"

The rawboned woman looked around.

Greenstreet lowered his voice to a whisper. "Hookers?"

For a moment he thought she was going to laugh at him, but he decided he must have imagined that. Her eyes widened. "That's what Billie tells me they are. They do seem to have different men with them all the time. But they seem like girls nice to me. They found a place for Billie and me to crash until the hotel gave us our room back after Frontier Days. It's better than living on the street or in an abandoned house like some kids have to do. Would—would you please come up to the room while I pack? Billie's boyfriend Shawn runs in and out as he likes, even when Billie's away working, like now, and I don't like being alone with him."

Greenstreet did not see how he could refuse her, but he slunk through the lobby hoping no one he knew would see him.

She unlocked the door and opened it cautiously. "Shawn? Are you here?" When no one answered she grinned with relief. "Good; he must be out drinking and hustling pool. Come on in. Packing won't take me a minute."

Following her inside, Greenstreet peered around and shuddered. This might be better than living on the street, but only just. The decor could best be described as fade-to-grey and while not threadbare, the two easy chairs, kitchenette table and chairs, drapes, and double bed had all clearly seen better days. He perched gingerly on the arm of an easy chair while she scooped the contents of a dresser drawer into a large denim tote.

He found himself eyeing the bed. "Where do you sleep when Shawn and Billie are..."

She grimaced. "In one of the chairs...and try to pretend I don't hear them, or if he's drunk and trying to drag me in to make it a threesome I go sit in the hall." She shuddered, then tossed her head, laughing. "But now I won't have to worry about that anymore. I'm going home, going home, going *home*!" She danced around the room. "And did I tell you Daddy divorced Raegene? After I left she started trying to keep him from seeing all his old friends and not only them but his sister in Douglas and his parents in Gillette. So he kicked her out. This is the happiest day of my whole life! We need to celebrate!" Almost before Greenstreet realized what she was doing, she pulled two beers from a little refrigerator and presented one bottle to him.

He frowned. "You're too young to drink."

She laughed. "It's just *beer*. Come on, let's toast that mugger. If he hadn't stolen my purse—no, no, better yet, I want to toast *you*." She held her bottle toward him, beaming. "To Mr. Gerald Greenstreet, a modern knight in shining armor and next to my father, the most wonderful man I have ever known."

Her joy infected him. He found himself chuckling, and politely taking several swallows before putting down the beer. It tasted flat. Someone must have been careless about refrigeration.

Valerie set hers down, too, and to his startlement, threw her arms around him. "Thank you for rescuing me." Standing on her tip-toes, she kissed him lightly. A surprised expression crossed her face. "Oh...that's nice." She smiled, then kissed him again, harder this time. "That's very nice." Her arms tightened, and she kissed him once more, this time parting her lips to tickle his with her tongue. "You taste good." She rubbed against him. "You feel good, too."

So did she. She wore no bra under her sweatshirt, he discovered. The hard points of her nipples pressed into his chest. He found his breathing and pulse quickening. A part of him said this was wrong...she was just a child...but his head swam and his body felt out of his control, as if it belonged to someone else. She laughed softly against his mouth and guided his hands up under her sweatshirt. Then hers reached for his belt.

Greenstreet wiped sweat from his upper lip with his napkin, swallowing hard. "I just don't know how it all happened. It never crossed my mind until she—"

"Unfortunately that doesn't wash with the courts," Bradshaw said. "Being a minor, she was legally unable to consent to sex. Which makes you, the adult, responsible for anything that happened...if we were to pursue the matter. What happened afterward?"

Greenstreet stared down into his coffee cup. "I fell asleep. The next thing I knew it was after midnight. She'd gone, just leaving a note on the pillow saying thank you for everything, she would remember me in her prayers the rest of her life, and she'd left for the bus station because she didn't want to take the chance of missing her bus. I—uh—have to admit I was relieved. I couldn't have faced her. I couldn't believe I'd let that happen. I still can't." Greenstreet frowned at Bradshaw. "And I can't believe she'd kill anyone. She was a sweet child."

"A sweet child who, while you were asleep, maybe drugged by something in your beer, stole your checks," Bradshaw said.

Not to mention her cute trick of drinking the blood of dying cops.

"I'm surprise she didn't take credit cards, too. Or did she?" Bradshaw raised his brows at Greenstreet.

Greenstreet hesitated. "Not take the cards, no, but for a while I wondered if she copied off the numbers. Some mail order purchases turned up on them from places I didn't recognize and when I called to find what they sold I knew they weren't orders either my wife or I placed."

Garreth could see the albino instigating that. Copying the numbers and leaving the card kept Greenstreet from realizing he had been victimized until the next statement came in. "What kind of mail order purchases?"

"They weren't things I can see any reason for her to be ordering either. So I think there was just a computer glitch and someone else's order ended up charged to my card."

"Still...what kind of things?"

Greenstreet shrugged. "Theatrical supplies...wigs and make-up."

"You never saw anyone like the male suspect or the other girl?" Bradshaw asked.

Greenstreet shook his head. "Though I suppose he played the mugger and her father. God, what a fool I was!"

No shit. And Bradshaw's blank expression had to be hiding the same emphatic agreement.

But Garreth also felt frustration flare in him. Wigs and make-up. Disguises...such as the black hair the albino had in Colby. Disguises were going to make them a hell of a lot harder to find.

Mocking laughter echoed in Garreth's head.

15.

Watching Greenstreet leave the cafe, Bradshaw rolled his eyes. "'I just don't know how it all happened.'" He forked the last piece of danish into his mouth.

Garreth finished off his tea. "I think he really doesn't understand." And he could not decide if that made him feel more contempt or pity for Greenstreet.

Bradshaw snorted. "Well of course he's clueless. Even if he realized he had this taste for jail bait he'd never admit it even to himself. But she sussed him out. And...played...him...like...a...violin." He grinned. "You have to admire artistry like that."

Garreth kept his expression neutral. Admire? Ordinarily, maybe, but not when he kept seeing Maggie in the ICU bed...and that vision of the albino. *He brings death and pain.* The bb's only "artistry" could be how well she danced to the albino's tune.

"It's a slick scam," Bradshaw said. "At the time the marks don't know they've been taken, and if, when they discover they've been victimized, they figure out the when and who, they're not likely to report it and have to admit they've been bonking a minor."

Garreth frowned. A slick scam, yes, but..."But this isn't something they can run on random men. They have to pick their victim...make sure he's vulnerable, learn his name and schedule. It seems a lot of trouble for no more than Valerie and the albino got out of Greenstreet."

"Maybe he was just practice for a bigger score."

A possibility, of course. "But if that's the case, they haven't pulled it off yet. Because I think a big hit *would* be reported. Their scam goes unreported because the sex offense looms larger for the victim than the monetary loss, right? If Greenstreet discovered they got his PIN or wrote a check emptying his bank account, you know he'd have filed a complaint and managed to think up a story that fingered sweet Valerie without ever mentioning the Niobrara. She passed his table in Rusty's and dropped her bag, and while he helped her pick up everything, he noticed her close to his coat, where he had his checkbook."

Bradshaw nodded. "We're lucky he was feeling too guilty to think of something like that yesterday. By the way, I can't believe he just rolled over for you like that. How'd you do it? More to the point, can you teach me the trick?"

Garreth's gut knotted. He should have expected this. Now he had to duck the request without a lie Bradshaw would catch. He made himself meet the detective's gaze with a grimace. "I wish I could but...I don't know exactly how it works myself. It's just something I've always been able to do." Mostly the truth.

Bradshaw eyed him a moment, then shrugged. "You're a wasted resource in a rural department. But getting back to our perps and their apparent reluctance, or failure, to go after a big score, let me shoot your original argument back at you: why go to so much trouble for peanuts?"

Garreth sighed. "I don't know. If they pulled the scam often enough the total might not be peanuts." He raised a brow at Bradshaw. "Is there a prayer the desk clerks at the Niobrara can tell us how often Valerie brought men in with her?"

"After a year, with all the traffic through that lobby?" Bradshaw snorted. "But we can ask."

The clerk on the desk at the Niobrara politely refrained from laughing at Garreth's question. He laid down his paperback and solemnly studied the sketches and the twenty-dollar bill Garreth handed through the grille. "Sorry...I don't remember them. I don't if they pay their rent and don't make trouble."

So for all its entertainment value, wringing the truth out of Greenstreet brought him no closer to learning who and what the albino was. "What?" he asked, realizing he had missed a comment Bradshaw made.

Bradshaw raised a brow. "I said, even though the Niobrara doesn't remember them, it's safe to say your suspects pulled the scam regularly. They took the time to get all the details right, including the senior citizens living at the hotel and the bit about renting to tourists during Frontier Days. Claims to the contrary, the hotel knows exactly who's living there and who's just using it for business, because it's only the hookers they kick out. So if they really included Valerie..."

Then they considered her one of the working girls. That gave him a thought. "I wonder how much of the rest of her story was true." Learning who Valerie was might give him a way to the albino. "She told Greenstreet she's a runaway. I'd put the odds of that being true about ninety-nine point nine per cent."

Bradshaw's brows arched. "So you're wondering if there's a Kaffley near Douglas?"

Garreth reached into the back seat and hauled up the case with his laptop and its little portable printer, stashed between his cooler and overnight bag. Pulling out the laptop, he punched it on, then while it booted, he dug the disc caddy out of a side pocket and slid the Western U.S. disc of his map program into the CD-ROM drive.

Bradshaw sighed. "And they give you cool toys, too? Does Bellamy County need another deputy?"

Grinning, Garreth typed "Kaffley, WY" into the program.

The drive light flickered, then: *No matches found.*

Garreth backspaced to erase the Wyoming abbreviation and slid his finger across the glide pad to point the cursor at *Search* again.

This time the computer came up with one match...in North Dakota. Garreth turned the screen toward Bradshaw. "Shall we give it a try?"

They called the Kaffley PD from Bradshaw's cubicle at the CID building.

The dispatcher they talked to had no record of a juvenile female of Valerie's description missing in the last two years, nor any record of a juvenile named Valerie Daniels.

Bradshaw, who had gone to another phone while Garreth talked to Kaffley, came back shaking his head. "Juvenile doesn't have any record of a Valerie Daniels or any female with her descriptors, or warrants for any juvie female with her descriptors. So I sent off an inquiry to the National Clearinghouse and faxed them the sketches."

Garreth nodded. Good thought. The Clearinghouse listed missing children from all over the country. "There's one other thing we might check. If they've run this scam anywhere else, maybe they haven't scared all their marks into keeping quiet."

Bradshaw eyed Garreth. "Elsewhere such as?"

Garreth told him about the dead girl in Billings.

"Let's try them," Bradshaw said, and reached for the phone.

From the laptop case he had brought in with him came a warbling. Garreth started. What? Then he remembered the digital phone he bought in Bellamy yesterday morning. No one had the number except the PD and SO dispatchers. He pulled out the phone. "Mikaelian."

"This is Bellamy County," came Emma's voice. "Sheriff Reichert said to tell you we've found the van."

16.

During the trip home, Garreth recalled Irina's suggestion that he take flying lessons and wondered if this counted. Surely driving at these speeds qualified the Porsche for status as some kind of low-flying aircraft. Since he had to travel by daylight this time, he had abandoned I-80 for hopefully sparsely-patrolled back roads. A road atlas lay open on the passenger seat but he used it mostly to warn him of up-coming towns while he zig-zagged cross-country on a long diagonal, navigating as his Grandpa Doyle used to do, heading "the right general direction." Much as it annoyed him to slow down for towns, it let him relax his concentration and take a hand from the wheel to call home on the digital phone.

"Found the van where?" he had asked Emma.

"Behind A-1 Auto Repairs."

"A-1..." He stared at the phone. "In *Baumen*?"

"Yes." Emma's voice had sounded amused. "You should have heard Reichert when your Chief Danzig called him with the news. 'Son of a bitch! They dumped it right under our noses and we didn't notice for *three days*!'"

But what better place to abandon a damaged vehicle than among other damaged vehicles. If the albino had left it in a salvage yard, they might never have spotted it. Which made Garreth wonder why the albino had not done so. But almost as soon as he asked, he realized why not; salvage yards had no vehicles one could drive away. "So do we know what vehicle they stole out of A-1's lot?"

"Your office says it's probably a blue and gray '97 Ford F-150 pickup with a topper, tag number King Boy Adam five four six. It has a dented passenger door and missing side mirror."

Damage that did not affect its driveability. Why abandon the van in Baumen, though? True, Baumen lay closest to the crash site, but Bellamy, only slightly farther away, had several body shops, most larger than A-1, which would have probably meant an even greater delay before discovery of the van. Since the switch could not be made until dark, however, bringing the van to Baumen meant they had to hide somewhere the rest of the day, risking discovery. Why take the chance?

Unless the albino specifically wanted to leave the van on the doorstep of the police department whose officers he had attacked. That sort of mocking gesture went along with the ones the albino made on I-70 and with the grin he wore gunning toward the ZX.

"And we have an ATL out on the pickup?"

"To most of the Great Plains states and Missouri and Iowa. And your Lieutenant Toews and Officer Melanie Hayes, a Bellamy PD evidence tech we use, are processing the van."

With Bradshaw an avid listener, Garreth had called Baumen to see what, if anything yet, they had learned from the van.

Wendy Bessler, the Day dispatcher, said "They're searching the area around the van first. Ed Duncan's the only one who's been near it so far, and that just long enough to get the VIN. The VIN comes back negative from NCIC."

The van's description had not given them a hit from NCIC, so it did not surprise Garreth that the vehicle identification number failed to either. Apparently the albino acquired the van legally. But had he registered it anywhere? Garreth never doubted Danzig and Reichert were trying to find out. "Any luck running the VIN through the state DMV's? Or is the SO running them?"

"We are, with no luck so far."

"And we still think the suspects are driving that F-150 pickup?"

"That's the only vehicle missing from A-1's lot." Her voice went wry. "Which is the whole reason we even found the van. The mechanic Kyle Hague assigned to work on the pickup couldn't find it when he went to bring it into the shop. Hague had a look and couldn't find it either so he called in here asking for his good buddy Ed to contact him. He wanted Ed to tell him how much trouble he was in for losing the pickup. It never crossed his mind anyone would steal it. Twenty minutes later Ed calls in asking if we have any wants involving a tan Dodge conversion van. He's spotted this familiar seeming vehicle behind A-1 without tags. Then as soon as he's described the vehicle to me I can hear brakes squealing in his head. 'Oh my god!' he says...in soprano. And then, of course, it turned into a circus here."

Garreth imagined so, and after thanking Bradshaw for all the courtesy and help, and giving Bradshaw his digital phone number for when the Clearinghouse reported whether the sketches matched any runaways in their computer, he had headed home to join the circus.

Wendy updated him each time he called in. "The van isn't currently registered anywhere. The VIN check came back negative from every state. Is Bellamy County paying for all this phone time, by the way?"

He should probably have expected someone to wonder about that sooner or later. "No, me. Between this and buying the car I'm probably using up all of the legacy from Anna Bieber...but Maggie's worth it. Have you run the van through the computer's VIN program yet?"

"Ten-four...and I'm about to call the factory that built it."

Who could tell them where they shipped the vehicle. The dealership in turn could tell them the name of the initial buyer, then they would try to locate him or her and learn if he/she still had the van or to whom it had been sold. With luck, they would follow the ownership chain to the albino.

When he phoned Wendy during a gas stop, she reported: "Things got crazy and I still haven't called the Dodge factory. The van's been hauled to Sterling's for printing."

Sterling-Weiss's location across the street behind City Hall made the funeral home a natural for an unofficial forensics annex. They were already collecting the unattended deaths and letting the county coroner from Bellamy use their embalming table for autopsies. So in the last few years their garage, windowless and wide and deep enough for six vehicles, had proven convenient for processing vehicles...out of cold or wet weather, shady in summer, dark enough when closed up to use the blue light for hunting prints and trace evidence, and well-lighted enough for night work.

On his next call Wendy gave him the name of the dealership the van went to. Garreth felt himself double-take on the name. "Excuse me?"

She laughed. "Boggus Dodge—that's two g's—Bismarck, North Dakota."

"Has anyone called them yet?"

"As soon as I hung up from talking to the factory. They're searching their records for the sale. Oh, Danzig and Sheriff Reichert came through about fifteen minutes ago. Not too happy. So far it appears the van's been wiped inside and out, but Nat's still working on it."

Garreth swore, though it would have been more surprising if the albino had *not* wiped the van. No doubt he gave the task to the bobbsey bitches while he chose their replacement transportation and started it.

Wendy went on, "They're also going to Super Glue it in hopes of finding prints in spots the suspects overlooked."

Super Glue turned the processing into a waiting game. It would take hours for the cyanoacrylate fumes to fill the closed van and react with the proteins and amino and fatty acids to bring up any latent fingerprints. He would be home before then.

By the time they heard back from Boggus Dodge, Sue Ann had taken over dispatching. "They sold that van four years ago to a Mr. Travis Thone. He's negative NCIC. Nat's been trying to reach Thone. Just a minute."

Nat came on the line. "How are you holding up, and how did it go in Cheyenne?"

"Fine and so-so." Garreth gave him a quick report on the interview with Greenstreet. "What luck have you had with Thone?"

"None. The phone number, according to the answering machine that picked up, now belongs to a family named Carpenter. I left a message for them to call us if they know how to contact Thone. But Directory Assistance has no listing for him in Bismarck and the DMV no valid drivers license for him. The Bismarck PD got me the current phone number for the address Boggus had and, no surprise, Thone doesn't live there any more. The baby sitter I talked to says the owners moved into the house three years ago. I left a message for *them* to give us a call, too. Maybe they know where he went. The PD has Thone in their computer as the victim of a burglary six years ago and his description rules him out as our suspect: late thirties, five-ten, heavyset, brown hair, grey eyes."

That he would be the albino was too much to hope for. "Did you find anything useful in the van?"

"Yes and no." Garreth could picture Nat pulling at an ear and rubbing the back of his neck. "A few prints. They thought to wipe the jack, incredibly, but I found some on the spare tire, and on the oil filter. But judging by the size of those, unless some garage employs delicate mechanics, they're just more of the females'. Nothing yet that might be the albino bastard's. I'm pinning my hopes on the Super Glue turning up some. Aside from that we have some long fibers that look like hairs from wigs. There was also alfalfa and brome caught underneath on the frame."

Once he disconnected, Garreth floored the accelerator. Only to come over a hill and find himself bearing down on the rear end of a wagon stacked with round bales, and another hill dead ahead. He stood on the brakes. The car skidded, fish-tailing as the tires grabbed at dirt and scattering gravel, but finally halting bare inches from the hay wagon. Heart thundering, Garreth settled behind the wagon at a crawl to wait impatiently for a place to pass.

Then, staring at the back of the hay wagon, he thought of the alfalfa and brome Nat mentioned finding under the van. Both were kinds of hay. Wherever the trio hid until dark had to be off the road, and presumably the van picked up the stems there. But alfalfa and brome did not grow in the same field. The one place to find them together was a hay barn. He knew of several hay barns on the two routes they could have taken into Baumen. Only one of those, however, sat out of view of a farm house...Dell Gehrt's at the junction of county roads 16 and 17.

17.

Coming down County 12 gave Garreth a lump in his throat and a chill down his spine, even after he turned off on 17. He made himself ignore it and think, instead, of the barn. If the albino and bb's hid out there, they had surely left traces of themselves. And those traces might give him information helpful in tracking them.

A road sign announced the junction with 16 ahead...and off to the right sat Gehrt's barn. A big barn...as long as the width of a football field, its high corrugated metal roof supported on a colonnade of telephone poles. Ranks of massive round bales filled the area between the barn and the barb wire fence along the road. Big as they looked, no van could hide behind them. But the barn afforded plenty of cover. Rectangular bales filled about half of it in irregular stacks, almost to the roof on the ends, lower in the middle, with an area near the center clear all the way through the barn. The gap looked wide enough for a hay wagon, which made it no trouble for a van. Drive in, stack bales behind, and a vehicle would be concealed.

A barb wire gate barred the lane leading to the barn. It had no lock, however, just a loop of wire over the gatepost and the post at the free end of the gate.

"You think those bastards hid in *my barn*?" Gehrt had said indignantly when Garreth called asking permission to search. "If they did, you find evidence that nails their asses!"

Garreth parked the Porsche, pulled his Stetson down to his glasses, and climbed out. Even approaching evening, the sun felt like a hammer. Carrying a Polaroid camera and a carton of gallon plastic freezer bags he had bought en route, he climbed between the barbed strands of the gate and slogged up the lane to the barn. If nothing else, it offered shade.

At the edge of the barn he bent to examine the ground. His pulse jumped. The loose hay scattered in the dust included both alfalfa and brome. But excitement became a grunt of frustration moments later. Beneath the layer of dust and hay the dirt felt hard as concrete, and the wind, hot as a blast furnace, smelling of dust and sun-baked grass, funneled through as if in a wind tunnel. More than hard enough to destroy any tracks left by the van. Still, if it had been here it surely left some trace of itself. Garreth started a slow sweep that would cover every inch of the clear area.

But his first turn back ended that phase of the search. He stopped short...grinning. Beyond the leading edge of the bale stack the central area widened out another ten feet to his right. And the "leading edge" consisted of just a wall one bale deep. *Built by guess who?* He saw no reason for Gehrt or his hands to have built it.

As he suspected, the wind had virtually cleared the space, blowing the loose hay against the surrounding bales, but he quartered the area carefully, watching for anything that seemed unusual in a hay barn.

Such as a triangular shard of glass gleaming near the bale wall. The curve of the surface and shape of the smooth edge identified it as a piece of headlight. He charged the flash on the camera. After taking Polaroids of the headlight shard *in situ*, Garreth picked it up by the edges, though he doubted any of the three had touched it to leave a print, dropped it in a freezer bag, and pressed the seal closed.

Glancing around, he tried to imagine himself in the bb's place that day. What would a pair of juvenile females have done with themselves while waiting for dark? Sleep? Go through Maggie's shoulder bag? The albino no doubt had first crack, but he might have handed it on after taking out all he wanted. If so, maybe when they finished in turn they discarded it...without thinking to wiping off fingerprints first. Maybe those prints even included the albino's.

A long shot, probably, but what better place to be grasping at straws? He shuffled through the loose hay. When that yielded nothing he eyed the piled bales. Would those attract the bb's? Maggie had often talked about the games she and cousins played in an uncle's hay barn, building forts, climbing to where they seemed to be looking down on the whole world. The appeal sounded similar to that of his tree house. At the southwest corner of the open area bales tumbled down like a stairway. Coincidence or the suspects' doing? Either way it provided access to the bale stack, as opposed to the sheer wall elsewhere on this and the other side.

He climbed onto the bales. Would they have stayed on this first level or, assuming height held the same appeal for them as it did for Maggie and him, climbed on up to the far end? He started up but quit halfway. While heat itself did not bother him, he felt it, and that up near the metal roof felt like an oven. Lower down the wind coming through offered some relief. So if they came up here, they most likely stayed on one of the lower levels.

On the way back down Garreth peered around and below him, hunting any sign of the bb's presence. Most of the bales had been stacked tight together, but gaps showed here and there. A variation in color in one such space caught his eye. He scrambled down to the space with mentally crossed fingers. Let it be Maggie's bag.

But when he reached the object, it proved to be made of denim, not black leather. Garreth grimaced. Still, it gave him something and he had been lucky to spot it since it lay almost an arm's length into the gap. He would never have seen it without looking straight down. While fishing it out he kept hoping that he *did* have something from the suspects and not just a ranch hand's jacket lost in the process of stacking the bales.

The object came free. Garreth grinned. Not a jacket, a tote bag. Greenstreet said Valerie had shoved her clothes into a denim tote. This might be an even better find than Maggie's bag. The tote had seen better days, so perhaps Valerie replaced it with the shoulder bag. Fine. When they captured the trio that bag would link them to the crash. He had given it to

Maggie for Christmas four years ago, one of a kind. A custom boot and saddle maker in Hays created it according to Garreth's design, with a side pocket molded to holster the Desert Eagle. Remembering her delight on opening the package turned a knife in him. Maggie had sat holstering and drawing the gun over and over, eyes sparkling, admiring the perfection of the holster's fit, snug yet permitting a smooth, fast draw.

With an effort, he jerked his attention back to the tote. It provided a link to the van and suspects, establishing, along with the piece of headlight, that they hid here after the crash. Valerie had removed all her property from the tote—Garreth checked inside to be sure—but trace evidence must remain, most certainly hair. Every juvenile female's purse he'd ever searched had contained a hairbrush or comb.

After taking Polaroids of the tote and a more distant shot of it sitting by the gap where he found it, then shots of the barn and bale stack, he started to shove the tote in one of the freezer bags. But stopped as he felt an edge through the fabric. In surprise he pulled the bag open and peered inside again. It still looked empty, but he definitely felt something. Possibly a matchbook from its size and shape. The lining had torn at one end and worn through several places near the bottom of the tote. The object must have slipped inside the lining through one of them.

Handling only the edges, Garreth teased the object toward the tear, then fished it out by a corner. A matchbook, stamped *Raddison Northern Hotel, Billings, MT.* Not the hotel where the black girl died but still...Billings. So it appeared Valerie had been there, and if she had been, the tall, pale man at the Sheraton almost certainly had been the albino. Anyone else would be too great a coincidence.

Garreth laid it on the tote and took a Polaroid of the two items together. Then holding the matchbook by the edges, he opened it. One match had been removed. He grinned. This might be a break. It might have few enough prints on it to read some.

He bagged the matchbook separately, then slipped its folded container into the bag with the tote and pressed the freezer bag closed. Then carried everything back to the car to head for town.

18.

Garreth drove up the alley behind Sterling-Weiss and parked at the driveway into the employee lot and garage area. Two tall traffic cones blocked the driveway itself, yellow plastic tape stretched between them declaring: POLICE LINE DO NOT CROSS. Although pointed toward one of the two roll up garage doors, the van sat outside. Garreth pulled his Stetson down to his glasses, over the adhesive strip bandage he had stuck on his forehead, and stepped around the end of the barrier. Even with trees to the west casting shadows across the paving, it still felt hot enough to cook on, but he had no trouble understanding why they left the van baking out here instead of putting it in the shade and security of the garage. The glue-impregnated paper strips suspended from the van's headliner needed a heat source to release the fumes, and what better heat source than the August sun. He did wonder, glancing around, why it appeared to sit here guarded by nothing more than the barrier tape.

Then the rear door of the funeral home swung open and Duncan, wearing jeans and a ball cap and t-shirt emblazoned: POLICE, lounged in the opening...obviously having kept watch from the air-conditioned interior of the building. Not that Garreth blamed him. "Well, well...look who came flying home." Duncan glanced at his watch. "And I do mean flying. I won't even ask how many citations you badged your way out of." He pulled a thin cigar from a box in his t-shirt pocket and lit it. "Did they tell you you've got *me* to thank for finding the suspects' vehicle?" The sweet aroma of brandy-soaked tobacco curled around Garreth. "You're not the only detective in this department."

Whether because Garreth had to spend the whole day awake, or focus so hard for so long on the road, or endure the headache the sunlight gave him despite his glasses and Stetson, Duncan crowing about his investigative prowess when he had merely fallen over the van set Garreth's teeth on edge. He pleaded to an imaginary judge, as a suspect he once arrested had, *It was aggravated battery, Your Honor. He aggravated me into battering him.*

But aloud he said only, "I heard you located the vehicle, yes." Then turned away to circle the vehicle.

A film of white forming inside the windows indicated progress of the fuming, but unfortunately it also prevented seeing inside and learning what prints might be developing. Or did it? Standing on the bumper and leaning across the hood to peer through the thinner film on the upper center area of the windshield, Garreth spotted a fine tracery of white lines on the rearview mirror.

He forgot his irritation, headache, exhaustion, and the press of daylight. "Hey, Duncan!"

Duncan came on the run, took a look in turn, and jumped off the bumper to high five with Garreth. "We got the bastard! They forgot the fucking *back* of the mirror!" He thumbed the mike of his portable radio. "Sue Ann, tell the Chief and Toews we're hitting paydirt over at Sterling!" He dragged on the cigar. "So you've gotten a piece of the action after all, Frisco. But the grand opening ain't gonna be for a while yet so why don't you go hit the rack? You look wiped out."

Such solicitude, Garreth reflected wryly as he headed back to the car.

When he let himself into the PD through the rear entrance, Sue Ann's eyes widened. Nancy glanced around from the computer, then down at his watch.

Garreth sighed. "None, if you're wondering about speeding citations." He set down his laptop case, laid the bags holding the denim tote and glass shard on a desk, and pulled evidence forms and tags from the forms shelves. "Is the evidence kit back?"

"Sorry." Sue Ann gave him a regretful smile. "I expect it's either in Nat's vehicle or he left it in Sterling's garage."

Garreth grimaced at himself. Of course...either place being logical until they finished with the van.

Nancy said. "What've you got?"

Garreth spread the Polaroids on the desk. "The albino and bobbsey bitches left them behind in Dell Gehrt's hay barn when they hid up there Monday afternoon. There's a matchbook we need to check for prints."

"I'll call Nat," Sue Ann said.

She must have notified Danzig, too, because almost before Garreth finished the evidence forms and tags both the chief and Nat blew into the office. Garreth found himself explaining once more how and where he found the items, and reassuring Danzig he had permission from Dell Gehrt to search the barn.

Which Danzig confirmed by calling Gehrt. "Not that I don't trust you, understand," Danzig said. "I just want to make damn sure all the i's are dotted and t's crossed when we finally haul this scumbag's ass to court. Nat, since that ET's gone back to Bellamy, take Nancy to help you go over that barn again while we still have daylight. Serk should be able to handle the watch alone for a while. When you get back, see what you can do with the matchbook."

Nat nodded and started for the rear entrance with Nancy. Then just short of the hallway he turned back. "Garreth, I almost forgot. The female half of that couple in Bismarck called. She says Thone told them he took a job in Canada. Now we're just waiting for Canada to track him through his passport and social security number." The door closed behind Nancy and him.

"Give me a mini evidence kit and I can process the matchbook," Garreth told Danzig.

Danzig shook his head. "It'll be simpler in court if we have just Nat and Melanie Hayes testifying on the physical evidence. But I'd like to hear how it went in Cheyenne."

Garreth told him, finishing with: "I'll make copies of my report for both you and Reichert."

"Good. But as soon as you've finished the report I think you ought to go home to bed."

Everyone wanted to send him to bed. It was like being five years old all over again. But Garreth nodded and turning to the computer, started his report. As soon as Danzig left, however, he opened his laptop on the desk, plugged the phone into it, and with Sue Ann eyeing him curiously, logged on to the Internet.

"And now you're up to what?" she asked.

"Not waiting for the Canadian government." Using the people finder programs, he worked at locating Thone. Most of the search engines had US listings but hunting harder gave him Canadian listings. Toggling back and forth to his map program for province names, he started with the southern tier and worked west one province at a time. No Thone, no Thone, no Thone. And then, in British Columbia, Vancouver had a listing for a Travis Thone. It had to be his man, Garreth reflected. How common could that name be?

He returned the phone line to the phone and punched in Thone's number. Vancouver ran two hours behind Baumen but the man ought to be home from work by this time.

On the fifth ring, a man answered.

"Mr. Travis Thone?" Garreth asked. He introduced himself. "Do you still own the 1995 tan Dodge conversion van you bought at Boggus Dodge in Bismarck?"

Total silence greeted the question.

"Mr. Thone?"

Slowly, Thone said, "No, I don't own it anymore."

"Who did you sell it to?"

"No one." His voice went sardonic. "You might say I lost it in the Twilight Zone."

Garreth stared at the receiver. "I beg your pardon?"

"A poker game with dead men in a hotel suite that doesn't exist. Weirdest damn experience I've ever had. I clearly remember the suite Kerrigan and I went to, and the face of the guy I lost the van to…though I didn't identify him and the other players in the game until the manager asked me to describe them. The next day when I went to try getting my van back the hotel said that room wasn't a suite and it had been vacant for three days. When I argued them into letting me into it, it *was* just a room and didn't look anything like I remember it. I tried contacting Kerrigan but he wasn't registered on that floor or anywhere in the hotel. Then I found that all the money I remember losing was still in my wallet…and I put a name to the guy who won my van. At which point I dropped the whole thing because I knew the hotel and police would write me off as wacko."

"Why?"

Thone hesitated a moment. "Because he's dead. The only reason *I'm* sure I didn't hallucinate everything is because my car keys were gone and so was the van from the parking lot, and the guys in the hotel bar with me remembered Kerrigan and the girls."

Girls? Garreth felt his ears prick. "Describe this Kerrigan and the girls, then. Do you know their names? And tell me what happened from the beginning."

After a long breath, Thone started reciting in the tone of someone who has endlessly gone over everything in his mind. "I don't know the girls' names. Staci and Tracy, Jeri and Geri, something rhyming, but the way they giggled telling us, I'm betting those weren't their real names anyway. One was a big busty redhead and the other petite and dark-haired. She looked part Hispanic or Indian or something."

The redhead sounded like no one they had heard of yet, but could the other one be the Billings victim?

"The redhead said Kerrigan was her brother. Daniel Kerrigan…twenties, skinny, tall but stoop-shouldered, stringy longish reddish hair, Coke bottle glasses. Talked like an encyclopedia."

It could be the albino…slumped, wearing a wig and glasses. The supplies he bought with Greenstreet's credit card number indicated he liked disguises. The so-called uncle in Billings with the dead girl could have been the albino in a more elaborate disguise.

"Two years ago I drove down to Spokane to give a presentation. My company does computer graphics for commercials."

Spokane. Garreth's neck prickled. Two years ago in Spokane a male of the albino's description had stolen credit cards.

Thone said, "After the presentation four of us went to the hotel bar. The girls were there and started joking around, with the redhead pushing her cleavage at everyone. Then in walked this Kerrigan and the redhead called him over. He bought a round and we all sat talking, then after a while I ended up alone at the table with him while the girls dragged everyone else out to dance. Kerrigan started playing with gold coins he said he'd bought that day and rambling on interminably about them. God knows why I didn't just get up and leave. He'd bore a corpse stiff. He invited me up to his room to see some coins too valuable to carry around. I don't know why I went— too numbed to resist, I guess—but as we reached his room a guy taking ice into the suite across the hall hailed Kerrigan like a long lost brother and invited us to join his poker game. I don't know what made me accept that, either, because I'm not a gambler and I don't like poker. But I not only played, I bet heavily, losing all the money I carried, and when I drew a straight flush, I threw my car keys into the pot. I didn't count on one of the other players having four aces."

"The dead man."

Thone grunted. "They were all dead."

"Who were they?"

Thone sighed. "Faces out of history books. Wyatt and Morgan Earp, Doc Holliday, the James brothers. Jesse held the four aces. I know I was had...I just don't know how. Like I said, I lost the van in the Twilight Zone. Now, why are you asking about it?"

Garreth kept his answer simple. "It was used to kill a police officer and we're trying to identify the man who drove it." Who, though not Jesse James, might indeed be a dead man.

After hanging up, Garreth wrote his report, brooding over the computer screen and his notes. What a piece of work this albino was. Whatever else came out of his trip to Cheyenne and talking to Thone, he had learned two things about the albino. First, the albino liked playing games. Knowing that did not help identify him. He could equally be a human wanting to prove himself smarter than other people or a vampire toying with humans to amuse himself. But now the effort put into the Homesick Runaway scam outweighing its profit made sense, and the elaborate charade perpetrated on Thone when the van could almost certainly have been acquired more simply. In playing games, economy of effort would not interest him, nor the amount of the take. The take counted only as an indication of success. The process of playing with the mark was what really mattered. His payoff came in the quality of the game's performance.

Or...it *had* been in the performance. With the introduction of blood games, that could have changed. Probably had, as the games themselves changed. Cold ran through Garreth. Having killed a dog for its blood, then drunk from dying accident victims, why stop there?

He might learn soon enough, because the albino also liked flaunting his cleverness. Why else populate his poker game with dead men, advertising the scam to Thone, or risk discovery waiting in the area Monday until he could leave the van in Baumen?

Garreth preferred to find the suspects before they went for anyone else's blood. How to do that, however, when the albino used disguises so effectively? A wig, glasses, a change of posture appeared to completely alter his appearance. And changing female companions as he had between Spokane and Cheyenne, or shedding them altogether, would make him even harder to recognize.

What concerned Garreth was *how* the albino might rid himself of unwanted females. He kept thinking of the dead girl in Billings. Could she have been the smaller of the pair in Spokane?

He reached for the phone and called Thone again. "Do you have a fax machine there at home?"

In a puzzled tone, Thone answered, "Yes."

Garreth pulled the case file out of his laptop case and extracted the fax photo from Billings. "I'm going to send you a picture. Tell me if you recognize the person."

Five minutes later Thone said, "That's the girl with the redhead."

Although he expected the identification, Garreth felt a surge of anger at the albino. For whatever reason, he had killed that girl. He gave her champagne, had sex with her, and slit her wrists...or made her do it. So where was the redhead now?

Garreth teletyped the Spokane and Billings PD's asking if a female of the redhead's description had been found dead in their jurisdictions between a year and a half and two years ago, then went back to his report worried whether the bobbsey bitches were still alive. Killing them would not only break the trail by reducing the trio to a solo, but if the albino were a vampire, it eliminated the threat of former flunkeys revealing that fact.

Sue Ann called, "Garreth, phone."

On the other end of the line, Sheriff Reichert asked, "How did Cheyenne go?"

"I'm working on the report now." The weight on him vanished. Stretching—sunset, finally!—Garreth gave Reichert a synopsis that included searching Gehrt's barn and both phone conversations with Thone...editing the account of the poker game, as he had in the written report, to reflect only the basic truth, that Thone lost the van to the albino in a poker game. No need to confuse the issue by mentioning dead men and phantom suites.

Though even if he had mentioned them, Reichert might not have noticed. His focus zeroed in on dead girls. "You think this turkey's killed these girls, too?"

Garreth shrugged. "I don't know. I hope not. But it could explain why we haven't had any response to the ATL."

"Continue to follow up on the redhead, then. And add the items from the barn to the other evidence we're sending up to the KBI lab."

Garreth sighed. The KBI techs could find the trace evidence in the tote, match the glass to fragments taken from the van's broken headlight, and scan any prints on the matchbook into their computer for transmission to the FBI. But everyone here could die of old age before results came back, the lab was so overworked.

"How's the Super Glue doing, do you know?" Reichert asked.

There, at least, he had something good to report. "I think we have prints developing on the back of the rearview mirror." Though wanting a print warred with the fear that it would end up matching some police record a half century old and raising uncomfortable questions...

"Well, let me know when we know."

Garreth went back to his report.

He was printing it out when he heard Sue Ann's voice. "Go ahead, Four."

Duncan's number. Garreth spun in Sue Ann's direction.

She nodded at him. "Great! I'll let One and Two know." She reached for the phone. "Ed says we've got prints."

Garreth headed for the rear entrance.

Behind Sterling's he found Duncan leaning against the van's undamaged front fender with a proprietary smirk. "I think you ought to buy me a beer for handing you Lebekov's killer."

"If this van gives us prints that identify the albino," Garreth said, "I'll buy you a *case* of your favorite."

Duncan blinked, his expression momentarily disconcerted, then grinned. "It's Coors."

Nat's Silverado rolled up the alley to the driveway. He swung down from the truck and around the tape barrier. "You say we've got prints?"

Duncan pointed. "Back of the mirror."

Nat stepped up on the bumper to peer through the windshield, then he jumped down and walked around the van opening all the doors. "Let's have a look."

Garreth stepped well back. Though supposedly nontoxic, these fumes always smelled overwhelmingly strong to him. "Did you find anything more at the barn?"

"One more piece of headlight, plus Nancy pulled up some of the bales where you found the tote and farther on down found Maggie's address book/planner and other items apparently dropped down that gap along with the tote."

While they waited for the van to air out, Nat brought the evidence kit from the Silverado. Danzig arrived, pulling up behind Nat's truck. They watched while Nat unpinned the strings on the glue paper from the headliner and dropped the strips in a plastic baggie. And they crowded around the van's side door while he sidled up between the front seats and, carefully grasping the rearview mirror by the side edges, pulled. It came loose from the windshield with a crunch. Once he had it free he turned the mirror over and held it up close to the dome light to study the fine white lines Garreth could see on the back, where the glue fumes had reacted with the organic compounds left behind by whatever member of the trio touched the mirror.

His sigh felt like a punch in the gut.

"What?" Danzig said.

Nat turned around grimacing. "They're smudged."

Duncan swore. Mocking laughter echoed in Garreth's head.

Danzig said, "If they missed wiping one place, maybe they missed others."

Nat nodded. "Hopefully. I'll go ahead and lift these anyway, because even smudged you can tell one is a tented arch."

And arches of all types making up just about five per cent of prints, a right hand tented arch turning up anywhere else could help make their case.

The laughter in Garreth's head died away.

"I need light to hunt for prints, so, buckaroos, if you'll give me a hand, please."

They raised the garage door and pushed the van inside. Duncan hung around a few minutes longer, but when Nat checked the dash and the front seats with no more results, he left mumbling about heading to Kickers for a beer.

While Garreth and Danzig watched Nat work his way around the interior of the van with a spotlight he plugged into the cigarette lighter, moving seats and checking the undersides of arm rests and storage space lids, Garreth told the chief about Thone and their conversations. "I've included it in my report." He frowned at the van. "The more of this albino's work I learn about, the more I worry about our chances of locating him. Disguises...maybe killing the females...and certainly driving a different vehicle now. You know that pickup's probably parked behind some auto repair shop or in a salvage yard." Instead of sitting here watching Nat in what more and more appeared to be a fruitless hunt, he should be out searching for that pickup. If only he knew what direction *to* search.

An hour later Nat slid out of the van shaking his head. "It's a bust. There are some partials scattered around that they missed wiping off, but the lanolin from the baby wipes they used for cleaning has leached into them."

Blurring the partials to useless smudges.

Danzig sighed. "I'll go phone the bad news to Reichert."

Frustration snarled in Garreth. It raged, cursing their bad luck, while he helped Nat pack up the evidence kit and secure the garage and funeral home's rear door, and riding back to the office with Nat. Nor did it help the frustration that no word had come yet from Spokane or Billings about the redheaded female. He climbed into the Porsche and gunned it to life.

Pulling out of the parking lot he thought of Duncan drowning disappointment with a beer and wished *he* could go someplace and drink. Well, maybe he could. He still had a couple of pints in his cooler. He drove to the cemetery, parked, and carried one pint back through the cemetery to the far corner where Lane's grave lay. Sitting cross-legged beside the rose bush planted on top of the grave to keep her in it, just in case cremation did not destroy her, he broke the seal on the pint, raised the bottle in a toast toward the profusion of blood red American Beauties blossoming on the bush, and took a big swallow.

The scent of the blood filled his nose...salty, metallic, delicious. Flowing cold and fiery sweet down his throat, it sent soothing warmth spreading through him. Beneath him, the soil drew at him, cool, soothing, relaxing, inviting him to stretch out and lose himself in it.

"Do you have any suggestions to help me find this bastard?"

But instead of imagining some mocking reply from Lane, he seemed to hear Maggie's voice...angry, hurt. *You're out here again? I still don't understand. She ruined your life. She tried to kill you. Yet you're sitting toasting her and asking her advice? Why don't you talk to* me *and ask* my *advice?*

Guilt pricked him. "I'm sorry." Why *did* he talk to Lane instead of Maggie? Habit?

No, because you're mine, lover. Her arms slid around him from behind. *You always will be.* Her breath tickled the back of his neck. *I made you; we're bound forever. Blood calls to blood, even from beyond the grave.*

Garreth started. He stared at the bottle in his hand, skin prickling on his neck and down his spine. Irina had said that, blood calls to blood. She claimed to have located him at the wake that way. And he had felt her in his apartment. If one or more of these suspects carried his blood now, could he feel their presence, too?

He closed his eyes and let his senses reach outward. Something tugged at him...very faint and tenuous. Garreth turned toward the sensation and...

Saw the albino with a bloody-tipped knife, and a naked man blindfolded and gagged with duct tape. Blood streamed down the victim's arm while the albino dragged his tongue up the liquid, eyes reflecting red as the blood he drank. Grinning, he licked his lips. "Belly up to the bar, children. Drink it while it's still warm."

The vision vanished. Garreth found himself on his feet staring at Ursa Major and Ursa Minor in the night sky...north, icy knots in his gut. If he felt them, then at least one of them had definitely drunk his blood. And the albino and bobbsey bitches were somewhere in Nebraska escalating the violence of their games...or about to. He needed to find them *now*, before the games turned lethal.

19.

For about five minutes Garreth contemplated calling Reichert to discuss heading north after the suspects and argue how that lay within the limits of his involvement in the investigation. But he could not imagine Reichert agreeing without being looked in the eyes and all the persuasive power Garreth commanded. Which meant either descending on Reichert at home tonight or waiting until morning. Or he could follow the advice he overheard his Grandmother Mikaelian say had kept her sane living with his miserly and despotic grandfather: it is easier to apologize than ask permission.

While he doubted he would have to pretend meek contrition while Reichert screamed abuse at him, the principle sounded workable. Trying to put himself in the suspects' place, he left at eleven, by which time on a Monday night the section of 282 along the east side of town would be as dead quiet as the stretch north. He called the SO just before starting and left a message with Cheryl for Reichert.

"Tell him I have this hunch the suspects have gone north and I want to check all the auto repair shops and salvage yards between here and Kearney for the pickup." Not all that difficult a task with only half a dozen towns on or near 282 in Kansas, and another three between the Nebraska state line and Kearney. "I'm sure they've ditched it somewhere in there so they have a free run on I-80. I'll keep him apprised of my progress and fax him copies of my reports, and I'll call when I've located the pickup and when I have a description of their new vehicle."

Gospel truth, as far as it went. They did need to know the suspects' current vehicle, so he might as well try to identify it.

Heading out with the Porsche packed for an indefinite trip, including cash, credit cards in two other names, and the rest of his blood supply stowed in the cooler, he laid the road atlas on the passenger seat, open to Kansas with a gas receipt bookmarking the Nebraska page. If he were the albino, Garreth would hope the van went unnoticed indefinitely, but plan strategy on the premise that he had only until morning before someone discovered the switch and broadcast a description of the pickup. So as he put distance between himself and Bellamy County, the albino would be watching for the chance to switch to a new vehicle. Stealing another was easy enough with night for cover. Many people in these small towns never locked their cars, and when he first moved to Kansas Garreth had been astonished to discover that older farmers left the keys in their vehicles. But a small town also meant people knew the local vehicles by sight, so a strange one would be noticed instantly...and a theft even sooner. Garreth credited the albino with the intelligence to realize that. In his place, then, Garreth would look for a vehicle that no one would miss. With anonymous wheels, and maybe minus the bb's, he could then disappear.

The sky clear and moonless overhead tempted Garreth to run without lights again. Had the albino also done so? Been able to? It would make him invisible on the highway and let him slip unseen through the dark and sleeping towns as he searched for the pickup's replacement. Duplicating what he guessed to be the albino's movements, Garreth made one pass down the main street of each town and along several side streets. When a local gas station also served as the auto repair shop and salvage yard, he had one stop checking, but if he spotted anything else worth closer inspection, he parked the Porsche in deep shadow and explored the town on foot. With their populations mostly around 400, even a human could walk them.

Though a human might have trouble with the dogs. They lunged at their fences and to the end of tie-outs, barking in challenge. Loose dogs charged into the street. But he could shush them with a word, so he had only the problem of becoming conspicuous because the loose dogs wanted to tag along with him.

His jog-through in the first several towns revealed a few possible places to ditch a vehicle....unused barns and garages, an overgrown yard filled with automotive carcasses—pull off the wheels and tags, break or bend the other outside mirror, and rake upright the grass flattened by driving in and walking around the vehicle and the pickup would blend right into the collection—but none them hid the F-150. Thinking of farm trucks with keys in their ignitions, ripe for theft, he eyed ponds between towns, but he doubted that this heat had left any deep enough to hide the pickup.

He also eyed the *For Sale* signs on cars along the way...an '86 Fairlane backed into a driveway in Natoma and an '82 Chevy S-10 parked on the shoulder at the highway end of a farm lane north of Eden. Although the albino had bypassed both those vehicles, Garreth could imagine his attention being drawn to them and him considering the advantages of legal ownership through a private sale. Law enforcement officials would have no way to know about the transaction for thirty days, Garreth could imagine him thinking, or what vehicle it involved...short of blind luck. Garreth saw no way to know, either, short of blind luck...or canvassing every farm and town along 282. But luck could start with finding the pickup. Then he would know the albino had acquired another vehicle by some means, and the area in which he had to have acquired it. *Then* he could canvass.

He needed to find that pickup.

Cyrus had a real salvage yard. An eight-foot corrugated metal fence with matching, chained gates surrounded it, but by jumping up to catch the top on a side where trees gave him cover, then swinging over, Garreth satisfied himself that even an ordinary human could scale it. The pole light above the cinder block office cast enough light for human eyes to see by.

While the chained gates barred a vehicle from the yard, Garreth had no doubt the albino knew how to pick locks. The trick was not to be caught at it. Coming through town he had seen the police department sign on a former bank building and glimpsed a woman behind the counter inside. A dispatcher meant an officer on patrol.

Conscious of criminally trespassing, Garreth slipped along the criss-crossing paths...between vehicles in varying stages of cannibalization and past piles of fenders and frames and doors. Bins in a long shed held smaller parts like pistons and mirrors. His search turned up several F-150's. None, however, of the right year or right damage, or with a topper. But as he explored, his sense of discomfort grew. Not discomfort like guilt...more like his spooked sensation the night Grandma Doyle died. Something about the salvage yard felt...wrong. But what? The area smelled of dust and old oil. Crickets rasped among the metal hulks and listening close, he could also catch the scramble of mice feet. It all seemed perfectly peaceful.

Too peaceful, he realized. Behind the office sat a dog run with food and water dishes in it. Where was the dog?

Looking around for the animal, he discovered that he felt more uneasy toward the front of the yard. So then he played Hot-Cold, tracking the sensation to its point of greatest intensity...a spot a few yards inside the front gate...where a patch of the asphalt drive stretching from street to office showed darker than the rest.

Garreth squatted on his heels, the skin on his neck prickling. Even baking in the sun since...Monday?...night, a faint scent remained. Tasting a finger he licked and drew across the spot confirmed what his nose told him...blood, animal blood—the dog's—but...not just animal blood. He rubbed a wetted finger on the stain and tasted it again. A trace of other blood mixed with the dog's...human blood. Familiar blood. And saying that to himself, he suddenly saw the word's derivation from "family".

He swiveled on his heels, staring from bloodstain to the gates. So they had what?...come over the fence to see if this looked like a good place to ditch the pickup. The dog attacked one of them, someone human, not vampire, and they killed it. And then spooked? Because they had not brought in the pickup. But excitement sparked in Garreth. The fact they contemplated ditching it here meant they had either acquired another vehicle or were about to.

Jumping to his feet, he dusted his hands off on his jeans and raced for the fence. An old Suburban made a handy springboard from which to vault the fence. Back at the car, he slapped on the Bellamy SO emblems, then drove downtown to the police station.

The dispatcher, a wiry little woman in her sixties, sat at the communications desk dozing over a novel.

Garreth lifted his hand to knock on the glass over the counter when her radio crackled to life. "Four Cyrus."

The dispatcher did not stir.

"Four Cyrus."

Her head sank lower.

"*Abby...wake UH-HUP!*" the voice on the radio sang.

Abby started, and hurriedly answered the call, then started again when Garreth rapped on the glass. "Who are you?"

He held up his ID. "I'd like to meet with the officer on duty."

Five minutes later Garreth lounged against the Porsche while a white Crown Vic pulled into the adjoining parking place and Officer Eugene Younger climbed out. Younger looked in his late fifties, with an air of experience and authority...possibly a former sheriff or deputy, highway trooper, or even a retired city cop looking for less excitement ...hair thinning, waist thickening.

He eyed the Porsche with the expression of someone who has now seen everything, but his brows climbed even higher as Garreth explained the reason for being here. "The middle of the night's a funny time to be tracking suspects isn't it?"

"This is when they'd have been through here, so people who are up now are the ones most likely to have seen them. Did anything unusual happen here Monday night?"

Younger's eyes narrowed. "Someone shot the dog at Koloski's Salvage."

Garreth felt himself start. "Shot!"

Younger nodded. "At one in the morning. It sounded like a cannon. I heard the shots five blocks away."

"Shots, plural?"

"Three of them in rapid succession. Whoever fired them had fled by the time I arrived and looked over the gate, though. We had the vet dig the slug out of the dog next morning—only one of the shots hit him—and..." His expression went thoughtful. "Come on."

He led the way inside through the counter, and from a locker in the old bank's vault brought a plastic envelope. Two smaller envelopes in it held the lead portion of a bullet and three .44 magnum shell casings. "The casings were near the dog's body. What kind of weapon again was it they stole from the officer who died?"

"A Desert Eagle." Something knotted in Garreth's throat. "She carried .44 magnum ammo."

Younger hefted the envelope. "Son of a bitch. I wonder what were they doing in Koloski's."

"Hunting a place to ditch the stolen pickup, I think. Do you have anyone in town who's had a van or RV, pickup with a camper, or some similar vehicle for sale?"

The dispatcher said, "There's Lloyd Farrell's delivery van. Except I don't know how serious he is about selling it. He's had the for sale sign taped inside the passenger window all summer but he keeps the van hidden in his garage."

Younger grinned. "Except Monday night I saw it at Marcotte's. I guess he finally took the warnings about his muffler seriously." He turned to Garreth. "It's an Aerostar extended cargo van. When he sold his bakery to young

Hochauser and his wife after they came back this spring from the baker's school up at Kansas State they had a brand new van of their own so they didn't want the Aerostar."

Electricity ran down Garreth's spine. "Let's see if he still has it."

Younger parked his unit in the Farrell driveway and shined his flashlight in through the row of windows in the overhead garage door. Only a late model Escort sat inside.

"Looks like he sold it," Garreth said. "How pissed will he be if we wake him up to ask who bought it?"

Younger switched off his light. "Nothing compared to the neighbors, who'll wake up before he does. Lloyd lost his hearing in Korea and Claudia sleeps with ear plugs because she claims he snores so loud."

Garreth tried to swallow his impatience...despite the urgency hissing in him and the image of the albino with the bloody-tipped knife running through his mind.

But something of his feelings must have shown in his face because Younger said, "I know these are cop killers, but you need to learn to relax, son, or you'll fret yourself into an early grave. Go ahead and smile, but it's true. Now, Lloyd'll be up in just a couple of hours—habit after all those years of baking before dawn—and we'll talk to him then. In the meantime, why don't we have a look around town. I don't remember seeing the van since Monday but that doesn't mean he didn't sell it to someone local."

They looked but did not see a white Aerostar with *Sunrise Bakery* painted on the sides parked in any driveways or around any businesses. Passing Marcotte's Auto Repair, Younger's expression went thoughtful. "You know, I remember seeing a Ford pickup with a topper and damaged side mirror here Monday night, too. But of course I didn't think anything of it because it had an Osborne County tag and the vehicle in your ATL was a conversion van."

Garreth sucked in his breath. Thinking of the dead dog, he gave thanks Younger had not approached the pickup. While he liked evidence of being on the right track, he did not want it at the cost of another officer's life.

At four-thirty they drove by Farrell's house again. As Younger promised, a light showed in the kitchen. He led the way up the back walk. "Five-thirty was the best time to drop by the bakery. The first batch of cinnamon rolls and bread would be just out of the oven and he'd have coffee brewed and welcome an opinion on the rolls while he put his feet up for a minute waiting on the second load in the oven and bread to raise. Hochauser is a good baker but like you...doesn't know how to relax." He pushed a door bell beside the kitchen door. A light flickered inside.

Moments later the light over the stoop switched on and a craggy face peered between the curtains on the door. Farrell opened the door, shaking his head and grinning. The rest of him, oddly, looked just as craggy as his face. Garreth would have expected more flesh on a baker. As the scents of coffee and yeast flooded out past him, Farrell yelled, "YOU'RE TOO EARLY, GENE. THE DOUGH'S STILL RAISING."

The blast of sound drove Garreth backward, catching his breath in pain. Farrell sounded loud enough to be heard back in Baumen.

Quickly, Younger held his hand horizontal in front of Farrell's face and brought it toward the ground. "Sorry about that. He can't tell how loud he is."

Garreth nodded. "I understand. It's all right. He just caught me by surprise."

"Sorry about that!" Farrell said. "I can't tell how loud I am! Come on in!" He opened the door wide and stood aside for them. His voice had dropped to a more bearable level, though it still remained loud.

"It's all right." Garreth fought the urge to raise his voice to match. Instead he concentrated on forming his words precisely. Presumably Farrell read lips. "I understand."

Younger, though, matched Farrell's voice, as they moved past him. "I didn't come for cinnamon rolls today!" In a lower tone, he said, "I guess I didn't mention that he still bakes those every morning. He and Claudia love them with their breakfast. Lloyd!" The voice went up again. "This is Officer Garreth Mikaelian from the Bellamy County Sheriff's Office! We need to ask you about your van!"

Farrell strolled to a cupboard and took down two coffee cups. "I sold it!" He filled the cups from the carafe in a coffee maker and brought them to a kitchen island where he plopped them front of Younger and Garreth. Then he picked up a third cup already sitting on the island amid baking ingredients and utensils.

Younger nodded. "We know! Who did you sell it to!"

Garreth wished he had Mrs. Farrell's ear plugs. This shouting across him would give even someone with normal hearing a headache.

"Fellow name of Jim Strawberry! He and his wife run a greenhouse in Eunice!" Farrell sipped his coffee. "Why do you want to know!"

"Officer Mikaelian's looking for some people involved in a little problem down in his county who could be looking to buy a van like yours!"

Farrell's brows rose. "Well, that might explain the mystery! He was supposed to come back that afternoon to pick up the title and have his wife drive the van home, but he never showed up here and he took the van in the morning! Marcotte called me when he came in to work and found it gone! I don't know how Strawberry managed that! He was here alone as far as I know! He hadn't left me a phone number so I called Information but they didn't have a listing for anyone in Eunice named Strawberry! I thought then that maybe his phone's under the name of the greenhouse, which I didn't know, but...maybe there's no greenhouse, you think!"

Younger nodded. "No greenhouse! Tell us about him! What did he look like!"

Farrell frowned into his coffee cup. "Hippy looking...poor posture, gut hanging over his belt, reddish hair he wore in a pony tail, sunglasses even when the sun wasn't up yet, and a tie-dye shirt!"

Younger glanced at Garreth. "That doesn't sound much like your suspect."

Garreth shrugged that away. "My suspect is into disguises. Mr. Farrell!" He stopped himself, waved to catch Farrell's eye, and resumed with his voice pitched normally. "Sir, how did he explain knowing your van was for sale?"

Farrell shrugged. "He said he was passing through on his way south to Natoma Monday evening and saw the van at Marcotte's! He said since no one was around and he noticed the van was unlocked, he took a peek at the registration in the glove box to get my name and address because he's been thinking about buying another vehicle for hauling plants! He knocked on my back door about six in the morning on Tuesday! Said he was on his way back home—driving early while it was cool...better for the plants he was hauling—and swung by in the hope I was an early riser so he could ask about buying the van! We drove over to Marcotte's in his pickup..."

Yes! Garreth interrupted with a wave. "What kind of pickup?"

"A Ford F-150!"

"With a topper?" Younger asked.

Farrell nodded. "He looked at the van, said he wanted it, and paid me a thousand in cash then and there! I wrote him out a bill of sale, we Xeroxed it at the Jiffy Trip, and he brought me home! Do you think he's the person you're looking for!"

Garreth nodded. "I'm pretty sure. Will you please find that bill of sale?"

While Farrell went to look, Garreth reflected that the albino could have stashed the bb's in the back of the pickup, or left them somewhere temporarily, to keep the male-accompanied-by-two-juvenile-females combination from setting off alarms with any local law enforcement officers he encountered while hanging around to buy the van. Garreth assumed temporarily. Since it did not appear they left the pickup behind in Cyrus, the albino obviously had someone to drive a second vehicle.

Farrell came back with the photocopied bill of sale. Garreth noticed that Farrell's signature had not been notarized. It might be an oversight on Farrell's part, but if "Strawberry" had any intention of registering the Aerostar, he would have seen to it. Something that *did* appear in the bill of sale interested him, too...the words *as is*.

Garreth pointed them out. "Does this mean the muffler wasn't fixed yet?"

Farrell grinned. "Marcotte was going to put it on that day! Saved me a few bucks!"

"Sir, may I photocopy this? We'll return it afterward."

Farrell grinned. "I'm sure Gene will see to it! He knows I'll be putting the cinnamon rolls in the oven pretty soon! You're welcome to have one, too, son!"

Garreth nodded, but back at the PD office with a photocopy of the bill of sale stashed in his computer case for attachment to his next report, he said, "Thank Mr. Farrell for me and tell him I'm sorry to miss the cinnamon rolls, but I have to keep moving." Especially when he still had a while yet to enjoy the night before sunrise.

"Good luck," Younger said. "Though you're making a big mistake being in such a hurry. Taking the time for bits of Heaven on earth like Lloyd's baking is what makes life worth living."

The words twisted in Garreth, razor edged. He felt his smile slip awry and quickly added a shrug. "Thanks for all your help." Backing the Porsche out of its parking space, he gave Younger a salute, then headed up the main street out of town.

20.

For several miles he just drove, breathing deep and slow, concentrating on feeling the tires' contact with the road and through it, the earth beneath the paving...cool and fragrant and healing. Whether he actually contacted the earth or just imagined so, the effect felt the same. Calm flowed through him. Irina seemed to be right.

And when he felt his grip on the wheel relax, he examined his reaction to Younger's words. He would have thought himself beyond wasting energy on regret over food. He barely remembered the taste of it. The question of what made life worth living must be what still touched a raw nerve. After he first came across and Grandma Doyle asked why he still walked, his belief had been that he survived as an instrument of vengeance, to track down Lane. Now it could be argued that he served that purpose again in tracking down Maggie's killers. But aside from that, what *did* make his life worth living? The night runs on the prairie? Driving without lights at night? Life with Maggie could have been a good one, if he had wised up sooner, if he had not, as always, brought too little too late to the relationship.

He shook himself irritably. Wax philosophical later. Right now he had a job to do. Having failed Maggie so often before, he must not do so now. For once, he was determined to be where he needed to be, when he needed to be, ready to give everything for her.

He pulled in at a pasture gate and after peeling the SO emblems off his doors, turned on his phone and called home.

Kit Bauer, the Graveyard dispatcher, answered. "Well, well...the prodigal."

"Prodigal?" Garreth filled his voice with astonished innocence. "Why do you say that?"

"Oh, an impression I got from Cheryl at shift change. She says when she passed on your message about going in pursuit of Lebekov's killers, Reichert wasn't happy. He apparently tried repeatedly to call you."

"Oh, I'm sorry. I had the phone turned off to save the batteries." He turned on the radio, keeping the volume just barely audible to him, and tuned it to a frequency broadcasting only static.

"Whatever." Skepticism filled the word. "Anyway, Reichert told Cheryl that when we heard from you he wants you to call hi—"

"What? Speak up. I'm getting interference." Garreth turned up the volume and held the phone to the hissing speaker.

On the other end of the phone, Bauer hissed, too. "Come off it, Mikaelian. I'm not falling for that. It's the oldest trick in—"

"What? What did you say? Damn piece of high tech junk." Garreth rapped the phone casing.

"Stop playing games! Reichert wants—"

"I'm sorry!" Garreth raised his voice. "I can't hear you at all now! I hope you can hear me!" Lloyd Farrell could have heard him at this volume. "As of Tuesday morning the suspects were driving a 1988 Aerostar extended delivery van, white, with a bad muffler and the name *Sunrise Bakery* painted on the sides! But I expect they'll have painted over or removed the sign by now! They could be using almost any tags! I'm now trying to find where they ditched the pickup! I'll call..." But instead of finishing the sentence, he held the phone to the radio speaker and turned up the volume still more. Then turned off the phone.

As he laid the phone in the passenger seat, Garreth discovered a quick surge of impatience at searching for the pickup. It was history and all his impulses shouted at him to keep hot on the suspects' trail.

But the pickup might have fingerprints.

Garreth spread the road atlas open across the steering wheel and grimaced. *Where are you?* In the albino's place, he would not be content with merely delaying discovery, as with the van, but would want to make the pickup disappear altogether, so law enforcement agencies would not learn he had changed vehicles. Making the pickup disappear became a tall order around towns so small that every non-resident person and vehicle might as well have a neon arrow overhead announcing its presence. Still, there must be a few places to bury a vehicle.

As the thought formed, he found his eye caught by a patch of blue on the map. Kirwin Reservoir.

Seeing it Garreth knew, with the same certainty that he had known the albino would duck off I-70, that the pickup rested somewhere on the lake bottom. But how to find it with miles of shoreline and countless little inlets to search? On the other hand, the map designated the reservoir as a national wildlife refuge, so not all of it would be accessible by car.

With the laptop set up on the passenger seat, he ran the map program, focusing on the reservoir with maximum enlargement. The reservoir's shape resembled a frog's torso with kicking hind legs. Roads ran along about half of the northern shoreline, from the dam to the top of the "thigh", and along the southern shoreline from dam to the toe of the lower "leg". That cut his search area by two thirds. Plugging the phone into the computer and logging onto the Internet, he tried to learn if the reservoir had organized campgrounds that would eliminate more area from his search, but found little more than its designation as a wildlife refuge, which presumably allowed fishing and boating as some other refuges in the state did, and the name and address of the Fish and Wildlife officer assigned to the area.

He closed up the computer and gunned for the road to Kirwin. Limiting his search to shoreline with road access still left him with plenty of area and he preferred to search as much as possible before the sun and fishermen rose. The southern side seemed the place to start. The town of Kirwin lay below the northern end of the dam and across access to the northern shore...full of possible witnesses the suspects would have wanted to avoid.

Steering along the twisting shoreline road a short while later, Garreth saw that the landscape gave the albino one way to dispose of the pickup. Limestone layering and erosion had carved the area hills into stair steps, with broad benches sloping to limestone risers. Around the reservoir the water lapped almost at the bottom of some risers. Send the pickup down one of the benches with the accelerator jammed to the floor and momentum would carry it well out from the shore before gravity pulled it down. If he had done stunt driving, the albino might even ride it into the water. Garreth did not expect the ground, hardened by the summer heat, to bear any marks, but would the parched grass still show tire prints? None of the inviting dropoffs he had passed so far showed any.

"All right, Grandma. If you're hovering at my shoulder playing guardian angel, I could use a push in the right direction."

But no sense of pushing came. As the sky lightened, he tried not to hurry. Hurrying he might miss something vital. Though he could well miss just as many signs at any speed.

Then he spotted a sign...a printed one, reading: *boat ramp*. Something in him felt like it came on point. What could be easier than just driving the pickup into the lake? The vehicle would not have to stay afloat long to drift twenty or thirty feet out, where the water would be deep enough for the keels and motors of boats in use on this lake to pass over it. But had they driven in here? Garreth knew only one way to find out.

He parked in the lot at the top of the ramp, stripped to his boxers, and waded down the ramp into the water...giving thanks that he did not mind cold. The sun's heat had not noticeably warmed the lake. Diving in the water around the island in Baumen's Pioneer Park hunting lost objects and one missing child had already shown him how much longer he could stay under than ordinary humans. So taking a deep breath, he submerged and swam out from the ramp in a careful zig zag. As he had when diving around Pioneer Island, he felt like he entered a dream world…all monochrome, misty shapes, and slow motion. Vampire night sight also let him see well under water, within the limits of the water's clarity, with the green glow from his watch dial casting its color over everything around him. Here suspended silt restricted visibility and if not careful, he could well swim within a few yards of the pickup and still miss it. Though at least he did not have the handicap of light from a lamp reflecting back at him off the silt.

And because of that, within minutes he spotted a squarish, dark shape lying on the bottom and parallel to the shoreline about fifty feet off the end of the ramp. Swimming closer and circling the object confirmed that he had found the pickup, sitting mostly upright but tilted toward the passenger side. The tags had been removed, but the F-150 had a topper and a damaged passenger door and side mirror. And close examination explained how it drifted so far out before sinking. All the doors and windows and the edges of the topper had been sealed with duct tape to keep it buoyant as long as possible. But the albino had also made sure it sank. The driver's door had two holes punched through it, the truck bed four. Fingering them, Garreth pictured the albino standing on the boat ramp with Maggie's Desert Eagle, firing into the pickup below the water line. Chill spread through him. The gunfire would have been loud, especially here on the water, and could have brought the local Fish and Wildlife officer to investigate. The albino had taken a big gamble. Unless he knew how to make himself a quick silencer by sticking the gun barrel into the neck of a plastic liter soda bottle and firing through the bottom. Still, this series of firearm incidents disturbed him even as he wondered if being caught up in the power of a weapon, such a human thing, meant the albino was human. What might the albino choose to shoot at next? Or could he have already used the gun, say on the bb's, before he sank the pickup, so he could travel more lightly?

Garreth surfaced to take another breath, then dived down on the pickup again. Peeling off his boxers gave him something for wiping silt from the windows but the interior remained too dark for even him to see anything inside. That left him no choice but to open the car. Carefully, with one trip to the surface for another breath in mid-task, he loosened the tape from the door frame while leaving it attached to the door itself and although swimming should have washed the salts and oils from his fingers, pulled the door open with his hand wrapped in the boxers. Only trash floated inside. He closed the door again and swam around to the back and lifted the topper door open. But the back proved empty, too.

Surfacing, he treaded water while he caught his breath. So it appeared the albino still did not consider the bb's a liability. Maybe because being a vampire, he felt he needed their aid? Or vampire or wannabe, he wanted an audience to appreciate his cleverness?

Garreth swam back for shore. There he dug a dry pair of boxers out of his bag and quickly dressed, debating his course of action. The wet boxers he wrung out and tossed in on top of the cooler. By rights he should not have plunged into the search on his own but contacted the Fish and Wildlife officer about his suspicions and let *him* organize the search...but having by-passed correct procedure, did he now backtrack and contact the officer, then tag along on the search and act gratified when they found the pickup? Or should he by-pass procedure some more and keep on the albino's trail?

Garreth wrestled with the question during the drive back toward the dam, and while he halted there for a quick breakfast, eyeing the town of Kirwin on the far end, where the Fish and Wildlife officer lived. He pictured himself standing around observing organization and execution of the lake search, watching the pickup hauled back to land, watching it processed it for prints and trace evidence which had in all probability been destroyed by immersion anyway. Against the time necessary for that he balanced the albino's apparent fascination with Maggie's gun, and the vision of the blindfolded man. It made the choice an easy one.

Taking a deep breath, he drove down into Kirwin and from a pay phone called the administrative number of the Phillips County Sheriff's Office. "A buddy told me something this morning that it seemed to me you ought to know," he told the male voice who answered. "He was out fishing on Kirwin Tuesday morning and heard a whole bunch of popping sounds." In case they found a soda bottle silencer in a trash barrel. "When he pulled up his line and headed his boat the direction of the sound, he spotted this tall, skinny, white-haired kid with a huge handgun standing on the boat ramp on the southern shore with a couple of young girls. They were watching this blue pickup sink about fifty feet out. He didn't say anything to anyone but me because he'd called in sick to work in order to go fishing, but I thought you ought to know about it."

"And what's your name, sir?"

Garreth hung up.

Hopefully the albino and pickup's descriptions would ring a bell, then the Phillips SO would notify the Bellamy SO and the pickup would be retrieved. He headed back for 282 and the albino's trail.

21.

Golden clouds above the eastern horizon threatened imminent sunrise. Garreth slipped on his glasses. With the pickup hopefully taken care of, he could focus on the suspects. They needed to do something about the muffler and the bakery sign on the Aerostar, so how and where would they be most likely to do that? According to the road atlas, Eunice up near the Nebraska state line had a population of about 1000. That might be big enough for a dedicated muffler shop...but would the albino want to risk them having a suitable muffler in stock, let alone waste hours, or even a day, while the shop worked on the Aerostar? It would be faster and cheaper just to patch the muffler. They could not have bought the materials in Cyrus, though. The stores there would not have been open yet when the albino took possession of the Aerostar. But they would be open in Eunice by the time the albino reached there. And according to his map, Eunice had a state lake outside of it, which would provide a secluded place to work on the muffler and spray paint over the bakery signs. Spray paint would not stand up to close scrutiny but it could pass until they reached somewhere with a good variety of auto services and large enough for strangers to go unnoticed...such as Kearney or Grand Island.

The sun had risen by the time he reached Eunice, mercilessly golden and oppressive. Should he bother checking in with the local police and going with them to the local Wal-Mart and Orscheln to see if one of the bb's showed up on a security tape buying white spray paint and Fiberglas patches? Would that further the investigation other than, maybe, providing him with a photo image of dubious quality? Why should he spend any time here when he knew the three had left? By closing his eyes he could feel the thread stretching on north.

Forget Eunice.

Across the state line in Nebraska he called the PD office. "Have we had any reply to my query to Spokane or Billings?"

"Both of them replied," Wendy Bessler said. "Neither had a dead female matching your description. You need to call the SO. That stolen pickup may have been located."

Garreth filled his voice with astonishment. "That's great! Where?"

"Kirwin Reservoir."

"Well I'll be damned. I passed right by there. Right now I'm in Eunice checking muffler shops. I'll give Reichert a call." But he called Cheyenne instead and traced down Bradshaw.

Bemusement edged Bradshaw's whisper. "Yes, the Clearinghouse sent us some possible matches on those females. I had no idea before how many small blonde females of twelve and thirteen disappear each year. They gave us about a dozen from the northwest region alone. Only about four possibles for Valerie, though. I'll run those by Greenstreet a little later. Where do you want me to fax everything?"

Just ahead lay the Republican River and the town of Pony Ford. "Let me call you back."

The locked door of the town marshal's office bore a notice that he had gone to court and law enforcement complaints should be directed to the sheriff's office. But the local Dillon's had a fax machine.

"It's ninety-nine cents a page," the clerk said.

"No problem." He called Bradshaw back on the digital phone and gave him the fax number.

The photos wrenched at him. They all looked so very young...just babies. He hated to think of the sweet faces gone street hard and innocent eyes turned old, and how many were probably dead or dying...from malnutrition and abuse, from drugs, from AIDS or venereal disease or hepatitis. But none of the blonde females' photos looked more than generally familiar, in the way that many pre-pubescent children resembled each other, and he recognized none of the four dark-haired possibles, though two of the photos, obviously school photos, might have come close if they had not been so stiff that Garreth doubted they bore any resemblance to the living children. He hoped that one of the two, Deborah Adkinson of the fixed Beauty Queen smile or sullen Rebecca Newman with the skinned back hair, was Valerie. He hated to think that her family would not care enough to report her missing.

He gathered up the photos and information sheets, thanked the clerk, and resumed the drive toward Kearney.

On the way he finally called Reichert. "I hear the pickup's been located. You know, I kept looking at farm ponds but dismissing them because they didn't look deep enough. It looks like the suspects found water deep enough."

"The question is, did *you* find it, too, then phone an anonymous tip to the Sheriff's Office?"

"Me?" Garreth filled his voice with surprised innocence. "Do you think I'd locate the vehicle then not stay around to see if it has useful evidence?"

"So you won't resist being asked to stand by representing our department while Phillips County processes the van?"

Garreth's gut knotted. However phrased, Reichert had clearly issued an order. But somehow that order had to be evaded, without seeming to evade it. He must not lose his authorization to work the case. "You want me to backtrack all that way?"

"All..." From Reichert's tone, Garreth visualized the sheriff frowning. "Just where *are* you?"

"Kearney." Close. He would be there in an hour.

A long silence came from the other end, then: "Mikaelian, turn around and head back to Kirwin. You were pushing our agreement when you wanted to go to Cheyenne. I'm not sure why I let you...maybe because it wasn't active pursuit. But this time you've gone too far."

"With all due respect, sir, I disagree." If only he were face to face with Reichert, staring the sheriff in the eyes. He felt so helpless having only the power of his voice. "Okay, I've fudged on our agreement but nothing I've done or am doing is over the line. And I *have* learned what vehicle they're driving now, which we might not have discovered otherwise."

"Though we'd have started looking for another vehicle after that tip led us to the pickup," Reichert said dryly. "I grant you it might have been a long process, but...now we know and every agency it in Kansas and Nebraska will be watching for it, so you've done your job. And now I want you there seeing what evidence the pickup will give us."

But it's a waste of time for me to be there! He pumped all his persuasive power into his voice. "That's just it...everyone will be *watching* for the Aerostar and the suspects. No one will be *hunting*. Let...me...hunt. I'm figuring out how this bastard's mind works. I can find him! But I have no intention of trying to approach him myself. I didn't even bring a weapon along with me." Absolutely true. "I'll check in with the local agency wherever I'm following up leads, keep in daily contact with you, and when I find the suspects, step back and turn the show completely over to the locals." If the albino were human, that should work. If a vampire, then by being in the background Garreth would escape the albino's notice and have the element of surprise when he moved against the albino. He held his breath waiting for Reichert's response.

After a long pause, Reichert said slowly, "All right, I'll let you go on to Nebraska...on one condition. First you go back to Kirwin."

Garreth swore silently. But he clenched his jaw to hold back the hiss of exasperation. "Yes, sir. I'll keep you posted on what we find."

"Let's hope we find something useful. Oh, one more thing...leave your phone on."

As he pulled into a field road and slapped the SO emblems on the Porsche's doors before heading back south again, he reflected that maybe the delay was a small enough price to pay for staying on the hunt. Maybe fortune would smile and they would find some of the albino's prints on the under side of the tape. But with the memories of the blindfolded man and the bullet holes in the pickup playing behind his eyes, impatience and protest howled in him.

He passed through Pony Ford, crossed into Kansas, passed Eunice. Daylight dragged at him, feeling twice as oppressive as usual.

Five miles south of Eunice, the phone warbled at him.

"Okay, forget Kirwin," Reichert said when he answered. "Head for Lincoln. Our suspects apparently spent the last several days there. Only this time they didn't leave a bloody glass and towel in their hotel room...they left a bloody man."

Garreth caught his breath. "Alive or dead?" It had to be the blindfolded man in his vision, and once more he heard the albino say to the bb's: *Drink it while it's still warm.* Anticipating that the man and his blood would soon be cold? Had his vision caught the last minutes of the victim's life?

"Alive, fortunately," Reichert said.

Garreth let his breath out in relief. "When was he assaulted?"

"Last night. He was found tied up in his hotel room about an hour ago."

And Lincoln had notified Reichert already? "How did they link this incident to our suspects so fast?"

"According to the sergeant I talked to after their teletype came in, they made the connection because the victim's assailant was a man over six feet tall dressed as a woman and calling himself Margaret Lebekov."

22.

The scene could be Cheyenne all over again...parking the car, slogging across the street through the press of daylight to a police building, showing his ID at the desk inside and asking for an officer, this time a Sergeant Kreutzer. Though as opposed to the early morning quiet in Cheyenne, driving through the bustle of Lincoln's noon hour, the Bellamy County emblems on the Porsche's doors earned him a whole succession of double takes, and a state trooper pulling out of the parking lot as Garreth turned in followed the double take with a grin and thumbs up...a gesture that struck Garreth funny as an echo of the phallic state capitol building dominating the emblem directly below it on the patrol car's door.

But one thing had changed dramatically from Cheyenne. There he studied an old, cold trail to learn the shape of the suspects' tracks. Here he breathed down their necks. If he had any doubt they had been involved in that attack, it would have vanished as soon as he arrived in the city. He could feel them...or rather, feel their trace, left behind like a scent. Closing his eyes, he focused on that trace, reaching out for the link, sensing its direction. East...and north...

He started at a voice piercing his concentration. "Mikaelian? Emil Kreutzer." *A*-mill *Kroit*-zer.

Opening his eyes, he found the voice's owner bearing down the corridor toward him....a rich chestnut complexion and the slim elegance of a dancer contrasting sharply with the Teutonic name. And with every step Garreth could feel himself growing scruffier by comparison. Like his Homicide lieutenant in San Francisco, Kreutzer possessed a sartorial gene that let him wear an off-the-rack suit so it looked like an Armani.

"The car's this way." Kreutzer swept Garreth up in passing, like movie footage Garreth had seen of trains snagging mailbags hung from poles, and dragged him back into the crush of midday light. "I don't know which you're most interested in, the crime scene or the victim."

We don't need either, Garreth wanted to say. *All we need to do is head northeast.*

But Kreutzer never paused for an answer of any kind. "The truth is, we'll just be underfoot at the hotel—fortunately we connected these perps with your suspects in time to secure the room for processing—so I'm headed to Lincoln General for another interview with the vict—Mikaelian?" He stopped in mid stride and swung to peer at Garreth over the top of dark glasses. "The same Mikaelian this turkey tried to kill? And you're working the case?"

Garreth made himself smile as he lied. "Not working it." He could hardly go around trying to exert mental control over everyone in the world. "Sheriff Reichert is just having me shadow other agencies as they become involved in the pursuit. Because when we do catch the suspects, I can identify them."

Kreutzer pushed the sun glasses up his nose. "Oh yeah? If you don't mind me asking, exactly what went down? The ATL information—there's the car—hasn't gone into much detail."

When they turned north out of the parking lot, then east, for a minute Garreth hoped the hospital lay the direction the suspects had gone, but Kreutzer was only heading for a street he could take south. Sighing inwardly, Garreth filled Kreutzer in on his encounters with the albino and bobbsey bitches and their victims.

The detective grimaced. "This guy's some piece of work. Let me give you the latest chapter. Victim's name is Lowell Becker. He's one of the exhibitors at the New Security Technologies exhibition opening at Pershing Arena today, hawking a pepper foam and security version of silly string, I gather. A housekeeper found him in his room at the Cornhusker Hotel this morning. The door had a Do Not Disturb sign on it but she said that since he'd left early the last three days and no one answered when she knocked, she went on in to make up the room. She thought at first she'd caught him asleep, since he was covered with the blanket...and then he moaned and she saw his head wrapped up in duct tape. She called hotel security. The hotel called us. Our responding officer and the paramedics arrived about the same time. A hotel security officer had already freed Becker's wrists and ankles and pulled off the gag and blindfold."

"Laying the tape out flat, I hope."

Kreutzer grimaced. "You're thinking about latent prints on the back side? Unfortunately he balled it up as he pulled it off. But he hadn't touched the duct tape wrapped around the biceps on the victim's left arm, and Officer Reece made sure the paramedic cut it off carefully."

"Why was the arm wrapped?"

"The tape and a folded pair of jockey shorts under it made a pressure bandage for a gash on the victim's arm. The paramedic told Officer Reece that without it Becker would probably have bled to death."

Garreth blinked. The albino left Maggie and him to die but not Becker? Why? "What does the victim say about what happened?"

Kreutzer grunted. "Next to nothing, just that a pervert transvestite calling himself Margaret Lebekov stuck a Desert Eagle in his face—Mr. Becker obviously knows enough about firearms to be able to identify them even staring into the muzzle—forced him back to his room and made him strip naked, then wrapped him up in duct tape and cut his arm with a knife. After a bit he also stated that the assailant licked his arm and might have been drinking his blood. But the name Margaret Lebekov and mention of the weapon your ATL said had been stolen from her alerted Officer Reece to the possibility of Becker's attacker being the same as yours, and he called it in to the office."

Waiting at a red light, Kreutzer drummed his fingers on the steering wheel. "I don't know what's with the guy. I understand this is pretty traumatic and he'd probably like nothing better than to get the hell out of Dodge and try to forget it ever happened to him, but I don't understand why he won't give us all the information possible to help us catch his assailant. Becker's not injured seriously enough to require hospitalization. A gash on his left arm took a number of stitches but as gory as the bed looked, he didn't lose much more blood, the doctor estimates, than he would donating a unit. So we're holding him in the ER for 'observation' until we can pry more details out of him."

If the albino knew Becker's business in Lincoln, no doubt he would enjoy the irony. Or perhaps he did know, Garreth reflected. Perhaps he picked on Becker for just that reason.

A car ahead swerved into their lane, almost into their bumper. Kreutzer's hand shot toward the siren switch, hovered, then fell away as he shrugged. "But we've learned a few facts even without Becker's cooperation. At one point he suggested Officer Reece quit wasting time with him and 'go catch the bastards before they check out.' Reece says he doesn't think Becker realized he used the plurals, and doesn't know why Becker was sure they were at the hotel, but Reece called the desk. Good move. They told him that a Margaret Lebekov and her son and daughter had been registered there since Tuesday evening, but had checked out several hours earlier."

Garreth frowned. Passing as female...turning one of the bb's into a boy? The albino had as many twists as a corkscrew.

"Luckily the housekeeper on that floor hadn't cleaned the room yet."

"Good luck processing it. They clean up very carefully behind them." But maybe not this time. He could always hope. "How did they list their vehicle and tags on the registration?"

"No vehicle. They left by cab."

Garreth stared at him. Cab? What did they do with the Aerostar?

Ahead a sign on a driveway marked the entrance of the Lincoln General ER. Kreutzer turned in. "The Capital Cab who picked them up took them to the bus station."

"Which is where from your headquarters?"

Kreutzer raised his brows, clearly surprised by the question. "North about three blocks. Why?"

Garreth grimaced. Wrong direction. They did not stay there long.

"We know that." Kreutzer parked in the doctor's section.

To his horror, Garreth realized he had spoken his thought aloud.

Kreutzer set his Kojak light prominently in the middle of the dash. "But they didn't buy bus tickets and no cab has picked up an adult of either sex accompanied by two adolescent juveniles. They had some large pieces of luggage, according to the hotel doorman, so even with wheels on the big suitcase, I'm thinking they wouldn't have wanted to walk very far. What do you mean, *wrong direction*?"

No reasonable lie came to mind. The best Garreth could do was shrug. "I don't know. A stray thought. They could have left separately." But heading where? To pick up the Aerostar? They spent three nights at the hotel. Maybe something happened to the van and they had to put it in a shop for repairs. Or, came a sudden thought, for alteration? Could the albino have felt safe enough to take time for that? Nothing major could be done in just three days, but they could remove the bakery signs and decal on a stripe set. "What car shops in the area do auto painting and decals?"

Climbing out of the car, Kreutzer straightened and stared across the top at Garreth. "I have a buddy in the police garage who'll know the places to check. Otherwise we're in for a lot of phone time. There are probably two dozen auto repair shops within fifteen blocks of the hotel alone."

But they could ignore everything not northeast. This time Garreth made sure he kept the words in his head.

As they approached the ER doors he braced himself. The outer and inner doors hissed open...and the flood of scents poured out to engulf him...a symphony of blood. He waded in through the flood, drinking in the symphony, separating its elements. Raw blood there and there, fresh and still flowing...from bodies or down tubing into bodies...sharply metallic, salty, mouth-watering. Setting his throat and teeth aching in hunger. Coagulating blood over here, soaking clothing...blood jelly. He licked his lips. Rancid blood there...dead blood in a dead body. Bloods variously soured by disease wafting at him from lines of chairs over there.

"Hey, man, are you all right?"

Garreth started at the interruption. "I'm fine." He tucked his Stetson under his arm. "Why?"

Kreutzer pulled off his dark glasses. "You're looking, I don't know, like my dog does when we start our evening walk. He stops at the top of the steps and sniffs before he heads out, reading the neighborhood I guess."

Sorting through a hundred different scent stories. Garreth could identify with that. An analogy he preferred to the maybe more accurate one of someone standing at the door of a candy store. "Where's Becker?"

Kreutzer hailed the security officer, and stopped at the desk to show his ID, then tucking his dark glasses in his breast pocket, strolled on back through the ER. Moving with him, Garreth peered into the rooms, hunting the face in his vision.

And quickly spotted it. He started to push open the door.

Kreutzer caught his shoulder. "Mikaelian, Becker's *this*—oh...that *is* him. They moved him. How'd you know?"

Garreth thought fast. Damn...he should have just trailed along, letting Kreutzer lead the way. "I—he—I don't know; he looks like the albino's scam victims."

And Becker did resemble Greenstreet, Garreth realized, despite being years younger. Prematurely thinning hair and a well-nourished sleekness created an air of middle age, and with the grey of fear gone from his face, his expression had become one of complacent self-importance. His bandaged arm was the only outward sign of trauma.

He looked around as the two of them pushed into the room and scowled, complacency turning to petulance. "Why am I still here? Some officer who came in and took my fingerprints wouldn't tell me anything. The doctor says I didn't lose enough blood to worry about but he won't release me. I have an exhibit to supervise, you know!"

Kreutzer gave him a bland smile. "I guess they just want to make sure there's no delayed reaction and you won't pass out into your pepper foam literature. You've had a pretty traumatic experience, after all. But it's just as well you're here. I need to ask you more questions. We need to know more about the attack on you."

Becker stiffened. "I've told you everything that's important. I don't know any more. The pervert dressed like a woman so I don't have any idea what he really looks like and he didn't happen to hand me his card with his name and address on it."

Garreth always tried to regard victims sympathetically. He could understand displacing anger on the people closest at hand. But Becker raised his hackles.

Kreutzer's jaw had tightened, too, he noticed, though the detective kept his voice pleasant. "Mr. Becker, we'd rather be the judge of what's important. You said he pulled the gun on you and forced you to take him to your room. Where were you when he pulled the gun on you? Did he hide it so no one else noticed? How did you discover he was a man and do you have any idea why he approached you as a woman in the first place?"

Becker stiffened. "How the hell should I know? Maybe he's got a thing for this Lebekov bitch and—"

"Mr. Becker." Garreth made himself imitate Bradshaw's near whisper to avoid a whip-cracking snarl. The slur sent anger hissing through him. He pulled off his glasses and hung them on the breast pocket of his sportcoat, moving deliberately to keep from backhanding Becker. Though how much more satisfying it would be to tear the albino apart. He not only killed Maggie but stole her identity...and presumed to use it in the commission of a *crime*!

Becker barely glanced at him...seeing what, a skinny kid in cowboy boots, dusty jeans, and a rumpled sportcoat, holding a Stetson tucked under his arm? The glance dismissed him as insignificant and returned to Kreutzer.

Garreth's gritted his teeth. The arrogant son of a bitch!

Becker scowled at Kreutzer. "Just go do the job you're paid to do and—"

"Mr. Becker," Garreth interrupted again, in the same Bradshaw voice.

Becker glanced around again, staring down his nose. "Who are you?"

"The partner of Maggie Lebekov." He punched every word at Becker. "The *real* Maggie Lebekov...a fine, dedicated police officer murdered by the same man who attacked you."

Becker reared back, clearly startled.

Garreth caught his eyes, held them, drilled his own gaze into them. "Knowing that, you're going to stop worrying about your own ego...aren't you? Because you realize that not only lets this son of a bitch get away with killing her and attacking you, but with profaning her name. Neither one of us are going to let that happen...are we? You...will...answer...all ...our...questions." He discovered that he wanted Becker to resist, wanted to have to beat the man down and break his will. "Tell us everything that happened. Right...now."

But Becker caved instantly, as if hollow inside. The story poured out in a rush. "Last night some of us from the Security Technologies exhibition were sitting around in the hotel bar, the Five Reasons, and up came this babe who looked like a showgirl...the longest legs I'd ever seen...and you could see almost every inch of them in that skirt. She started talking, asking what we're in town for, and when we told her about the exhibition she said she's in security herself, and showed us her badge. At first she sat around joking with all of us, but after a while it was just her and me, with her rubbing her leg against mine and her boob against my arm. She suggested we go up to my room. But when we got there and she starting working on my belt and zipper—" He squirmed. "—I pulled up her skirt and..." He stumbled into silence, going scarlet.

"Found more than you bargained for?" Kreutzer said.

Becker winced. "The next thing I know I'm staring into the muzzle of a Desert Eagle and he's laughing. He has a real ugly laugh. 'Surprise,' he says, then, 'Okay, I showed you mine; you show me yours.' And he made me strip, laughing the whole time. He used my phone to call someone else in the hotel, gave them my room number and said to bring the duct tape."

"Who came?" Kreutzer asked.

Becker shook his head. "I don't know. He said close my eyes and he'd shoot my dick off if I opened them. But I think there were several and one of them was a little girl. None of them said anything, at least not then, just him. They wrapped the tape around my eyes and mouth. He said it was better I not see what was going to happen."

Thereby terrorizing Becker by letting his imagination run amok.

"And what did happen?"

Becker swallowed. "He threw me on the bed and taped my ankles and wrists. He told me he had a knife and started running the tip of it all over me, singing a song about a red robin bob, bob, bobbing along. Then he started getting weird."

Kreutzer caught Garreth's eye with an expression that said: *Then* he started?

Garreth drew in a breath. Had the albino done something that would reveal, finally, definitively, whether he was human or vampire? He found himself lowering his voice still more. "Weird how?"

Becker stared through Garreth, vision turned inward. An artery throbbed below the angle of his jaw. "He started talking about blood. At first I thought it was to me, but then I decided it was to the others...about how blood is life and power and the taking of a person's blood brings the ultimate power over that person, and how blood makes a fountain when a throat is cut or torn open and how it feels to have that fountain pumping in your mouth. 'Splashing at first,' he said, 'hot and hard and salty sweet, then softer and softer and ever slower as the bottle empties.'" Becker's voice slowed and lowered in concert with the words.

Beyond him, Kreutzer listened with an expression that said: *sicko*. Garreth heard through the haze of a sudden ravenous hunger scalding his throat. His vision locked on the artery throbbing in invitation in Becker's neck while his head filled with the man's blood scent and his imagination with the taste of it. With an effort, he wrenched his eyes from the artery.

"'But the last is best,' he said," Becker went on, "'...the final oozing drops telling you that you have it all...all this person's life.' But then he *was* talking to me...right down by my ear, whispering in it. 'Total power over him,' he says." Becker's voice dropped to a whisper, too. "'Nothing tastes as sweet as death.'"

Psycho, Kreutzer mouthed.

Vampire. He had to be. Garreth sucked in a breath. The bastard *knew*. He sounded just like Lane.

"I just knew he was going to cut my throat." Becker covered his face with his hands. The whisper leaked between his fingers, hoarse with the memory of terror. "He kept dragging the point of that knife back and forth across it. When he stabbed my arm I thought he *had* cut my throat." He shuddered.

"And then you think he licked the blood off your arm?" Kreutzer said.

"They took turns. Then...they just walked away" Becker lowered his hands and sat slumped on the bed, spiritless. All arrogance gone.

But Garreth still felt no pity for the man. Controlling Becker was too easy to use up his anger.

"Left, you mean?" Kreutzer asked. "After bandaging your arm?"

"No, they stayed in the room but they walked away. I could feel blood running down my arm but they ignored me, just letting me bleed while they searched the room. The guy warned the others to put on gloves, then I heard drawers opening and closing, and the guy said, 'Well, well, look at this. I'll just take it since he won't be needing it.' I guess he found my travel cash and spare credit cards in the false bottom of my shaving kit. When the stretcher went out I saw everything from the kit scattered on the bathroom counter."

"How much cash?"

Becker shrugged. "Five hundred. He got my billfold, too. I spotted my pants across a chair with the pockets inside out. There was a couple of hundred and a credit card in there, too. Then I guess they'd had enough fun. They left." He sighed. "Is there anything else? I think you're right about after-effects. I don't feel well."

"Did they ever call each other by name?" Kreutzer asked.

Becker shook his head.

"What about the bandage on your arm?" Garreth said.

"Oh." Becker sighed again. "When the guy went in the bathroom this girl's voice said, 'The sight of him makes me sick. Can I cover him up?' The guy said yeah if she wanted. There was a gasp and a shushing sound, then the girl whispered in my ear, 'You're a pig but I guess you don't deserve to die for it.' and she started wrapping my arm with tape. When the guy called out he'd found my cash, I thought she wouldn't have time to finish the bandage before he came out of the bathroom. But then the guy decided to take a leak. I could hear him whizzing. She whipped that tape around my arm and yanked the sheet up over me."

Garreth eyed him in disbelief. One of the bb's had a heart? But that did not answer his original question: why save Becker when they were perfectly willing to leave Maggie and him to die? The question kept anger simmering in him as he and Kreutzer left Becker and made their way back through the ER.

Kreutzer eyed him. "What about that doesn't make you happy? That was slick. I just don't understand how you made him roll over like that."

"What doesn't make me happy?" Garreth grimaced. "The man *is* a pig. He could have told you everything when he was found, but no, Mr. Pecker couldn't admit that he invited his assailant up to his room thinking he was about to get laid."

Kreutzer pursed his lips. "I think groping a man freaked him out."

"Whatever...you wasted hours waiting for him to come clean. Instead of being down here, we could be out hunting the shop that worked on the Aerostar, learning what it looks like now so we can update—"

They froze. A male in his twenties...clothing over-sized enough to bag even on his big frame, rings in his nose and ears, straggling beard...stalked through the ER doors holding a gun. Seeing them, he thrust the weapon out arm's length, aiming at first Garreth, then Kreutzer, then the security officer stepping automatically forward. "Everyone back!" His eyes glinted, white-rimmed. "I'm coming in! I want a nurse with the key to the drugs and I don't want any fucking nonsense or someone's going to *die...understand!*" He shrilled the last word.

The sudden silence behind him told Garreth that everyone in the ER had frozen. He imagined the fear on all the faces, staff and patients alike. But fury boiled up through him. Another of the world's stupidest criminals! The moron appeared not to know that his Colt Pony had double-action mechanism and needed to be cocked before it could be fired. But he had also left the safety on...and the magazine protruded abnormally below the gun butt. "You worthless piece of crap!"

The gunman swung to aim at Garreth. But not fast enough. Two steps had brought Garreth in arm's reach. His left hand grabbed the Pony's barrel and twisted the weapon up and into the male's thumb, ripping it free with a force that audibly dislocated the thumb. At the same time his other hand grabbed the male by the throat, cutting off the scream of pain. The throat gave in his grip, the outer flesh doughy over the inner stiffness of cartilage. With only a little more pressure he thought he could make his hand could completely encircle the adam's apple, thumb and fingers meeting between trachea and spine. The male gurgled, his eyes bulging. Then an inner voice sounding like Maggie cried, *No, Garreth!* accompanied by Lane's, warning, *Witnesses!* Shit. But he released the throat and grabbed the beard instead. He jerked the gunman forward, then as the gurgle turned to a squeal, pivoted, dragging his captive along on the spin and slinging him into the ER. "You want in...then *come on in*!"

Still squealing, the male hit the tile sliding backward and on his side...caromed off an empty wheel chair and into the waiting area, into loose chairs...sending them sliding, too, through scattering patients, successive rows piling up ahead of him until they all hit the wall in a tumbling, rattling crash of metal.

A part of Garreth noticed Kreutzer had secured the entrance and was calling for backup on his portable radio but Garreth's focus remained on the gunman...following him with measured strides. "Let me suggest, you bungling cretin, that if you presume to enter a life of crime, you take the trouble to learn the tools of your trade!" As he talked he grabbed the protruding bottom of the magazine and wrenched it free—the imbecile had put it in backward! He longed to reinsert it correctly, but—*witnesses!*—settled for pretending to do so while letting the magazine drop into his coat sleeve, flipped off the safety, pulled the slide back as if chambering a round—reassuring himself he had an empty weapon...cocked it. "There...now it'll work." He aimed at the screaming male and pulled the trigger.

Kreutzer yelled, "No!" Nurses and patients gasped. The male doubled, screeching.

The hammer fell...*click*.

"See?" Garreth said. To his satisfaction, a pungent smell and spreading stain on the male's trousers indicated that the would-be thief had fouled himself twice over. Garreth released the grip so the Pony flipped over and dangled from his index finger by the trigger guard. Turning, he extended the weapon toward a gaping Kreutzer. "Sir, I'm not sure about this, of course, because I've never met you before and I'm sure you don't know me from Adam, but I thought I heard someone say you're a police officer. Maybe you'd better take possession of this. And this." He shook the magazine out of his coat sleeve. "And that dog shit under the chairs. Now please excuse me."

He scooped up the Stetson from where he dropped it, settled it down to his mirrored glasses, and headed out through automatic doors. As they hissed closed behind him, the voice of the hospital guard slipped through, wry: "Say, who *was* that masked man?"

23.

Eight blocks from the hospital Garreth heard a vehicle approaching behind him slow. As it pulled even the passenger window hummed down. "Feel better?"

Garreth could not blame Kreutzer for the dry tone. *Did* he feel better? In one respect, yes. But the "no's" outweighed the "yes." Since leaving the hospital he had kept thinking: how could he let himself lose control like that? It could have been worse—he sweated blood thinking of the worse—but he should have stopped at just disarming the bastard. "Any guesses how bad the fallout is going to be?" Lincoln's Internal Affairs did not apply to him but depending on how Kreutzer reacted, this could make trouble for Danzig and Reichert.

"What fallout?" Kreutzer's brows rose. "I'm cool since I don't have much sympathy for scumbags who stick a gun in my face...and you didn't make me witness to a homicide." An undertone suggested he might not be feeling quite as cool as he claimed. "It's just personally embarrassing. I mean, this unarmed civilian disarms a drug-crazed thief then walks away while yours truly of Lincoln's Finest stands there with his thumb up his butt. And I can't even help track down the civilian. It all happened so fast I didn't get a good look at the guy, and I know the security officer didn't either."

Garreth eyed the empty rear seat. "Speaking of our perp...what did you do with him?"

"Turned him over to a member of the Southwest Team, of course. I didn't want him stinking up *my* vehicle." Kreutzer paused. "You want to get in or are you planning to walk back downtown?"

Garreth climbed in.

As the door closed, the lock thunked down. Startled, Garreth glanced at Kreutzer.

The detective's hand came back to the steering wheel. His eyes remained fixed forward as he pulled back into traffic. "Never, *ever* do that to me again."

Garreth slunk down in his seat. "I'm sorry." Kreutzer did not respond and Garreth waited several blocks before speaking again. "Where are we going?"

"The Cornhusker." He switched on the car radio and they listened to police calls against a background of classical music the rest of the way downtown.

In the hotel lobby Kreutzer left Garreth to stare at the soaring ceiling, woodwork, and grand sweep of stairs while he used the house phone, punching in two numbers. Garreth heard him mutter, "How's it going?" to whomever answered the second number, and for the first time since leaving the hospital, smile. Hanging up, he crooked a finger at Garreth and headed for the elevators. "Let's go. Lady Fortune has smiled."

Upstairs Garreth did not need the uniformed officer in the corridor to indicate where they were going. As soon as they neared the door...he knew. That room. And it had been *their* room. The sense of menace raised the hair on his neck.

"Mikaelian!"

He realized Kreutzer and the uniformed officer were staring at him. "What?"

"That's what I want to know." Kreutzer stuffed his glasses in his breast pocket. "You just—well, to use another dog metaphor...you went on point. What gives? I think you owe me."

Garreth felt as if Kreutzer had just locked another door on him. He could hardly admit the truth. Or could he in this case? "You'll laugh."

"Try me."

The uniformed officer, who appeared about to smile and whose eyes seemed to have a permanent crinkle of amusement, eyed him with obvious curiosity.

Garreth took a breath. "Sometimes I...sense things. Courtesy of my Irish blood, probably. My Grandma Doyle had Second Sight. Whatever the source, it told me this is the suspects' room. Am I right?"

No doubt about the smile now. And over it the uniformed officer peered up at Kreutzer. "Hey, Cruiser, you ought to introduce him to *your* grandmother."

Kreutzer did not share the amusement. Face deadpan, he strode past into the room. "Okay, Sparacino...so we're just in time for something exciting. Thrill and impress us. Oh, this is Officer Mikaelian from Bellamy County in Kansas, where these suspects killed an officer."

A dark-eyed woman looked up from checking an evidence list against a room sketch and numbered hinged lifter cards holding fingerprints. "It's up to you to be thrilled and impressed. We've already done our part. I found plenty of prints in the victim's room, but except for the ones on the back side of the duct tape from the victim's arm, I doubt any of them will be the suspects'. So many had overlying smudging from someone wearing gloves. In here the Piece turned up just some partials—your suspects cleaned up very carefully...polished almost everything to a fare-thee-well— and thought he'd have to be satisfied with those. That is until—but it's his find so I'll let him do the Show and Tell. Reece, baby, you're on! And Kreutzer has a newcomer shadowing him."

Reece? Garreth glanced back toward the officer in the open doorway. That was the name on *his* name tag. Then he noted everyone watching him expectantly.

When the evidence tech in the bathroom opened the door Garreth understood why. They wanted to see his reaction to double vision...the same amused face as at the door, the same compact build. Only this version wore a t-shirt and jeans. "That's cute. Not many departments have identical twins."

Kreutzer and Sparacino grinned. "Meet the Reeces Pieces," Kreutzer said.

Garreth could imagine civilians running into them separately at a crime scene thinking: *Man, that officer gets around...but how did he change clothes so fast?*

Sparacino dropped the fingerprint cards into a bag. "There's a younger sister, too, who's in the document examination section. Fortunately she doesn't look anything like these two."

Obviously an old familiar insult. The Pieces rolled their eyes. The one in the bathroom said, "Try to focus, okay? Ev, get the door and the lights." Then as his brother came in, closing the room door and flicking off the lights: "Now if I can have everyone in here..." In the darkened bathroom he switched on a blue spotlight and pointed it at the raised toilet seat, then handed it around to let each of them peer through the orange filter attached to the top of the spotlight. "Today's blue light special."

When Garreth's turn came his pulse jumped. The bb's had forgotten to clean under the seat! Fingerprints fluoresced on it. And several faint ones on the right side of the seat had a tented arch.

He handed the light back to ET Reece. "We lifted a tented arch from the rearview mirror of the van that ran Maggie Lebekov off the road but that one was too smudged to do us any good."

Reece squinted through the filter toward the seat. "I'll lift those first. They're going to take some work. This guy isn't much of a secretor. Okay...the party's over. Out of my way and let me work."

They cleared out. Back in the room Kreutzer asked Sparacino, "Did you find anything else of special interest?"

"Some fibers that look like wig fibers...hardly a surprise when we know the suspect was wearing one."

"But useful for comparing to the wig fibers *we* found in their first van," Garreth said.

Kreutzer glanced toward him. "Speaking of vans, now would be a good time to check car shops." He reached toward the phone. "Deb, is it all right to touch the phone?"

When Sparacino nodded he picked up the receiver and punched a number.

Calling his buddy at the police garage? Garreth pulled the Lincoln Yellow Pages from the bottom of the bedside table. They did not need the best places for painting, just what someone new in town would be likely to use. Because of a billboard, or visibility from the highway, or an ad in the Yellow Pages. Garreth leafed through the auto section. It had a staggering number of listings, even limiting the search to the shops specializing in body repair and painting. He could picture the albino pulling in somewhere off the Interstate, opening to these same pages. What would catch his eye? A name that put that shop at the front of the listings…A-1, like the body shop in Baumen where they left their first van? Flashiness of the ad? The inclusion of a map to find the place?

Then a small ad jumped out at him…a frame of elaborate swoops like pin-striping around five lines of text with a look of skilled hand lettering. *Night Wolf Custom and Paint.* Below that an address, the information *motorcycles welcome*, a web site: *www.nightwolf.com*, and at the bottom a phone number in one corner and in the other: *Evening hours.* Garreth stared at it. Evening hours.

Kreutzer hung up the phone and turned to Garreth. "My buddy's given me a dozen names. Come on. We'll call them from the office."

Garreth ran his fingers across the ad. "Is one of them Night Wolf Custom and Paint?"

Kreutzer turned to eye him. "No. Why? That guy I'm familiar with and he's into the art of motor vehicles, not repairs…chopping, fabricating, pinstriping, flames…murals on the sides of semi trailers. He'd sooner cut off his hands than 'repaint' a car."

"What direction is his shop from here?"

Kreutzer's eyes narrowed. "Let's go." He led the way out. At the elevators he stabbed the *down* button. "The shop is northeast. Is that the 'right' direction?"

Of course Kreutzer would remember that comment. Garreth gave him a shrug. "I know it sounds weird."

Kreutzer leaned into the elevator button again. "So I suppose you want to skip calling these other places and go straight to check out Night Wolf's."

"If you'll indulge me."

The elevator doors opened. Two men and a woman in the car stepped back to let Garreth and Kreutzer on, never missing a beat of their discussion on barrier and alarm efficiency.

Kreutzer said nothing during the ride down, but out starting the car, said, "I'm going back to the office. In the first place, the guy doesn't get up before mid-afternoon. Second, I don't believe in this psychic bullshit. It's just lucky guessing and you know it. You had a fifty-fifty chance of being right about the room...and if it'd been the victim's room you could just claim you 'felt' the suspects because they left such a strong psychic scent or somesuch."

Garreth blinked. Kreutzer's voice could have scratched diamonds. Something had pushed his buttons big time. Something *Garreth* had done...aside from almost choking Dog Shit?

"It's one thing for an old woman who grew up around voodoo mumbo-jumbo to believe in this stuff but someone who's supposed to be educated and logical has to be playing games. It isn't a game I'll play! We work my way or you can go back to Kansas. Do you have a problem with that?"

Now Garreth understood. Even though he tapped the button, Reece's wisecrack jammed it home. *Where* was *your grandmother raised?* he wanted to ask. *What does she do that embarrasses you so much?* But Kreutzer's declaration to the contrary, they were playing a game...Kreutzer's. So Garreth folded. "No problem." Hopefully he had never acted embarrassed about Grandma Doyle's Feelings.

Back at Headquarters, Garreth swung by his car and picked up his laptop before heading for Kreutzer's desk. Standing there at the car with the door open, he toyed with the idea of not catering to the detective's hangup, just climbing in and going to visit Night Wolf on his own. But the LPD had that print from the toilet seat. He needed to stay allied at least until they heard back on it. So he slung the computer case's carrying strap over his shoulder and trudged across the street to where Kreutzer waited inside the front door.

At least the daylight had dimmed. Clouds rolling in from the west covered the sun in an ever-thickening layer. To the west they looked almost purple. A thunderstorm coming. His choice for daylight weather.

Inside, Kreutzer watched warily while he set the laptop on one corner of the semi-cubicle's desk and plugged the digital phone in to it. "What's that for?"

Garreth shrugged. "I thought I'd check out the Night Wolf web site."

Kreutzer's mouth thinned. "You people just won't let go of it, will you."

Garreth sighed. "Look, I'm just—"

"So let's take care of this right now." Kreutzer grabbed the phone book and checked the Auto listings....dialed. From the length of time he waited, the phone must have rung close to ten times. Kreutzer started to hang up, then stopped. "Good afternoon, Mr. Francis. I'm sorry if I woke—...Oh, good. This is Sergeant Kreutzer of the Lincoln Police Department. Tuesday afternoon or evening, or any time this week, did anyone bring you a white, 1988 Aerostar extended delivery van to work on?...We're not sure. It could be either a man or women, but he or she would have been over six feet tall and probably thin....We don't know that, either. Maybe to remove a bakery sign on the side or paint over the sign. Have you see the vehicle?...Well, thank you very much." He hung up. "He hasn't seen any Aerostars lately, let alone agreed to work on one. Satisfied?"

"Are you satisfied he was telling the truth?"

Kreutzer sighed. "Yes, I'm satisfied he told the truth. Why would he lie? Now, do you want to help me canvass the places your albino *would* have gone to?"

"Sure." He could be wrong about Night Wolf. He had no justification for concentrating on the shop other than thinking a vampire—real or wannabe—would be attracted by the hours. Taking half Kreutzer's list, he dialed the first number. At the same time, however, he logged onto the Internet and typed in *nightwolf.com.*

The web page opened with a bang—but not before Garreth noticed it had been updated on Wednesday—*Sprach Zarathustra* accompanying a morph that transformed a rusted hulk labeled *1953 Allard* into a gleaming restoration. Then the site introduced Night Wolf, born Marion Wolfgang "call me Wolf" Francis, in the back seat of a 1965 Riviera and car crazy ever since. It trumpeted his artistic talents, expounded his beliefs on the Automobile As Useable Art, and bewailed the homogenization of body design that now made one make of car virtually indistinguishable from another. Judging by the pictures in his gallery pages, he followed rhetoric with action by waging a campaign for individuality, decorating cars with not just pinstripes and flames and airbrushed murals, but stringing garlands of mums and bronze roses across the hood and along the doors and body of a Rolls Royce bus with its body repainted a variegated cream-to-amber. Garreth had never realized Rolls Royce made buses...one roughly the size of the short buses used for special education student transport, but with the seats running lengthwise down each side. Judging by its body style it came from the World War I era or early twenties. Night Wolf had also wood-grained the sides of a Falcon station wagon to mimic a Woody. He also chopped and reshaped, creating a Mustang station wagon and, shades of Travis McGee, a pickup from another Rolls Royce.

At the bottom of the gallery pages appeared a link to Works In Progress. Garreth clicked on it. Like the opening gallery page it showed a group of thumbnail pictures. A sleek shape teased him into clicking on the one labeled *Atlantic reproduction.* And for a minute he could only sit and stare at the machine the text said reproduced a 1995 Chrysler concept vehicle...all sleek, swooping lines, slung low between four huge wheels. Even with its exterior dull with primer and no seats in it yet, he wanted to climb in for a test drive. Just looking at it he could hear the rumble of the engine and snarl of its exhaust.

Reluctantly he backed up to the thumbnail page.

Then the square white shape in the last thumbnail, labeled *Watch This Space*, caught his eye. He clicked on it...and as the extended image loaded like a lowering shade, Garreth found himself staring at a white Aerostar expanded delivery van, a ghost of lettering spelling *kery* visible on its side under an area of brighter white. *A blank canvas*, the legend under it said,...*an opportunity pregnant with boundless possibilities. What can we create from it? Stay tuned and see!*

Garreth waited for Kreutzer to finish his call, then turned the laptop to show him the screen. "Sergeant?" He kept his voice even...carefully free of triumph or smugness. "Check out this page of Night Wolf's web site." As Kreutzer stared at it, mouth tightening, he longed to say *I told you so*, but opted for tact instead. "Obviously the man's an accomplished liar."

The narrowing of Kreutzer's eyes said the diplomacy had not fooled him. He stood, kicking back his chair. "All right, we'll go see—" He broke off, frowning past Garreth. "What's up?"

Garreth turned to see ET Reece trotting into the room grinning. "Good fortune. Since your buddy here said they lifted a tented arch off a vehicle the suspects used, we went ahead and scanned one of our tented arches into AFIS and sent it off to NCIC as soon as we got back here." He paused.

Garreth's heart leaped. He held his breath.

"And we got a hit."

Reece paused again, obviously to draw out the suspense. Garreth waited in agony, longing to learn the name, but at the same time fearing the suspect's record would raise questions difficult to answer...though Garreth saw none of the confusion in Reece's face he would have expected if previous arrests occurred, say, before someone the suspect's apparent age was born.

Kreutzer showed no appreciation for suspense. "Give it to me!"

Reece's smile faded. Rolling his eyes, he pulled out the fax sheets he had tucked into his belt behind his back and handed them to Kreutzer, and a photocopy of the fax to Garreth. "According to the FBI, the print belongs to a Cameron Dark, arrested buying crack in San Francisco three years ago and skipped bail."

No arrests before then? Garreth stared at his photocopy. That blast of menace hit him again, looking at the mug shots. And angry satisfaction. *The scent's heating up, Maggie*! It was the face he remembered...and the one in his visions. "That's the bastard who ran us off the road."

"I'll query the SFPD for details." Kreutzer headed for the door. "We should have them by the time we're back from Night Wolf's. I'll meet you at the car."

"Wait." Garreth logged off the Internet and began shutting down the laptop. "Let's take my car. It may catch him off guard, or at least amuse him. I'll be waiting for you at the front door."

Kreutzer's upturned eyes said: *Why me, Lord*? He sighed. "Okay. Fine." And disappeared out the door.

"You're welcome," Reece called after him.

"Here." Garreth reached into his computer case for the photocopies of the bb's prints on his car. "Use these for comparison with prints in the suspects' room." Then he tucked his photocopy of the fax away and headed out the door, too.

The clouds continued to thicken and darken, Garreth noticed with satisfaction as he crossed to the parking lot, and from the west came a distant rumble of thunder. Music to his ears.

When Kreutzer stepped out of the building five minutes later, a trench coat over his arm, he stopped cold in the middle of the sidewalk for a moment, staring at the car, then came around it and folded himself into the passenger seat. "We'll amuse him, I think. Head north and catch 180 to the Cornhusker."

While he drove, Garreth thought about the albino. The print had a name attached to it, but did they finally have *the* name, or was Cameron Dark just another alias? It sounded like a name a vampire might adopt. The arrest bothered Garreth, however. Why would the albino be buying crack? A vampire would not use it, and had no need of it to render someone else compliant. Maybe the albino was just a wannabe after all?

By the time they reached the interchange connecting to the Cornhusker Highway, the storm clouds had darkened the afternoon to twilight, turning on the streetlights. Motorists had begun switching on headlights, too. Kreutzer frowned out the window. "Look at that. And it started out such a nice day."

But Garreth reveled in the gloom. It made the afternoon bearable, and almost as pleasant as sunset. "It's *still* a nice day. Look how much progress you've made on the case...a name for the suspect, and now details about his vehicle."

"Assuming Wolfie talks."

"He'll talk."

"Like Becker?" Kreutzer eyed him, grimaced, then cleared his throat. "Ah...look. About popping off on the psychic thing...you have to understand. I've caught a ton of grief ever since my grandmother waltzed into the department one day and offered to help find a murder weapon for us. She—she thinks she can find things..." He grimaced again. "...by dowsing for them. She even brought along her wires to demonstrate how they worked."

So that was her big offense, and the reason for Reece's comment. Garreth tried to imagine how he would have reacted if Grandma Doyle had done something similar. Certainly not with anger and embarrassment, but then, he believed in her Feelings. "I take it the department didn't accept her help?"

The color across Kreutzer's cheekbones darkened. "I didn't let them. I hustled her away before she could make a bigger fool of herself."

He did not even let her try, not even in private, with just him watching? "Was the weapon ever found?"

After a long pause, Kreutzer said, "No. Oh...in case you haven't felt it, you need to take this upcoming exit."

Garreth took the exit without comment. Overhead, thunder grumbled closer, audible even above the snarl of the Porsche's engine.

Night Wolf Custom and Paint occupied a former car dealership building, fifties vintage judging by the semi-circular showroom and the black-and-white tiled floor. Now the Mustang station wagon from the web site sat on display there, even cooler looking than in its picture. Garreth parked in front of the two roll-up doors in the garage area of the building and they tried the showroom doors, but found them locked. So was the standard door between the garage doors and showroom. Kreutzer finished shrugging into his trench coat and leaned into the car and across to hit the horn three times.

A minute later the door opened. The man standing there reminded Garreth less of a wolf than the cartoon Tasmanian Devil...head about level with Garreth's shoulder, no neck, shoulders almost as wide as the doorway, straining at his paint-stained t-shirt, but almost no hips or legs in his jeans. He leaned on crutches secured to each wrist with a metal cuff and eyed them through a fringe of hair protruding below the bandana tied around his head. The scent coming from him mixed blood and paint. "Yeah?"

Kreutzer started forward, badge case in hand. Garreth jumped in first, pointing up at *Motorcycles welcome* on the building sign. "Hogs are welcome. What about pigs?"

Why the double take? Garreth wondered as Wolf—presumably Wolf—started, then frowned at them. Thunder boomed closer. "From what department?"

He had certainly caught on to that reference fast. Stepping back, Garreth pointed at the Porsche.

Wolf's eyes narrowed. "I never heard of Bellamy County. What brings you into Lancaster County?"

Kreutzer reached over Garreth's shoulder to dangle his ID in front of Wolf. "Let's discuss it inside."

Wolf did not move except to peer up past the ID at Kreutzer. "I just talked to you on the phone."

"Right...but now I want to talk to you again."

Thunder boomed even closer, and a sudden gust of wind slapped them. Wolf looked as though he were contemplating shutting the door in their faces. "I don't know why. I already told you I don't know anything about your Aerostar."

"What about the one on the Works In Progress page of your web site?" Garreth asked.

Wolf stared at them a moment, then sighed ruefully and worked his way backward. "Who'd have thunk you'd check my web site."

They followed him. Another gust of wind caught the door and slammed it behind them.

The only lights inside flooded down over a Model A...where a tracery of green looping across the paler green door, ending at a stool and tea cart with paint cans on it, indicated that Wolf intended to decorate this vehicle, too, with flower garlands. Beyond the Model A, the rest of the garage disappeared in darkness. Garreth's vision, though, let him see the Atlantic reproduction standing with the hood off and a small block V-eight engine hanging from a hoist beside it...racks of tools, welding and cutting equipment, other hoists, one end of the garage walled off with a compressor outside and breaker boxes on the wall with the arms up in the *Off* position. A paint room?

Wolf led the way around a corner past a lift up to a loft area and into an office with sketches and photos pinned all over cork-covered walls and every horizontal surface, except the computer section of the L-shaped desk, piled high with

car magazines. A window looked out into the showroom.
He plopped behind the desk in a high-tech looking swivel
chair and, peeling the cuffs off his wrists, hung the crutches
on the edge of the desk by their grips. "Clear yourselves a
place to sit."

Garreth moved a stack of *Hemmings* from an oak side chair
to the floor. Kreutzer continued to stand, hands jammed in
the pockets of his trench coat. "Why'd you lie about the
Aerostar?"

Wolf leaned back with his hands behind his head. "I remember you. You used to be on the Northeast Team...always
coming around looking for evidence of a chop shop." He ticked
his tongue and shook his head. "Just because I've got outlaw-
looking friends and like to work nights. But..." He focused
on Garreth. "...exactly who are *you*, deputy?"

"Wolf—" Kreutzer began.

But Garreth had already pulled out and handed over his
ID.

Wolf glanced over it. "Mikaelian. Sounds Armenian."

"I think my great-grandfather—"

"Doesn't matter." Wolf tossed back the ID. "I don't have
anything to say."

Kreutzer stiffened. "You ought to reconsider that. I can
take you in for obstruction."

Wolf shrugged. "You do what you have to." He reached
for his crutches. "Just let me go up and tell my old lady what's
happening."

"I'll go with you."

"What do you think?" Wolf's mouth twisted. "I'm going
to take to my heels?"

"No need to come upstairs, Wolfie darlin'." In the office
doorway stood a woman in her mid-twenties, wrapped in a
terrycloth robe, a mane of dark honey hair falling down around
her face and shoulders. A faint scent of honeysuckle drifted
from her. She strolled over to Wolf and leaned down to kiss
the tip of his nose. The action opened the top of her robe

enough to show she wore nothing under it. "And I've heard enough to assess the situation." Honey filled her voice, too.

Wolf stroked her forearms. "You're up early."

"Well, it's such a lovely day I decided to enjoy it with you." She pulled his hand into the robe to her breast while a deafening crack of thunder shook the building.

Garreth glanced out through the office window to see the first few raindrops hit the showroom windows.

She flipped up the arms of the chair and swung astride Wolf's lap, baring both her legs to the hip...quickening Wolf's breathing. "But before afternoon delight, we need to send these good gentlemen on their way. So why don't you go ahead and talk to them?"

Despite the obvious flare of desire in him, a heat Garreth felt echoed in himself, too, watching her, Wolf scowled. "But he's from the same—"

She wrapped her legs around both him and the chair and worked her hips deeper into his lap. "But I doubt very much that he's the one, darlin'. Deputy, sugah." She glanced over her shoulder at Garreth. "Do you have any children?"

Garreth blinked. What? "A son."

"How old?"

The conversation had been bizarre from the moment the woman entered but this took it a quantum leap beyond. "Twenty-two."

Both Wolf and Kreutzer stared at him in disbelief. But the woman nodded, smiling. "I did suspect he's older than he looks. Now just one more thing, deputy. Why are y'all lookin' for the Aerostar?"

Kreutzer's stare switched to her. "Who are you?"

"Savannah."

"Savannah what?"

She smiled languidly over her shoulder. "Mercy, sugah, I've been married so many times I can't keep track of my last name. But my first one is almost always Savannah." And as she turned the smile toward Garreth, her eyes reflected red.

Recognition jolted Garreth. Vampire! Some detective he was, he reflected in disgust. He should have realized the moment she walked in smelling only of perfume, and how could he have kept missing it after all the clues in their conversation? How could he overlook the old eyes in the young face? She obviously recognized *him* right away.

Suddenly unwrapping her legs, she swung to her feet, and Garreth watched her catch Kreutzer's eyes. "We want to cooperate, sugah, really we do, but...it's only fair you tell us why you want the Aerostar."

She had clearly been around for some time. For all its honey, her voice carried so much power Garreth felt compulsion tug at him even without eye contact.

Kreutzer never had a chance to resist. "The driver unlawfully restrained and battered a man here in Lincoln and he killed a police officer in Kansas."

Wolf sat upright in his chair. "He?"

Anger flared in Garreth. Had the albino had pretended to be Maggie here, too? "The officer who died was named Margaret Lebekov."

Wolf caught his breath.

Savannah snugged her robe around her. "Darlin'...I think you'd better tell them everything. But," she told Kreutzer, "you have to understand Wolfie thought he was doing a good deed, helping a lady in distress keep some kids away from an abuser. My knight in shining armor." She ruffled his hair, smiling. "Even as...negative as some of his contacts with the police have been, he'd never help a cop killer. Hear?" Her eyes narrowed. "Or do we have to wait for his lawyer before he says anything?"

"All right, we'll ignore the fact he's aided a fugitive," Kreutzer said. "Talk."

"Okay." Wolf took a breath. "Tuesday evening I'm working on the Model A with the doors up to get air inside. This Aerostar pulls into the drive and the tallest woman I ever saw climbs out...legs all the way to her shoulders. She strolls up to the door and says, 'I see by your sign you welcome hogs. What about pigs?'"

The hair raised on Garreth's neck. He and the albino opened the same way? No wonder Wolf looked startled. "And she showed you ID for a Margaret Lebekov."

Wolf nodded again. "She said, 'But I'm not here as a police—'"

"Darlin'," Savannah interrupted gently, "they'll be just as happy with the Reader's Digest version. She told you she needed help to keep two children—a couple of girls she brought out of the van—away from an abusive father...a superior officer in her department. No one would believe her story and take the girls away from him, so she took off with them. She said he had her charged with kidnaping and probably other trumped-up charges. She traded her known car for the van in Grand Island but as an added precaution, wanted to change the appearance of the van to make identification of it more difficult. All a pack of lies, it seems now."

"I'm surprised he took *you* in," Garreth said. If he could find a way to talk to her alone, she could tell him if the albino were human or vampire.

She raised her brows. "But I never met the 'lady'. Tuesday evening I was out...shopping, and then on my way to bed this morning when she came in for the van. I only saw her from the loft."

"The big question," Kreutzer said. "What did you do to the van?"

"Well, she couldn't afford to wait long so I had to keep it simple." Wolf swiveled to his computer, Savannah staying with him, hands on his shoulders; picked a disc from a carousel of them; and slid it into the tower's floppy drive. The blank screen lighted as he spun the track ball on the mouse, and the pointer flashed across the screen, through a succession of menus, until the drive light flickered and Wolf sat back.

Presently an image filled the screen...a white extended Aerostar but no longer a delivery van. The panel area now had windows.

Kreutzer's brows rose. "You call putting in windows simple?"

Wolf grinned. "It is when they're trompe l'oeil. And it's a first rate job if I do say so."

"It is," Savannah said. "You can't tell they aren't real until you're right up to them."

The shake of Kreutzer's head said he cared nothing about the artistic value. "So now we're looking for an Aerostar with painted on windows."

"Well, not necessarily," Wolf said. "I didn't paint the windows on the *van*. A friend of mine down the street does magnetic signs. I did the windows, two for this side, one for the passenger side, on sheets of material I got from him. So she— he could use the windows or not."

Kreutzer sighed. "So the Aerostar may or may not have windows."

"Or maybe a florist's sign. My friend had some he'd made that never got picked up for one reason or another and we sold those to her—him, too."

Kreutzer rolled his eyes.

"But I believe you copied down the license number, didn't you, darlin'...on the check?"

Dismay twisted Wolf's face. "Oh, my god. The check. I don't suppose it's any good?"

Garreth shook his head. "It's stolen."

"Son of a bitch!" He jerked open a desk drawer and started to reach in.

Kreutzer blocked him. "Wait." He reached in the pocket of his trench coat and pulled out a plastic bag. "Never leave home unprepared." Picking up the check in the drawer by the one corner, he slid it in the bag. "This should give us some nice prints to compare with Dark's. Thank you for your cooperation, Mr. Francis."

Wolf shook his head. "My father always said no good deed goes unpunished."

Savannah kissed the top of his head. "Let me comfort you. You put yourself in first gear, darlin', while I see the gentlemen out." But she hung back, letting Kreutzer move ahead, and lifted a inquiring brow at Garreth. "You look like a man with a question you don't want to ask in front of Mr. GQ," she murmured.

Kreutzer pushed open the outer door and swore. Rain poured down. He glanced back at Garreth. "Are you coming or what?"

"Be right there."

Turning up the collar of his trench coat, the detective dashed for the car.

Garreth asked, "Could you tell at all if this customer had a blood scent?"

Her eyes widened. "You mean there's a chance he's one of us?" She frowned in thought, then shook her head. "I'm sorry. I was too far away this morning or too sleepy to notice."

"Thanks anyway." He started for the door, then stopped and pointed toward the office. "Are you going to bring him across?"

Her gaze measured him, clearly trying to analyze the reason for the question. "Were you going to bring *her* across?"

Those eyes saw even more than he thought. Pain wrenched at him. "When she was dying I wanted to save her. I had the blood ready. But...she didn't know about me or anything about this life and—"

"It's a perilous decision even when they do know. Living the life being a whole lot different than observing it. And Wolfie...can I do that to him, dear as he is to me? Even if he asks? I don't know. Coming across rejuvenates, but it doesn't regenerate."

He saw her point. "Well, thanks."

She touched his arm. The scent of honeysuckle curled around him. "I'm sorry you lost her. It always hurts. Good luck finding her killer."

Driving back downtown, Kreutzer said, "Next to that chick, you don't seem so weird anymore."

Back at the office he headed for Communications to send out the van's descriptions. He came back with information San Francisco had sent on Cameron Dark's arrest.

Reading it did not take long. The arrest occurred almost by accident. The dealer had been the objective and Dark merely caught in the net. He was observed buying crack and arrested along with the dealer. On making bail, he disappeared.

The tag number Wolf wrote on the check belonged to a white '89 Aerostar registered to Jeremy Phillips of Grand Island. Only an answering machine responded when Kreutzer tried calling the telephone number. Garreth was willing to bet Phillips had flown off somewhere and they would find his Aerostar, minus tags, in the long term parking lot of the airport.

Garreth called Bellamy County, but found Reichert out of the office. So he left a message promising a report. Kreutzer let him use a desk to write up the report and print it out, and their fax machine to send copies to Reichert and Danzig.

Writing up about the fingerprint identification reminded him of the remark to Duncan at Sterling's. Garreth called Information for the number of a Baumen liquor store. Calling the store, he ordered a case of Coors for delivery to Duncan, wishing he could be there to see Duncan's expression.

Then Garreth asked directions to Reece and Sparacino to reclaim his photocopy of the bobbsey bitches' prints taken off the ZX.

Returning to Kreutzer's desk, he found the detective on the telephone with eyebrows skipping from frown to arch and back. Kreutzer hung up, stared at the phone for a long minute, then turned to Garreth. "The van's been seen."

Garreth's pulse jumped. "Where?"

"A gas station off the Interstate in Iowa. But the officer who attempted to arrest the suspects is in the hospital—I don't know how seriously injured—and one of the suspects is dead."

24.

The rain made the night as dark as any Garreth had experienced in years, it and the midnight paving swallowing light so completely he might never have turned on his headlights....and all the darker in contrast to lightning's intermittent glare. The car felt as though it hydroplaned more often than made solid contact with the highway, but the urgency pounding in him kept his foot hard on the accelerator, pushing the Porsche to the edge of control. He had lost so much time already, first in Omaha waiting for the president of the local Philos chapter to come down and identify him as a Life Member so he could restock his cooler, then outside Council Bluffs, joining two other off-duty officers in assisting Iowa State Patrol troopers and emergency personnel at a twelve-vehicle accident. Ten had piled into each other and/or the eleventh, a semi trailer jackknifed and overturned across both eastbound lanes, with the twelfth and cause of it all, a Miata that cut too close in front of the Peterbilt on a downhill grade, wedged between the Peterbilt's front wheels. By some miracle, however, in all the nightmare tangle of metal, surreal in the freeze-frame brilliance of lightning and glare of emergency floods, the only fatality was the Miata's driver. With the scents of blood and gasoline fumes still filling his head, lingering on his jeans and the cheap plastic raincoat he had picked up coming through Omaha, Garreth shoved images of the pile-up aside to concentrate on what lay ahead.

The teletype gave a few more details of the incident...the name of the town, that a deputy sheriff had been the officer injured, and the gender of the fatality...female, not the albino, unfortunately. But *was* she dead? If not, he had to see to it.

The thought made him queasy, remembering his own death. By all medical definitions he had been dead—no heartbeat, no respiration, no bleeding, no pain response, flat line EEG—and yet...he heard sound, he saw movement. And...he thought. She would feel no pain as he broke her neck, crushing the spinal cord and destroying her nervous system, but she would be aware to the end of what he was doing to her. Peering into the rain for the Edgemoor exit, Garreth hoped the bobbsey bitch had died a true death already.

The exit came almost without warning. Garreth stood on his brakes and steered the right tires toward the shoulder to use the rumble strip for slowing down. He still entered the exit ramp almost sideways...then, agile as a cutting horse, the car pivoted on its haunches, straightening, and settled into a decorous roll to the stop sign at the bottom.

Across the highway a Conoco sign glowed blurrily though the rain, and below it, *Gas 'N More*. Garreth eyed the station. That had to be the scene of the incident...but all that mattered now was reaching the body as soon as possible. A sign to his right said: *Edgemoor 1 mile*. He turned.

The highway skirted Edgemoor's western edge and intersected Main Street. Garreth headed up Main and found the police department on a corner at the edge of the two-block downtown area.

At the counter inside he shook water off his Stetson and held up his ID. "I'm here from the Bellamy County SO to identify the suspect killed at the gas stop. Can you tell me where to find the body?"

The young woman on the other side regarded him wide-eyed through the glass. "You'll need to ask Sheriff Sechrest and I heard her on the radio telling her office that she's at the hospital waiting for Deputy Andersen to wake up from surgery. The hospital is one block back toward the highway and left for three blocks."

Cold shot through Garreth along with an image of Maggie's Desert Eagle. "How was the deputy wounded? How serious is it?"

She started to speak, stopped—clearly deciding she should not give out information too freely—and said, "The sheriff can tell you more than I can." Then added, "but it's my understanding his condition isn't critical."

Relief washed through Garreth.

When he reached it, the hospital looked small, fewer than fifty beds. He parked outside the emergency entrance beside a dark brown Crown Victoria with *Travis County Sheriff* on the side.

The nurse at the desk inside directed him to the patient wing, and the nurse there sent him across the corridor to a waiting area. "I'll tell Sheriff Sechrest you're here, deputy."

A pregnant young woman in her early twenties huddled in one of the upholstered chairs, hands clasped together white-knuckled in her lap, face equally white. The deputy's wife? If his injuries were not critical, why did she seem so terrified?

Garreth laid his raincoat across one plastic chair and sat down in another next to her. "Mrs. Andersen?"

She looked around, and he saw not just fear but anger in her eyes. "Why are they doing this to him!"

He blinked at her ferocity. "Doing what?"

"Crucifying him! Troy didn't mean to kill the girl. He said so over and over while he was coming out of the anesthetic. 'I didn't mean to kill her! Christ, she's just a kid!' He was crying he was so upset about it."

Garreth could well imagine. Finding yourself responsible for a death hit hard under any circumstances...but especially when it involved a juvenile. Garreth could picture Andersen lying in bed thinking of his own nearing fatherhood and putting himself in the place of the father who had just lost a child. "How long has your husband been on the job?"

She stiffened. "Eighteen months...but he's a good officer! Look at the way he pulled those kids out of that farmhouse fire in May. But they won't remember his commendation for that, will they. They think he panicked when that girl attacked him!"

"Did someone say—"

Her eyes flashed. "No...but why else would Stan House-holder be in there along with the sheriff? And they made me leave while they talk to Troy."

Now he understood. "Stan Householder is with Internal Affairs?"

She stared at him a moment, then her face slammed shut. "You're not with Travis County. I don't know you."

He shook his head. "Bellamy County. But in every law enforcement agency I know it's standard procedure for IA to investigate when an officer is involved in an injury or fatality. The Sheriff's Office just needs to be sure what happened."

Theoretically...though it never felt like "just" when you were the subject of the inquisition. He had not forgotten one grim moment of his grilling following Harry being shot. But then, he fully deserved to have the shooting team rake him over the coals.

Andersen's wife needed to think about something else. "When's your baby due?"

Magic words. She smiled down at the bulge of her stom-ach and ran a hand across it. "The last part of December. The doctor has an actual date but I don't believe it. I mean, it isn't like one of Dad's Red Devon cows, where you know the exact breeding—" She broke off and pushed to her feet, eyes focus-ing past Garreth. "Is it over? May I go back in to him?"

Garreth turned in his chair...and stood, too. At the en-trance to the waiting area a small, stocky woman with salt-and-pepper hair, tan shirt, brown trousers, and a sheriff's star smiled at the deputy's wife. "Certainly." Then as the young woman hurried out past her and a taller, younger man wearing the same uniform, she raised her brows at Garreth. "I'm Sher-iff Sandy Sechrest. You're the officer Lincoln teletyped about?"

"Garreth Mikaelian." He handed her his ID. "How's Deputy Andersen?"

She shifted the slicker draped over her arm to take it. "It could have been worse. He has a broken nose and cuts and scratches on his face and arms."

"Cuts?" Involuntarily, Garreth glanced down at his own arm. "Knife wounds?"

"Broken glass." She returned the ID. "Sorry all we have is one dead suspect for you instead of three live prisoners."

"Better that than another dead officer. What happened? And when may I see the body?"

"We can head that way now." She pulled on her slicker. "It's over in New Prospect, the county seat. We'd transported it there to the coroner before Lincoln teletyped us." Sechrest paused. "I don't know that it's really necessary for you to identify the body. Lincoln faxed us some prints that I understand your department lifted from the car this trio ran off the road, and about twenty minutes ago my office informed me that some of those prints match the body's. The body's also match ones Lincoln found on duct tape on their assault victim. So her prints put her at the scene of your officer's death and the Lincoln assault."

Not go to the body! Cold ran through him. Would it seem suspicious if he insisted? If she had not truly died, how much longer did he have to reach her? Although he had felt he lay there forever, it had probably been around eight hours when that first new breath and heartbeat broke the terrible silence of his body. Could he count on the same time period now? "If you don't mind, I'd like to see it anyway, since I'm here."

Sechrest nodded. "No problem. And on the way you can hear the interview with Deputy Andersen. Do you have a cassette player in your car?" When he nodded she turned to the man behind her. "Stan, I'll take the tape."

He frowned. "Sheriff—"

She arched a brow. "I know, I know. Of course you need it. And I promise to give it to you when we're done at the hospital." As soon as he ejected the tape from a portable cassette recorder he carried and handed it to her, she turned and started briskly up the corridor. "Coming, Mikaelian?"

Garreth snatched up his raincoat and hurried after her.

Outside, she never paused between the ER door and the Porsche, but once in the passenger seat, said, "I think my favorite police vehicle has to be the tank in the movie *Dragnet*...the one with *Have a nice day* on the end of its ram. Go back on Main to the highway you took down from the Interstate, but turn left. That puts you on 83. Follow it to New Prospect. It'll seem like forever and the road twists a bit but keep going." She turned on his radio and slid the tape into the console's cassette slot.

The distress Andersen's wife reported to Garreth came through sharply as the tape began, an anguish in his voice that wrenched at Garreth. Then as Sechrest and Householder drew the story out of him, he gradually caught the trick of insulating himself from the event's emotional impact by answering in dispassionate professional terminology. But even couched in official language, the encounter played out vividly in Garreth's mind.

Troy Andersen always made the Gas 'N More a frequent stop on his rounds. Sheriff Sechrest liked maintaining a visible presence there since its location off the Interstate made it a tempting target for felons wanting a quick score on their way cross-country. Today, however, weather concerned him more than armed robbery. The darkening sky told him better than Dispatch's announcement of a thunderstorm watch that he had rain coming any time, and he worried how that might affect traffic as exhibitors funneled toward New Prospect for tomorrow's opening of the county fair.

Parking at the end of the building, he noted the white Aerostar at the pumps. All week he had been following the continually updated ATL's from that officer killing in Kansas, but the latest teletype, coming from Lincoln, sharpened his interest even more. It suggested the suspects were headed east. This Aerostar had the ATL's described color and extended body style, but the windows made it a conversion van, not a delivery van, and it carried Iowa tags.

All the same, he ran the tags. They came back for a white Aerostar conversion registered to Alan and Jessica Nelsson in Mineola, no warrants, no report of their tags being stolen. Andersen sighed. Well, it had been worth checking.

The dispatcher continued, "We have a new update on the ATL for the three suspects in a white Aerostar."

As she gave him the new information, he shook his head. How could they think anyone would be fooled by painted windows? Then he froze, staring at the Aerostar. The rearmost side window did appear...odd. Moments later he identified why. The darkening sky had switched on the station's lights and that window did not reflect them the same way the others did.

Andersen thumbed on the mike of his unit's radio. "I'll be on high band taking a closer look at this Aerostar."

Approaching the vehicle shifted the reflections on the other side windows, but not that rearmost one. And as he reached the van the window's three dimensional appearance suddenly proved to be indeed just painted...a clever optical illusion. Running his hand across it confirmed the flatness. And his finger found an edge...and with a fingernail under the edge, he could lift it from the side of the vehicle.

Heart racing, Andersen reached for mike on his shoulder, but stopped before activating it. Presumably the van's occupants had gone inside the Gas 'N More, but if one remained in the van, he did not want them warned they had been identified.

A quick glance at the building spotted no one near the windows. So hopefully any suspects inside had not seem him by the van. He eased away from the vehicle, then dropped into a casual stride and headed into the building.

"Hi, Cass," he called to the clerk and strolled toward the restrooms. He did not see the male described in the ATL, but two juveniles dressed almost identically in wide-legged jeans and camisole tops stood looking over the potato chip choices and they matched the females' descriptions: both petite, the very small, blonde one looking anywhere from nine to twelve, the dark-haired one, fifteen or sixteen. And while they never turned their heads, he saw them watching him from the corner of their eyes. The older one carried a large black leather shoulder bag similar to the one described in the ATL, with a zipper top and a leather flap on the side.

His heart raced even faster. Under that flap would he find a pocket sculpted into a holster for a Desert Eagle?

The male suspect was not in the men's restroom. Andersen locked the door to make sure the male could not walk in on him and thumbed his radio mike. Good thing he had not called this in out by the van. "Travis Twelve requesting backup! I have the wanted white Aerostar van at the Gas 'N More. They have the fake windows on it and it's carrying the Iowa tags I ran a couple of minutes ago! The two juvenile females are here inside. There's no sign of the male suspect. He may still be outside in the van."

No other Travis County deputy might be close enough to assist, but his call would be picked up by all the area agencies and he could count on Edgemoor PD officers and maybe a Shelby County deputy to respond. He just had to make sure the suspects did not escape before backup arrived.

He took a deep breath, strolled out of the restroom, and put on a friendly smile. "Hi, girls."

Though almost colorless blue, the small girl's eyes made him think of a deer's...huge and filled with panic. She took a step backward, clearly ready to bolt.

But the older girl caught her hand, stopping her. "It's all right, sis." She smiled at Andersen. "She's kind of shy. Do you want in here to pick out some chips?" She hid her feelings better than the small girl, but her voice still betrayed tension.

He shook his head. "Thanks, no. What's your name?"

The small girl went even paler. The older girl's grip on her hand tightened. "August. August...Morgan. And this is Beth."

"And I guess that's your Aerostar out front?"

The smile fixed slightly. "Well, we're traveling *in* it, but it belongs to our uncle." She paused and he watched her mind race before she continued with an undertone of satisfaction, "Alan Nelsson...of Mineola."

Proud of being able to recite the tag owner's name and address? They must have stolen not only the tags but broken into the Nelsson van and taken the registration as well.

"Sis, what kind of chips do you want?" When the small girl shrugged, "August" sighed. "Well, choose *something*." And releasing the small girl's hand, she moved down to the drink cooler.

The small girl stood rooted by the chips...staring at the packages but judging by her fixed gaze, seeing none of them. Andersen remained near her where he could watch both girls.

"August" opened a cooler door and fingered the soft drink bottles inside. "Is something the matter with the van?"

"No." Where the hell was that backup? He could not keep them talking much longer without giving up the pretense of this being casual chitchat. "You're traveling with your uncle, then?"

"Uncle Alan loaned the van to my brother." The tension thickened under the off-hand tone.

"And he's in the van?"

"Oh yeah." She picked out two bottles of Pepsi and after a moment of hesitation, an Arizona Tea. "Plotting route and mileage. The Great Navigator." She rolled her eyes. "Like there's any mystery to finding Des Moines. Oh, Bethie." Sighing, she came back to the smaller girl and thrust the two Pepsies at her, then a bag of chips. "Take these to Donny while I pay for them."

Andersen cursed silently. Still no backup! It appeared action was all up to him. He needed to catch the male in the van by surprise, though. Thought of the weapon stolen from the dead Kansas officer sent cold down his spine. Fortunately the girl gave him a perfect approach. "You have your hands full there, Miss Morgan. Let me open doors for you."

The small girl's nerve broke. Dropping soft drinks and chips, she bolted for the entrance.

One thought shot through Andersen's mind: *Don't let her warn the suspect!* He caught her arm.

The girl screamed in a piercing note of fear.

"Let go of her!"

He glanced around into blazing dark eyes, and only a split second later registered the Arizona Tea bottle held club-like by its neck...swinging toward his face. A split second too late.

His nose flattened under the blow and he reeled backward, blinded by the explosion of excruciating pain. He struggled to breathe while wet warmth poured down over his lips, filling his mouth with the metallic tang of blood.

"Run, Amber!"

Beyond the pain Andersen heard feet scrambling on the tiled floor...felt movement past him. He grabbed at it...found his arms wrapped around a body larger than the little blonde's. The bottle hit him again, this time across the temple. He groped for the arm, found it, followed it up to the hand. "Give me the bottle. Give me the bottle!" He forced her hand backward, then grabbed for the bottle as her grip loosened. But she clawed for it and at him with the other hand and the bottle slipped away from both of them...fell, shattering as it hit the floor. Then he lost his footing, slipping on the spilled tea, or maybe his blood, and the two of them went down together.

Pain pierced his arms, but it seemed inconsequential compared to the agony enveloping his face...or the effort of hanging on to the girl. She writhed, clawed, kicked...struggling in wordless, panting desperation.

"Stop fighting! Quit resisting!"

But hanging on became harder by the moment as she turned slippery. From his blood? He wished desperately he could see more than this red haze, but even it dimmed as he felt his eyes swelling shut. He gave up trying to talk and concentrated on just hanging on however he could until backup arrived, praying it would be soon.

Then abruptly, she stopped struggling...sagged motion-less. At first he thought she was playing possum, waiting for his grip to loosen. But she remained limp...and he gradually became aware that he had an arm around her throat.

Cold flooded him, fear overriding his pain. Hurriedly releasing her, he groped for the carotid area of her neck. And the cold deepened. Where he should feel a pulse, he felt none. The hand on her chest detected no breathing.

No. *No*! Frantically he rolled her onto her back and felt for her mouth, took a breath through his own mouth, blew into hers, pressed the heels of his hands down on her breastbone, breathed for her some more, pumped her chest. What was the ratio of chest compressions per breaths? He could not remember.

"Breathe, kid...breathe! Come on, come on! Please breathe! And give me a heartbeat!"

He kept going, pleading with her. She could not die. He refused to let her. Whatever she was involved in...Christ, she was just a kid!

An eternity later he became aware of sound around him...footsteps, voices, exclamations of horror. Hands pulled him away from her to a stretcher. "Troy...Troy! Come on...we'll take over now."

He yielded reluctantly. "Just don't let her die. Okay? Don't let her die."

"But of course she already had," Sheriff Sechrest said as the tape ran out. She shook her head. "God what a mess, both of them covered with blood—his, mostly—blood and glass all over the floor."

"And the van long gone, of course."

Sechrest grimaced. "Of course. We're not even sure in which direction. As soon as she saw the suspect hit Troy with the bottle, Cass Stephens called 911 but didn't think to run outside to see which way the van went." She sighed. "Poor kid. He's taking this hard, though I guess I'd be more worried if he didn't care. But I hope this doesn't finish him in law enforcement. He's a good deputy, just young. Oh, there's New Prospect. Beyond the second stop sign turn right, then left on 7th, then right again on Chestnut to the hospital."

They parked outside the St. Francis ER. And as soon as they stepped through the automatic doors, the sense of presence tugged at Garreth, so overpowering he even forgot the flood of blood scents washing at him. His stomach lurched. Blood calls to blood. No doubt about it now. Those had definitely been the bobbsey bitches at the Gas 'N More, and this one, at least, had drunk his blood. Urgency drummed in him. He had to reach her as fast as possible, had to ensure she remained dead. Circling the ER desk, he headed up the corridor, following the pull.

"Mikaelian!"

He turned.

Sechrest had stopped at the intersection with another corridor. "Where are you going? The body is in the autopsy room, this way and downstairs."

Fear bloomed in him. Suddenly he could hardly breathe. "What's in this direction?"

"Most immediately? ICU and Surg—"

"Sheriff!" A nurse hurried down the corridor toward them. "Your office said you were on your way so we didn't have them radio you. You won't believe what's happened."

The fear hardened into certainty and dropped into Garreth's gut like a stone. "The girl isn't dead after all."

The nurse stared at him. "How did you guess?"

Sechrest frowned. "That's impossible. I know dead when I see it and that girl *was*. The paramedics called it, too."

The nurse shrugged. "Well, they mis-called it. A few minutes ago one of the aides headed for the laundry heard screaming in the autopsy room and went in to find the body bag rolling around on the floor and the girl fighting to get out.. We have her in ICU...under sedation because she was so hysterical."

A whole catalog of emotions played across the sheriff's face, starting with disbelief and settling finally into amazed relief. "I'll be damned. Let's have a look at her, then...after I call this down to the Edgemoor hospital."

Garreth groaned inwardly. While the news should help Troy Andersen sleep better tonight, it left *him* sick with dismay. Breaking the neck of a corpse was easy...uncomplicated. But now what did he do?

25.

The bobbsey bitch lay in the ICU bed with her eyes closed. Despite sedation, she did not rest, however, but lay groaning and twisting. Outstretched hands seemed to be pushing something away. She looked smaller and thinner than Garreth remembered, dwarfed by the bed and every bit the waif Gerald Greenstreet had described in Cheyenne. A heart monitor attached to her beeped at long intervals.

Blood scent curled around Garreth from the nurse standing beside him at the window. "I can't believe how much sedation we've had to give her, or that we'd dare to. That dose was enough to send a grown man into coma...and her vital signs are so low I'd have thought it would kill her. But it took every bit to calm her. She's probably having nightmares about coming to in that body bag."

And, kiddo, that's only the start of the nightmare. But she was *alive*, Garreth reflected angrily. Undeservedy alive. Thirty minutes sooner and he could have prevented this. If only the chapter president in Omaha had settled for a phone authorization. If only that Miata's driver had exercised a little caution and good sense. He grimaced. And if wishes were horses, as Grandma Doyle used to say, beggars would ride. Nothing could change the delays or the fact that the bobbsey bitch revived sooner than he expected, or that as a result, a newborn vampire writhed in her sleep on the other side of the window. Now he had to decide what to do about it.

He could picture Irina puzzled that he had anything to decide. Their few philosophical discussions revealed that while she took no pleasure in killing, considering it often wasteful and likely to attract unfavorable attention, she had no qualms about acting in self-defense or expediency.

I'd *kill the little bitch*, Lane's voice whispered in his head.

No doubt. But then, Lane enjoyed killing.

The whisper turned to a sneer. *Sanctimonious, aren't we. Admit it...you want her dead. And doesn't she deserve to die for Maggie? You're just squeamish about* doing *it.*

Because it would be murder, Maggie's voice came in sharply, *and Garreth's whole life has been upholding the law.*

So...he's supposed to leave her to your precious criminal justice system? Give me a break. Just what do you expect them *to do with or to her?*

Garreth winced. Now he not only imagined Lane and Maggie talking to him, he had them arguing with each other. But they did articulate his conflict. Yes, he wanted the bb dead! She deserved it. But how could he murder her in cold blood? A whole different situation than killing Lane as she tried to kill him. On the other hand, following proper procedure and sending the bb through the criminal justice system was not only pointless but—

Footsteps behind him interrupted the thought. Sheriff Sechrest joined him at the window. "Well, she does indeed appear to be alive. I don't think I've ever been as happy about making a mistake. How are you doing?" She glanced sideways at him. "Disappointed?"

"Yes." He might as well admit the truth. Then he made himself shrug. "But this way maybe she can give us information that will help us track down her boyfriend." Not that he could ask any of the questions important to him in the sheriff's hearing. "How's Deputy Andersen?"

She smiled. "Feeling a whole lot less pain. Any idea when the girl will wake up?" she asked the nurse.

The nurse shrugged. "It's anyone's guess. As much sedative as she took, she might sleep a week."

Sechrest eyed the girl, then headed for the nurse's desk. "May I use your phone?" Returning shortly, she said, "The PD is letting me borrow one of their officers to stand guard and notify us when the girl wakes up. We'll wait until the officer shows up, then if you'll drive me to the office, you can help me go through the suspect's property."

For a minute Garreth debated whether he could risk leaving, then decided he could. Even having lived with the albino she needed a while to realize what had happened and sort out the changes in her. She had no fangs yet and in any case, hunger would come later.

Twenty minutes later the two of them sat in Sechrest's office on the lower floor of the courthouse annex, with everything removed from the bb spread on the desk between them. Garreth's hands went automatically to the shoulder bag, fingering the soft leather, lifting the flap to reveal the holster molded into the side pocket. It smelled of saddle soap and gun oil. Touching it felt almost like touching Maggie again...feeling her skin, smelling the mixed skin/blood scent of her.

Belatedly he realized the sheriff had asked a question for the third time. He smoothed the flap back down. "Yes, it's Officer Lebekov's purse." He longed to bundle up the purse, take it with him as a piece of Maggie, a link to her as the ZX had been to Marti. But he made himself lay it aside and turn to the bag's contents.

The amount of stuff girls and women managed to fit in their purses always amazed him. Much of it he anticipated...the comb and brush, cosmetics, mirror, cigarettes and matches, billfold, sunglasses, and ballpoint pens with the names of businesses and high-end hotels. The three condom packages did not surprise him, either. But she had also fit in a miniature folding hair dryer; a Mini MagLite; a folding multi-tool in a carrying case; a dog-eared paperback novelization of the movie *The Lost Boys*; a small spiral notebook with directions written in a round, girlish hand for running half a dozen scams including one titled "Homesick Runaway;" and three tape cassettes, two of them albums, the third with the title hand-written.

"Do you see anything that identifies her?" Sechrest asked.

"Plenty of identification." The billfold held five drivers licenses from three states. "None of it worth anything. Though there's a photograph we can use in the ATL info in place of the younger juvenile's sketch." Four actually, a photobooth strip, cut into two pieces to fit it into the billfold, of both bobbsey bitches laughing into the camera, looking for all the world like any two young girls hanging out at the mall. But he palmed one piece before laying the billfold in front of Sechrest. "Unfortunately she didn't write her name in the notebook."

"Nor on her cassettes." Sechrest turned them over in her hands. "We have just the name of the younger female, and Amber is probably a street name." She handed him the cassettes. "Odd taste in music for someone her age. This one group I've never heard of, but they don't sound like any modern band, and the two Blue Steel Perdition albums have to be twenty years old."

That would be about right. Garreth remembered the rock group...not for their music but because back in San Francisco he and his partner had been one of four patrol units dispatched to the Mark Hopkins Hotel to arrest the band and their party guests when the group began breaking windows and furniture in the band's suite. He also recalled reading a few months later that the group broke up after one of them OD'd. It did seem odd that someone the bb's age would even know about them, let alone own probably the only albums they ever made.

Unless the albino had been a member of the band? None of the images in memory looked like the albino, though, and neither did the faces scowling out of their shoulder-length hair in the photos on the back of the cassettes. One face flickeringly rang a bell...not as the albino but someone else he had seen recently. Identification eluded him, however.

And he forgot about it when he read the title and band name written on the third cassette in a hard, angular hand: *"Shades of Midnight" by Cenotaph*. His skin prickled. The tune Emma caught him humming Wednesday morning at the SO came running back through his head, along with what she re-called of the lyrics...and that same sense of menace.

Sechrest examined the clothing...wide-legged jeans, a spa-ghetti-strap camisole, and clogs-*cum*-loafers with thick, lugged soles. "Name labels. She obviously shoplifts at the upscale stores in the mall."

He barely heard her through the noise in his head. If he did not remember the song, had he dreamed about it because the bb knew it...and was cold-blooded enough to sing it while bleeding Maggie and him?

"Hello...Mikaelian...Earth calling!"

He blinked at Sechrest. "What?"

She shook her head. "I said, don't you think it'd be a good idea to let your boss know your suspect's alive so our respec-tive county attorneys, and Lincoln's DA, can start discussing who gets first crack at her?"

He discovered that without knowing why, he suddenly felt reluctant to talk to Reichert. But he picked up the phone, dialed the Bellamy SO, and left a message with Cheryl Hannes.

She must have passed it right on because five minutes later Reichert called. "She just seemed dead and came to in the body bag? It's an epidemic. But it's nice to have one of the trio in custody. Have you talked to her?"

"It hasn't been possible yet."

"Then let me speak with whoever's in charge of the case there."

"That's Sheriff Sechrest. Here she is." He extended the phone to her.

She started out talking in a normal tone, telling Reichert about the attack on her deputy, but after listening for a bit, she sent a sharp glance Garreth's direction and with seem-ing casualness, swiveled her chair away and dropped her voice. He still heard her clearly, though her one and two word contributions to the conversation gave him little to listen to. Not that he had any trouble guessing the subject under discussion.

Garreth left her office to give the two of them more freedom to talk about him and dashed out to the car to bring in his laptop. The rain came down as hard as ever. He might as well use the waiting time until the bb came around to write up a report. With no one else in the squad room he had plenty of desks to choose between.

But after turning on the laptop and starting the word processing program, he found himself just staring at the screen...until it filled with the turns and walls of the screen saver maze. He ran his finger across the touchpad to kill the screen saver. Too bad the maze in his life could not be banished as quickly.

No, not a maze, he decided. However they twisted, mazes offered a continuous path, and hope of escape. Even a dead end let you backtrack. He stood in a blind end with the tunnel behind him caved in and the three doors leading out all labeled *Lose*, *Lose*, and *Lose*.

The screen saver came on again. He let it run. Now he understood his reluctance to talk to Reichert. How could he sit there saying yes sir and no sir and don't worry I'm doing it all by the book when he knew full well that as of tonight, he would be throwing away the book. And no matter which door he went through, it would lock fast behind him, preventing him from ever going back. Was this what Grandma Doyle meant by the albino destroying him?

But what other choices did he have? Door Number One...follow the book and let them treat her like a human juvenile offender. Disaster! As soon as she realized what had happened to her—which after running around with someone who was or pretended to be a vampire, could not take long— of course she would begin exploring her new powers and walk away. Anyone attempting to stop her stood in danger of being attacked. Worse, she might attempt to drink from them, and between her hunger and inexperience, the result would be butchery. If she killed them, he doubted it would occur to her to make sure they stayed dead, resulting in more vampires

...but, reanimated by only a small inoculation of the retrovirus, not rational beings, just mindlessly blood-hungry. He could not bear the thought of that happening to anyone, and even if he prevented it by cleaning up after her, a trail of bodies with broken necks would attract just as much attention. Scratch door number one.

That left him with two choices. The first...kill her. Logic made that the most practical choice. Irina would certainly agree. And he had no doubt he could accomplish it without drawing suspicion to himself. It would be even safer, of course, to engineer circumstances so someone else took her out...say during an escape...though that would have to be handled carefully, making sure they literally blew her head off.

Disgust washed through him. No...forget killing by proxy. It was chicken shit to make someone else do the dirty work and suffer the emotional trauma. If he opted to kill her, he should do it himself. But the idea tied his gut in knots.

So did his other choice. It violated just as many ethics and laws. Yet...if he could not afford to leave her to the criminal justice system nor bring himself to kill her, he had only this one other course of action...become her keeper.

The choice carried a kind of justice. After all, however inadvertently, he was responsible for her existence. His blood had created her. His knowledge, strength, and experience in the life should let him control her. As no human agency had a prayer of doing.

The choice also sounded insane. Did he really want to drag her along everywhere he went? Because he would have to...and he had ground to cover...the albino to find. She would be like wearing leg irons. Unless maybe he could use her to find the albino. After that...well, he could decide then what to do with her.

Sechrest leaned into the squad room. "Officer Mikaelian, your boss would like to talk to you some more."

Garreth's stomach knotted. *Cool it, man*, he told himself. *You haven't done anything wrong.* Yet. Taking a deep breath, he followed the sheriff back across the hall to her office and picked up the phone. "Yes, sir?"

"Sheriff Sechrest has briefed me on the situation there and I've filled her in on some facts about your relationship to the case that you neglected to mention to her."

"With the suspect dead it seemed immaterial."

"But she isn't dead so now it *is* material. Nothing against you, but...we both feel it isn't wise for you to participate in interrogating this suspect."

"I wasn't planning to." Absolute truth. "I'm not even going to be in the room." Though not for the reason Reichert might think. The less interest he showed in contact with her, the lower the chance, hopefully, he would be connected to her turning up dead or missing.

"Good boy." Reichert sounded relieved. "We don't want to risk compromising prosecuting her."

"No, sir. And what do you think of this idea? After we question the girl I'd like to check out this Cameron Dark's arrest in California to see what I can learn about the man."

"Good idea." The speed of the answer suggested Reichert wanted to approve before Garreth changed his mind. "Maybe he has friends in this area of the country that can be contacted or watched."

"I'll let you know."

With the debate over what to do about the suspect still echoing in his head, Garreth had trouble focusing on the report, but he slogged through a narrative he decided worked and printed it out.

Handing the report over the desk separating squad room from business office so the clerk could fax it had a chill feeling of finality. It might be the last truly honest one he sent.

Through his gloom he heard the phone ring. A minute later Sechrest came out of her office. "The hospital just called. Our girl's waking up."

On their way out she detoured into the squadroom, and, unlocking a locker, took out an alphanumeric pager and a palmtop computer. She clipped the pager on her belt and handed him the palmtop. "Even though you won't be in the room during questioning, I'd like you where you can listen…so you can feed me information or questions you want asked."

Back at the hospital, Sechrest frowned through the ICU window. Their suspect lay curled on her side in the bed, the eyes tightly closed behind the curtain of hair falling over her face. "I thought you said she's awake."

The PD officer, a tall young women with hair shorter than Garreth's and muscular arms that proclaimed she spent her free time in the gym, said, "She is…but I think she's hoping that if she sleeps long enough, or pretends to, this will all turn out to be a bad dream."

If only that *could* solve the problem, Garreth reflected wryly.

Sechrest grunted. "Then it's time to make her wake up and face reality." While Garreth strung a phone cord from the palmtop to the phone jack at the nurse's desk and turned on the palmtop, she switched on her pager. "Benton, you come in with me."

The PD officer nodded and followed Sechrest into the room.

Reaching the bed, Sechrest touched the girl's shoulder. "August. I'm Sheriff Sechrest. Open your eyes."

The girl did not move.

Sechrest sighed. "Ignoring us won't make us go away. You're in too much trouble. You can help yourself, though, by cooperating with us."

No response.

Garreth typed quickly on the palmtop and hit the *send* key. Shortly, Sechrest glanced down at her belt and read his message: *Try alias not on DL's, Valerie Daniels, used in Cheyenne.*

Sechrest leaned down near the girl's ear. "Maybe you'd rather be called Valerie Daniels."

That hit a nerve. The heart monitor beeped faster. The girl's eyes popped open and Garreth heard her sharp intake of breath as she twisted to stare up at the sheriff.

Sechrest straightened, nodding. "That's right. We know about your games in Cheyenne."

And Billings, Garreth typed into the palmtop.

The sheriff glanced down again. "And the game in Billings."

And Colby.

"And Colby."

The girl's glance darted from Sechrest to Benton, her expression that of a trapped animal.

Sechrest leaned over the girl again. "We also know all about running those two officers off the road in Kansas... leaving them to die...drinking their blood."

Reichert must have told her about that.

The girl's eyes widened until they seemed to fill her face. Then suddenly she squeezed them shut and curled up on her side again, whispering, "I...don't know what you're talking about."

Benton snorted, but quickly fell silent under the icy glance Sechrest sent her.

That displeasure never marred the smooth assurance of the sheriff's voice, however. "Oh, I think you do, Valerie. Yours and Amber's fingerprints were all over their car. But we know it was your boyfriend who actually ran them off the road. He's the one we're inter—"

The beeps on the heart monitor jumped. "Amber?" The girl sat up in bed. "She didn't get away? Where is she? I want to see her!"

Sechrest stared down at the girl and Garreth watched sheriff's mind race, calculating how to take advantage of the girl's erroneous conclusion. With barely a pause, Sechrest shook her head. "I'm sorry; it isn't possible right now. You and I have to discuss your boyfriend first."

Now Garreth saw the girl's mind working. A moment later she lay back down again with a sly, streetwise smile. The heart monitor slowed. "Because Amber wouldn't talk about him?"

If that response disappointed Sechrest, she did not show it. "Because we always like corroboration of our information …hearing it from more than one source."

The girl stiffened. "I don't believe Amber told you anything. She'd never do that!"

"Someone had to tell us about drinking the officers' blood."

A light blazed up in the girl's eyes, firing off alarms in Garreth. Being behind her, Sechrest could not see it.

But before he could reach the door and warn Sechrest, the girl rolled over and sprang like a cat, ripping loose from the heart and blood pressure monitors attached to her. *What did you do to her to make her talk?*

Even caught by surprise, Sechrest reacted instantly and jumped backward. Benton leaped between girl and sheriff, hand chopping toward the girl's throat. But in a lightning move, the girl ducked, then as the officer's arm passed overhead, came upright almost against Benton's body and drove both hands into her chest. Benton flew backward to smash against the wall, then collapse onto hands and knees, mouth gaping as she fought for the breath knocked out of her. The girl stared open-mouthed from her hands to the officer, clearly astounded by what just happened.

Garreth and the nurse scrambled for the door. The girl's pause gave Sechrest time to act. She charged at the girl's back.

The girl heard, however, and whirled. And whether her arm swung out from the centrifugal force of the spin or she intended to backhand the sheriff, the result was the same. Her hand connected with Sechrest's face. Head snapping sideways, Sechrest catapulted back into the foot of the bed.

Gasping and still on the floor, Benton clawed for her pepper spray. And seeing the canister in the officer's hand, the girl leaped at her.

Just as Garreth and the nurse entered the room. Everything had happened in a matter of seconds.

The girl started to reach for the pepper spray, but suddenly changed direction toward the officer's hair, then finding it too short to hold, grabbed her by her shirt collar and duty belt...heaved around and flung her into the stunned sheriff.

It confirmed all Garreth's fears about the danger the girl posed. In under a minute she had discovered her strength and though astounded by it, had begun using it. And now she charged the nurse and him, hands outstretched like battering rams, obviously expecting to throw them aside, too, and escape.

So much for maintaining distance from her. Garreth shoved the nurse to safety behind him, then caught the girl's wrists as she came at him. Anger flaring in her eyes, she jerked back...and stopped short, eyes going startled when she could not break free

He used the moment their gazes met to trap her. "It's no use running. Amber isn't here. We don't have her." He dropped his voice to a whisper only she could hear. "Go...to...sleep. Stay...asleep...until...I...wake...you."

And obediently, she closed her eyes and went limp.

He caught her and carried her back to the bed. "Sheriff, Benton, are you all right?"

The two climbed to their feet. Sechrest rubbed a bruised cheek, grimacing. "Mostly."

Benton's bruises appeared more than physical. Angry color splashed her cheekbones. "I don't fucking believe the way this kid tossed me around."

Garreth eyed her. "Obviously you've never had to wrestle some druggie pumped on PCP."

"Adrenalin will do it, too," Sechrest said. "I've seen a man tear the door off a car at an accident scene to free his kid trapped inside. You'd swear he turned into the Bionic Man. What I don't understand is what *you* did to *her*, Mikaelian." She stared down at the girl.

He put protest in his voice. "I didn't do anything, just grabbed her wrists. You saw me. I wasn't even using pressure points. When I told her we didn't have the other juvenile, she just went out like a light."

"A highly volatile and unpredictable young lady." Sechrest turned to the nurse. "Get me a stretcher or wheel chair. I'm moving her to a security room."

The nurse frowned. "Only the doctor can release her from ICU. Her vital signs are so low—"

Sechrest cut her off. "Anyone capable of throwing Officer Benton and me across the room has vital enough signs for me. Find a doctor fast because I'm moving her before she really hurts someone."

The nurse had one there in five minutes. Five minutes after that they were on the second floor pushing the girl's wheelchair into one of the hospital's two rooms designed for psychiatric patients. While he helped put the girl in bed, Garreth glanced around, assessing the room, from the reinforced glass of the window to the inner and outer doors. None of that presented a problem, but what did he do about the monitoring camera? He could see its tiny eye—presumably a CCD camera with wide-angle lens to cover most of the room—gleaming from the corner of the ceiling above the door.

"Do you watch her from the nurse's station?" he asked the nurse as they left.

He nodded, locking both doors. "The monitor is at the desk."

They all went to have a look. On the screen the girl twitched in her sleep. Garreth could imagine the inner conflict between his order to sleep and her body's desire to be up and prowling the dark. The wide-angle lens did not cover the area directly beneath the camera, Garreth noted.

As off-hand as possible he asked, "Do you tape this?"

"We probably can, but I never have." The nurse glanced at Sechrest. "Do we need to?"

She shook her head at him. "Just watch her. If there's an emergency, call me at home. Otherwise I'll come back in the morning to talk to her. Benton, there's no further need for you to stick around. Thanks, and sorry it got rough."

Benton shrugged.

Sechrest had driven her own vehicle over this time. As she and Garreth headed back out front, she said, "I'm heading home. There's a cot at the office you're welcome to use tonight."

"Thanks, but I'll just find a motel room." Where no one would notice his coming and going. "What's the best place?"

"With the county fair opening tomorrow, I'm guessing our two motels and bed and breakfast will all be filled by exhibitors who'd rather stay here than drive home tonight in this weather."

Under which circumstances it might seem suspicious in retrospect if he insisted on trying for a motel room. He made himself smile. "In that case...thanks for the cot." He would just have to find a way of dealing with it.

Instead of heading straight back for the office, though, he drove around town, letting the debate between the Lane and Maggie voices run in his head. He noted locations of the fairground, the high school, a cemetery up the street from the hospital with a Greek temple of a mausoleum dominating the high ground in the middle, a housing addition where footings and basements were being dug for some new homes, being poured for others. Seeing the muddy holes the rain had made of the basements, he realized what he was really doing...hunting somewhere to take the girl, alive or dead.

I vote for dead, Lane's voice whispered. *Then it's done with, fini.*

No! Maggie's whisper protested. *You can't kill her, Garreth!*

He sighed. "Well, I have to do *something*. You see how dangerous she is. And she isn't even hungry yet."

Oh, yes, came Lane's satisfied whisper, *and once she has her appetite and teeth, and learns locked doors can't hold her, well...I always made sure those dinner partners I killed died the true death. Look what happened to me the one time I didn't.*

She had a point. Much as everything in him screamed against murder, it would take care of the bb once and for all. He would not even have to hide the body, he realized. With the security rooms on the upper floor, if he smashed the window and dropped her out on her head, it would appear she had broken her neck trying to escape.

That's my boy!

No, Garreth, please! Oh, no!

They made his head ache. He headed for the Sheriff's Office, longing, for the first time in years, to sleep at night, just to escape the debate.

The clerk buzzed him into the office from the waiting room. "Sechrest called in that you'd be sleeping here," she said over the desk between the squad room and business office. "The cot's in the room at the far end there. The restrooms are off the locker room down the hall toward the rear entrance."

The "cot" turned out to be bunkbeds sharing a storeroom with equipment shelves. Setting his computer case and carry-on bag on the top bunk, Garreth realized the foolishness of trying to sleep. It would give him no more escape than it did the girl. But maybe being here had an advantage over a motel. It gave him an alibi if any question came up about his whereabouts late in the evening. The clerk would testify that she had buzzed Garreth in only once, well before the suspect died trying to escape.

Only as the thought formed did he realize that subconsciously he had made his decision about the girl. His gut knotted, but...he had so few choices, none good. This was the cleanest. She should have died hours ago anyway...and what difference was there between this and shooting a vicious dog?

The rationalization failed to relax the knots. He had pushed the line a number of times, but this would take him over it into betrayal of every ethic he believed in. Maggie's voice wailed unhappily in his head.

He made a show of heading out to the locker room and calling good night to the clerk on returning, then in the bunk room he pulled a dark, long-sleeved shirt over his t-shirt and jeans and locked the storeroom door on the inside to make sure no one, such as a deputy at watch change returning or picking up something from the storage shelves, could find him gone. But to be doubly safe, he pulled back the sheet on the bottom bunk, rumpled the bed, and punched the pillow to make it appear he had been sleeping and gotten up for a minute. He also left the raincoat. They would not expect him to leave the building without that.

Wrench.

Once through the door, he slipped across the squad room, keeping low, then down the corridor to the rear entrance. *Wrench.* Outside he peeled the SO emblems off the car and drove to the street behind the hospital, parking where the car faded to invisibility in the shadows.

Almost 11:00. Hopefully this hospital changed shifts then, like most he had dealt with. Garreth drank half a pint of blood. Too bad it could not be alcohol. A stiff shot of Irish whiskey would be nice about now. He raced across the grass for the hospital...passed through the ground level stair door at the same end of the building as the security rooms...climbed to the second floor. And sat down on the stairs to wait. Guilt twisted in him but he tried to ignore it. What had to be done, had to be done.

The seconds ticked away. His mind ticked, too. There might be periods when no one watched the security room monitor but the only time he could count on was shift change, when everyone should be in report. He hoped.

At 11:00 he eased open the door to the floor and peered toward the nurse's station. Nurses and aides milled around it. Presently, however, they trailed across the corridor to their conference room. He could not see into the station itself to tell if someone remained there but he had to gamble not. Heart thundering he dashed into the corridor and flung himself at the security room door. *Wrench.* And hit the inner door, *wrench*, with barely a pause between. The cumulative effect of the two passages brought him through the second door staggering. Garreth caught himself and pressed back into the blind spot of the corner below the camera. His meal did its job. The energy flowing out through him quickly dispelled the discomfort from the doors. Once recovered, he darted forward, snatched the sleeping girl from the bed, and hauled her back to the corner.

She felt small and fragile as he grabbed her forehead and the back of her head. Remembering Maggie and the attacks on local officers, though, he tensed his muscles to twist her neck.

Suddenly the room vanished. He stood with fire enveloping him, staring through a tall window at the girl, though with her hair short and smoky blonde, braced angrily before the albino, her fangs extended, while he stared down at her with murderous fury in his face and glowing eyes.

As the vision vanished he released the girl's head and caught her under the arms to hold her upright. His heart leaped. Did the vision mean she could lead him to the albino...that she *would* if she lived? But what a dangerous burden she made in the process. Could he afford the risk?

Voices rose in the hall. "She was in the bed a minute ago. She can't have left the room so she must be under the camera."

The lock turned in the outer door.

Garreth swore...stared down at the girl. He had to decide now. The vision flickered through his head again. Oh, hell; he might as well trust his grandmother's gift.

Heaving the girl over his shoulder, he charged across the room and hurled himself at the window. For a tense moment he feared it would not break...but then it shattered, falling away before them, and amid a rain of shards, they plunged out into darkness.

26.

They seemed to fall for an eternity before the ground jumped to meet him. He landed prepared to collapse and hit rolling, but the lawn gave beneath him like a wet sponge and Garreth found himself still upright without pain—nothing broken!— albeit sinking into a squat. Someone shouted from the broken window. Garreth let gravity finish pulling him into the squat, then used the flexion of his knees and hips to rebound to his feet and sprint for the car.

As he shoved the girl across into the passenger seat and started the motor, his mind raced. Had the rain helped hide him or had they seen him? If so, how clearly? And even as- suming he had escaped cleanly...now what did he do with the girl? He had to stash her somewhere secure but close and make it back to the SO in time to be "wakened" by news of her escape. The seconds ticked off in his head like a time bomb. He had to hurry! Any minute someone would start knocking on the bunk room door.

Only one hiding place close occurred to him...the Porsche.

On a dark side street he moved the seats forward and wedged her in behind them on the floor, covering her with the blanket he kept in the luggage compartment up front for emer- gencies. Her bent knees made a hump in the material but its dark color should help keep her invisible to all but a close scrutiny. He gunned on downtown, hoping the rain muted the snarl of the engine.

The parking lot behind the courthouse sat almost empty, as it had his last two trips here. Sechrest's deputies, like Reichert's, apparently drove their units home. But the hand- ful of current vehicles included three patrol cars, two that had not been there before. If the graveyard shift, however many deputies that included, had left on patrol, two units must belong to deputies on the swing shift finishing up reports. He would have to find a way past them.

He parked in the far corner beyond a battered International Travelall he'd noticed his first trip in tonight. Any accusations that his car had not been in the lot around 11:00 he could counter with the claim that it had simply been hidden by the Travelall.

After slapping the Bellamy County emblems on his doors, he started around the edge of the lot toward the SO's rear entrance...but dropped flat as two deputies banged out through the door toward their patrol units. He lay motionless until they peeled out of the parking lot, then dashed for the rear entrance. Outside he paused just long enough to make sure no footsteps approached on the other side, then leaned forward. *Wrench.* No one in sight. Keeping low, he raced for the squad room.

The rapping warned him before he reached the doorway. He stopped short. Someone knocking on the storeroom door?

A male voice confirmed that. "Hey, Mikaelian! Wake up! Hell...what does it take to wake this guy?"

He did not sound like someone talking to himself.

A voice from the direction of the desk between squad room and business office said, "Just go in and shake him, Sarge."

The clerk. Damn. The man at the door could be persuaded into believing he found Garreth in the bunk room, but that would not work with a witness at the other end of the room. Time for plan B.

He stripped off the dark shirt, then stepped on the heel of one boot with the toe of the other and pulled up, but the wet boot clung to his foot as if glued. Shit! Dropping to the floor, Garreth wrenched at the boot with both hands.

Metal rattled. "He's locked the door."

The boot came off with agonizing slowness, pulling his sock along with it. He dropped them and grappled with the other boot.

"You could get the key and unlock it."

The boot came free. Garreth sprang to his feet and in t-shirt, jeans, and bare feet, strolled into the squad room, kicking boots and shirt first ahead of him, then sideways under a desk. He just had to gamble the deputy did not notice the jeans were wet. "Hi. I'm Mikaelian from the Bellamy SO in Kansas. Your sheriff's letting me crash—" He broke off with raised brows as the husky man by the door stared at him. "What's the matter?"

The deputy nodded toward the door. "We thought you were in there."

"No, I've been in the can. Why?"

"The door's locked."

Garreth put on a frown. "It is?" He padded down the room to the door and tried the knob. "I'll be damned. I wonder how—"

"Never mind that now. I'm Maurice Collins, the First Watch duty sergeant. I was trying to wake you to tell you that your suspect's escaped from the hospital."

Garreth stiffened. "Son of a bitch! I thought that was supposed to be a security room! Can you help me with this?" He pointed at the door. "I need to dress."

Collins disappeared across the hall and returned with a key.

Once inside, Garreth rummaged in his bag for dry socks. "How'd she manage it?"

"I don't have details but somehow she broke the window and jumped."

Garreth pulled on the socks. "Shit."

Collins nodded. "Yeah. But we're hunting her. Both patrol units on First Watch and most of the ones from Third Watch have gone over to search the area around the hospital. The PD's helping, too."

"And I'm on my way as well. Sergeant?"

Looking down at him, Collins went motionless as their gazes met and locked.

Garreth stared deep into his eyes. "You will remember that I put on my boots in here. You won't notice me picking them up in the squad room." He put on his raincoat, now dry from being hung on the frame at the foot of the bunk.

As they walked out through the squad room together, Garreth kept Collins between himself and the business office desk, and used the sergeant for cover as he ducked to retrieve his shirt and boots. In the corridor he headed for the rear entrance.

"Be careful," Collins called after him.

On the porch outside the rear entrance he jammed his feet into his boots...twice as hard to do as pulling them off had been.

At the hospital a Sheriff and PD car sat at the entrance while up on the floor the deputy and officer from the units stood at the doorway of the security room with a nurse. He joined them, showing them his ID. In the room, hospital maintenance personnel taped a sheet of plastic over the shattered window to keep out the rain.

"I don't understand how she broke the glass," the deputy said.

The nurse shrugged in bafflement. "Especially someone her size. We thought at first maybe she used a chair to break it, but there isn't one by the window or on the ground outside. She had to have just jumped through it."

"Won't the tape show you for sure?" the PD officer asked.

Garreth's heart skipped. If they *had* gone ahead and taped...

To his relief the nurse said, "Since the sheriff didn't ask us to tape her, we didn't."

The deputy sighed. "At least she ought to be easy to spot in a hospital gown and she can't have gone too far."

"Did you see which way she went?" Garreth asked.

The nurse shook her head. "Not really. We couldn't see much of anything outside."

So he had dodged *that* bullet.

"I'm just surprised she could jump and not break something," the nurse added.

The deputy grimaced. "I think she's pretty well proven herself one tough little bitch."

"And the sooner found the safer we'll be," Garreth said. "I'm going to join the area search." The sooner he moved her out of his car the safer *he* would be.

But...where to take her? It had to be a place he could leave her unattended and feel certain she would go undiscovered. Thinking back through his tour of the town he thought of the Greek temple mausoleum in the cemetery up the street. It seemed like one place unlikely to be searched.

He drove over to check it out. Gates closed off the entrances on the streets on the east and south, and the cemetery wall stretched unbroken along the north side. He would have to park on a side street and carry the girl in. That bothered him. Even at night in the rain he might be spotted crossing the street. Could there be a way in on the west side?

No street bordered it there. Instead, the western wall abutted the grounds of private homes. He halted on the nearest street west to pull the emblems off the car, then cruised on north.

What he could see of the wall here looked unbroken, too, and lined with tall trees screening the cemetery from the view of the homes. Two east-west streets dead-ended at the wall. But a third narrowed to an alley running between hedge on one side and towering rhododendron bushes on the other...and led to a gap in the cemetery wall. An equipment shed inside explained the reason for this entrance...and only a padlocked chain crossed the gap.

Seeing crumbling mortar around one end of the chain, he wiggled it experimentally and without too much surprise found that the anchor bolt pulled out of the wall. Someone before him had worked it free; at a guess, a hormone-driven adolescent male from one of the neighborhood homes, seeking a secluded place to bring his dates. Replacing the chain behind him, Garreth hoped he met no one parking tonight.

He spotted no one, but following the drive toward the Greek temple, he discovered that more mausoleums sat along two branching drives, smaller and built into the slope. He stopped in front of one group. Trees and the curve of the hill hiding them from casual view appealed to him. Peering into them, however, he found the first two too shallow; just a few feet of space between the doors and vaults. Four others provided more of a vestibule, but one near the far end sitting separated from its neighbors intrigued him most. It looked so small within its Grecian portico, not quite two vaults wide. Why, then, all the space around it? The thick stained glass in the double doors blocked all view of the interior.

Garreth sighed. He would have to go inside to see it. Gritting his teeth, he leaned into one of the doors. *Wrench*.

When he opened his eyes a few moments later they met something he had almost never saw...blackness. Night and the storm blocked so much light from entering through the door glass that even with his vampire vision he had trouble seeing. But gradually he made out details...and the reason for the mausoleum's isolation. Inside the entrance, steps led downward to a chamber with vaults on three sides.

He liked it...roomy, more secluded than the Greek temple, and unlikely to be disturbed. According to the vault dates, the last interment occurred in 1947, with four vaults remaining unoccupied, and judging by the dust on a granite meditation bench, no one had even visited here in years. The air smelled wonderfully of rain and damp earth. The building must be ventilated.

But he needed the door open to bring the girl in. Foremost, he wanted to avoid, for as long as possible, letting her learn she could pass through doors. But it also might not be possible to *carry* her through.

Once outside again he examined the lock. It had two, an old-fashioned rim lock in the door with two or at most three tumblers—no skill necessary to pick it, just brute strength to turn it, considering how long it must have gone unopened—and a padlock from the fifties or sixties on a chain run through the door handles. The padlock should be no problem, either. He still carried the lock pick set he bought as a rookie...which had probably been used more often breaking into colleague's lockers for practical jokes than in police work.

Garreth brought his tool kit from the car, grateful for the portico shielding the tools from the rain. Though the rain did appear to be letting up. After spraying liberal amounts of lubricant into both keyholes, especially up between the tumbler plates of the door lock, and carefully wiping away all traces of it outside the locks, he went to work on the padlock. From the feel of the tumblers, it might not have been opened since before he was born. Almost half seemed frozen in place. But he sprayed in more lubricant and patiently slid the pick back and forth, pushing up until he felt the tumblers start to move. Then he worked at turning the cylinder. In fifteen minutes, he finally had the padlock open. Hardly a world record. The ghosts of burglars past must be snickering in the Great Beyond.

The door lock went faster, benefiting, no doubt, from the long wait with lubricant soaking through the dirt and rust in it. The tumbler plates complained, scraping loudly past each other, but the generous tolerances within the lock let him feel where each plate cleared the stop inside, which let him bend a piece of baling wire to the configuration of the key. And though it still took pliers to turn the lock while the wire "key" raised the tumblers, he had the door open in less than five minutes.

Despite feeling relatively secure from discovery, he let his breath out in relief...and hurriedly carried the girl down inside, followed by a few other items, including his pallet—on which he laid the girl—and a couple of pints from the cooler. Then he closed the door, leaving it unlocked, relocked the padlock, and passed back through into the mausoleum.

Downstairs he switched on the SnakeLight from his tool kit and coiled it to sit on the meditation bench, pointing down toward the girl. Sitting cross-legged beside her, he took a minute to drink in the sensations of the earth surrounding him beyond the concrete walls...sweet, soothing, refreshing. His next home, he decided, should be underground. Then he shook himself back to business. "Valerie. Valerie, wake...up."

She stirred. "Ice?"

He blinked. What did she want ice for? Then a thrill shot down his spine. Not ice...Ice. A name. A name that described one person perfectly...the albino.

Her eyes opened. And instantly shut. When she opened her eyes again, she did so more cautiously, squinting, blocking the light with her hand. "Where am I?" Her nose wrinkled. "It smells like a cellar." She turned to peer at the wall behind her...and jumped up with a squeak to back away from the vaults. "Those are—this is—"

"A fine and private place, perfect for an undisturbed chat."

She started to turn. "Who the hell are you? Chat about wha—" Suddenly she seemed to become aware that she wore just a hospital gown. Snatching it together behind her, she spun her back away from him.

He pulled off his raincoat and tossed it to her. "Here." He wanted her to focus on him, not worry about her modesty.

She eyed him as she put it on and snapped the front, then scowled at him through her hair. "I know you. You're the cop that knocked me out at the hospital!"

Her expression reminded Garreth of the picture on the Blue Steel Purgatory tape, and he realized why one of the band had seemed familiar. If that musician were her father, it could explain why she carried the tapes, though by the time she was born Blue Steel Perdition was ancient history. He considered asking her father's name but decided to save his knowledge of that relationship for a time when the revelation had useful shock value. "You want to tell me how I could do that while holding your wrists with both my hands?"

The scowl deepened. "How else did I end up unconscious? And look what else you did, you son of a bitch!" She pulled her hair away from her face, then baring her teeth, used her tongue to wiggle first one upper canine, then the other.

And suddenly he knew who she was. With the scowl and her hair skinned back, she matched the National Clearinghouse photo of Rebecca Newman. More knowledge to save for a strategic moment! Though it would be handy to have some name to call her, without asking her for it and ruining the illusion of being all knowing. Maybe he could maneuver her into volunteering whatever name she currently called herself.

"And after you sock me you break me out of the hospital." She crossed her arms. "Why? Is this where you pretend you're my friend and that you want to help me?"

"No. I'm definitely not your friend, cupcake." He relished being blunt with her, and the flash of annoyance in her eyes. "But I find myself in the position of having to help you so you can help me—"

Her contemptuous snort cut him off. "Help *you*? No. Fucking. Way."

He repeated, "So you can help me find Ice."

The sneer vanished with an indrawn breath. "How—" Her face blanked. "They sell ice at any convenience store."

Very cute. "You know what I'm talking about, cupcake. This Ice is two-legged, albino, and kills cops. I want him."

The annoyance in her expression morphed into a smirk. "No you don't. You might know his name but you don't have a clue what you're dealing with. Ice is the last person in the world you want to meet."

He can destroy you. But despite the danger, Garreth felt a rush of relief. *Finally* he knew. "Because he's a vampire, you mean?"

She stared at him. "You know that? How did you know?"

He tried to keep his voice free of irony. "Past experience. How old is he?" That would give him a true picture of how much power he faced...how much danger.

The smirk returned. "Two thousand years."

Cold shot down Garreth's spine. Two thousand years. More than double Irina's age. Did he stand even a chance against someone with that much experience? *He can destroy you.*

"He's been *everywhere*." She sat down on the end of the meditation bench and leaned toward him, expression smug. "Ice rode with Genghis Khan and knew Ivan the Terrible and Louis the something, the Sun King. And he was a general in the Roman army in Nero's Rome and knew all the famous artists like Botticelli in Florence. He's got *millions* stashed away in Swiss bank accounts."

Garreth's bullshit alarms went off. All that, yet now he lived as a petty criminal? "You believe him? Did he offer any kind of proof, cupcake?"

She frowned, then sniffed. "Proof? You mean like a year zero birth certificate or pictures of himself with Genghis Khan, or Roman army dog tags? Ice has fangs, and his eyes glow blood red. And he never eats regular food. What do *you* need for proof?"

He sounded like a vampire. But was he really as old as he claimed? "You've never wondered why he steals money when he already has so much?"

"Of course." Her lip curled. "I'm not stupid. I asked him why he wasn't living on the Riviera and driving Ferraris. He said he got bored. 'The trouble with being immortal,' he said, 'is there's so much *time*. It's hard finding interesting new things to do.'"

That had a discouraging ring of authenticity. Irina once voiced something of the same sentiment when Garreth asked about the origin of the Philos Foundation.

She crossed her legs and leaned back on her hands. The foot of the crossed leg bounced, as though keeping time to some unheard music. "He saw this movie, *Badlands*, about a couple that go on a cross-country crime spree. It looked like fun. So he decided to try it, too. Greedy people and perverts and fools all deserve what happens to them, he says."

"The police, too?"

The foot stopped moving and her expression went wary. Hearing some dangerous note in his voice despite his effort to keep his tone even? "Every game needs risk, Ice says. There's no point to playing otherwise. Like when he fought as a gladiator, and helped sneak aristocrats out of France during the French Revolution." She smirked. "Not that there's been much danger to him this time around."

Little bitch. Garreth held on to his temper. "True. You're the only one who's died."

That took her back. She stiffened...but recovered fast. "No thanks to that goon deputy I didn't!"

"Now that's where you're wrong, cupcake." He made no attempt to hide his satisfaction.

This time she stared at him longer. Her legs uncrossed. "What do you mean?"

Garreth unfolded and moved up to sit on the other end of the meditation bench. "You *did* die."

She frowned. "That's just what everyone thought."

"What everyone else thought doesn't matter, cupcake. I'm telling you what you *experienced*."

Her frowned deepened. "You don't know *shit* I've experienced! And quit calling me 'cupcake'!"

What a pleasure it would be to wipe that sneer off her face. He smiled. "We'll see. I'll tell you what happened and you let me know if I'm right, cupcake."

Her voice went shrill. "My name's *Raven*, asshole!"

Bingo. "Your felt your heart and breathing stop. That's being dead."

With just a moment of hesitation, Raven shrugged. "An hallucination, because he choked me. Besides, I could still—"

"You could still see, sort of, right? Just not focus or move your eyes, and you could still hear and feel people touching you, but vaguely. How am I doing so far?"

She did not reply, just sat staring at him.

"Then after they zipped you into the body bag and transported you to the hospital for an autopsy and you were lying there maybe wondering—I'm guessing a bit here—wondering if this was what death was like...no Heaven, no Hell, not even oblivion, just eternal awareness...maybe wondering what it would be like feeling your body putrefy and decay. Or maybe you thought: what if they cremate me? Do I feel myself cooking, hear the meat sizzle and—"

"Stop it!" She jumped up, away from him, shuddering, retreating until the wall stopped her. "You fucking *bastard*! I didn't think anything *like* that." Her voice carried relief.

Maybe he was laying it on a bit strong. "All right. At some point in the nightmare, you felt yourself finally take a breath, and your heart squeeze into beat. Then it beat again, and you took another breath, and another. Eventually you could move again, which is when you tried to get out of the body bag and rolled off the gurney onto the floor. And now..."

He saw her hold her breath.

"Now everything is weird." He put his hand over the lens of the light. To ordinary vision, the crypt would have plunged into darkness, but with the bright pool gone, he saw a generalized twilight grey. "Night isn't dark anymore. And there's so much sound...things you never heard before, that you never *could* hear...like people talking way down the hall. There are more smells than you ever noticed before, too. But most of all, people smell different...salty-metallic. If you haven't identified it yet, it's the scent of blood. You're smelling the blood in people."

Her whisper trembled. "How do you know all that?"

"Past experience. Are you thirsty?"

Her hand went to her throat. After a moment she nodded.

Garreth reached under the bench for the pints he had brought down from the cooler and handed her the one he had opened earlier. "This is only half full but take my word that it's more than enough to satisfy you."

She twisted off the cap and raised the bottle toward her mouth, then stopped, sniffing. And flung the bottle down. "You psycho! This is *blood!*"

Garreth's dive caught the bottle before it before it hit the floor. "I thought you liked blood." Some had splashed out on his wrist. He licked it off.

Above him her face twisted in revulsion. "That's *nasty!*"

He sat back on his heels to peer up at her. "Then why'd you drink it before...the dog's and those officers' and Mr. Becker's in Omaha?"

She hugged herself. "That was different."

"How? You drank the blood and liked it then."

"No I didn't, but—" She broke off, shrugging...then grimaced. "You have to be with Ice to understand. Whatever he wants you to do, you do. But he isn't here now and I won't drink that stuff!"

"But blood is what vampires drink."

"I'm not a vampire!" Her tone said she had no desire to be.

This should be interesting. Garreth retrieved the bottle's cap and twisted it on as he stood up...then stepped well back from her, in case she went berserk. "Yes you are."

Instead she frowned in puzzlement. "What?"

"You're a vampire...bloodsucker...undead." A bit melodramatic, but he needed to make the point.

After a frozen moment she said calmly, "No I'm not."

Denial, denial. Garreth sighed. "Come on, Raven. I know you haven't been in the life long enough to experience the desire to sleep through daylight and discover the soothing qualities of earth, but how can you live with a vampire for a year and a half and not recognize other signs? You never had such sharp hearing or night sight like this before today...and yesterday little you could never have thrown that fitness nazi across the room. Those teeth are loose to make way for your new fangs."

Her voice hardened. "It's impossible. Ice hasn't bitten me."

"That isn't the only way to come across. Another is to drink a vampire's blood. And you did. Mine."

She stiffened. "I've never seen you before today!"

"You just don't recognize me. About all you saw of me Monday was my arm hanging out the car window."

He could see in her face that she made the connection almost instantly, but did not believe him. "That cop was dead!"

"A common impression when we're asleep or unconscious."

Fear flickered in her eyes, then her jaw set. "I don't believe you're that cop…or that you're a vampire. You're trying to trick me so I'll help you find Ice. It won't do any good. There's *no fucking way* I'll ever help you."

Stubborn! He handed her his ID. "I *am* that officer. And check this out." He opened his mouth wide, extending his fangs.

She recoiled, throwing down the ID and retreating to the corner beyond the bench. "No! Maybe you're a vampire, but I'm not. I'm *not!*"

As he retrieved his ID he watched her eye the stairs. No doubt gauging her chances of making a break for it. He better be careful. If she reached the door, a frantic enough desire to escape could take her through them.

He moved between her and the stairs. "Raven, deny it all you want—though I'm not sure why you're upset; isn't the promise he'll bring you across the reason you're with Ice?— but you're a vampire. You are. Now and forever, world without end, A—"

"Shut up!" She launched at him, fists hammering. "*Shut up*! That's blasphemy!"

In his astonishment he almost missed grabbing her wrists. Of all he might have anticipated her saying, that statement never occurred to him. Blasphemy? A vampire's servant with religion?

"And I'm *not* a vampire!" She flailed at him. "I can't be. NO!" He heard the hysteria in her rising voice. And seconds later her control vanished. She screamed, a piercing siren that in the restricted space threatened to shatter his eardrums.

"Raven." He shook her. "Listen to me. Stop!" But she screamed without slackening and he shook her harder. "Rebecca!"

For a moment she froze.

He used the moment. "Rebecca, calm...down. Go...to...sleep. Sleep."

And like a balloon leaking air, all the rigidity went out of her. She quit screaming, quit flailing, and wilted. Garreth caught her, grimacing in relief, and carried her to the pallet. Was it worth keeping her alive to fulfill the vision? He had no time to deal with hysteria. Now would be a good time to finish her, while she felt nothing.

But the vision replayed in memory...vivid, insistent. The need to find the albino beat at him. And he recalled his own initial horror. While not hysterical, he had certainly yelled and ranted, repulsed by the idea of the vile, damned creature he thought he had become. Okay, give her some time to adjust.

Time. He glanced at his watch. Time to check in with the Sheriff's Office. The girl ought to be secure here. Even if he had not commanded her to sleep, the processes altering her body used up most available energy and would probably keep her naturally out for hours. He had slept thirty hours straight at one point.

He leaned down to Raven. "I'll be back, cupcake, and whatever I have to do to you, you *will* help me track down Ice. Sweet dreams."

27.

As soon as the clerk buzzed him into the office, Garreth noticed the glow down the corridor that had to be coming through
the frosted panel of Sechrest's door. She was back down here?
Garreth knocked.

Her voice called, "Come in if you have good news."

Garreth opened the door enough to stick his head in. "I
don't, sorry, but I was hoping someone had."

The sheriff sat leaning back in her chair, feet propped on
her desk, eyes closed. Opening her eyes, she dropped her feet
off the desk. "It's you, Mikaelian." She covered a gaping
yawn. "Your suspect is playing hell with my sleep. I don't
handle all-nighters as well as I used—Lord!" Her eyes snapped
wide. "You're a mess. Where have you been wallowing? And
is that blood on you?"

He peered down. The spots on his t-shirt must have come
from the pint Raven dropped. "I had a collision with a low
branch and gave myself a nosebleed." He did looked as if he
crawled out of a mud wallow, thanks to a combination of wet
jeans and dust from the meditation bench. Grime smeared his
arms, too. He grimaced. "I saw a shower stall in the men's
room. I think I'll use it, and then I'm going bail out of the
hunt and hit the rack for a couple of hours. You don't need
me and I haven't slept for..." Shit, how long *had* it been?
"...days. Will you have someone wake me when something
happens or the day shift starts, whichever comes first? And
tell them to shake me hard. I sleep really deep. Sometimes I
don't even seem to be breathing."

"I'll tell them." Her feet were back on the desk and her
eyes closed before he had shut the door behind him.

The shower and shave felt wonderful. And the clean clothes. And whether Irina's The Mind Rules theory worked or sheer exhaustion overrode the need to sleep on soil, it seemed he had just thrown himself on the lower bunk and begun reaching down to feel the earth beneath the building when an earthquake and distant shouting interrupted him.

Not an earthquake, he discovered, but a female deputy shaking him. The room had no window but obviously the sun had risen. He felt as if the earthquake had brought a building down on him.

"Jesus," the deputy said. "No shit you sleep deep."

"Yeah. Sorry." Garreth used the bunk frame to haul himself out and upright. He groped in his sportcoat for his dark glasses. "What time is it?"

"Seven-fifteen. There's coffee in the business office if you ask them politely for it. No insult intended, but you look like you *really* need it."

He found the glasses and slipped them on. Sometimes he regretted not being able to drink coffee. He certainly needed something to energize him. "How are things going?"

"You mean the search for the fugitive? There's no sign of her."

The girl! That woke him. He needed to retrieve her and sneak her the hell out of Dodge while daylight reinforced his command for her to sleep.

He hurriedly packed up and presented himself to Sheriff Sechrest again. Three mostly empty coffee cups sat on her desk.

He eyed them. "Have you been here all night?"

She grimaced and shrugged. "I kept thinking: I'll give it another half hour. And here we are." She poured the dregs from two of the cups into the third and slugged it all down like a shot of whiskey. "One advantage to being female at times like this, though, is no morning stubble. You're heading out? Going to San Francisco to check background on the male suspect?"

He nodded. "Maybe I'll learn something useful. Thank you for your hospitality."

"Good luck."

The sun shone hot and bright in a cloudless sky as he drove to the cemetery. With the gates open he used one of the regular entrances, but drove around for a few minutes before parking in front of the Ward mausoleum. Cars lined one of the drives toward the north side of the cemetery but he saw no one in his immediate vicinity. He still kept watch while working on the padlock.

This time it opened in less than a minute. Aware that every minute he spent here increased the risk of discovery, in another three minutes, despite daylight dragging him, he had scooped up everything in the mausoleum together and moved it to the car. The girl went back on the floor, the pallet tucked around her, and the blood in the cooler. In daylight the blanket filling the space in front of the back seat looked odd, especially the hump caused by her bent knees. Hurriedly he unclipped the shoulder strap from his computer case and tucked most of it down between blanket and front passenger seat, leaving some showing to suggest he had more luggage under the blanket, then dropped his sportcoat in a casual heap on the hump of her knees. That looked better. Fortunately he did not have to worry about her feeling suffocated by the space and the heat under the blanket. Now, did he have time to go back down and remove any evidence of recent usage?

No. He could see a vehicle headed up the drive his direction. "Damn!"

While trees momentarily blocked its occupants' view of him, he threw the chain back through the door handles and snapped the padlock shut.

And moved to the next mausoleum.

When the car reached him he stood with his forehead pressed against the glass in its door, hands cupped on the sides of his eyes, as if trying to peer inside. He waited for the conversion van to pass. But to his dismay, a woman's voice said, "Look at that one, Frank," and in the window reflection, he watched the van halt and a middle-aged couple slide out of their captain's chairs to climb down with cameras in hand.

The female half said, "Excuse me, young man, but could you step back for a moment while we take a picture of this mausoleum?"

Garreth obediently retreated to the rear end of the Porsche. "Are you members of the—" He checked the name above the portico. "—Schwartz family?"

The male half squinted into his viewfinder and twisted the rings on his lens. "No. We're in town to watch our grand-daughter ride in the horse show at the fair and thought we'd check out the cemetery. They're kind of a hobby."

"The animals here caught our eye," the woman said.

Garreth supposed the builders had in mind the text about the lion lying down with the lamb, but putting one animal on each side of the doorway created an effect of adversaries eye-ing each other.

After the woman snapped her picture, to Garreth's dis-may, she wandered over to the doors of the Ward mausoleum. "Frank, there's some beautiful stained glass here."

He could only cross his fingers and hope the door did not move!

Frank joined her but to Garreth's relief, turned away shak-ing his head. "They're nice but we need light behind to show up the colors for pictures." Suddenly he stopped, staring in through the car's rear passenger window.

Garreth's heart went into spasm.

The man looked over at him. "Is that one of those elec-tric coolers that plug into the cigarette lighter? I've been considering buying one of them for the van. What do you think of it?"

"It's very handy." He had to get rid of these people!

He pulled off his glasses, but before he could catch Frank's eyes, the man turned away and strolled on toward the last mau-soleum in the row. "They went Egyptian on this one, Caro."

Shit. Should he just forget the door and trust no one would discover it was open? Even if someone did and checked out the inside, given enough time no one was likely to associate it with Raven or him. Given enough time. A big risk. "Caro."

The woman turned to look at him.

He trapped her gaze. "One of the mausoleums on the south side of the hill has a Tiffany window. You...want...to ...see...that."

"Frank!" The woman flushed with excitement. "There's a Tiffany window. Come on!" She headed back for their van.

After a moment Frank hurried after her.

Garreth sighed in relief.

The moment the trees and slope blocked their view of him, he raced for the doors with his pliers and baling wire "key". He made himself breathe slowly and work deliberately, but his heart thundered with urgency. And raced faster every second the bolt resisted him. Daylight pressed on him. When his hands started to shake he made himself stop, take a deep breath to calm down, and then try again.

This time pliers and wire worked together and after a grate of complaint, the bolt slid home.

Panting with relief, Garreth raced to the car...but made himself drive decorously toward the closest gate. Then he followed streets around the edge of town until he reached the highway leading north to I-80.

Once on the Interstate he called Reichert. "I'm afraid I have bad news. The suspect escaped."

The sheriff's sigh came through the phone. "I know. We got the word by teletype last night. How'd she get away?"

Garreth gave him official, non-vampire, version.

Reichert grunted. "I suppose you want to stay there and help hunt for her?"

"No, sir. Cameron Dark is who we want most, right? I'm headed for San Francisco as soon as I take care of my car." He needed some excuse for not leaving right away and running through the possibilities between New Prospect and the Interstate, the car emerged as most reasonable.

"Is there a problem with it?"

"Unfortunately. But that's the price of buying a vehicle the previous owner probably drove the hell out of." He put a shrug in his voice. "Of course there's no place in New Prospect to have a Porsche worked on so I'm trying to make it back to Omaha. Once they've told me what's wrong, I'll leave the car to be repaired and catch a plane."

"You have enough money for a ticket?"

Garreth grinned at Reichert's wary tone. "Don't worry; I haven't spent all my legacy yet. I'll let you know before I fly out."

Then he called Irina's pager and left a message. She might not know all the vampires in the world, but a two-millennium albino must have come to her attention, by rumor if nothing else.

While he waited for her to respond, he kept moving. First and foremost on the agenda, moving the girl out of his car before he died a true death of a heart attack! Another mausoleum would be nice...except for having to pick a lock in broad daylight. More Franks and Caros *would* give him a heart attack.

Another underground structure as suitable as a mausoleum occurred to him, though. During the Cold War the Philos Foundation had sought to ensure survival of its blood inventory and personnel to distribute it by building bomb shelters under their chapter offices. However, he needed permission to use Omaha's, which meant taking the chapter president into his confidence. Philos rules forbid using vampire persuasion on human personnel or chapter friends. And even though Philos chose its presidents for their discretion, it made him nervous to reveal his activities to a stranger, especially if she refused him.

Still, he had few other options.

So an hour and a half later he sat in the president's office of the Omaha chapter with his glasses hanging on his sportcoat pocket, his gaze fixed on her nose, and anxiety crawling down his spine. Despite her kindness in closing blackout curtains, Joanna Lovings' rawboned six feet made her seem like a model for *American Gothic* or Frau someone from a Mel Brooks movie, at whose name horses neighed in panic. Did Philos also choose presidents for their ability to intimidate even individuals centuries older than themselves? Garreth had no doubt that holding a job which brought her in contact with individuals who had to live by lies made her as expert as a school principal or police officer at spotting not only direct lies but those of omission and half truths. Any of which would certainly earn him a refusal.

Her brows rose at him. "What problem is so big that you have to use the bomb shelter? You know we have members and friends prepared to take guests."

He nodded. "But I have charge of a newborn vampire in hysterical, violent denial. When I stopped here yesterday I was on my way to prevent her reanimation. Unfortunately I was too late." He took a deep breath. Here came the chancy part. "She's also wanted by the police, and if they learn I have her, I will be, too." They. The word stabbed him. When before had he ever had to refer to his fellow officers as "they".

Lovings frowned. "Yet you want us to risk accommodating you?"

He winced inwardly. That did not sound promising. "Yes, ma'am...because there's an even greater danger involved here."

She sat back, elbows on her chair arms, fingers tented. "Go on."

At least she had not summarily ordered him out. With the lie-detector eyes boring into him, he told the story from the moment Maggie spotted the van, all the time sweating at the thought of the car sitting in the parking lot, locked but with the girl inside unattended. Lovings listened with her expression going grimmer by the moment and the tented fingers becoming arms folded across her chest. A negative posture if Garreth had ever seen it. Despite a sense of futility, he plowed on. She must surely see the importance of finding and stopping the albino.

When he finished she sat eyeing him for a minute before speaking. "A two thousand year old vampire doesn't reach that age by calling attention to himself."

Did that mean she doubted his story? She certainly appeared to be missing the point. "Maybe he isn't that old. That's just what he claims. We don't know for sure he's even a vampire. If he is what he says, having survived this long he might feel invulnerable, or be bored enough to take risks. Whatever the truth, he needs to be taken out of circulation."

She considered, then nodded. "I agree."

"His age and whether he's a vampire affect how I have to deal with him..." Garreth leaned forward over the edge of the desk. "...so I need to see what I can learn in California. Hopefully that's where I acquire the ammunition that convinces the girl to help me find the albino."

Her brows rose. "That's odd phrasing. You acquire? Convinces her? You know the future?"

He hesitated, then nodded. "I have psychic flashes and I've seen her lead me to him. Crazy as that seems."

The brows leveled. "When I was twenty it might have, but not when I've spent over half my life selling blood to vampires. 'There are more things in Heaven and earth, Horatio, that you and I have dreamed.' This psychic flash is why, I presume, you're letting this girl live, despite the risk?"

He nodded. "At this stage, she isn't too much of a risk, though. She ought to sleep naturally for at least twenty-four hours, keeping her out of trouble. Which is time enough for me to fly out to California and—"

"No."

A stone dropped into Garreth's stomach. "We can't use the shelter?"

Lovings' mouth thinned. "I'm willing to let the *two* of you use it for a day or two, while you help this girl come to terms with her change of life. But if you're proposing that I warehouse her, goodbye. She isn't luggage you can just store, nor am I a jailer. When you leave, she goes with you."

The thought of flying with the girl, or driving cross country, dropped another ton of rock into his gut. Control would be a nightmare! "May I leave her at least long enough to buy something for her to wear besides the hospital gown and raincoat?" He could *not* leave her in a mall parking lot!

After a long moment, Lovings nodded. "Since we don't want witnesses seeing you carry in what looks like a body, bring your car around to the back."

Behind the building a ramp sloped down to a roll-up door on the basement level. Standing at the open door, Lovings motioned him in. The garage looked built for trucks. The space dwarfed the Porsche. But that gave him plenty of room to maneuver with the girl hanging over his shoulder.

Lovings led the way through basement past shelves of office supplies, the dusty corpses of old computer monitors and keyboards, and cartons of needles, test tubes, and blood collection bags waiting to be used in the donation room upstairs. "Your presence won't be general knowledge so always come in this way. I'll loan you a remote opener. Using the door shows up on the security panel at the receptionist's desk but Laura will be told you're down here. She knows about Life Members."

She unlocked a door nearly invisible in a dim corner under the stairs. An exterior that looked like distressed wood with peeling varnish opened to reveal steel bulkhead construction. Beyond it a long set of steps led down to a second door opening into a narrow room with shower heads along one side and hooks on the opposite wall. The door at the end opened into the shelter.

Garreth laid the pallet and girl on the lowest of a triple-decker bunk. "This is quite a setup." Far more elaborate than the one in San Francisco...three roomy barrel vaults, with plenty of soil and concrete over them.

Lovings shrugged. "For all the good it would have done. With the SAC base here, we'd have been almost ground zero."

"I see it's still cleaned and provisioned." He pointed at cartons of canned goods stacked in the vault with a cooler door in the partition built across halfway down its length.

After a moment she shrugged again. "The bear may be only sleeping." She handed him the garage door opener and the door key. Conical depressions on sides and edges of the shaft instead of a sawtooth edge guaranteed it could not be copied at the local convenience store. "The phone over there has speed dial entries for all our extension numbers. If you need something during the night, call Doug Curtain at 05. He'll be on duty all week end. Right now, when you go out, call Laura or me, and then let us know when you're back."

"I'm on my way out now. I just need to know where to find a garden store, mall, and laundromat."

Following her directions, he hunted up the laundromat, and while his clothes washed, he wondered that the hell to do with the girl. Maybe he should find a mausoleum after all? Except he had no guarantee she would sleep for twenty-four hours and he shuddered at the thought of her waking with him half a continent away. And what if checking out California needed more than a day? No, if he had no one to watch her, he had to take her along.

Playing on her inexperience and insecurity probably gave him his best chance for control of her. She must have other buttons he could push, too. To find them, though, he needed to know more about her.

He brought in his computer case and dug out the fax copies of the National Clearinghouse photos, sorting through them to the sullen face of Rebecca Newman. The accompanying data told him little except that her father Edward Newman had reported her missing from Crow Ford, Montana, in January two years ago. Garreth frowned. January? Good weather produced plenty of runaways, but what impetus sent this girl off in the middle of winter?

He switched on his phone and called Directory Assistance in Montana.

A woman answered the Newman number. "Living Word Parsonage."

Parsonage? Garreth whistled soundlessly. "Then Edward Newman is the Reverend Edward Newman?" Even more religion in the girl's background than he expected.

"Do you need to talk to him?"

"I'm not sure. Who am I speaking with now?"

"I'm Marian Newman."

Presumably Mrs. Newman. Who would be best...the mother or the father? He sent a trial shot to test the reaction. "Rebecca's mother?"

"*Ed!*" The scream almost made him drop the phone. "Have you seen her!" He pictured her clutching the receiver in both hands. "Is she all right? Dear Lord, is she all right?"

In a surge of sympathy, mixed with anger at the girl, he imagined how many hours in the past two years Marian Newman had spent agonizing over where her daughter was and what was happening to her. At least he did not have to inflict the anguish he had on other mothers when the answer to that question was *No*. "She's alive, yes."

A sob came through the phone, and a whisper clearly not meant for him. "Thank you, dear Lord." And then, also not to him, "It's a man who's seen Rebecca!"

A rich tenor voice came on the phone. "I'm Edward Newman, Rebecca's father. Who are you, sir? And where's Rebecca?"

"I'm sorry but I can't answer either question. Please hear me out," he said as Newman started to protest. Garreth had put his story together while dialing their number. "I'm the director of a shelter for runaways. Our ultimate goal is returning these kids home, of course, but most immediately we want them off the street."

"Well of course, but—"

"And while some come in just needing a little support to call home, others are too full of anger or fear to even mention home to them in case it makes them take off again." His washer stopped. Holding the phone with one hand, he transferred clothes to a dryer with the other and fed in quarters. "Rebecca is one of the latter, and even though I'm encouraged by the fact she carries tapes of your band's music with her, I won't tell her I know her real name or that I've contacted you. And I won't tell you where we are in case you can't stop yourself from coming after her. Going home has to be her idea."

"Wait." Confusion filled the voice. "If she didn't tell you her name how—"

"I check every new resident against the National Clearinghouse files, and I know you used to be in Blue Steel Perdition because of the resemblance between your daughter and you in the album photos. We even met once, though I doubt you remember the officers who arrested you at the Mark Hopkins in San Francisco and I don't remember which one of the band you were."

After a hesitation, Newman said, "Teddy Rivers," and made a sound close to a groan. "That was our last concert before Doug Wayne OD'd, and I almost did." Somewhere in the background Marian Newman mumbled something even Garreth's hearing could not distinguish and Newman sighed. "Not wicked, Marian. We were just young and wild and stupid." He grunted. "You know, for almost twenty years after I walked out of that hospital I didn't think about the band or my past. As far as I was concerned, I'd left it all behind, changed my name, become a new man. But we're fools to think the past is dead."

"Does the band have something to do with why your daughter ran away?"

Newman sighed again. "It started everything. Marian found a tape of *Perdition Bound* in Rebecca's room in a case for a spiritual album. I've always banned rock music from this house. Look what it did to me...and how Rebecca reacted when Marian confronted her. Rebecca grabbed the tape and started screaming at her mother to stay out of her room, then when Marian tried to take the tape away again, Rebecca slapped her and locked herself in her room. Even when moving to a new church has made her unhappy, Rebecca never behaved that way before.

"Marian called me home. Rebecca still had the door locked. She shouted at me that if rock music was evil so was I because I made that album, and accused me of being Teddy Rivers. I didn't try to deny it. I regret so much of what I did, but I won't lie about doing it. It shocked Marian, of course, because she didn't know about Blue Steel Perdition. I'd just told her I ran away from home as a teenager and lived a wild life until I found Jesus. That night at church instead of giving a sermon I confessed everything...my past, and my rebellion in not acknowledging that past. I begged forgiveness from my congregation. Then we destroyed the tape to symbolize my renunciation of all I had been. I thought Rebecca would faint she went so white. The next morning she was gone, along with Marian's grocery money. She left a note saying: *You had your fun. Now I'm going to. Whatever you did, think of me doing twice as much. I hate you. PS: I'll send back the money when I can.*"

In the background Marian Newman sobbed.

The note sounded like verbal histrionics Garreth had heard teenagers hurl at their parents in domestic disputes, but the PS surprised him. And if he did not know where she ended up, he would have found it even encouraging...conscience amid her anger. "Did she repay you?"

"Yes. About four months later a money order arrived from Billings. We called the police there and I went down and searched all over the city, but never found any sign of her."

She and the albino had probably left by that time. Interesting. She claimed to hate her father but carried his albums with her. She lied and stole and seduced for the albino but repaid money she took to run away.

At the other end, Newman was talking to his wife again, voice chiding. "Marian, Valerie isn't wicked either, just—"

Garreth started. "Valerie?"

"Rebecca's best friend. We later learned they found the *Perdition Bound* album at a garage sale and she suggested Rebecca hide it, and other rock albums they bought, in religious music cassette cases."

"...to smoke, too," came Marian's angry voice.

So Raven called herself by the name of a friend she admired for daring to indulge in forbidden pleasures and avoid being caught. Did she use other names from her past, too? "Did you ever live in a town called Kaffley?"

Newman's tone said the question surprised him. "Yes. In North Dakota. That was my previous church. We'd moved here to Crow Ford just that spring." Then his voice went pleading. "Look, I promise not to try seeing Rebecca until she's ready but can't you tell me where she is, or give me your name and phone number so I can call you to check on her?"

Regret pricked Garreth. "I'm sorry. I'll have to call *you*."

Disconnecting, he grimaced. He hated doing that to them, much as he needed the information they gave him. It must be like glimpsing their daughter off in the distance with no way to reach her. But at least they knew she was alive.

With his clothes clean and potting soil from the garden store stashed in the car, he headed for Westroads Mall. He knew the girl's size from the clothes in New Prospect, and similar jeans and tops ought to be available in the mall stores. One look around confirmed that, and that most of the juveniles in the mall wore similar clothes. So she should look indistinguishable from countless others her age. With every law enforcement officer in the region on the lookout for her, she needed to be anonymous. Except...officers would be watching for her face, not looking at clothes. He needed to alter her appearance somehow. Maybe a change of height to start with. The shoe stores displayed plenty of shoes and boots with towering heels and platform soles.

A wooden zebra in the window of a home decorations shop gave him an additional idea. Camouflage. Break up the lines of her face to make it harder to recognize. Distraction could help, too, he decided, eyeing a poster in the window of a video store...divert attention from her face.

He started shopping in earnest.

Back in the shelter two hours later, he called up to Lovings...a great relief to her, judging by her voice. What did she think, that he might just abandon the girl?

Raven still slept soundly and would until at least sunset, he estimated. If they could feel sunset down here.

After tossing the bags onto the top bunk above the girl and hanging up the suede blazer he had spotted and bought for himself, he set about one last task...cutting open the end of the air mattress he bought, pouring in potting soil, and sealing the slits with duct tape. It made a crude pallet, but one like this served him for months in the beginning and could do so again until he acquired another quilted pallet for the girl. Garreth tossed the mattress onto another top bunk, hauled himself up after it, and with relief let himself sink into its comfort. He had better sleep while he had the chance. Once the girl woke no telling when he might be able to relax again.

The familiar, welcome lift of pressure woke Garreth. Stretching back into consciousness, he noted the fact, and wondered how far underground sunset continued to register.

The sound of movement cut through his speculation. Peering over the edge of the bunk he watched the girl crawl out of her bunk and stare around in confusion. Peering at herself, she ran her hands down the raincoat, then a bulge slid under her upper lip. Her tongue exploring her front teeth, he guessed...feeling the points of the fangs coming in. Her breathing quickened as her expression turned to one of trapped-animal panic. Garreth braced himself, expecting her to try bolting for the door, but instead she backed against the bunk, whimpering, and slid to a huddle on the floor, head buried in arms hugging her knees.

Her terror brought a rush of memory...his first days, still vivid, and the drop of his stomach even yet when he woke from some sunlit dream to reality.

"I'm sorry, kiddo." And he realized that for now he meant it. He dropped to land soundlessly on the balls of his feet. "This isn't a nightmare you can wake from."

Her head snapped up at his voice. "No!" She jumped to her feet, breath pumping ever faster.

"Raven." Garreth caught her eyes. "Stop. Hold your breath."

She froze.

"Good girl." He held her eyes. "Now listen to me. Just listen. You are what you've become. Nothing can change that. But—listen to me," he repeated as she whimpered again. "You're still you. What you've become is just...well, a mutation. An enhanced human, if you want. Not undead. Not eternally damned. I'll prove it to you. And I can teach you what it takes to survive if you're willing to learn. Because if you aren't willing to learn, you won't survive. Most humans think vampires are myths, but some know better, and some of those believe we're Evil and will hunt down and destroy anyone they identify as a vampire."

She stared saucer-eyed at him.

Did that mean he had sufficiently impressed her to keep her at heel for a while? He broke eye contact and turned away. "Are you thirsty?"

Of course she was. At the edge of his vision he saw her wrap her hand around her throat.

But when he opened the cooler she recoiled. "I won't drink blood!"

Having been where she was, he could almost read her thoughts, the desperate twist of logic telling her that if she refused to drink blood she could not be a vampire. He felt a surge of sympathy. "Have some tea, then." Anticipating that she might react as he had, he bought tea bags at a convenience store he passed.

She grimaced. "I don't like tea."

But he still lit a burner on the propane stove and filled a small pan from the single tap in the sink. "Try it. Warm liquid soothes the throat and helps the hunger pangs..though those won't be really bad for another day, not until your teeth are fully—" He spun at her intake of breath and caught her eyes again. "Raven! Keep calm."

She sat down shivering on the edge of the bunk. "Okay...prove I'm not damned."

"I can't, here, but—"

"What is this place?" Hugging herself, she stared around.

"A bomb shelter."

She scowled. "Don't you stay anywhere that isn't underground? Where is this bomb shelter anyway?"

"Omaha."

"You bastard!" She jumped up. "You're taking me back to that podunk town you're from...*aren't* you!" Now she bolted for the door.

He caught her around the waist in two strides, pivoted, slung her into the nearest bunk. "Settle down! We're in Omaha because we can catch a plane from here for San Francisco."

The anger vanished in bewilderment. "San Francisco?"

"I'm going to see just how powerful your master is." He turned back to the stove. "Three years ago he was arrested there for buying crack."

She snorted. "No way could any cops could lay a hand on him!"

"We'll see." As the water came toward a boil, he dropped in a tea bag and turned off the propane. When the water colored, he poured some into a mug from the shelf of dishes and handed it to her. "Here."

"I don't like—"

"Drink it! Believe me, your throat will feel better."

After a moment she accepted the cup and took a sip. Then another, and another.

All the acknowledgment she would give that he was right, he saw. No matter. He had her drinking it. He brought down the shopping bags and set them on the floor. "See if this stuff fits you."

After a moment of disbelief she dug into the bags like a kid at Christmas, pulling out a large sling style shoulder bag and a carry-on bag, toiletry and makeup items, underwear and jeans and shoes...her eyes widening more with each item. "These are all my size! How'd you—long-sleeved shirts in summer?" She held up the two he had bought, grimacing. "That's dumb!"

"You won't feel hot in them, and sun on your skin *is* uncomfortable."

A shiver went through her. Hurriedly she peered into the next bag. And stared, then pulled out the black leather pants, camisole, and duster. "These are for me, too?"

"A new look, as the fashion people might say...especially if you add some of these." He reached into the bottom of the bag for several packages of temporary tattoos. "We need to make it harder for the police to recognize you."

She caressed the leather. "I want to try these on."

A new look indeed. Sheathed in the black leather and her hair pulled up into a topknot secured with a strip torn from the bottom of the hospital gown—since Garreth had not thought to buy anything for her hair—she became an affluent version of the outlaw look...and a close copy of the movie poster he had seen. She would also be conspicuous, but the boots added height and a tattoo, a rose whose stem grew up her left jaw and across her temple to a red-black blossom over her left brow, drew attention away from her features.

He shrugged into his new blazer, crossed his fingers, and led the way upstairs.

Seeing the Porsche, Raven stopped cold, eyes lighting. "Cool! I didn't know cops could afford—" She broke off, smacking her forehead with the heel of her hand. "Duh. But you're not like a regular cop, are you." She drifted around the car, caressing it. "It isn't new though. The newer 911's have an adjustable spoiler. Can I drive it?"

"No."

She frowned. "I won't hurt it. I'm a good driver. Ice taught me and he's an expert. He's raced at Le Mans."

Being a professional race car driver would explain that flawless one-eighty. "You still can't drive it. Get in."

Rolling her eyes, she did so. "Can I at least help work on the engine?"

He blinked. "You like playing with cars?"

She grinned. "Oh yeah. Ice let me do all the oil changes and stuff on the van. I have a natural mechanical ability Daddy—" Her animation died like a switch snapping off. She huddled in the seat. "Where are we going?"

He backed out of the garage and triggered the door closed behind them. "Somewhere that will prove you're not damned."

She shivered.

And when he pulled into the parking lot of their destination, it took his hand over her mouth to stifle her scream.

"Raven!" He could not catch her eyes so he poured all his power into his voice. "Listen to me. Be...calm. It's...all...right."

She thrashed her head, freeing her mouth. "No! That's a church!"

"Right. And even though we're not really dressed for it and have arrived late, we're going attend evening Mass."

Her voice climbed into hysteria. "I can't! I *can't!*"

"Yes you can." Her own kind of church, probably not, but she should be all right in a Catholic church. Being snared by a rosary had reduced Lane, raised Catholic, to screaming in torment but he, an indifferent Episcopalian, had touched it without harm. It all hinged on the belief in the symbols and rituals. The mind rules. "Trust me."

Not trusting *her*, rather than walk around the car to her door he grabbed her hands to prevent her from clutching at anything and dragged her from her side across the driver's seat and out his door. Then standing her up against the side of the car he caught her chin and forced her gaze to his.

"Raven, you will walk into the church with me. You will not resist. You will not scream."

He backed across the street, holding her hands as well as her gaze. They must look strange to any witnesses but he did not dare relax his focus. He could feel her terror fighting him every inch of the way, struggling to break free so she could bolt. Step by step he pulled her up the steps, and through the one door left open. She moved like a robot. From the interior came the sing-song voice of the priest and the ting of a bell. He pulled her across the outer vestibule and into the sanctuary. No one in his peripheral vision seemed to be watching them, all attention forward. Still holding her eyes, he dipped his fingers into the Holy Water and crossed himself, starting by firmly touching his forehead.

Something clicked behind her eyes, perhaps the dawning realization that they stood inside and no lightning had come down to strike them, that he had touched Holy Water without going up in smoke. The rigidity in her started to melt. When he touched her forehead with Holy Water, she barely flinched. He pulled her into the rear pew and releasing her gaze, sat down.

She sat, too, staring around her with wonder...then down at herself as though astonished at finding herself still whole. Her posture and face relaxed and as the Mass progressed, she looked almost at peace.

Just before the end of the Mass he shook her arm and pointed toward the door. They slipped out.

She walked slowly down the steps, chewing on her lower lip. Then at the bottom she stopped, grinned, and suddenly jumped straight into the air, fists shooting skyward. "Yes!" And danced into the street, giving the finger to a car that honked as it swerved to miss her. "Who needs the light! Give me Midnight! This is gonna be so much *fun*!" she shouted back at Garreth.

Shock jolted him. What? Shit! He raced across the street after her. "Raven this life isn't *fun*."

She spun back toward him, eyes smoldering. "Sure it is...sleep all day, stay out all night, never go to school, stay young, and live forever. I'm gonna party like my father never *dreamed* of!"

Garreth felt as if a bomb had gone off in his face. Had he screwed up by curing her terror? He never thought that would change her attitude so fast and so radically. What had he let loose?

29.

Daylight had at least one virtue, Garreth discovered. It hammered Raven. He had barely managed to keep her on her feet and alert enough to board the plane. Now she sagged torpid in her window seat, head cushioned by a neck pillow with a sealed bag of soil added to its padding. Giving him peace for the first time in twelve hours.

He took advantage of it to settle against his own augmented pillow and close his eyes.

His plan had been to show Raven she would not be struck down for entering a church, then worm information about Ice out of her while teaching her how to deal with her new life. But Raven grabbed the initiative, starting questions as soon as they climbed in the car...everything she wanted to know about being a vampire that Ice kept saying he would tell her "when she needed it." And while she shrugged off the disappointment of not being able to change into a bat—"Ice said everything you read about vampires isn't true."—she sneered at the idea of bottled blood. "Vampires are supposed to be hunters! And like Ice says, humans are out there for us to prey on."

That echo of Lane's sentiments brought a cold rush even in retrospect.

But Raven quickly lost interest in how to be a vampire. "Let's check out some clubs and bars. See what kind of night life Omaha has."

"Your can't go into bars; you're underage," he had reminded her.

Her lip curled. "So much for *your* vampire powers. Ice took Amber and me into clubs all the time. So, okay, then let's go to a mall. I need a different lipstick and eyeliner to go with black leather."

Fair enough. He took her. But before reaching the department store she located on the mall map she had stopped at the window of a beauty salon and stared in, or so he thought at first, then as she reached up to touch her hair, he realized she was looking at her reflection.

"You're not surprised you reflect?" he asked.

She had rolled her eyes. "Well hey, Sherlock, I could see Ice in mirrors, so duh." She frowned back at her reflection. "I ought to change my hair. I suppose you've got to okay the do, warden?"

"No, do what you want." He saw no harm in that.

"And you're paying for everything, right?"

He nodded.

She grinned. "Then go get in touch with a mall marshall or something for an hour."

Much to her obvious disgust he had stayed, watching the transformation with skepticism. But he had to admit, handing a credit card over to pay what seemed to him an exorbitant amount for hair mutilation and the cosmetics Raven also bought in the shop, that a fluorescent red spike changed her appearance...and along with the near-black lipstick and black hole eyes, suited her outfit. So did the pierced nostril and row of rings up each ear she acquired at the jewelry boutique on down the concourse.

She admired her reflection in shop windows. "This is so rad. My parents would shit cows if they saw me now. But I can't believe you actually bother to pay for stuff. *I'd* have given those clerks a couple of ones and hypnotized them into thinking they were hundreds, then I'd not only have everything free, the change would give me a profit."

Oh really. He had better step on the head of this snake right now. "Not paying is called theft!"

She arched her brows. "And your point is...? What do vampires care about human laws?"

He wanted to shake her. "Vampires not only have the same choices between right and wrong anyone else does, our greater power gives us greater responsibility in the use of it."

"Responsibility? Give me a break." She brushed past him, rolling her eyes. "You wouldn't be whining about responsibility if you had the guts to use your power the way Ice does, and the way *I'm* going to."

He caught her shoulder and spun her back, so hard she would have fallen without his grip on her. "You think it takes guts to steal that way when the clerks don't have a chance to resist? That's something to be *proud* of? The store doesn't write it off when a drawer comes up short, you know. The clerk has to make up the difference."

For a moment he caught dismay in her eyes, but it vanished in anger. She jerked loose and backed away, rubbing her shoulder. "Get out of my face! Just get out of my face! And shove your Brady Bunch sermons between your ass cheeks!"

Recalling the scene, Garreth sighed. That had won him no ground in the war for her cooperation.

Nor did he later when he refused her demand to go back to New Prospect for her belongings. "It's too dangerous and there's nothing we can't buy replacements for. Most of it we already have." Except the tapes, of course. He waited for her to mention them.

"*Replacements*!" Hysteria built in her voice. "I don't give a flying fuck—*ow*!" She rubbed her head where his knuckle cracked down on it. "You son of a bitch!" But she calmed, settling into sullenness. "I want *my* stuff!" No mention of the tapes.

Lord, what could he do with her? How did he handle her? *You raised sons and daughters, Grandma. Any suggestions?*

Apparently not. No inspiration came.

He turned the questions over in his head the rest of the night while he stashed the Porsche in the Philos garage for safekeeping and Doug Curtain, the Life Member friend on night duty, helped him create a photo ID for Raven to use at the airport. They scanned the photobooth snapshots he had taken from Raven's billfold into an office computer, cropping down to one image of Raven's face, and adding it to a school ID. A school was easier than faking a driver's license and by using a hopefully fictional one, the Bradford Academy, he could set up any form he wanted.

"Pick a first name for yourself that you haven't used before," he told Raven.

So to match the credit card he was using, because he wanted no evidence of a Garreth Mikaelian buying *two* plane tickets, she became Tiffany Ballinger.

In the course of making the ID she had tried to catch his eyes. "Give...me...the...pictures."

She had a long way to go to exert any control over him, but he had Curtain print her a copy of the photobooth snapshots. For which she grudgingly thanked him.

Relaxing against his neck pillow, he considered how he might use Raven's fondness for Amber. And perhaps the tapes, too? Even in her temper tantrum she never mentioned them but what else in her effects could she want enough to go back to New Prospect for? Why *had* she said nothing, though? Because she did not want him to know they were important to her...or perhaps could not admit it to herself?

"Here's your tea, Mr. Ballinger."

Garreth had almost forgotten he asked for it. He opened his eyes and thanked the flight attendant as he set the cup on the table between his seat and Raven's. He bought First Class tickets because it had the only two seats together on this flight, but he decided he could easily learn to prefer it.

The flight attendant eyed Raven...who winced and squirmed as she slept, sometimes whimpering, not entirely comfortable despite the neck pillow. "Is your...sister all right?" Behind the concerned tone Garreth could imagine the attendant wondering what drugs this girl used.

"Niece, and she's fine." Garreth picked up the cup and sipped the tea. It felt warm in his throat and stomach, comfort amid the pressure of daylight. "If we're lucky, she'll stay that way until we land. Not that she's dangerous," he added as the flight attendant's expression went wary. "She just tends to be loudly profane when she's unhappy, and right now I'm not her favorite person."

Reassured, the attendant smiled. "If there's anything else you need, let me know." And she moved on.

Garreth checked his watch. Harry ought to be awake by this time. He inserted his credit card into the phone in the seat ahead and punched in the Takananda number.

Lien answered. Her voice warmed with pleasure. "Garreth! How are you feeling?"

He knew immediately she meant Maggie, and with a sharp pang, wished he had let Maggie meet Lien. *I cheated you out of so much. I'm sorry.* Not even scars remained of the lacerations on his forehead and arm, but the list of Things Not Done regrets kept growing. "Maybe I'll feel better when I've dealt with the individual responsible. Is Harry there?"

"Sorry, no. They called him out at five-thirty on a case. Is there anything I can do?"

"You can refresh my memory on his phone number. I'm going to be landing there in a few more hours to—"

"Oh, that's wonderful. The guest room is always ready for you."

If only he *could* stay with them and wrap up in the healing warmth of Lien's hospitality. "I'm sorry...but this time I have to stay at Holle House. I'm not alone. I—" This needed to be phrased to match the Ballinger persona, in case fellow passengers overheard. Hopefully Lien's intelligence would prevent her from being completely baffled. "—I'm temporarily responsible for Tiffany...you know, my brother Don's daughter...the wild one."

After a long silence, she said drily, "There's more to your family than I realized. Nevertheless, despite the wild child, I insist you stay here. You know Harry will be hurt if you don't. So will I. We'll work out sleeping arrangements later."

Harry would figure out in about five seconds who "Tiffany" was, and then be put in the agonizing position of having to choose between upholding the law and protecting a friend.

Garreth refused to do that to him. "Believe me, Lien, you don't want this girl—"

"Did you hear me? I insist you come. Don't worry about Harry."

After his first start, Garreth realized that even worse than read his mind, Lien had deduced the girl's identity sight unseen. "So...you realize who Tiffany is?"

A soft laugh came over the phone. "Garreth, dear, it's a nobrainer. Harry's been having Vanessa Girimonte monitor the police teletype in Denver and pass on all bulletins relating to your case. And of course he tells me. After experience with you, Irina, and the Philos Foundation, a miraculous recovery from death suggests one thing. Then she escapes and you turn up with a juvenile companion. Who else could she be?" Lien paused. "I guess my only concern is her origin...the pale gentleman or you?"

He sighed. "Me...but accidentally."

"I'm looking forward to hearing all the details." When he did not respond, she said, "Garreth!"

He gave in. "All right." Like that line from *Star Trek*: *Resistance is futile*. "I'll see you in a few hours."

After hanging up he settled back into the neck pillow and closed his eyes. Why did he ever worry about baffling Lien? She had always thought a step ahead of Harry and him. Or maybe she had a Chinese equivalent of Grandma Doyle's Feelings to assist her. Whatever the source of her wisdom, it gave him a sense of relief and assurance and comfort... like going home.

A feeling Raven did not share when they landed in San Francisco and he broke the news. "He's a *cop*! You said we'd be staying in a cool mansion these Philos people own, not with some fuck—*ow*!"

Fastest knuckle in the west. He blew on it like a gun barrel. "Harry and Lien are dear old friends." He herded Raven from the car rental depot toward its parking lot.

"Yeah..." She rubbed the top of her head. "You'll think they're old friends when they turn you in for aiding a fugitive.

Look, you don't really want me around. I'm not going to help you find Ice. You might as well let me go. In fact, let me go or I'll start screaming rape."

He found himself more amused than irritated. "And when I wave my badge, who's going to look more credible? Besides you don't know nearly enough yet to survive on your own."

"I didn't know *anything* about getting along by myself when I left home, but I learned." She tossed her head. "This won't be any harder."

"Even though you've been refusing to drink blood?"

She hesitated, then shrugged. "I'll learn that, too."

After being driven into a frenzy of thirst and tearing out victims' throats? "No, I think you'd better stick with me a while. There's our car."

Above her dark glasses, her brows rose. "Cool." She ran a hand across the gleaming hood of the red Mustang. "Not cool as the Porsche but okay. Will you let me drive this one? I'll be polite to your old people if you do."

"We didn't make a drivers license for you." He unlocked the passenger door.

She tried to flounce in but ended up collapsing in the seat. And immediately reached to flip down the visor. "Daytime sucks. Why didn't you find us a night flight?"

He sighed. If he put her under one of those full spectrum lights for treating winter depression, would it keep her zonked all the time? "The people I need to see work days."

She huddled in the seat. "This sucks. Big city, bright lights, lively night life and I suppose I won't get to see a fu—" She ducked sideways as his hand started to lift from the wheel. "...any of it."

Garreth put his hand back on the wheel. "We're not here for fun."

She scowled. "You suck, too. I hope you do catch up with Ice and I'm there to watch him tear you apart."

"It's good to have a goal."

With a glare, she lapsed into torpid silence.

When they pulled into Harry's driveway she roused enough to grunt, but otherwise did not move while he pulled himself out of the driver's seat and walked up to the door.

Lien answered only seconds after he pushed the bell, hurling herself out into his arms. "Garreth!" She grinned. "You look pretty good considering the time of day. Do come—"

Garreth whispered in her ear. "Don't invite us; just go in."

Without hesitation, she stepped back and looked past Garreth to Raven hauling herself out of the car. "And you're Tiffany. I'm delighted to meet you. Garreth, I'm putting her in the guest room. You'll have to rough it on the family room couch." She stepped back into the house.

Garreth collected the luggage from the car and followed Lien inside.

Raven started to, then close to the doorway stopped short. Her forehead furrowed above her dark glasses. She took another step forward and jumped back with a yelp of pain.

"Now it's okay," Garreth murmured.

Lien hurried back to the door. "Oh, I'm so sorry. I forgot. Tiffany, please come in. Come on. It'll be all right now."

Raven reached out gingerly, then charged through the door and at Garreth. She swung her sling bag at his head. "You damn bastard! You did that on purpose!"

Garreth sidestepped the bag and started to point at the dwelling barrier as one of many things she had yet to learn. But before he could speak, Lien said, "No, it's my fault, really. Garreth has been welcome here for so long I forgot you have to be invited in on your first visit. That's a beautiful tattoo. It makes your face very striking. I would love to sketch you while you're here. But I'm sorry for rattling on; you look exhausted." She bent to pick up the rolled pallets and peeled loose the quilted one. When Garreth picked up Raven's bag, Lien took it from him. "You go into the family room. I'll take Tiffany to her room."

Raven scowled at Garreth, her expression still accusing him, but let Lien lead her upstairs.

Ten minutes later Lien came back down. Seeing Garreth slumped on the couch, her brows rose. "I expected to find you stretched out under your favorite tree in back."

He sighed, shaking his head. If only he could. "I can't sleep right now. The albino's fingerprints match those of a Cameron Dark who was arrested here three years ago. I need to check out the arrest and the life this Dark character led here. I've had a vision that I'll catch up with the albino, but before that happens I need to know if he's really a vampire, and if so, how old. I can't go out and leave you alone with Raven, though. Her teeth will be ready to use by the next time she wakes and she'll be ravenously thirsty."

"I'll be fine." Lien sat down beside him. The scent of her blood eddied around him. "In the first place, she went out cold the moment she lay down. From the look of her she won't stir before sunset. Secondly, I know how to protect myself. I have blood in the fridge and an atomizer loaded with garlic juice. If Tiffany-Raven won't drink the bottled blood, I'll zap her with the atomizer and keep her dosed until you come back. You know how incapacitating that is. And that's assuming she makes it out of the guest room...which, because I suspected you might want some security measures, has a vase of roses on the window sill and a rose spray, thorns intact, hanging on the door. Have you told her about the barrier properties of roses yet?"

He shook his head.

She smiled. "Good. Then she'll think they're just decorative and not feel imprisoned."

"I don't care if she does." And when Lien's brows rose he not only gave her the full story about what had been happening, but found himself pouring out his frustrations in dealing with Raven. "She's right; I don't want to drag her around. I have to watch her every minute. But I can't turn her loose. Every time she opens her mouth she sounds like Lane. People are cattle. The consequences of her actions on others doesn't matter." He hunched his shoulders, cold running down his spine. "It almost makes me wonder if Lane's soul was too strong to be destroyed and lived on in my blood, just waiting for a suitable host like this girl to come along. And now she's alive again, ready to take up her blood hunt where she left off. Vision or not, I think I should have broken Raven's neck in that hosp—"

"No!" Lien grabbed his arm. "You couldn't murder her! Even illegitimate children are still our children."

Of course Lien, with her love of children and sorrow over having none, would be against destroying any child. But the rest went too far. "Forget me ever thinking of her as my daughter!"

"Oh?" Lien smiled. "From what I've observed, you already are."

What? "I'm her warden." He grimaced. "Just ask her."

Lien ticked her tongue. "Father...warden...one and the same sometimes to an adolescent. But surely you don't want to go on that way? Always treating her like a felon."

He frowned. "She *is* a felon."

Her eyes narrowed. "Oh, that's very righteous. But so are you, my dear."

Garreth felt as though he had been slapped. "It isn't the same thing! I didn't have any choice! I couldn't leave her—"

"I'm not saying you weren't justified." She laid a hand over his. "I'm just pointing out that by human law, you're both equally guilty."

Human law. Mocking laughter in his head tied a knot in his gut. "Shit. I hate this. I don't want Lane to be right about the law being irrelevant to vampires. But I keep seeing this gulf between what I believe is right and how I seem to be forced to act...and it feels wider all the time, pushing me away from you and Harry, my parents, fellow law enforcement officers. From everyone. I'm scared one day I'll look around and find—"

"Garreth." Lien put her arm around him and gave him a hug. The warm scent of her blood filled his nose. "I think that as long as you're afraid of losing your ties to humanity, you won't. Even if you have to break a law now and again. And even when the life forces you to give up friends and colleagues and jobs you like."

It did not surprise him that she guessed the wider extent of his unhappiness. "I really like Baumen. This life stinks," he said bitterly. "But *she* thinks it's the coolest thing since MTV. Perfect freedom...power without accountability. Just like Lane."

Lien leaned back to look him in the eyes. "I've heard you and Harry talk about cases, and how you've won cooperation from even suspects you despised. Are you so angry at this girl that you can't put it aside to use some of those techniques on her? Maybe then you wouldn't have to guard her so closely."

She had a point. He sighed. "I suppose it's worth a try."

"And consider this in trying to relate to her: that being a vampire and an adolescent are very much alike. You're both struggling to adapt to changed bodies and new emotions and physical needs, and with feeling isolated in a world you think condemns you for being what you are without even trying to understand you."

He stared at her. What amazing insights she had! He kissed her cheek. "Lien, next to Grandma Doyle, you have to be the wisest woman I know."

Her smile went inscrutable. "Maybe part of the wisdom *is* hers now. But...you go do what you need to do so you can catch a little sleep before the wild child wakes up."

Garreth called Homicide first. Harry was still out of the office but Garreth drove downtown anyway, hoping Harry would be back by the time he arrived.

Years ago, coming back to Bryant Street the first time after resigning from the SFPD had felt like a homecoming...walking familiar halls, seeing familiar faces. Today, though, even while old reflexes still took him straight up to Homicide, he realized he had become an outsider. The bustle in the halls; the flood of body and blood scents; the sounds of footsteps, voices, telephones, doors opening and closing, piled on each other; and most of all, all the unfamiliar faces, brought an unexpected longing for the cozy familiarity of the Baumen office. Even in Homicide a stranger sat at the desk where Art Schneider had worn the same rumpled suit, or endless copies of it, year after year, and there were strangers, too, at the desks Earl Faye and Dean Centrello had used, who in addition to being fine detectives had striven to keep alive and well the art of oral storytelling. And visible through the windows of the lieutenant's office, someone huskier and blonder than the darkly dapper Lucas Serruto sat behind the desk.

"Oh my god. I don't believe it. Garreth Mikaelian!"

He turned around to find a face he did know...Evelyn Kolb...heavier, going grey, now wearing glasses, but still familiar.

She shook her head, grinning. "You're looking pretty lively for being declared dead again—when was it?"

"A week ago tomorrow." It felt like a month. "Harry told you?"

"Of course." She set down a black binder crammed with reports. "So are you visiting him and Lien while you recuperate?"

He shrugged. "Not exactly. Maybe Harry also told you that another officer in the car with me did die?"

Kolb nodded. "I'm sorry."

He swallowed the lump her sympathy brought. Maggie would have like Kolb, too. "She's why I'm out here. The suspect who ran us off the road was arrested here three years ago on a drug charge. I'd like to see the case file in the hope it'll give me background on him or names of some local associates who might have information to help us track down the bastard."

Her brows rose. "A little extracurricular investigation?"

How nice to be able to say: "No, it's official." He paused. "I was going to ask Harry to help me look at the file but since he's not here, will you?"

"Sure." She sat down at her computer. "What's the name?"

"He called himself Cameron Dark."

She typed it in with Garreth peering over her shoulder. "Just the one arrest it looks like. There's the address he gave. No listed associates except Candy Bratton, the drug dealer he was arrested with. Let's see if there's anything helpful there." She typed in the dealer's name. "Oops...I guess not."

Seven months ago Bratton had made his last drug sale, which had culminated in death by gunshot.

"How about the names of the arresting officers?" Garreth asked.

She brought the Dark file back. "They were Enrique Aguilar and Philip Cho."

He wrote down the names, then using Kolb's phone, called Narcotics. He caught Aguilar in and while introducing himself crossed his fingers that the officer would remember the case.

After being given details of the arrest and the albino's description, Aguilar said, "Oh, yeah, now I remember. Phil and I were after Bratton. I was supposed to approach him for a buy but this skinny dude strolls up from the bus stop and starts negotiations so we looked at each other and said work with what you got and busted them." He snorted. "What a son of a bitch."

"What happened?"

"Well," Aguilar said in disgust, "the minute we appear this schmuck starts toward us and in front of Bratton with his hands up screaming don't shoot, don't shoot, he isn't armed, and then he trips and falls flat and clutches at his face howling he's broken his nose. Bratton bugs out and Phil takes off after him. When I finally get Weeping Willie spread-eagled on the ground and search him, the pill bottle with the crack we both saw Bratton give him isn't on him. He's managed to toss it away during all the sniveling. Which stops, by the way, the minute I have him cuffed and in the unit. I grab a flashlight and hunt around the area until I find the bottle...for all the good it does me as far as Dark goes. Later when he has his Public Defender demand we print the bottle, the only ones on it are smudges and a few partials of Bratton's."

So the arrest had come at night. That might or might not be significant. "He just let you cuff him? Didn't try to, oh...stare you in the eye?"

"What? I don't know. He was wearing shades. But he just smiled when I cuffed him." Aguilar's voice went disgusted again. "I found out why when he handed the fucking things to me at the station, smirking, like the whole thing was some kind of game. And it obviously pissed him off that we didn't find it cute."

It might well have been a game. "Any idea how he got them off?"

"A pick he had hidden on him and I didn't catch patting him down, I expect."

Or maybe Ice had just passed through them.

Aguilar growled, "When he made bail he waltzed around shaking everyone's hand, thanking us for treating him so considerately. Arrogant son of a bitch. I'll bet he sings a different tune when he loses. He's just the kind to turn nasty then."

"He came by bus you said? He didn't own a car?"

"Not registered in California or any other state in the western U.S. We checked that after he jumped bail. Which was a stupid move on his part, you know, because if he'd stuck around, I don't think the DA would have prosecuted him on the basis of the evidence we had."

Garreth could not see a vampire with as much experience as Ice claimed making that kind of mistake. Unless Ice just decided that a police record might make him vulnerable to future investigation he did not want to risk. "Who was the bailbondsman?"

Aquilar ticked his tongue. "Ah...Silverman Bailbond, I think."

"And one more question. This may sound strange, but do you remember what Dark ate while he was in custody?"

Silence stretched out at the other end of the phone. While Aguilar stared at the receiver? Finally he said, "You're right; that's a weird question...and I don't know the answer."

As Garreth hung up, Kolb asked, "Why do you want to know what he ate?"

Garreth concentrated on writing down Dark's listed address in his notebook. "To see if he has some dietary restrictions that've been mentioned as a possibility." He looked up the Silverman number and address in Kolb's phone book, then scribbled his own phone number on a page of the notebook and ripped it out before tucking the notebook into his blazer. "Thanks, Evelyn. If you see Harry, tell him I'm sorry I missed him. This is the number of my digital phone if he wants to call me. Otherwise I'll see him at the house later."

He stopped at Silverman's office, but other than impressing a clerk that a country sheriff would send an officer so far from home checking such an old offense, learned only that the bailbondsman had had no luck tracing Dark after he left San Francisco. "It was like he dropped off the face of the earth," the clerk said, reading through their file.

Next he visited Dark's address. It lay in the Haight-Ashbury district. Like himself, the Haight seemed to stand outside of time, its radical bookstores, cafes, used clothing boutiques, and record stores making it still echo eerily of the sixties. As with many of the Victorians of the area, the one at Dark's address had been subdivided into small flats. The landlord did not live on the premises but Garreth found a tenant home who gave him the landlord's number and he called it on his phone once back in the Mustang.

The landlord at first drew a blank. "Cameron Dark? Do you know how fast some of these kids come and go? Three years might as well be a lifetime ago."

"He was very tall and thin and pale, an albino."

"Oh, him." The voice on the other end paused. "I don't know what I can tell you about him. I remember he paid his rent on time and then moved out with only a message on my answering machine for notice. He was paid up, though, and forfeited his deposit, so it wasn't any problem for me."

Carrying the photocopy of the fax on Dark, Garreth trudged to the shops and cafes in the area, wishing one of San Francisco's fogs would roll in...and the thicker the better. The sun had no business shining so brightly here in August.

He held little hope of many people remembering the albino, but gambled that a few would. A bookstore clerk recognized the face but remembered nothing about him. Checking the clothing boutiques he came up with a clerk who remembered a little more. "He came in sometimes, always with a girl that he'd buy a sexy top or pants for, but mostly I used to see him pass here in the evening, headed up the street that direction. Like maybe he was going to work."

Garreth supposed that even if he had no need to work, Ice might have found a job amusing. Working his way "that direction," Garreth visited a record store, Vintage Vinyl, that gave its hours as noon to midnight.

"The night people deserve somewhere to shop, too, man," the shop owner said. He looked in his late forties, old enough to have been part of the hippie influx. And judging by his waist-length pony tail, tie-dyed shirt, and jeans decorated with flowers and peace symbols, he remained stuck in the era. He peered at the mug shot Garreth showed him. "I think I remember a guy like that working in the video store across the street."

Garreth thanked him and turned to leave...then noticed a poster for the soundtrack CD of *Midnight In the Garden Of Good and Evil*. It made him think of Raven's tapes. "Do you have Cenotaph's *Night Gardens?*"

The owner raised his brows. "Now that's a group I'd never have expected a kid your age to ask for. But, yeah, I think I've got it." He headed down the tables of albums and tapes.

"What about anything by Blue Steel Perdition?"

A search turned up the Cenotaph record, and one Blue Steel Perdition tape, *Steel and Stone*. Garreth bought both. Harry and Lien had a stereo/tape player. He could do what Raven had done before, record the *Night Garden* album on tape.

Paying for the albums, he left his card with his digital phone number written on the back. "Just in case you think of anything to do with this dude...or come across the *Perdition Bound* tape."

Carrying the bag with his purchases, he headed across the street to the video store. After Garreth explained the purpose of his visit, the clerk there dialed the owner and handed over the phone.

"Dark?" the owner said. "Sure I remember the freak."

Freak. Garreth took a deep breath. Was he close to proof about Ice? "A freak how?"

"Well first was the way he looked, dead pale but always dressing in black, and he wore dark glasses even at night. We run movies on TV sets all around the store, recent arrivals to push rentals of them. But Dark ran vampire movies instead. *The Lost Boys* was a big favorite of his, I remember, and movies like *Bonnie and Clyde* or *Badlands*. And he had this group of— well, I wouldn't call them exactly friends...more hangers-on. They all looked pretty freaky themselves...street kids, stoned or crack heads. Mostly teen-age girls. They'd sit on the side- walk outside or wander around the store...disappearing the minute I walked in, but if I passed again a while later, they'd be back. They made me think of a wolf pack lying around waiting for the alpha male to make a move so they could fol- low. I always wondered if Dark was pimping for the girls, though I never saw any proof of it. But when he didn't show up for work one night and the police came around I can't say I was surprised." The voice on the other end paused, then added, "Something that did surprise me, though, was how many people were looking for him."

Garreth's brows rose. "You mean there more than the po- lice and bailbondsman?"

"Yeah. A few weeks later some private detective showed up asking questions."

The hair lifted on Garreth's neck. Who would hire a private detective to find Ice? "Did he or she say why?"

"No...just showed me a photograph and asked if that was the guy who worked for me."

"Do you remember his name, or did he give you a card?"

"I don't remember the name but he did give me a card. I may still have it somewhere."

If only! "Mr. Singer, will you do me a favor and look for it? And if you find it, please call me...whatever the time. I'll give you my phone number. This is very important."

Visits to the rest of the shops in the area added nothing new to what he had learned. He headed back for Harry and Lien's. On the way his mind churned, trying to imagine why a private detective would be hunting the albino...and who could have hired him. A vampire hunter, maybe...someone with a loved one the albino had killed...or allowed to reanimate as a thirst-driven undead? He crossed his fingers that the video store owner found that card.

His phone warbled.

Garreth activated it eagerly. "Mr. Singer?"

"No," answered an accented female voice. "Irina. How goes hunt?"

He sighed. "I don't seem any closer to finding this bastard and the questions keep multiplying instead of being answered." He gave her a quick recap of his activities and findings.

A long silence greeted the recitation, then Irina said, "You are keeping girl alive?"

The question sounded disapproving, accusatory. He heard his voice go defensive. "I've had a vision that she'll lead me to the albino."

"True vision? I recall you spoke at Grania's funeral of making companions."

Make *Raven* a companion? "Give me a break. She drives me crazy. After I find this albino...I don't know what I'll do with her. I'll decide then. Ice may destroy her and take care of the problem. I hope you called because you know if an albino V2K does or doesn't exist."

After a moment, Irina answered, "Only newborns count years. I know if acquaintances are of great age only by life experiences they mention. I have made inquiries about albinos, however, and learned of two."

Garreth held his breath.

"Female one obviously you can ignore. Male is known mostly by rumor. Exact age is unknown. None of my contacts can remember meeting him in recent history. One recalls him among Praetorian Guard of Caligula, but not since."

Cold ran through Garreth. So an albino vampire had existed a thousand years ago. And if he still did, he could now be Ice. Maybe as powerful as Raven claimed. "Thank you for asking around. If Ice is this vampire, it would be nice to have reinforcements when I take him on."

She hesitated a moment. "Perhaps yes. I will come if possible. But opportunity to strike may be limited so you should plan to act without me. Perhaps is good you have girl. She can be ally."

"An ally?" Garreth grimaced. "I don't see that happening."

"You should try for it, child. Very hard."

30.

Irina's words echoed in his head all the way back to the house. He grimaced in frustration. An ally? Right. She hero-worshiped Ice for his power, for his total disregard for rules...and it looked very much as though he was indeed the biggest baddest dude around. That could be useful, of course...just set her loose somewhere in the albino's vicinity and follow her to him. But it did not make her anything like an ally.

At the house, Lien sat on the patio, turning a charcoal stick over in her fingers and frowning at paper pinned to the easel before her. The beginnings of a face already existed and as always, Garreth marveled at how she managed to convey so much with so few lines. The face, he saw, leaning down to peer over Lien's shoulder, was Raven's...defiant and yet unutterably lost.

"Does she really look that way to you?"

Lien turned. Her frown turned to one of concern. "You look exhausted. Why don't you pull the afghan off the glider and stretch out on it under the tree."

The shade and earth did call him. But he held up the bag from Vintage Vinyl. "There's an album I want to tape."

She reached for the bag. "I can do that. You rest." She pulled out the album and the blank tape he had bought. "Cenotaph? My college freshman crowd considered all that social doom-crying very sophisticated but I'd have thought you spent those years listening to the Beatles and—were the Monkees on TV then?"

"It isn't for me." He told her about the tapes in Raven's bag.

Her brows rose. "It's even more surprising *she* knows the group."

"Maybe she doesn't. Ice could have given her the tape. There's one cut on the record, 'Shades Of Midnight,' that a vampire, or wannabe, might consider a theme song. My subconscious heard someone singing it while the girls drained blood from Maggie and me."

After Lien carried the album inside, Garreth stretched out face down on the afghan and let the weight of daylight push him into the soothing welcome of the earth. He sank into sleep on the music drifting out of the house...haunting melodies sung almost *a cappella* by intense, cautionary voices.

But sleep put him back in the wrecked ZX with the crackle of grass and gravel marking the footsteps of someone circling the car. He tried to sit up but the smashed top pinned him against the steering wheel, and the jammed door would not open no matter how hard he threw himself against it. He thrashed harder, snarling. Since he recognized this as only a dream, why was he so powerless? No real daylight stripped away his power. Surely he should be able to do what he wanted, including pass through the car top and door.

The footsteps slowed as they neared. "It's all right," Raven's voice said reassuringly. "They're dead, or almost dead, and Ice needs their blood."

"And we hate them, don't we?" a childish voice said. "Like Ice says, they've rejected us." She started singing, and the words curled around Garreth in a high, breathy voice...almost a whisper....*shadow brothers/Disenfranchised from the light/Pariahs, outcasts, misfits, exiles...*

"They deserve whatever happens to them." Raven said.

Nameless faces/Shadowed places/Lives enclosed by sunless spaces.

Pain shot up Garreth's arm.

"And like Ice said, drinking enemies' blood shows we've beaten them."

...reject the light/Choosing to embrace the Dark/And welcome lives in shades of Midnight.

The song followed him away from the dream into deeper sleep.

Violent shaking pulled him out of the blackness. "Garreth!"

Lien's voice and blood scent. Garreth hauled himself up toward consciousness. And daylight! But alarm stalled his snarl. Lien would not wake him before sunset without good reason.

He forced his eyes open. "What's the matter? What's wrong?"

"It's almost sunset and I thought you'd want to be up before Raven is."

Right. He pushed to his feet. "Is Harry home yet?"

"No. He called a while ago to say—surprise—that he'll be late." She shook her head, smiling. "The evening he's home on time I'll probably drop dead with surprise."

Yawning and stretching, Garreth dragged himself upstairs to the bathroom with his bag and grooming kit. But coming back downstairs fifteen minutes later, shaved and showered, and more to the point, with the sun slipping over the horizon, he felt ready to take on the wild child.

In the doorway of the kitchen he stopped short in alarm. Raven already sat at the kitchen peninsula...gulping down a mug of...tea, judging by the odor. He frowned at Lien. "Lien, you shouldn't have—"

"Are you hungry, my dear?" Smiling serenely across the peninsula, she headed for the refrigerator. "I heard Raven stirring and invited her down for something hot to drink. She's very thirsty. Tea is all she's asking for but I assume you prefer something more substantial?"

Without waiting for an answer, she took a familiar pint bottle from the refrigerator, broke the seal, and poured half the blood into a ceramic mug. Gently swirling the contents, she walked back to the peninsula and set the mug in front of the stool next to Raven.

The scent rising out of the mug drifted to Garreth. Raven smelled it, too, he noticed. She watched him sidelong while he lifted the mug, and her throat worked when he swallowed.

He started to offer Raven the mug, but Lien caught his eye and shook her head in a microscopic *no*.

What was she up to? He lifted the brow on the side away from Raven.

Her eyes focused on the counter almost in front of the girl. "So what are your plans for the evening?"

Garreth set the mug down where she indicated. "I think I'll make another canvass of that area, this time to talk to the night people."

Raven's eyes had followed the mug down, he noticed. She stared fixedly at it. Now Garreth saw the plan.

"Go on," Lien said.

Beside him Raven chewed her lower lip but did not move toward the mug. Garreth shrugged inwardly. *Okay, don't drink.* Why should he care? Starvation had to be very unpleasant for a vampire since no death would end the agony, but that was her choice.

He focused on Lien. "I may have a better chance now of finding someone who remembers this Cameron Dark since night appears to have been when he got out and about."

Movement caught his eye. Raven's hand inched toward the mug. Her mouth and throat worked. Lien made some comment and he replied, but automatically, unaware what he said, focused sidelong on Raven.

Her hand closed around the mug's handle. Then, as if that committed her and she feared it being taken away, she seized the mug with her other hand, too, snatched it up, and gulped down the blood. Astonishment spread across her face. Slowly, she lowered the mug and stared into it, licking her lips. "It tastes different. I mean, it tastes the same, but—"

Garreth said, "I know."

Lien poured the rest of the pint into the mug, then opened another pint for Garreth.

Without hesitation Raven emptied the mug again, then ran her finger around inside and licked the finger clean. "Now I know what Ice meant when he talked about delicious fire. I can't wait to try warm blood again."

Dismay flashed through Lien's eyes. Garreth emptied half the pint from the plastic bottle and carried it back to the refrigerator. Now maybe Lien understood his problem with this girl.

But none of that showed in her voice as she said, "You two had better go so you'll have plenty of time to canvass that neighborhood. I presume you're taking Raven with you, Garreth?"

It was the last thing he wanted to do, but he would not leave her here alone with Lien, garlic juice atomizers at Lien's hand or not.

Raven's face twisted in disgust. "This should be a load of fun." Then she eyed him. "Unless we can go check out the real nightlife afterward?"

"I'm sure he'll be happy to show you the city," Lien said. "I'll give your excuses to Harry, Garreth...both yours and Raven's, who is, let's say, an acquaintance of Irina's she sent along to help you out. But let's call you, oh, Elspeth. That sounds like someone born in another century."

Raven grinned. "Cool. I can tell him I was born in Salem and hung for being a witch."

"Don't tell him any such thing," Garreth said. "The more you say, the bigger your chance of tripping up." Was this what Lien meant by not worrying about Harry? Lying to him? Conscience twisted in Garreth. But it was a lesser evil than making Harry choose whether or not to aid a fugitive. "We'll try to stay out until he's asleep, anyway."

Lien shook her head. "Don't bother. You know he'll stay up until you *do* come back so he has a chance to visit. But before you leave, was there something you planned to give Raven?"

He had almost forgotten. Quickly he brought her the Vintage Vinyl bag from the family room.

Her eyes widened as she peered in. Pulling out the two tapes, she stared at them, and at the Walkman she brought out next. He had bought that at another stop before return-ing to the house.

"That's in case you actually want to play them," Garreth said.

She laid down the Walkman. "Thanks...but I don't need to play them. I don't even *want* to play this one."

The Blue Steel Perdition tape. Garreth eyed her. "You just carry it?"

He thought he asked a simple question but she bristled. "That isn't a crime, is it! Are we going out or not!"

So much for softening her up by doing her a favor. But Garreth noticed that Raven stuffed the Walkman into her sling bag along with the tapes.

In the car she pulled *Steel and Stone* out of the sling bag and smirked at it. "If you could see me now...you damned lying hypocrite." She glanced sideways. "I suppose you wonder who I'm talking about."

Garreth shook his head. "No. The resemblance between you and Teddy Rivers is too obvious to miss. When I was on the department here I helped arrest him once."

Her eyes widened, then she grinned. "Cool." Then her lip curled. "So do you know where he is now? What he's pre-tending to be? A preacher! All goody-goody...and sooo damn humble. Every time one of our churches got a big congrega-tion and everyone adored him, we'd have to leave. He'd drag us off to the middle of nowhere and an even littler church in an even worse dump of a town. Because Jesus is supposed to be what's important, not him, he'd say. Only I found out what he *really* is."

So much anger. Garreth felt almost seared by it. It must have made her easy for Ice to manipulate. Do this or that and get even with your father. Now *he* needed to find a way to use the anger *against* Ice.

But for the moment Garreth concentrated on just keeping track of her while he worked his way along the same streets he had during the day, showing the Cameron Dark photo around the cafes and the shops still open. But he had no better luck at this time of day finding people who remembered Dark. Even some loitering juveniles who looked the type to have been part of Dark's wolf pack neither knew him nor could suggest anyone who might.

Raven's expression became increasingly disgruntled, but to her credit she said nothing until Garreth called the canvass quits after two hours. Then she sighed in relief. "If this is what detective work is like, I'm surprised you don't all shoot yourselves in the head out of boredom. So." She brightened. "Where's the night life?"

He parked on the Embarcadero and took her for a walk up Broadway. Though not as lively as on a Friday or Saturday night, the blaze of club signs, streams of tourists, bar crawlers, and hustlers on the sidewalks, the calls of barkers proclaiming the titillating delights of their shows still impressed Raven. Scents of car exhaust, tobacco, liquor, perfume, and most of all, of blood, swirled past them, ever changing.

Maggie would have enjoyed this so much, he reflected. What a fool he was. He could have brought her here. He should have.

Raven stared around in wide-eyed delight. "Now this is what I call night life. Let's go in some of the bars."

Well here came the end of her good mood. "You're too young."

She snorted. "You can't pull that again. If you won't hypnotize the bouncer, I'll do it myself."

"You can't hypnotize a surveillance camera." He had no idea if the bars here used them, but it sounded good.

Raven scowled. Then her lip curled. "Then be sure to let me know when we start having fun. I didn't come along for a fu—frigging hike. I want to see some shows...maybe *be* the show. Like this one piano bar Ice took us into in Denver. It was *so* dead. The piano man played like a zombie on 'ludes. Ice said why didn't I liven it up...so I jumped onto the piano man's lap and got it on with him right there at the piano." She smirked. "That had to be the jazziest version ever of 'I Write the Songs.'"

"Did the police appreciate it?"

She laughed. "No one called the police. They were too busy cheering me on."

She had to be making that up. How could Ice take obvious juveniles into a bar, and encourage one to put on an indecent performance, without being challenged? Even a vampire with centuries of accumulated power surely could not hypnotize an entire crowd of people. Yet Raven sounded sincere.

Rather than call her bluff and escalate the argument, however, he said, "You'd have a hard time out-doing the stage shows in these clubs. We're going to have to settle for just walking. Personally, I've always enjoyed the street more than the clubs. It's such great people watching."

Raven glanced around. He watched the lights from club signs and cars reflect in her eyes and saw her take a deep breath...tasting the symphony of blood scents? "Well...I guess it's a little interesting. There are sure a lot of people. I wonder why Ice didn't bring us back here. It's a perfect hunting ground for him, and a motherlode for marks." She eyed a passing couple who were staring around avidly, obvious tourists. Her expression went thoughtful, then she smiled warmly up at him. "If I can't be the show in a bar..." Sliding her arms around him, she pressed against him. Her voice went husky. "Let me show *you* a thing or two. You must know somewhere we can go."

He peeled her arms loose. "I'm not interested."

"Yeah?" Her lip curled. "What are you...*homo!*"

Hell hath no fury. "No, just selective. What was your plan...go in the bathroom to undress and slip out the window?"

She jerked back, eyes flashing. "Look, Sherlock, there's no way I'm ever going to help you find Ice and I'm tired of being your *fucking prisoner!*" Her voice rose.

Several passers-by turned to look at them. Garreth met their eyes then rolled his in a long suffering expression.

Almost without breaking stride the pedestrians walked on.

Raven declared, "This is a great place and I'm staying here! Do I have to start screaming that you're demanding sex in return for not arresting me?" She smirked. "That'll take care of you trying to wave your badge around."

Now he *felt* long suffering. Did she ever quit? Time to fire a little ammunition across her bow. "You don't care if you never see Amber again? Aren't you worried about her?"

The smirk vanished. For a moment she stared at him with a stricken expression that said clearly she had not thought of that, then with a visible effort she shrugged. "She'll be all right. Ice will take care of her. She's devoted to him and he's the best thing that's ever happened to her."

Yeah, right.

His feelings must have shown in his face, because Raven's expression went bitter. "You don't think so? Well, Ice doesn't sell her to perverts who want sex with her because she looks like a baby, the way that pimp in Denver was, getting her high so she'd cooperate and not struggle and cry. And you know how she ended up on the street? Her mother, who let some anti-abortionist talk her into having her baby, spent Amber's whole life locking her in closets when she didn't want to be bothered taking care of her and telling Amber that she was stupid and too much trouble and *should* have been aborted. Until the mom caught her boyfriend in bed with Amber, which he'd been doing for weeks every time mom wasn't around and Amber was too scared to tell anyone about...then dear mom accused Amber of *seducing* him and threw her out on the street! In the middle of the night! An eleven-year-old child!"

Garreth had encountered plenty of children beaten, tortured, starved, and sexually abused...but he never ceased being shocked and enraged by it, nor could he understand how any parent could treat a child that way. A similar outrage blazed in Raven, he saw. He liked her for that. "I expect *you're* the best thing that's happened. You care about her."

Raven blushed. "So does Ice. He promised her she'll never have to let one of our marks touch her and none ever have."

Garreth was about to ask if she believed Ice when he spotted an approaching figure he quickly decided Raven should meet. "So you want to leave Amber with him and stay here, make this your hunting preserve?"

Raven tossed her head. "Yes! I'll be set for life."

"Which'll be very short," a voice behind them said, "because I'll fucking rip your head off!"

Raven spun...and stared at the speaker...a lean woman with a mane of platinum hair, chain belt draped around her waist, a lace-up bustier, leather miniskirt, and high heels.

The hooker hissed, "No one trespasses on my territory!"

Garreth backed away. "We're just passing through."

But Raven snickered. "You mean you think you can rough us up?" Remembering tossing Officer Benton across the room?

Garreth braced to take action if necessary but made no attempt to intervene.

The hooker's mouth twisted. "Not rough you up, gump. *Kill* you...and that's true death, fangette...forever and ever...no third coming." Her eyes flared red.

Raven started. "Hey...you—you're...like me."

The street vampire bared her teeth. "I'm nothing at *all* like you!" She glanced at Garreth with disgust. "Is this thing your fault?"

"Yes." He clamped down firmly on an urge to laugh. He doubted she would see any humor in the confrontation.

Her lip curled. "Shit for brains obviously runs in the family. Well, if you want it, you'd better keep it away from here or I *will* rip its head off." And shoving past them, she stalked away. No question that in Garreth's place, she would have dropped Raven out that window with a broken neck.

Raven stared after her, ashen, then tossed her head. "Bitch. You're just going to let her talk to you that way? Ice would kick her butt!"

"Not for just name calling, I'm sure. You don't survive two thousand years without learning to pick your fights. But if you want to challenge her for the territory, go ahead. Or maybe you're thinking of finding another block to stake out?"

Raven's expression went thoughtful. "Are there others like her along here?"

Intelligence had finally kicked in. "Oh, yeah...and in the Tenderloin and South of Market. I don't know how many...but they're there."

Her eyes narrowed. "You brought me up here hoping we'd meet one of them, didn't you?"

He could see how it looked that way. "No...but I'm not sorry we did. That's what you'd face living on your own here... and that's what you'd turn into."

She frowned. "Ice likes his blood on the hoof but he's not like that."

"Until now you haven't been in a position to compete with him." Saying it brought Garreth another flash of his vision, Raven snarling up at Ice and Ice staring down with murder in his eyes. Was competition what led to the confrontation? Not that the reason mattered, as long as it led him to Ice.

Raven's expression went thoughtful. And it remained so as they continued walking up Broadway and then down Grant through Chinatown.

Passing one alley, memory rushed back at Garreth. He sighed. "I used to eat at a greasy chopsticks restaurant up that alley that served the best fried rice in San Francisco."

Raven eyed him. "Don't you miss this place? Why are you living in that podunk town when you could live here?"

He considered. "Yes...but there are things Bauman has that San Francisco doesn't." Knowing everyone, Sue Ann dispatching, prairie runs with coyotes flanking him, silent shadows, under stars with the piercing clarity of halogen bulbs. He smiled at Raven's skeptical expression. "Bright lights aren't everything."

His phone warbled.

It was the video store owner. "You said call any time. I found that private detective's card if you're still interested."

Garreth dug in his blazer for his notebook. "I'm still interested."

"The name is Walter Daniels of the Bettencourt Detective Agency. They're in Seattle."

Seattle? "What's his number?" He scribbled as Singer dictated. "Thank you very much, sir. I really appreciate you taking the time to look for the card." He punched *reset* and punched in the Seattle number. Somewhat to his surprise, a live voice answered, and offered to switch Garreth to Daniels' voice mail. He told the voice, "I know it's late but can you page him for me? This is important. It's about a man named Cameron Dark that he made inquiries about here in San Francisco three years ago."

"I'll try to reach him. What's your number?"

As he disconnected Raven said, "If this guy's still alive, I'll bet he didn't find Ice."

A distinct possibility. But even learning who hired the detective might give him valuable information.

They headed back for the car while Garreth waited for a response. He crossed his fingers. Let the guy call back. Let him call.

Almost at the foot of Broadway, the phone warbled. On the other end of the phone a baritone voice said, "What's so important about a three-year-old case?"

Garreth introduced himself. "Dark is now responsible for the death of a police officer."

"Somehow that's no surprise. He was a cold, creepy bastard. Only his name's Bruette, not Dark...Mitchell Craig Bruette."

Yet another name. "So you traced him?"

"Of course. I'm good at my job. I located him in Portland a few months later and dragged him back to his family in Seattle. Never turning my back on him, let me tell you."

Family? Garreth found himself staring at the phone, his breath frozen in his chest. He felt as though the ground had just slipped sideways from under him. In wondering who might be trying to find Ice, the idea of a family never occurred to him.

"What is it?" Raven demanded. "What's he saying?"

Ice was human? Really the age he seemed? Garreth knew that information should relieve him, but somehow it did not. It felt...unreal. What about his visions? The eyes he saw in them. The fangs. What about the menace he felt from the bastard? "May I have the name and number of the person who hired you?"

"Sure. It was his father, Harrison Bruette."

His fingers feeling numb, Garreth wrote.

Raven danced in front of him. "What? What? Come on, damn it! Tell me what's happening."

Disconnecting, Garreth shoved both phone and notebook into his pocket. "In the morning we're going to Seattle."

She stared at him. "Seattle? Why?"

He took a deep breath. "To learn the truth about your two millennium vampire."

31.

"He isn't Ice! No way!"

Raven had made that declaration how often through last night and their dawn flight north? Far too many times...though he could understand her anger and anxiety. For the second time in three days she had had her sense of reality jerked from under her. Hell, he *wanted* Bruette to be Ice and looking forward to this interview tied his stomach in knots, however much he tried to relax.

Garreth sighed and settled deeper into the limousine's seat, eyes closed. The limo was well worth the expense, he decided...more fun than a cab and certainly easier than fighting daylight and driving around an unfamiliar city in a rental car trying to find the address—*It's in Magnolia*, Bruette had said, as though that should explain everything to Garreth. He could relax and enjoy the rain, which combined with the limo's dark windows, made daylight almost bearable.

He did miss the listless Raven of yesterday's flight, though! For the umpteenth time, he told her, "We'll see if it's Ice when we talk to Alexandria Bruette."

"Who says she's Ice's sister." She made the statement an accusation.

"She's Mitchell Bruette's sister. That's all we know right now."

About the relationship...but using the internet to look up Bruettes in Seattle had located a law firm with that name and the online Martindale-Hubbell lawyer listings named both Harrison and Alexandria Bruette as firm members. The whole group appeared to be related...from Harlan Littrell (practice suspended while he served on the state supreme court) to Catherine Bruette nee Littrell, Harlan Bruette, and five other Littrells and Effinghams.

"And why is it again we're talking to *her*?"

Garreth did not have the energy to be impatient. "Because according to her father, she's the family member closest to her brother."

In age, too, though her birthdate in the Martindale-Hubbell listing made her thirty-seven, a gap of fifteen years between her and Mitchell.

What Harrison Bruette had actually said when Garreth called him last night, fortunately catching him still awake, was: "Please don't bother telling me why you're hunting Mitchell, officer. Short of receiving his head on a platter, I have no interest whatsoever in his whereabouts or activities, and in any case, I haven't heard from him in nearly three years. But my daughter Alexandria was always close to him. She may have been in contact, though god knows why. She's working at home for a few weeks so I'll give you her address and tell her you're coming. In the morning, I presume?"

Garreth eyed the phone as he disconnected. All the courtesy in the voice could not hide the icy anger under it. And this was the man who hired a detective to find his son? What went on in this family?

Considering Harrison Bruette and Mitchell, if he were Ice, Garreth hesitated to think what Alexandria might be like, but when the apartment door opened the woman on the other side of the fire barrier jolted him more than he expected, and not because of her crutches or the bright fuchsia cast encasing her left leg to the hip. Lean and close to six feet tall, an angle here in her face, a plane there, and certainly the ashen color, echoed chillingly of the albino grinning at him through the windshield. Did Raven notice? It appeared so. The girl's face tightened into a stiff mask.

"You're the detective from Kansas?" Alexandria asked, then, "Please come in," after she studied his ID. She crutched backward carefully. "It's okay to lean your umbrellas against the wall there."

The same courtesy as her father, but this time Garreth heard fear under it. And saw fear in brown eyes that retained warmth despite it.

She eyed Raven. "And you are..."

"Tiffany Ballinger," Garreth said. "She's met my suspect and is assisting me in trying to establish whether or not he's your brother."

Alexandria lost even more color. Turning, she led the way to a book-lined study with a glass wall whose view of the city must be spectacular at night...but admitted entirely too much daylight for vampire comfort, even with the rain. Garreth drifted along the bookshelves carrying the computer case he had brought up with him, keeping as far from the windows as possible. Interestingly, the books, all pushed to the back to make room for photographs, small sculptures, and art glass vases at the front of the shelves, included almost everything except law books, but especially fiction. Then a title raised the hair on his neck. *Hotel Transylvania.*

Setting down the computer case, Garreth moved aside a small bronze sculpture and pulled out the book. After reading the front flap of the dust jacket, he skimmed through the first several pages inside. It was about a vampire in eighteenth century France. The first page of the opening chapter mentioned the Sun King. He pulled out the next book, one of six others on the shelf by the same author. According to the dust jacket, *The Palace* had the vampire running around fifteenth century Florence with the likes of Botticelli. The next book took him to the Far East in the era of Genghis Khan, and the next to Ivan the Terrible's Russia. Places Ice told Raven he had lived, people he claimed to have known. Garreth felt a stir of hope and relief.

Alexandria sat down behind a desk, crutches leaning again the bookshelves behind her, and smoothed her butterscotch hair like someone pulling on a protective helmet. "What kind of trouble is...your suspect in?" She visibly braced herself. "It must be serious to bring you all the way from Kansas."

"I'm afraid so." Raven had slouched down in a wingback chair with its back to the window. Garreth handed her the book set in Nero's Rome. "He—" He saw no way to soften this. "My suspect killed a police officer."

"Oh my god." The words emerged as much the convulsive exhalation of someone socked in the stomach as a sentence. Garreth thought she had been pale before, but now she went bone white. He worried she might faint. But her eyes closed rather than rolled up and she repeated, "Oh my god." This time on inspiration, and almost like a prayer.

None of her father's indifference here.

Thumbing through the book, Raven was going paler, too. She slapped it shut.

At the sound Alexandria opened her eyes. She licked her lips. "Why do you believe it's Mitch?"

Movement of Raven's hand suggested she wanted to throw the book, but after a moment she stood and returned it to the shelf.

Garreth pulled the police sketch of Ice out of his computer case and laid it on the desk. "This is the man who killed our officer. Subsequently, fingerprints at a scene connected to an assault our suspect perpetrated in Lincoln matched those of this individual." Beside the sketch he laid his mug shot of Cameron Dark. "And Cameron Dark is who your father's private detective made inquiries about after he skipped bail."

From the corner of he eye he watched Raven stare long and hard at the other titles, then, slowly at first, but with increasing agitation, thumb through each book in turn.

Alexandria could not lose any more color, though her stricken expression as she studied the sketch and mug shot suggested that if she could, she would have.

Garreth said, "We know our suspect and Cameron Dark are the same person, but the question is whether Dark and your brother are. Do you have any photographs of Mitch?"

She pointed at some photographs on one of the bookshelves on the other side of the desk. "There."

The moment he picked them up, Garreth knew with grim, smoldering certainty that he stared into the face, the eyes, of Maggie's killer. The eyes told everything. If Garreth had seen nothing else of the face, he would have still recognized Ice. In both photos, one with him in a cap and gown, standing beside Alexandria, the other showing him and an older man beside a Formula I race car, Mitchell smiled, but the pale blue eyes did not. They glinted cold and empty, as if the gene that failed to give him color had also left him without some vital spark of humanity. Or, Garreth reflected, thinking suddenly of windows to the soul and old souls, Mitchell had lost the lottery the day they drew for souls in Heaven.

"Who's this?" Garreth asked, holding out the photo with the race car.

She barely glanced at it. "Our uncle Sheldon. Outside of court, he's an amateur race driver."

"Did he teach your brother to drive?" He handed the photos on to Raven.

"Up to a point." Alexandria's voice had developed the same distracted tone as her father's last night. A finger traced the lines on the police sketch. "Then Mitch talked Dad into sending him to a professional driving course. He always had to be the best at whatever he set out to do."

After staring hard at them, Raven carefully laid the photos on the desk. "May I go to the car?"

No need to ask her if she recognized the face in the photographs, too, not with hers so tight it looked ready to shatter and her body rigid with the effort of containing her emotions. After all her tantrums, Garreth admired her self restraint.

"This will take just a few minutes, then we'll go."

She sat on the edge of the nearest chair and stared down at hands clenched white-knuckled in her lap.

Garreth felt the knots in himself unclenching, however. So much for Ice's terrible power. Not two thousand years old. Not even a vampire. At least not yet.

Alexandria slid the photos over beside the sketch and mug shot. "I taught him that...as defense against harassment by the other children. Yes you look different, I told him, but they have to respect you if you have better grades and shoot free throws." Slumping back in her chair, she grimaced. "Maybe I should have taught him to make friends instead. He was an honor student, basketball star, president of the chess and fencing clubs, but none of the people hanging around him were ever friends, I think. But he didn't care why they hung around...as long as they did." Pain crossed her face. "His senior year he told me he'd made himself the man who could get anything...except test answers—he considered that too much risk to his academic standing, but...candy in grade school and cigarettes and liquor in prep school, yes. Even...setting up dates for classmates with girls guaranteed to put out." The brown eyes looked up, wounded, into Garreth's. "So I wonder if your dead officer isn't my fault."

Now she had lost him. "Excuse me?"

"Because I raised him."

Definitely lost him. "But...Mitch is your *brother*, right?"

She took a breath. "You have to understand...my mother's pregnancy with Mitch came as a shock. She thought she'd had her family. She deliberately spent most of law school in maternity clothes having my brother Harlan and me so pregnancy wouldn't stall her career later."

Garreth recalled Judith at Grandma Doyle's funeral, radiant over her own mid-life surprise. Not Alexandria's mother's reaction, it appeared.

"But I thought it was wonderful!" Alexandria smiled, gaze turned inward. "I was fifteen and in love with the idea of babies. And he was so adorable, all pastels...that pale skin and hair and pale blue eyes! Like a Lladro figurine. He had a nanny but I snatched him away from her every chance I had so

I could play with him. I went to college and law school right here in Seattle so I could come home every night and be near him. I thought of him as my baby." Tears welled in her eyes. "I don't know when it went wrong. Maybe when I dressed him up as Dracula for Halloween when he was about five or six. He always wanted to do Dracula after that. He became obsessed with vampires and werewolves. Those are his books you were looking at. I took them to keep Dad from throwing them away." She stared blindly past Garreth. "Or maybe it was just growing up in our family. We're lawyers, born and bred to it for generations...all the way from Daniel Emmett Effingham, who founded the firm in the fall of 1889, a few months after the Great Seattle Fire. The only one of us I can think doesn't live and breathe law is Shel. Dinner at home is never just a meal. As long as I can remember it's always been a debating society or moot court session. Maybe Mitch grew up thinking that's what life is, playing power games, getting one up on everyone around you."

That sounded like Ice. "How did your father happen to be having a detective hunting him?'

Alexandria sighed. "The year before Mitch had declared he hated college and wanted to drop out. I think what he hated was being a lowly freshman and a small frog in a large pond. Dad wouldn't hear of it, of course, so Mitch took off. I got a postcard from him a few months later saying he'd been in LA but left because there were too many freaks. Another pond too big for him, I guess. We should have just let him go his way. Maybe he would have eventually come home on his own. But at the time I was frantic with worry and Dad hates people crossing him, so...the detective." Her eyes turned haunted. "I wish to god he'd never found Mitch."

All the building relief evaporated. Cold ran through Garreth. "Why?"

"Because he'd...changed."

The chill deepened. "Changed how?"

"Dad's a very intimidating person but...Mitch wasn't intimidated anymore. He had this...smugness about him, as if he knew something that put him one up on the rest of us for all time. He sat there at dinner that night talking about how he didn't mind leaving Portland because he'd gotten all he could out of being there, and when Dad asked him what that meant he just smirked and said he'd gained what might be called a new lease on life."

Raven lifted her eyes and stared at Alexandria.

Garreth's stomach sank. Had Mitch, obsessed with vampires, met one in Portland and managed to be brought across? Was he a vampire after all? "Do you remember if Mitch ate anything at dinner?"

Alexandria blinked. "What? No, he didn't. I remember Mother making some remark about it and him answering that none of this was on his new dietary plan."

Garreth swore silently.

"And the next morning he'd disappeared again. And we haven't heard from him since."

"Nothing?" Garreth frowned.

She shook her head, staring down at the photos on the desk. "Not a call, not a card." Her voice dropped to a whisper. "Nothing."

Garreth could understand why she might be hurt by that, but nothing in the story seemed to justify the father's attitude. Did he hate being crossed that much? "Why does your father want Mitch's head on a platter?"

Alexandria grimaced, then took a deep breath. "Before Mitch left he opened the safe in Dad's study. I knew he'd taught himself to pick locks in high school—he had this Houdini party trick with handcuffs he liked to show off—but I didn't know he could do combination locks, too...or maybe he'd found out the combination. Anyway, he stole ten thousand dollars in cash, a hundred thousand in bonds—which we subsequently discovered he cashed at banks all over Seattle the next day, flawlessly forging my father's signature. But what's really earned him Dad's undying hatred is: he stole my mother's heirloom jewelry, too. Some of the pieces dated from colonial times and the Civil War. And Mitch..." Her voice went bitter. "Mitch twisted them until he'd freed the big stones, then just dropped what was left in the gutter." She straightened in her chair. "Officer Mikaelian, I can't think of anything else that will help you. I'm sor—" She caught herself. "No, that's not true. While I *am* truly sorry about your officer and about everything else Mitch has done...in spite of all that, I hope you understand that I can't wish you luck catching him." She started to tremble. "Can you see yourselves out?"

"Yes. Thank you." Garreth gathered up his sketch and photocopy.

Raven said nothing as they left the apartment and rode down in the elevator, just stood rigid and white-lipped. But as they crossed the lobby she started trembling as Alexandria had and whispered, "That bastard."

Without bothering to open the umbrellas, Garreth hustled her out and up the sidewalk into the waiting limo.

"That *bastard!*" Her voice rose. "The God-damned lying *sack of shit!*"

"Take us on back to the airport," Garreth told the driver, and hurriedly ran up the window between the driver and passenger compartments.

"*He lied to me!*" She pulled the ring out of her nostril and hurled it to the floor. "He's a fake! A fraud! *Just like my father!*" She jerked out the rings in her ears, throwing each the direction the hand happened to be moving. With each one Garreth winced, but Raven seemed either unaware of or indifferent to the pain. "All those places and people he talked about were just from those *books!*"

Garreth ducked the rings coming his directions. "He's still a vampire."

"But he lied about his age!" Angry tears spilled down her cheeks from under her glasses, bringing streaks of mascara and eyeliner with them. "His age wouldn't matter to me. Why did he have to *lie!* The bastard!" She reached for the window switch and ran down the window. "Who's good for doing hair in this town?" she demanded.

In the rearview mirror, the driver's reflected eyes glanced toward Garreth. "Uh...Mr. Ballinger?"

Goosebumps ran down Garreth's spine. In his vision Raven had short, smoky blonde hair. *Maggie, I think we're close.* "If you know somewhere a little bribery will slide her into their schedule in time to make our two-thirty flight, go ahead and take us there." He ran the window back up. Now was his chance. "So, would you like to get even with Ice and help me find him?"

She threw herself back against the seat. "I never want to see that lying fucking bastard again!"

"Even though you know he's a liar and he has Amber? What if he's also lying about not letting the marks touch her? After all, she's his only girl now."

Raven sat bolt upright, sucking in her breath. "But...she's no good to him for that. She can't make anyone believe she *wants* sex."

"That might not count any more." While he talked, Garreth dug in the computer case. He had to push while he could. He thrust the fax photo of the dead girl in Billings under her nose. "Do you know her?"

Raven shrugged. "Sure. That's Twilight. She used to be with Ice but he sent her away because she got jealous and thought she should be his only servant. Where'd—" She frowned. "She looks dead."

"She is. She was found at the Sheraton with her wrists slashed."

Raven blinked. "You mean she killed herself because Ice sent her away?"

"I don't think she killed herself. It was just made to look like suicide. She'd been drinking champagne and having sex shortly before she died. There were white pubic hairs on her body and a man of Ice's description was seen near the suite."

She caught her breath. "Ice?"

"He isn't just a liar." Garreth leaned toward her. "The games have to be played Ice's way, right? But Twilight wouldn't anymore. Do you think he'd tolerate that?"

Raven said nothing but chewed her lower lip.

"He told you he sent Twilight away...but you know he's a liar. And a killer." Garreth rattled the photo. "You need to get Amber away from him."

She stared hard at Twilight's photo. "Tell me what to do."

32.

"How is it this link works?" Raven sat cross-legged on a picnic table at the rest stop west of Des Moines, eyes closed, forehead furrowed in concentration. Light from the crescent moon overhead glinted on the few remaining rings in her ears and turned her hair, newly cropped and smoky blond, to silver. "Like one of those direction finders in TV shows?" She had scrubbed off the rose tattoo and replaced it with a dagger stabbing down the right side of her face.

"No." Sitting with a hip propped on the other end of the table, Garreth stared up into the midnight sky. How could he explain it? "Imagine yourself a compass and Amber your north pole. Sit passive, thinking about her, until you feel a pull."

She grimaced. "I don't feel anything."

"Keep at it. It just takes a little practice, and your emotional ties to Amber should give you a good bond with her. It's the only way we'll locate them in a timely fashion."

Raven frowned, eyes still closed. "But you already said you think you know which—hey! I feel something!" She bounced on the table and twisted to point triumphantly. "That way!"

South. The same direction he felt. "Looks like they went to Kansas City." *We're closing in on him, Maggie. San Francisco yesterday, Seattle this morning, Kansas City tomorrow. We've almost got him.* "We'll head down there in the morning."

"Morning!" She swung off the table in a swirl of leather duster. "Why do we have to wait until then? Where are we going now? Can I drive, please, please?"

"Des Moines, and no, you can't drive." Garreth stood and headed for the car, marveling at the adaptability of the young.

The hysterics of Friday and Saturday seemed forgotten and she wore her new life as easily as if she had lived it for decades. "I need names of local officers to use in my reports home and I want to establish my presence here with the Des Moines police by dropping in on a couple of shifts."

"To keep you from being a suspect when Ice is found dead?" Her eyes reflected red in the light over the parking area. "You *are* going to kill the bastard, aren't you?"

She had turned against Ice with a vengeance. Perhaps her reason for choosing to wear the dagger tattoo. "Why don't we see if it's necessary first."

She climbed in the car with a snort. "What a choirboy. But what else can I expect from a cop who doesn't even pack a gat, for heaven's sake."

"A gat?" Shaking his head, he started the car. "Did you get that from the movie you were watching last night?"

She shrugged. "I had to do something while you and Harry talked all night. He seems like a nice guy for a cop," Her expression went sly. "Even if he didn't want to hear how I was hung for witchcraft in Salem."

Garreth refused to rise to the bait. "And how were you planning explain surviving a broken neck?"

With barely a pause, she came back, "A bad hanging. I was just strangled to death."

Give her credit for thinking fast.

"So," she went on, "what's there to do in Des Moines until dawn?"

From her disgusted expression when he reached the Des Moines Patrol Division offices, Things To Do did not include sitting in the parking lot of a police station. Leaving her worried him but taking her inside seemed an even bigger risk...and handcuffing her to the steering wheel out of the question.

So he kept his fingers crossed while he introduced himself to the lieutenant serving as watch commander and asked if they had any information on the hunt for the albino or the juvenile female who escaped from New Prospect. Informed with regret that the lieutenant had heard nothing, Garreth added the name Mitchell Bruette to the information on the albino, as he had also told Reichert, phoning the sheriff from San Francisco this afternoon before catching the flight back to Omaha.

"Will there be any problem with me canvassing the area hotels and motels with Bruette's picture to see if he's holed up here somewhere? If I learn anything, I'll hand everything over to your department, of course. I've seen Officer Lebekov's cannon in action on the firing range and busting this turkey is definitely not a job for one unarmed officer. I'll be introducing myself to your day watch commander, too."

"That sounds good," the lieutenant said. "If there's any news, where can I reach you?"

"I haven't checked into a motel yet, but here's my digital phone number."

Leaving the building he immediately peered toward his car to see if Raven remained there. And started in alarm. She sat cross-legged on the Porsche's hood in animated conversation with a police officer! He tore toward the car, undecided which horrified him more, her boots on the car or imagining what she might be saying to the officer. And he could not even yell at her because he might use the wrong name.

Seeing him coming, she grinned and winked at the officer. "Don't have a cow, bro. I'm not scratching your precious Porsche. See?" As she swung to the ground he saw that the duster had been tucked under her. "I've just been telling Officer Lefavre—isn't he a hunk—who stopped because it worried him finding me alone out here, that I'm safe because of how I happen to be named Elspeth."

Officer Lefavre, who looked too young to drink yet, went red-eared. "According to your sister it's because a fortune teller told your mother the baby would be the reincarnation of her great-something aunt who was hung for witchcraft in Salem?"

"Reincarnation?" Garreth arched a brow at Raven, who simpered back. "Now that you mention it, I can envision you being charged with witchcraft. Get in the car."

She rolled her eyes as she climbed in. "Get in the car. Up against the wall. You have the right to remain silent. What a bummer having the police for a brother." Leaning back out the passenger window, she blew a kiss to Officer Lefavre as he returned to his patrol unit. "Bye. You be careful out there, y'hear?"

Pulling out of the lot, Garreth said, "What the hell were you doing? What if he'd asked for some ID? The only thing you have says Tiffany Ballinger."

She scowled. "I was ready for that. I'd just have said I'm from our mother's second marriage and I've renamed myself because I hate the name Tiffany. Tiffany is for snooty, ditzy girls who wear ruffles and pink and I'd rather be boiled in oil than wear ruffles or pink! Loosen up! I was just having a little fun. Life is too—" She grinned. "Too *long* to be serious all the time."

"Amber and Ice," Garreth said.

Raven sobered abruptly. "Okay, when can we go to Kansas City?"

"In the morning, but it'll be early. Their Second Shift starts at six-thirty."

They left a little before seven. Garreth drove while Raven slept in the passenger seat with the sleeping pallet wrapped around her and her face covered by a cowboy hat she had bought at the Denver airport during the layover on the way back to Omaha. In conversations about Ice on the plane and the Denny's where they spent the rest of last night drinking tea and going over the Kansas City map and hotel listings on the laptop, Raven had said Ice always picked a good hotel for himself. Then if the city looked promising, he hunted a cheap room for the Homesick Runaway scam and started trolling for marks. Kansas City had plenty of hotels, but only half a dozen in the downtown area of the class Ice liked. Checking those should not take long.

As they neared downtown Kansas City, he prodded Raven awake. "Start feeling for Amber."

She struggled upright in the seat and substituted dark glasses for the hat over her face. Looking at her from the side he could see she closed her eyes. Presently she opened them and pointed ahead and to her right...south and a little west. "That direction?"

It matched what he felt. Interstate-29 merged with I-70 and a large area of downtown with its warehouses, office buildings, and first of the hotels, good ones and cheap, lay to their right. But the thread stretching from him to that other presence continued on south.

"What's the first hotel ahead?"

She opened his road atlas to consult the list they had drawn up . "The Hyatt Regency and the Westin Crown Center."

He and Maggie had come up to Kansas City a few times so he had a rough idea of the city layout and found both hotels without much trouble. But in front of neither did he feel any sense of presence.

"You want the next hotel?" Raven asked at the Westin.

Garreth shook his head. "First let's see if they have a room. Staying here we won't be running into Amber or Ice by accident, or have them spot us first." He parked on the drive and headed inside. "You'll like the waterfall in the lobby."

"You've been here before?"

He nodded. "One year for Maggie's Christmas present I brought her up to their New Years bash." And his throat tightened remembering the shimmering red slip dress that seemed to make her skin shimmer, too, and reflected in her eyes as she whooped at the confetti and balloons raining down on them.

Raven's eyes widened in horrified understanding. "That other cop was a lot more than your partner, wasn't she?" She sidled away from him. "You know, if I'd been you, I'd have killed me in that hospital."

He smiled wryly. "I almost did."

She went a shade paler. "Why didn't you?"

He shrugged. "One thing and another. The fell clutch of circumstance."

"What?"

"A line of poetry I read sometime." Where did it come from? He could not remember. "I guess cold blooded killing isn't my style."

Her forehead furrowed. "What about Ice?"

He felt his jaw tighten. "That's different. There's the waterfall."

This time delight widened her eyes. "Cool!" She stared up at the soaring ceiling and the top of the waterfall high above them. Moments later she headed for the escalator to ride up past the waterfall.

Garreth let her go and made his way to the desk. "No, I don't have reservations but I need two adjoining rooms," he told the desk clerk. On the drive he had decided he should not to use the Ballinger credit card. That would link this stay and the flight to the west coast. So on a rest stop he had dug under the false bottom of his luggage for a different card. He handed it over to the clerk along with the accompanying ID, a badge case containing a private security badge and picture ID card identifying Michael Stone as a bonded operative with Madrigal Executive Security Associates.

"How many nights, Mr. Stone?" the clerk asked.

"I don't know." He scribbled a false address and license tag on the registration. "However long it takes to locate my niece and retrieve her from her mother. Maybe a week."

And he left her with questions in her eyes. Which gave the desk clerks something to speculate about that ought to fix him in memory as someone hunting a child kidnapped by a non-custodial parent.

Half an hour later he and Raven had carried their luggage up to their rooms, grabbed a quick drink to fortify themselves against daylight, and were back in the car heading south. Farther and farther...until Raven started eyeing the street numbers anxiously. "Are you sure we haven't taken a wrong street and passed these hotels?"

But minutes later they reached the Saville Plaza. Again Garreth felt nothing but did not risk showing Ice's picture. In case of a police investigation hotel personnel would certainly recall Garreth's interest in Ice and describe him to the investigators. Asking about Amber carried some risk, too, but less. He showed the desk clerks the photobooth strip and gave them the kidnapped niece story.

"Her mother is very tall for a woman, over six feet, thin. She might be dressing as a man."

The hotel had no guests of fitting those descriptions and none of the desk personnel could recall any in the past week that would. He also came up empty at the next three hotels. But they had to be close. The area *felt* right.

Raven leaned forward to peer out the windshield. "She has to be somewhere arou—wow!" She sat upright. "Look at that!"

He nodded. They were coming up on the Country Club Plaza. Boulevard streets of restaurants and shops housed in eclectic architecture sprinkled with towers...Spanish and Moorish and French something...whatever the name of that ornate dome architecture. The crowds gave it the same electricity as areas of San Francisco, the same symphony of sounds and scents. Plus a profusion of fountains. "The Christmas lights here are spectacular."

He turned down 47th toward the Sheraton...and quickly remembered something less appealing about the Plaza...the traffic, and lack of traffic lights. When he and Maggie came down, they had quickly given up driving, parked, and just walked around.

Raven sat forward in her seat staring everywhere. "This is cool. But I don't understand. There's no way to work the runaway scam here—it's too busy—but...I can feel Amber somewhere around."

"It's an affluent area. Maybe Ice has invented a new scam."

If he had, he worked it out of somewhere other than the Sheraton. Out of somewhere other than any of the hotels, in fact. Every desk clerk looking at Amber's photograph shook his or her head. No child like that had come in recently with an adult of either sex.

Outside the Ritz-Carlton, their last hope, Raven scowled in frustration. "It doesn't make sense. They have to be staying somewhere."

Agreed, but until he had some idea where else to look…"It's time for plan B."

"Which is…"

"We canvass…work our way across the Plaza with Amber's picture, showing it to shop clerks, cab drivers, the drivers of the horse carriages, any street vendors, waiters at the sidewalk cafes. If necessary we'll canvass Westport, too."

Raven's mouth dropped open. "You mean during *daylight*!"

He shoved her toward the car. "I hate it, too, kiddo, but if we want to find Amber, we have to be willing to do whatever's necessary. You can tolerate daylight if you're determined to. We'll hang around for evening, too, in case that's when they're here."

"It'll take *forever*!"

He had to smile at her dismay. "It isn't like TV, a little thirty-second montage of people shaking their heads at the detective. The job takes persistence. But we can save some time by each taking a side of the street we're working. And at the same time keep alert for Amber. If she's close, you should be able to feel it."

Raven sighed, then squared her shoulders. "Where do we start?"

Along with persistence, some luck would be nice, of course. He crossed his fingers.

For all the good that did. They struck out the first day, accomplishing nothing more than some shopping—a pair of leather driving gloves for him, some slouch style suede cowboy boots and other clothes for her—even hanging around until the Plaza started shutting down for the night. And slogged through the second day with no better results. But Garreth had to give Raven credit. Wearing the new boots and a long-sleeved t-shirt and jeans, her cowboy hat pulled down to the top of her glasses, she marched doggedly from store to store without complaint. Even when she looked ready to crumple under the weight of daylight.

He watched her use her discomfort to evoke sympathy, extending Amber's photo to a clerk with a trembling hand and a voice on the verge of tears. "Please, miss, have you seen this little girl? She's my sister. Our mother kidnapped her and I know she has her somewhere around here."

The clerk clearly regretted having to say *no*.

Toward the end of the third day, however, when the two of them sat in the shade of a sidewalk cafe's awning, she pushed aside her tea and leaned folded arms and head on the table. "It's hopeless. If she's been around here, why hasn't anyone seen her?"

Garreth felt frustrated, too. He put an arm across her back and gave her a squeeze of encouragement. "These things take time. Sometimes a long time. We can't give up."

"I keep worrying what he's doing now, and what's happening to—" She broke off and jerked erect. "Amber!"

He stared at her. "You can feel her somewhere close?"

"Yes!" She stood, peering around. "I don't—wait...there."

He followed the direction of her finger. Down the sidewalk a small group of people milled in confusion. One seemed to be on the ground...Amber, he realized a second later, as a male pedestrian helped her to her feet. Raven had already scooped up her sling bag and charged down the sidewalk. Garreth threw money on the table and followed.

On the way he spotted something else in the excitement...a juvenile female brushing behind the good samaritan, and the wallet bulge visible in his hip pocket as he leaned down toward Amber had disappeared once she passed. A new game indeed. Ice had found himself a pickpocket.

And lost no time in finding a new girl. But of course. He needed pawns for his games and an audience to appreciate his cleverness.

While Garreth sorted through the street noises to hear Amber apologizing for her clumsiness at falling down in front of the samaritan, he homed on the dip. She never saw him until he snatched the purse off her shoulder.

She spun, yelping. "*That's my*—" but broke off as he shoved a badge under her nose.

He smiled at her. "Shall we see how many billfolds are in here?"

In a heartbeat she spun and bolted. Garreth made no attempt to follow but dug into the purse and made his way toward the good samaritan.

Amber's apologies had given way to breathy *thankyou's* that ended abruptly in a shriek of joy. "*Raven*!" She hurtled past the samaritan into Raven's arms. "You're alive! What happened? Where've you been?"

Garreth tapped the bemused samaritan on the shoulder and held up four billfolds. "Can you tell me which of these is yours?"

For a second the man stared at the billfolds, then his hand shot toward his hip pocket. "How—"

"I spotted the individual taking advantage of your distraction and intercepted her. Which one, sir?"

The samaritan could only point. Garreth handed him the billfold.

Amber and Raven headed back up the sidewalk toward the sidewalk cafe, chattering breathlessly.

Garreth spotted a patrol unit in the far traffic lanes. Dodging between cars, he made his way to it and handed the purse to the officer behind the wheel. "A young lady dropped this and when I picked it up I discovered it has several billfolds in it."

The officer peered inside. "So there are. May I ask your name, sir?"

But Garreth had already dodged back around a truck and used its cover to work back to the far side of the street. Would it seem to the officer that he had vanished into thin air?

He sat several tables away from the girls.

"...scored us a *house*!" Amber was saying, leaning eagerly toward Raven. "We were just coming into the city and saw this Mercedes on the side of the Interstate with the hood up and this guy just staring at the engine. It was almost evening so Ice pulled over to see if he could help."

A Mercedes would draw him, yes, Garreth reflected. The thought process must have gone something like: *rich dude in distress; there has to be opportunity in it for me.*

Raven doodled on a napkin. "Since when has Ice been willing to get his hands dirty with an engine?"

"Oh, he didn't do anything to the car. They just talked, and finally the guy used his car phone to call a garage and Ice stayed there with him while he waited for the tow truck and then we gave the guy a lift home...to this *mansion*. He's a professional house sitter and he'd just taken the owner and his wife to the airport to go to England for six months. I fell asleep while they were talking and when I woke up Ice told me he'd used his powers to make the guy turn the house over to us and go off to another house sitting job."

Cold slid down Garreth's spine. Vampire powers could not control a mind that much. What had really happened to the house sitter?

"So we've got this cool house for *six months*! You've got to come see it. There's two new girls, Silk and Onyx, but I know Ice will be glad to have you back, too. I can't wait to see his face when he sees you! I hope he likes your tattoo. I do."

"I've got another idea," Raven said. "Don't go back. Come away with me...now."

Amber gaped at her. "What are you talking about? Leave Ice? That's crazy."

Raven took her arm. "Come on. He doesn't need us."

"Of course not, but don't you remember what it was like for us before we met him? I do, and I won't go back to that!"

"We won't have to. I'll make us a new life...just the two of us. A better one than with Ice."

Garreth groaned. *Raven, give it up.* If only vampire powers included telepathy. Amber was not going to listen. He crossed his fingers and hoped Raven saw that and went back to their game plan...learn where Ice was and set up a meeting for later.

Amber frowned. "How could it be better? Are you mad at Ice? Is that it? Because he didn't come back for you?"

"No, no." Raven grimaced. "I hit that deputy so you two *could* get away. But I shouldn't have. I've learned some things about Ice since, and he isn't what you think. He's a fraud and a liar, and—"

Amber jumped up. "I don't know what's wrong with you! Did they do something to you before you escaped? Look, come home with me and talk to Ice. He'll straighten everything out."

Raven glanced Garreth's direction.

He read her thought in her eyes and groaned. *No! Don't! Set it up for later*!

But she turned away and doodled on the napkin some more. "Okay, sure. Let's go."

Damn it! What the hell did she think she was doing!

"How do we get there? Walk?"

Garreth hoped. Walking, much as he hated it in daylight, would work.

Amber giggled. "Hell, no. Onyx has a driver's license and we got the Mercedes back from the garage. And here's something else that's cool." She pulled a phone out of her shoulder bag and punched in a number. "Onyx, can you come and pick me up? I'm at Skelly's. I have someone Ice will want to see. Okay, sure. See you." She dropped the phone back in her bag. "We'll meet her on that corner over there."

Raven sent a glance Garreth's direction, then at the table, before following Amber. Garreth checked the table.

The napkin had writing, not doodles. *Sorry, choir boy, but I'll take care of Ice. I know I've got the guts. I'll do whatever it takes to save Amber from him.*

Damn her! The stupid fool! He slam dunked the napkin on the table and plunged into traffic after her.

Before he reached the corner a black Mercedes pulled up and the girls climbed in.

Now Garreth gave thanks for the traffic. It trapped the Mercedes, holding its speed down and delaying it at intersections enough to let him follow from the sidewalk, dodging between other pedestrians. Until the car reached the edge of the Plaza. Then it gunned away up Ward Parkway and he could only stare after it swearing in frustration, the vision of Raven and Ice flashing through his mind.

He hurried back for the car. At least he knew which direction the Mercedes went. If he were here officially he could run the tag and have the address, but without that, he hoped to hell he *could* use the bond between Raven and himself like a direction finder.

33.

Garreth drove slowly, studying the houses and cars in their driveways, trying to feel the bond without closing his eyes. A number of the houses looked worthy of being called mansions. Intersections were trickiest. Sometimes he missed. He would drive on and realize the thread now stretched behind him. Each time he had to turn around he cursed more passionately. It was almost sunset. Had Raven met Ice yet? Had she survived? Would he feel it if she died?

After casting back and forth across the area half a dozen times, he found a gate where he felt Raven's presence. Up the circular drive sat a black Mercedes. He looked around for a place to park. The Porsche fit the neighborhood but the locals did not park on the street.

Except at a house farther up the street, which appeared to be holding a party. Cars spilled out of the driveway to line the curb in front of the house. Garreth slid the Porsche in among them and walked back.

The fence and closed gate presented no problem. He passed between the bars. The landscaping included enough bushes and trees to give him cover to the house. A stone terrace stretched across the front and halfway back along one side. As he climbed the steps to the terrace, Garreth pulled on his driving gloves. Windows reaching nearly floor to ceiling showed him a living room on one side of the house and a library on the other...rich wood paneling, floor to ceiling bookcases, big leather chairs, a massive desk, a stone fireplace with weapons displayed from the mantle to the open-beam ceiling...battle axe, morningstar, cavalry saber, flintlock rifle, dueling pistols.

He sucked in his breath. Though he had paid little attention to the setting in his vision with Raven and Ice, recognition reverberated in him. The confrontation happened here. "We're there, Maggie. We've got him!" The fire and ice of adrenalin pumped through him. Triumph. Fear. *He can destroy you.*

Raven's cowboy hat sat on the desk with her glasses folded on the brim. Seconds later Raven herself appeared, pacing from somewhere between the windows to the fireplace and then the desk, hands behind her back with the sling bag swinging from them. Waiting.

Garreth edged up to the window nearest the desk and gritted his teeth against the flare of fire enveloping him. He could surely stand it long enough to rap on the window and bring Raven over to invite him in. He reached for the glass.

The door opened. Garreth jumped aside, then cautiously peered back around the edge of the window. Warning flame licked at him.

Ice strolled into the room to sit in the big executive chair behind the desk. His eyes glowed red. "Raven. We heard on the radio that the girl who attacked the deputy at that gas stop had been killed. How gratifying you weren't. Though I confess to being surprised you aren't in police custody."

He sounded, Garreth reflected, like his father...so neutral his tone barely cleared the frost point.

Raven beamed with childlike pride. "I escaped. It was like something from a movie. I smashed my hospital window and jumped out in a rainstorm in nothing but a hospital gown. And I had to hide in a mausoleum and steal the clothes from a corpse so I could hitchhike to Des Moines and shoplift better clothes, scam myself some cash, and...come find you."

Garreth grimaced. *Watch yourself, kiddo. Keep it simple.*

"And exactly how *did* you manage to find me?" Ice opened a drawer and casually took out Maggie's Desert Eagle.

Raven started to step backward as he laid it on the desk top, then stopped. She hiked the sling bag to her shoulder.

"Well, I tried to think like you. You need good hunting ground so you'd head for a city. I looked around Des Moines for a bit and you weren't there so the next logical place was Kansas City."

Ice stood and came around the desk. "Really. You won't mind if I check you for police wires?"

She gaped at him. "You can't think I'd lead the cops to you?"

"Oh, of course not." The red eyes gleamed. "But have you considered maybe they let you escape and bugged you? So let's just check...starting with your brand new purse there."

She shrugged and held out the bag...but as he reached to take it she stiffened, then hurled the bag at him. "Bastard! Lying *son of a bitch!* You didn't just lie about your age; you've been lying about *everything!* It's *all fake! You're no vampire!*"

Ice stiffened and stared down at her, blood in his eyes. "Where did you get a foolish idea like that?"

Almost the scene in his vision! Garreth hurled himself at the window...and smashed into the wall of flame. The glass seared like a hot grill.

Inside Raven hissed, "Because I can smell the blood in you, you stupid bastard! But you don't know what that means, do you, since you're an imposter, a bogus bogeyman."

"Raven!" Garreth shouted. "*Raven!*" If only she would shut up, hear him, and call him in!

But she focused completely on Ice. "You're a bigger fraud than my father's ever been! He just covered up his past, he didn't *make* it up. He doesn't parade around bragging on himself and pretending to be something high and mighty! And he's never deliberately tried to hurt anyone. But you damn well enjoy that, don't you!"

Nor did Ice appear to hear. He had gone dead still, his face congealing into white, icy, murderous fury. His voice dropped to a whisper. "That's enough."

"RAVEN!" Garreth tried pounding on the window but could only brush it. The fire shrieked through him...hissing, searing, consuming.

"Because you can't stand the truth? Because you want us gullible little runaways to think you're the biggest frog in the pond when you're just a *little* frog in a *very* little pond, nothing but a fucking phony, while *I*—"

"RAVEN, NO!"

"—am the *real thing!*" And she stretched her jaws wide, extending her fangs.

His vision, exactly! And having come, the moment filled him with a blast of foreboding. Disaster loomed ahead!

Raven snatched up the gun and aimed at Ice. She had to hold it in both hands for a secure grip. "But your games are over, Mitchell Craig Bruette. Your father wants your head on a platter and I'm happy to—"

"Sleeping beauty," Ice said.

And abruptly Raven went slack. She remained on her feet but her eyes closed and her chin and arms dropped.

Ice retrieved the gun from a nerveless hand and returned it to the desk top. Then he walked around her shaking his head. "Well. Well, well."

Garreth slid back from the window before Ice faced his direction. But he barely felt the flames ease. His skin still crawled...with dread now. Being human did not render Ice one bit less dangerous, but Raven was helpless...and so was Garreth Mikaelian. He pounded a doubled fist against the stone of the house. He had to gain entry! But how?

Inside Ice said, "So there really *are* vampires? And you managed to meet and become one. I wonder how. Not that it matters. You've really been a busy little bitch this past week. Becoming a vampire, learning my name, talking to my father, and tracking me down here. I'm impressed. But you have one thing wrong. I'm not a complete fake. I know hypnotism...and I've made myself very very good at it. And you know what can be done with hypnotism?" He bent to Raven's face. "*Any*thing. Post-hypnotic suggestions, for example—" He pointed at her with hands folded into gun shapes. "—are very useful, as we see. I'm happy to see the command held, by the way, even though you've changed...lifestyle? And you 'servants' are so suggestible. Tell you to sleep all night and you do, so I'm free to go have a good meal and pick up a real woman to screw. I can even create virtual reality without a computer...a poker game played with dead men, or turn our hotel room into a fancy restaurant and hamburger into steak, or make you believe we've gone out to a bar." He sneered at her. "You were so proud of the show you put on with that piano man—sex as a public spectacle was something even Teddy Rivers wouldn't dare to do. But guess what, it wasn't public, and not much of a spectacle, hard as I tried to help you out."

Though she never moved, color surged in Raven's face.

"But you're also right about one thing." He continued stalking around her. "The games are over. Now I'm going to do Vampire for real...and then we'll see who's a small frog. Listen to me, Raven. When I count to three you'll wake up and when I say: 'Here's my throat,' you will drink from me and bring me across. Do you understand?"

Hope flared in Garreth. *Do it! Do it! We can make sure he never revives!*

"You may speak and answer me."

Raven said, "Go to hell."

Garreth smacked the house again. Damn her. What a time to resist Ice's influence!

Color flared in Ice's face, then making an obvious effort, he shrugged. "Well, one drawback to human hypnosis is it can't make a person do what he wouldn't ordinarily do. And I've pissed you off, have I? Well you've pissed me off, too. But I know how to make you more cooperative."

Even as Ice left the room, Garreth knew, too. He pressed back against the window, into the fire. "RAVEN! You have to be able to hear me. You *know* what he's going to do! Fight free! Invite me in!"

But only a rush of color through her face suggested she heard him.

Ice returned leading Amber by the hand. Garreth jumped back from the window.

Amber stared at Raven. "What's wrong with her?"

"Oh, she believes some vicious lies about me and I'm giving her time out to reflect on her gullibility." Ice stroked the girl's hair. "Do you love me?"

Amber stared up at him adoringly. "Oh, yes."

He put an arm around her. "Do you believe I love you?"

The silky tone chilled Garreth. He stared at the window, clenching his fists. If no one would invite him in, he had to enter without an invitation. His gut knotted. *Could* he? Could the mind always rule? Even against the dwelling barrier?

Inside, Amber answered Ice. "Yes."

Ice moved up to Raven's ear, smiling, showing fangs. Garreth just managed to hear the whisper. "Think of all the fun I can have with her...for instance, telling her what a stupid little fool she is for believing anyone could *ever* love *her*, or, say..."

Not even Garreth's vampire hearing picked up the rest. But the suggestion turned Raven bone white. Garreth ran for the next window, to be out of Ice's line of sight, and pressed into the fire, straining for the glass. The mind rules. All he had to do was believe. A little pain—well, agonizing pain, but he could surely stand it long enough to pass through.

"Talk to me, " Ice said.

"You're a son of a bitch."

He smiled. "Oh I'm even worse than that when I don't get what I want." Still smiling, he walked over to Amber stroked her hair once...then grabbed a handful and jerked upward, lifting her almost off her feet. Amber screamed. At the same time his hand dove into his pocket and came out with a switch blade. It opened with a *snick*.

Amber's scream rose to a shriek.

Garreth shoved into the fire. Touched the glass. Pressed into the scalding inferno, teeth gritted. It could not stop him. The mind rules.

Ice jerked Amber by the hair. "Shut up, bitch!" He raised his voice above her screams. "This is all Raven's fault. She has something I want and won't give it to me. So I have to take away something she wants."

Raven's body trembled.

The fire of the sun, nuclear, but Garreth forged into it. The mind rules.

Ice waggled his brows. "Ready to cooperate? Or will innocent blood be on your hands?" He trailed the knife point across Amber's throat. "We can even make it Biblical, in honor of your father." His voice went sing-song. "This is her blood shed for you...unless you take and drink from me in the hope of my resurr—"

Screaming, Raven jerked upright and flung herself at Ice.

Through! Garreth charged Ice, too.

For a moment Ice froze in disbelief. In that moment Raven grabbed the knife and wrenched it away. Garreth chopped at the arm holding Amber. The girl dropped to the floor and huddled screaming.

Raven waved the knife like a sword. "You blasphemous son of a bitch! I'm going to gut you!"

Garreth grabbed her wrist. "No. Leave him to me."

She gaped at him. "How did you get in? No one invit—"

"I invited myself." The fire had not extinguished once inside, though. It remained as strong as ever, making every movement, every breath, agony. Taking the knife away from her, he struggled to talk. "Go on and take Amber out of here. Now."

Raven stared hard at him, then scooped up Amber, and hugging her close, crooning reassurances, started for the door.

Ice snatched the gun from the desk. "I was right; you did lead the cops here!" He took aim on her back. "See you in hell, you little cu—"

Garreth's backhand sent him flying sideways into a heap against the fireplace. The gun sailed out of his hand.

Ice glared up, blood trickling from a cut on his lip. One eye had turned pale blue, leaving him with one eye blood colored, one eye icy. But Ice seemed unaware he had lost a contact lens. Fingering his mouth, he climbed to his feet. "This is police brutality, and I don't see a warrant."

"That's because there *is* no warrant." Even wearing gloves Garreth wanted to wipe his hand on his jeans to scrub off the contamination where he touched the albino. But nothing could erase the sense of contamination that came from smelling Ice's blood scent...and feeling the thread that told him, beyond any hope of mistake, that the albino had drunk his blood, too...that all chance of being able to arrest, try, and imprison the albino like any criminal had disappeared. Bile rose in Garreth's throat at the very thought of any bond between the two of them. "But then, I'm not here in an official capacity." Garreth listened in surprise to how even his voice sounded with anger boiling in him and the fire scorching him. He put a foot on the gun while he folded the switch blade and dropped it in a pocket of his blazer. "I'm the officer driving the car you ran off the road...the officer whose partner you killed." He picked up the Desert Eagle.

Ice rolled to his feet, wary, watching the gun, but also glancing up at the weapons above the fireplace. "But that guy was dead."

"Not exactly."

Ice drew in a slow breath. "I see. You're the one. You brought her over." Light blazed up in the blood and ice eyes. "Bring me over, too."

The naked lust in Ice's face disgusted Garreth. "Not. A. Chance."

The lust turned to rage. "I'm right for it! I'm a hunter! I *deserve* it! I certainly deserve it more than that little piece of pussy does!"

The flames of trespass fused with Garreth's anger into incandescent fury. He aimed at Ice. "Mr. Bruette, you have a foul mouth. And you don't deserve anything except to die."

"For what?" Ice demanded. "Encroaching on your territory? For being a mere human who dares to hunt like you do?"

"For being a vicious piece of scum who's brought everyone nothing but misery and pain. But most of all, for killing my partner."

Garreth expected Ice to go defiant or defensive, or show fear, but the albino stared blankly back at him. "But...she was only human, wasn't she? You're going to shoot me for that?"

The bafflement in the question shocked Garreth. Ice had no idea why Maggie's death made Garreth want to kill him. The thought Garreth had looking at Ice's eyes in Alexandria's photographs came back to him...a man without humanity...without empathy...without a soul.

Fire and anger seared him, pushing Garreth to pull the trigger and finish this, so he could leave and end this unbearable pain. But how could he let Ice die without some understanding of *why*...without feeling punished...without pain of his own?

And Garreth could think of only one thing that might humiliate Ice...losing. Someone *else* winning the power game and being one up.

Garreth lowered the gun. "No, not shoot you. That's too easy. Let's try a little game. You like games. When I said I wouldn't bring you across I lied. Because you don't need me. By drinking my blood you're already halfway there, a latent vampire. When you die, assuming it isn't by some method that destroys your nervous system, you'll reawaken a vampire. As Raven did."

The blood eye flamed. The ice one glinted. Both narrowed. "How do I know you're not lying now?"

Garreth laid the gun on the desk. "Well, you don't. That could be part of the game. The only way to find out for sure if I'm telling the truth is for you to die. So you have to decide if you want vampirism enough to have the guts to gamble. But...that isn't the game. You know Raven drank my blood, and now she's a vampire. So how much of a gamble would you be taking?"

Could trespassing kill a vampire? He felt as if he were dying by inches.

Blood and ice eyes stared intently at him.

Garreth fought not to double over with the pain, fought to talk, even breathe. "Let me assure you it's no gamble. The vampire is in you, just waiting to be born. I want you to know that because..." He lowered his voice, Bradshaw-like. "...while you *could* become a vampire, you never *will* be. I won't let you. You're so close, just a heartbeat away from undeath and all the power you crave, but whenever you die, wherever, however long I have to wait—time isn't anything to me—I'll be there to destroy you before you cross over. You took away something I wanted, Maggie Lebekov, so I'm going to make sure you never have what you want more than anything else in this world." He made his smile thin and cold before he brushed past Ice. "Have a nice life."

He almost hoped Ice would let him leave...let him escape this consuming pain! But, gritting his teeth against the inferno in him, he listened for a rush of footsteps behind him and the scrape of the gun being snatched up from the desk. Instead, another sound reached him...a ringing hiss of tempered steel leaving a scabbard.

Adrenaline blasted him with searing cold. The cavalry saber above the fireplace! He spun barely in time to dodge Ice's rush. But with another rush of adrenaline, he realized he had moved much slower than usual. Because of the pain? Was it affecting his reflexes enough to give Ice a real shot at him?

He can destroy you.

He cut around the desk to the middle of the room to give himself maneuvering space. Ice's arm length plus the sword far exceeded Garreth's reach. Garreth had only speed and strength on his side. Maybe. He sucked in a breath full of flame.

Ice stalked him, blood and ice eyes glittering. "Maybe I'll destroy you first. Beheading ought to do it, don't you think?" He swung the saber.

Garreth dodged. Barely. Almost stumbling.

Ice grinned. The false fangs gleamed. "I thought vampires are supposed to be fast." He swung again.

Garreth dodged...and found the blade meeting him. It slashed his sleeve just below the shoulder. Ice had only feinted.

"Touché." Ice saluted mockingly with his free hand. "Did you know I fenced in high school?"

The sword hissed through the air...missed Garreth's neck again as he dodged but slashed the other sleeve.

"Touché."

Pain made Garreth's feet feel leaden. If at some point it became impossible to distinguish between extreme heat and absolute cold, he thought he had reached it. Anger and fear, fire and ice, had all become one torment. How long could he endure this before nothing mattered but ending the torture?

Long enough to beat this bastard! Maggie's voice whispered. *Come on; you can do it, lover. Let go. Be all that you can be. Shred that dog shit for me!*

The mind rules.

Ice danced away, back toward him, away, then suddenly lunged, aiming at Garreth's throat. Garreth ducked under the thrust...popped up again before Ice could draw back, and swung backhand.

The blow felt clumsy but it connected. The Ice's head snapped around and he flew sideways into a leather chair.

The blood and ice eyes blazed. The mocking smile disappeared. Working his jaw, Ice climbed to his feet and circled Garreth, feinting first one way, then another, all the while keeping his arm too low for Garreth to duck under it, and driving Garreth backward.

Garreth!

It could have been either Lane or Maggie but he saw the albino's trap even without the warning. Ice intended to pin

him against the paneling. Instead of trying to duck out of the
trap, he gave before the dancing blade until his back met wood.
A big leather chair blocked him sideways on the right, a li-
brary-sized world globe on the left. He blinked, as if astonished to find himself trapped.

And a split second later, eyes coldly triumphant, Ice swung
the saber.

Garreth gathered the fire to him, stared it in the face...made
it himself. Now...or never. *He can destroy you.*

The blade angled down, clearly expecting Garreth to try
dodging by ducking. But Garreth sprang forward, and by the
time the blade reached him, he had reached its hilt. He caught
the sword by the guard and shoved upward. At the same time
he grabbed Ice by the throat, fingers locking around the adam's
apple. Ice's yell cut off in a gurgle.

Déjà vu. But without witnesses.

"All right, you've had your try at me. Now it's my game."

Squeezing, Garreth shoved, driving Ice backward. Ice
stumbled, choking, eyes blazing, free hand clawing at Garreth's
wrist. His lips pulled back as though to talk, but Garreth tightened his grip and the attempt became a wordless snarl. Ice
jerked his sword hand, trying to twist free. Garreth tightened
his grip still more. Cartilage crumpled between his fingers.
The blood and ice eyes bulged and Ice released the sword to
claw at Garreth's wrist with both hands, mouth gaping wide in
a vain struggle for air. His knees buckled.

Garreth dragged him the last few feet to the desk and
hoisted him back across the desk top...laid down the
sword...picked up the Desert Eagle and shoved the huge barrel in Ice's mouth.

The albino stared up at Garreth with eyes almost popping out of his head...disbelieving...terrified...and both
eyes looking bloody now as capillaries ruptured in them.
He tried clawing for the gun but with the oxygen supply to
his brain failing, had no strength and his fingers only waved
feebly.

"You lose," Garreth said before Ice lost consciousness. "Everything...both this life and your chance to be a real vampire. You die just a humbug." He aimed for the spine. "This is for Maggie."

Reichert had wondered what monsters she expected to run into that made her pack such a weapon. Meet one. The roar of fire around and in Garreth drowned out the sound of the shot, but Ice jerked in concert with the gun's recoil and beneath his head, blood spread out across the desk top.

Garreth stepped back to avoid it, laying the gun on Ice's chest. Other than glazing over, he noted, the albino's eyes looked about the same as in life...no less empty of humanity.

He picked up the sword again. "And this is to make sure that you never, ever hurt anyone again." Holding the saber two-handed, he slashed down with all his strength.

The head tumbled backward and plopped into the desk chair.

Way to go, lover! Was it as good for you as it was for me?

"Put a sock in it, Lane." He searched himself for satisfaction or guilt, but pain left no room for either.

Trying to pick up the sword again, Garreth discovered that the force of his blow had imbedded the blade in the desk top. He left it. Let the detectives working the case speculate about a killer strong enough to crush a larynx with one hand, then chop through a neck with that much force. If they looked at Garreth Mikaelian as a suspect, let them compare the skinny kid to this exhibition of strength and try to make him a credible fit.

One more thing to do. He opened the drawer where Ice kept the Desert Eagle. As he hoped, Maggie's billfold and badge case lay in it, too. He pocketed the badge case. That would go back to Martin, handed over privately, and whatever the official theory of what happened here, Martin would know the truth. Maybe he would bury the badge with Maggie's ashes.

"Rest in peace, Maggie."

You, too. It's a righteous kill.

Garreth checked his gloves. They looked clean. To be safe, though, he used his handkerchief to turn the bolts on the front door, so it was locked tight from the inside before he passed through. Closed windows, locked door, bloody homicide. This should be an interesting investigation. Too bad he was not going to risk coming anywhere in a hundred miles of it. Maybe they would find the body of the house sitter stashed somewhere in the grounds.

Disappearance of the fire felt as if the bones had been pulled from his legs. Garreth crashed to his hands and knees. He had to crawl to cross the terrace, then cling to the balustrade to keep from pitching down the steps on his face. Every inch of his body ached.

As he reached the bottom step he remembered the other two girls still in the house, but shook his head. They were going to have to fend for themselves. Judging by the pickpocket's quick retreat when he grabbed her purse, they would waste no time clearing out when they found Ice's body in the morning.

"Garreth?" Raven came tearing up the lawn. "Did I hear a shot?"

"Oh yeah." He tried releasing the balustrade and walking. But he succeeded only in staggering and almost falling.

Raven slid under his arm to hold him up. "Where did he get you?"

Belatedly he realized how he must look to her. "He didn't. I got him." He still felt neither satisfaction nor guilt, only weary relief. In this life his choices always seemed to be between evils. But maybe not this time.

Raven blinked in confusion. "But if you got him, why—"

He grimaced. "I entered a dwelling uninvited, remember?"

"But you ent—Oh." She sucked in a sharp breath. "You mean even after you were inside it felt like at the door of Lien's?"

He managed a short laugh. "Every. Single. *Fucking*. Second. Where's Amber?"

She gestured toward shrubbery near the gate. "I made her go to sleep."

"Help me down to her, then you go after the car."

By the time Raven came back, lying full length on the grass had leached away some of his weakness, but he still felt wrung out. He stripped off the blazer and rolled it up inside out with the gloves tucked inside. Somewhere away from the city he would dispose of it.

"Okay, you can drive this time. Just don't get us pulled over. Head back for the hotel." And while Raven stared in astonishment he sank into the passenger seat.

She handed Amber in to him. "Ice is really dead?"

He cradled the girl on his lap. "Truly dead. For ever-more."

Raven slid under the wheel and headed north. "What happens to *us* now? What happens to Amber?"

"She's latent, so she can choose whether she wants to be a vampire. Like a living will. As for the two of you..." Garreth sighed. Lord he felt terrible, as if he lay sprawled somewhere in the full midday sun without hat or glasses. "Good question. I'm not about to turn you loose. The both of you are accessories to Maggie's death and helped Ice run all those scams, and you attacked that deputy. Though you did a good thing for Becker."

Raven shrugged.

"I can hardly turn you over to the juvenile authorities, either..." And he had no more stomach for death. A righteous killing did not make his hands any less bloody. "So until we find a better solution, you two will have to put up with being in my custody." A sobering thought. He had been a rotten father to Brian. Could he do any better a second time around?

Raven nodded. "I deserve it." She pounded the wheel with a clenched fist. "I've been so *stupid!*"

She made it such an ultimate sin that Garreth felt compelled to say, "I hope not. Stupidity is incurable. Foolish, yes...headstrong...rebellious. Young."

The Cenotaph song ran through his head....*Lives enclosed by sunless spaces.* Abruptly he remembered the poem that "fell clutch of circumstance" came from: "Invictus." Grandma Doyle used to read it to Shane and him. How could he have forgotten that? *Out of the night that covers me...*

Raven said, "Do you believe in redemption?"

He glanced down at his hands clasped around Amber. "I hope it exists. We can all use some."

"My father believes in redemption."

"Well, he's living proof of it."

"I wish I could talk to him." Her voice trembled. "I wish I could go home. Can I ever?"

"Not the way you'd like. None of us can. But visits, yes, sure."

She stared through the windshield. "Maybe after I've learned more about me, stuff you haven't told me...like how you came in though that window without opening it." Raven paused. "Do you think I'll ever be able to tell my parents what I am now?"

He shrugged. "It depends. But I think anyone who's been Teddy Rivers can understand that living on the edge of hell doesn't necessarily make someone a demon."

She drove in silence for a while, then asked, "Where are we going?"

"After we check out of the hotel—yes it is the dead of night, but having recovered your little sister, we don't want to give her mother a chance to re-abduct her—we'll boogie for Des Moines...so I'll be hanging around the police station there when that carrion back there is found. Then...I think San Francisco again. It's a nice distance from all this and it's time for me to dispose of things I've had in storage there far too long. Lien will be good for Amber...though this time we'll definitely stay at Holle House to keep from hitting Harry over the head with who you two are."

Outside the car the nighttime city flowed by. Presently Raven said, "I think I'll call my folks from there. So they'll know I'm—well, sort of all right, and sorry about being such a butthead. And that I love them."

A stoplight ahead turned red. While Raven sat waiting for the green, Garreth considered "Invictus." Maybe he could find a little book of poetry with that in it and leave it for Raven to "discover." A better theme song than the Cenotaph tune. Something he might do well to remember, too. In his head Grandma Doyle's voice whispered the last verse: *It matters not how strait the gate/How charged with punishments the scroll/I am the master of my fate/I am the captain of my soul.*

Author's biography

Lee Killough has been storytelling almost as long as she can remember, starting somewhere around the age of four or five with making up her own bedtime stories. In grade school the stories became episodes of her favorite radio and TV shows: Straight Arrow, Wild Bill Hickock, Sergeant Preston of the Yukon, and Dragnet. Beating the episode-writing practice of Trek fans by almost two decades.

Then, in keeping with wisdom that says the golden age of science fiction is about age eleven, a pre-teen Lee discovered science fiction. Having read every horse book in the school and city libraries, and repelled by the "teenager" novels that seemed to be about nothing but high school and boyfriends, she was desperately hunting for something new to read. The science fiction being shelved next to the horse stories, she started leafing through these future/space stories and decided to try one. The book was Leigh Brackett's *The Starmen of Llyrdis* and...lightning struck. Love at first sight. But along with the pleasure of devouring this marvelous literature came fear. She lived in a small Kansas town with a small library and she could see that as with the horse books, all too soon the section would be read dry.

So she really began writing SF to make sure she never ran out of science fiction to read. And because the mystery section adjoined the SF section, leading her to discover mysteries about the same time as SF, her stories tended to combine SF with mystery.

They still do...with a noticeable fondness for cops (the influence of Dragnet, Joseph Wambaugh's books, and TV shows like Hill Street Blues). A ghost cop in *"The Existential Man"*, a vampire cop in *Blood Hunt* and *Bloodlinks*, published together in the trade edition *BloodWalk*, space-going cops, werewolf cops. And the future cops Janna Brill and Mama Maxwell of *Dopplegänger Gambit*, *Spider Play*, and *Dragon's Teeth*, published together in the trade edition *Bridling Chaos*. Her current work in progress, *Wilding Nights*, features a werewolf cop.

Lee lives and writes in Manhattan, Kansas (notice how Kansas and plains/prairie settings do turn up in her books), where she lives with a non-human—a Miniature Schnauzer—and enjoys a committed relationship with, fittingly, a book dealer.

An excerpt from Lee Killough's
werewolf detective novel:
Wilding Nights
(Summer 2002 from Meisha Merlin)

Tuesday, August 28

1.

The victim had been a young man with thick dark hair and brown eyes, possibly good looking, once well dressed. His death changed all of that. The mauling of his face left just one eye intact, and dislocated his jaw so that it gaped open as though in a last desperate scream. Below it, from neck to groin, his sport shirt, leather blazer, and trousers had been shredded on the way to ripping open his belly. Beneath the blind stare of empty windows he lay in fallen masonry and rubbish blown and carried into the fire-gutted warehouse, draped with the bloody tatters of cloth, flesh, and half-eaten loops of entrails.

Standing well back from the body so the two evidence techs could examine the area around it, Inspector Allison Goodnight eyed the carnage angrily. Of all the stupid, terminally irresponsible behavior...

"It's hard to believe a *human* did this," one of the ET's said as she photographed coins scattered off to the side of the body. "But those are sure as hell human footprints...and a tall dude judging by size of them."

Yes, Allison agreed grimly, the two sets of tracks leading up to the body, intermittently visible in the trash and weeds, looked wholly human...both the victim's, shod, and his bare-footed hunter. Clearer bare prints, long and narrow, overlaid

each other around the body, but those leading to a rear doorway had been mostly obliterated by the bag lady who came in
that way to investigate what she said had looked like a pile of
clothes. Allison eyed the hunter's tracks. Why go barefooted?
Shedding shoes that interfered with running, yes, but why not
leave on socks or stockings to hide foot details?

She closed her eyes and drew in a long breath, sorting
through the stew of odors around her: fish and brine carried in
from San Francisco Bay along with traces of diesel, the scent
of smoke that still lingered in the blackened bricks even after
four years, the rich organic smells of mud and pioneer plants
that had taken root in the derelict building, the pungent ones
of the body, and those of the evidence techs...skin, aftershave,
soap, deodorant, the powdered latex of their gloves. So many
scents. She opened her eyes, grimacing. Too many scents in
this confined space.

Outside, grocery cart wheels rattled away up the street.
The bag lady leaving, her verbal statement taken down.
Allison noted the fact without letting it break her concen-
tration.

Nor did the male voice that said, "Not much help there."

A second voice, that of her partner Zane Kerr, carried a
shrug. "At least she reported the crime instead of walking all
over the scene and picking the victim clean."

Which made the first speaker the uniformed officer secur-
ing the crime scene perimeter...Lindsay, his name tag said?

A second breath, deeper and slower than the first, confirmed the odor problem. She needed to be closer to the footprints for any hope of reading the hunter's scent.

Lindsay's voice rattled on. "And speaking of clean, Zane
my man...nice suit! Deserting Patrol for Homicide ain't gonna
disgrace Dryden's finest sartorially anyway. But I got to ask
whose desk you assed on to get stuck with the Ice Maiden and
a case like this right off."

She headed for the footprints at the building entrance. The
ET's had finished with that area.

"The thought was that since I've just come from Darling Division, my familiarity with the territory should help the investigation."

Now why had Kerr passed over his buddy's Ice Maiden comment and implied they were assigned the case? Trying to make brownie points with her? She had volunteered them for the call. Hugh Bass and Andy Trembecka were supposed to be catching today. And though she used the excuse Kerr repeated, it had actually been Bass's wry comment as he hung up the phone—*Hannibal the Cannibal must be in town. We have a chewed up body off Cutter with only human tracks around it.*"— that made her want the call. She had even been prepared to use her leverage as Lieutenant Garroway's recent partner if necessary. But Bass punted it with his blessing.

Some blessing. Still, better she work this case than anyone else.

Hitching up her slacks, Allison crouched beside a barefoot print not overlying the victim's. She scraped her left fingers down the print, picking up some of the mud, and sniffed them. It gave her just a whiff of scent. Not enough.

Movement in her peripheral vision made her look up. Lindsay and Kerr stared at her from the sidewalk outside, her partner looking all shoulders and flaming hair...the color brighter than ever against the dark hair and skin of the uniformed officer and lingering grey of fog in the street.

She stood, swearing at herself. The long partnership that had blinded Garroway to her quirks had made her complacent and careless. She'd better start watching herself. Kerr's expression contained that mixture of curiosity and fascination she caught on his face every time they worked out at the same time in the gym at the Police Training Center. After she turned down several invitations to have coffee with him, he never approached her again, and when she ran into him on homicides up here, he kept all conversation strictly professional, yet she always felt him watching her. Why? Had something about her triggered suspicion? She'd better keep his attention focused elsewhere.

"Start canvassing for witnesses. You know, the street people who might have been sleeping in here or close by last night."

Only when he turned away and headed across the street did she lower herself to the footprints again.

2.

Lindsay followed Zane under the yellow barrier tape and part way across the street, grinning. "You sure you got your marching orders straight now?"

Much as he liked Lindsay, Zane felt a flash of irritation. He kept it out of his voice. "Well, she *is* senior and the lead investigator."

And of course he should have starting looking for witnesses as soon as the bag lady left, but...he wished he could stay and watch Allison work. She and Garroway had racked up an astonishing record of solved cases...and this one certainly needed solving. No one should die the way this victim had.

He hardly believed his luck in becoming Allison's new partner. Aside from her investigative reputation, she had intrigued him from the first time he saw her in the police gym. Even subsequently meeting other officers of similar coloring and build—all cousins of varying degrees, he gathered, and most assigned to Darling Division—had not lessened his fascination. A smoky blonde sylph over six feet tall would have caught his eye in any case, but a curious sense of recognition and a kind of electricity crackling around her had transfixed him. Even thirty feet away from her, waiting his turn at the climbing wall, the hair on hisbody had prickled. Though sweat soaked her cropped hair, the way she ran effortlessly while male officers on adjoining treadmills strained to keep pace with her, Zane had found himself with the crazy notion she sweated from the effort of *restraining* herself. For the rest of his workout and driving home he had searched his memory for a clue why he felt he knew her.

Recognition came in the middle of the night, jerking him out of a dream and upright in bed. Of course. Tall, slim, elegant, fair, almost-silver eyes...she looked the way he always pictured Tolkien's Elves in *Lord of the Rings*.

And now he worked with her. But he wished he understood what she was doing. What did she expect to see in that footprint? Others had better detail. Or was sight the sense she used? Once as a uniformed officer at a crime scene, he'd heard Garroway say jokingly that the way she knew a guilty suspect as soon as she walked up to him, she must be psychic. She could be just very intuitive. Zane remembered his psychology class in college discussing the correlation between left hand/right-brain dominance and intuition/pattern perception/creativity, giving Leonardo DaVinci as a prime example. She took notes the way he read DaVinci had, too, writing backwards and right to left. Or maybe her talent was—what was the term for sensing details about people through touching things they touched? Psychometry. She had run her fingers along that footprint. It sounded fantastic, of course, but Zane hesitated to dismiss the possibility. Shakespeare wrote it: *There are more things in Heaven and Earth, Horatio, than you have dreamed in your philosophy.* And was it Spock who said that the universe would always be bigger and stranger than they could imagine?

Lindsay's grunt recaptured his attention. "Senior dick. Sounds weird. She doesn't look much older than you are."

"But she's been in Homicide as long as I've been on the job."

Lindsay nodded. "Me, too, and I've been here longer than you. It's like she went straight to Inspector from the academy." His brows arched. "Makes you wonder how."

The implication sharpened Zane's irritation but he only shrugged. "I'm more concerned with learning what brought our victim slumming up here and turned him into some psycho's midnight snack." He grimaced. "Wish me luck finding someone who wasn't blind and deaf last night."

As Lindsay returned to his post at the barrier tape, Zane finished crossing the street, eyeing the building facing him. The company had gone out of business and chained the doors years ago, but he knew runaways and street people found ways in. They must have heard or seen something last night. He just had to find one willing to talk.

A face peered out a ground floor window. It ducked down almost immediately, no doubt having spotted him, but not before Zane recognized it. "Blue! Blue, come here!"

Instead, footsteps pounded away inside. Grinning, Zane sprinted up the street and around the corner to the alley. Sometimes the flight impulse could be useful...certainly preferable to Blue going to ground inside, where even a squad of searchers might never find him. Zane ducked into the cover of a nailed-up doorway under a fire escape. When a scrawny figure in grimy, outsized desert camos dropped off the fire escape, Zane sprang for the shirt collar. "I thought the fire door up there might be how you're getting in and out."

Blue squealed as Zane's grip jerked him to a halt, then went instantly into a whine, cringing inside the shirt. "I ain't done nothin'."

Zane lifted a brow. "You mean if I turn out your pockets I won't find a crack pipe?" but before Blue went more defensive, or lapsed into sullen silence, he said, "But this time round all I want to do is ask what you saw or heard out in the street or in that building opposite last night."

For a heartbeat Blue paused. "I didn't see or hear nothin'." But his eyes twitched sideways behind the greasy hair falling over them, and in that heartbeat pause, he had shivered.

Zane prodded him toward the end of the alley. "Let's go talk to Inspector Goodnight."

3.

Crouched over the tracks again and leaning down within inches of them, Allison drew in a breath. There. Now she had it. After another breath, she sat back on her heels, grimacing angrily. Of course she expected scent to confirm what the body's condition told her of the hunter's identity, but a small wisp of hope had remained that she might smell a human here. She hated losing that hope. Despite their appearance, these tracks belonged to feet that had left the hominid mainstream well before humans ever became human. One of her people made them. A volke. Historical humans and modern mythology called them werewolves.

On the plus side, the scent told her none of the Dryden clan were responsible, nor anyone in the Bay Area. She smelled no trace elements from the local environment. She did, however, detect sex pheromones. The hunter was female, in estrus. *But who isn't?* Allison reflected wryly. Full moon coming; ditto the clan's Harvest Gathering...

She shook off the surge of anticipatory heat. The hunter must be young for the pheromones to linger this long, maybe twenty or twenty-one, in one of her early cycles. That or she had repressed her sex drive for a long period and built up its intensity. *Is that how you lured him here, cousin? Who are you? How dare you come into my territory and hunt like this.*

"It is creepy, isn't it?"

She glanced over at the ET making a cast of a barefoot print. "Excuse me?"

He pointed to the tracks. "Weren't you looking at those? Only toe prints of the victim's shoes—he's running for his life—but the killer's almost flat footed, just loping along behind him."

Taking her time...enjoying herself. With no regard for the danger to the local clan! The image of Great-grandmother

Thérèse flashed in Allison's head, sole survivor of a clan slaughtered after just such a killing betrayed their identity to the human villagers. Her jaw tightened. She would not let that happen here! "How soon before we have access to the body?"

"Any minute now. Call the ME."

As she returned her cell phone to her jacket pocket after the call, Lindsay laughed outside. "Good hunting, Detective Kerr."

Allison grimaced. She had hoped he would come back empty handed.

"I hope you don't have to put him on the stand, though."

That sounded better. The witness might be just as good as being empty handed.

"I didn't see nothin'," another voice whined.

Oh, he did sound like a prize. She stepped out onto the sidewalk to see for herself, and almost smiled. A prize indeed. He stank of unwashed skin, soiled clothing, and rotting teeth. She raised her brows at Kerr. "And this is…?"

He shrugged in apology. *Up here, what else can you expect,* the gesture said. "He's called Blue."

"Or sometimes Tweaker Blue," Lindsay said.

A crackhead. Very good. She switched her focus to him. "What can you tell us about last night?"

Blue shrank inside his shirt. "Nothin'!" A lie. She smelled his anxiety.

Kerr pulled his billfold from a hip pocket and fished out a twenty dollar bill.

Blue stared hungrily at it.

"There's a dead man in this building, torn apart." Kerr pulled the twenty between his fingers. "And you didn't hear him screaming, or see the guy chasing him?"

Blue licked his lips, watching every movement of the bill. "Okay…yeah…I heard him. And I seen him. But it wasn't no dude chasing him."

Kerr blinked and glanced into the warehouse. Thinking of the footprints?

She could not avoid the obvious question so she might as well ask it. "Who *was* chasing him?"

"Wasn't any *who*." Blue hunched his shoulders. "I seen this movie once about this giant dog running around in England killing people. This was like that. Like the biggest fucking cop dog ever...coal black, huge fangs, eyes like fire." The acid reek of his fear assaulted Allison, overpowering all other odors. His voice dropped to a whisper. "Straight outa fucking Hell."

Behind him, Lindsay's eyes rolled. Kerr looked thoughtful.

Allison kept her expression deadpan, contemplating damage control. She must not dismiss him so fast that it seem *too* fast...and lose information that might help *her* track the hunter. "What time was this?"

She saw Lindsay frown. Not believing she would waste time on the crackhead? Good.

Blue scowled. "Hell, how do I know. I don't have no watch. It was dark."

"Was the moon still up?"

The bill in Kerr's fingers crackled. Blue slid a glance toward it. "Maybe. Maybe just ready to go down." His voice returned to a whine. "That's all I know. Can I go?"

Kerr glanced at Allison. She waited a moment, sighed as though in frustration, and nodded.

Kerr handed him the twenty. "You ought to try buying food for a change." Watching Blue scurry away though the rag-tag group of on-lookers they had begun attracting, he shook his head. "The Hound of the Baskervilles. Not much help."

Lindsay's lip curled. "Tweaker. His brain's fried."

Tension eased in Allison. "A prime example why eye witnesses provide poor evidence." Though not in this case.

"But he did see the chase." Kerr glanced skyward. "I wonder what time the moon went down."

"I believe about twelve-thirty," Allison said. She had seen it set while out for a run with the rest of the household.

The medical examiner's wagon nosed through the on-lookers and halted at the yellow tape. An assistant ME swung out of the passenger side. "Morning, Inspector. What do you have today, and where?"

Allison pointed Dr. Pedicaris into the building.

Pedicaris looked Kerr over on the way. "I heard about Garroway's promotion to lieutenant and Homicide commander. That your new partner?" She gave Allison a wink. "Nice upgrade."

Allison and Kerr trailed her in, followed by two attendants with the stretcher.

"But I know that hair, don't I?" she said over her shoulder. "Haven't I seen it in uniform?"

"Only for the past eight years," Kerr said.

Pedicaris grinned at Allison. "You do need to break him of the sarcasm, though. Oh my." She stopped short near the body's feet, then circled it as she pulled on two pairs of surgical gloves. "This isn't one you want to come across on a full stomach, is it. Not much question about the cause of death anyway. He fought it. Defense wounds." She started to pick up a savaged hand, but the arm did not move. After feeling her way up the arm, she tried the joints of a leg. "Pretty advanced rigor."

"He died running for his life," Allison said.

"Oh, in that case..." Pedicaris shrugged. "Violent exertion depletes ATP in the muscles, brings rigor on faster, " she told one of the stretcher attendants. "Plus he looks in good physical shape...present condition aside. That speeds it up, too." Muttering under her breath, she continued her examination, poking fingers into the mutilated flesh, peering at loops of gut, taking the temperature of the air and body, peered under his clothes at the back of his shoulders and buttocks. Finally she straightened. "Okay...looks like he's lying where he died. Time of death roughly between eleven and three. His stomach's still intact so I'll be able to tell you the what and when of his last meal. Anything else you want to know right now other than my opinion that you should be ve-ry careful around this psycho when you find him?"

"Why more than usual?" Kerr asked.

"Because you might lose body parts. This guy has jaws I don't believe." Pedicaris stripped off both pairs of gloves. "He bit clear through that right radius and ulna, and through some ribs on the right."

The eyes of the evidence techs and stretcher attendants widened. Kerr smiled wryly at Allison. "Except for the footprints, that could almost make you believe in Blue's hound from Hell."

She stared back at him. "Except for the footprints."

As though the footprints had any relevance to what Blue saw. Shifting involved energy planes and perception, not shape changing, no matter how it felt and appeared. Her people had always known that from their footprints, long before the invention of photography proved it. What changed was the power output...like going supercharged, kicking into a hyper-adrenalin rush accessible on demand and sustained for as long as one wanted. It affected perception because the Shift created an enveloping energy field that registered on the brain as: *Big Powerful Dangerous Creature*...which the mind then perceived as a shape that fit the criteria for that individual. And from the cultures of the Russian steppes and Europe, Big Powerful Dangerous Creature had come to North America translated as...wolf.

Allison pulled on latex gloves. "We don't need a Hellhound to explain this. We've all witnessed or been on the receiving end of the phenomenal strength of subjects pumped on adrenalin or feeling no pain...psychotics...junkies high on PCP." Steering their thoughts that way should make biting through ribs and a forearm less astonishing. Fortunately the hunter had not gone for the upper arm, or a femur. Sitting down on her heels, she started through the dead man's pockets.

"Hellhound?" Pedicaris said.

"It's just what a local crackhead claims to have seen chasing the victim," Allison said. She turned out an intact pocket of the leather blazer and found a set of keys.

"A giant German Shepherd thing," Kerr said. "Coal black with huge fangs and blazing eyes."

Pedicaris cocked a brow. "But if it turned human in here, surely we're not talking Hellhound but werewolf."

Probably it had been inevitable that someone say the word. Allison kept bent over the body. "In either case, we're talking nonsense."

"Besides, it wasn't a full moon last night," Kerr said.

Allison smiled to herself. Oh, the glorious fallacies of myth. The moon had nothing to do with Shifting. It just intensified the hunting urge for the obvious reason that it provided good light to hunt by. "Kerr, glove up and help me here."

The blazer yielded the keys, a comb, a squirt tube of breath freshener, and a cell phone. Rolling the body up on its side, they found his hip pockets intact, too.

Kerr fished a billfold out of one. "At least we'll know who he is."

The billfold flipped open to a driver's license for one Alexander Vincent Demry, age thirty-one, of 1532 Isley. The physical description matched the victim. The photograph, of course, was more problematic.

While the stretcher attendants scooped Demry's remains into a body bag and hauled him off, Kerr carried the billfold outside and spread the contents on the hood of Lindsay's patrol unit. Since the keys included one for a BMW, Allison used the unit's computer to check for vehicle registrations in Demry's name. It came back on a silver BMW Z8. She had Dispatch issue an Attempt To Locate on the vehicle.

Kerr shook his head. "An Arbor Heights condo, a hundred grand sports car. Until last night Demry was doing all right in the world. But then, sharks usually do." He flipped out a business card in the billfold.

It declared Alexander Demry, J.D., a specialist in Trademark and Copyright Law for the law firm of Caffey, Schroer, Wagner, Wentz, and Glass.

Lindsay ticked his tongue. "I thought you'd got past the bitterness by now."

Why Kerr disliked attorneys interested Allison not in the least but she suspected Lindsay was about to tell her anyway.

Sure enough, he cocked a brow at her. "Divorce is really hell when your father-in-law is a lawyer and your soon-to-be ex is studying to—"

"Drop it, okay?" Kerr interrupted. "I'm sure Inspector Goodnight isn't interested in my marital tribulations."

Lindsay shrugged and went silent. Kerr finished emptying the billfold.

In addition to the driver's license and business cards, it held seventy dollars in cash; a couple of credit cards and gas cards; a medical plan card; Red Cross blood donor card; a packaged condom; and a card listing his blood type and the names and phone numbers of his doctor, dentist, and people to call in case of emergency...a John Glass with two local numbers, one matching the law firm number, and Richard and Julia Demry at area code 210.

Kerr frowned at the backs of the driver's license and Red Cross card. "He has the organ donor box checked and was one unit shy of being an eight-gallon blood donor. A shark with a social conscience."

"A good Boy Scout, too." Lindsay pointed at the breath freshener and condom. "He's prepared."

Allison bet Kerr, being unattached, packed protection, too. The condom and naming a firm partner to be called for emergencies told her Demry must lack a significant other. Leaving him vulnerable to sexual enticement?

She punched the law office number into her phone. Before making the effort to trace Demry's movements, she wanted him officially identified.

But the answering voice informed her Mr. Glass had not come in yet. She left her name, without mentioning Homicide, along with her phone number and a request for him to call as soon as possible.

Lindsay shook his head. "You want his boss to identify him? I don't think even his *mama* would know him."

Kerr tapped the dentist's name on the phone numbers card. "At least there are dental records to compare to the victim's teeth."

So they needed to contact the dentist and see about obtaining those records for the ME. Maybe a good job for Kerr? Allison ran through a mental checklist of other investigative tasks where he might learn something useful without discovering too much. There should be enough to keep him out of the way while she followed her own investigative lines.

She tossed him the keys. "Find a judge to sign a warrant and have a look through Demry's apartment for an address book." That should keep him occupied for a while. "I'm betting he usually carries an electronic organizer, but since it isn't on him, if he didn't lose it in the course of everything, maybe he left it home for the evening. We need names to contact about where he went last night. I'll stay here until the Crime Scene Unit finishes then catch a ride back to Market Street with them to pick up another car. I'll visit the dentist and take the lawyer down to the morgue for the identification."

Kerr nodded and headed for their car.

4.

Instead of heading straight to the court building, which along with Headquarters shared part of the Civic Center, Zane took the car around the block and west toward the bay, reflecting that the change of cars made a nice transfer perk. Impalas and Crown Victorias made up Patrol's fleet but Investigations drove Camaros. He fished his cell phone out of his coat pocket and punched in Homicide's number. Asking a favor of a new boss might be a bit presumptuous but...why not, in the interest of efficiency? They wanted to find this maniac as fast as possible.

Garroway sounded surprised when he came on the line. "Kerr? What's up?"

"Allison will be briefing you soon. It's...messy. But we have a tentative ID of the victim and keys to his apartment. Allison wants me to check it out for an address book, either paper or electronic, so we'll have the names of friends and acquaintances to interview. She asked me to ask if you can put a warrant in the works." Surely she meant to. It was faster than waiting until he arrived there. "I have a stop to make, then I'm on my way downtown." He had one place to check for Demry's car first.

"You'll have your warrant."

Whatever reason brought the victim up here, if he drove himself, chances were he had parked at the Hilst Basin. Their lot was well lighted and monitored by video cameras. The Basin might even have been Demry's destination. Though it served primarily small to medium commercial vessels, and the occasional freighter, it also had a few slips for pleasure boats. Not that Zane could see someone of Demry's affluence by-passing the comforts of the Bayview Yacht Club or even the less exclusive South Shore Marina for Hilst's utilitarian facilities, but he could have a friend with a tighter budget.

5.

Standing inside the barrier tape, Allison made eye contact with the on-lookers in one sweep. Since the removal of the body, the number had dwindled. "Were any of you in this area last night and see or hear anything?"

No one spoke up. A few heads shook. Two pairs of eyes skidded away from hers and their owners, both clearly street people, remembered other pressing business.

Allison brought their sneakaway to a halt with a piercing whistle. More witnesses were the last thing she wanted, but she needed the appearance of hunting for them. She crooked her finger. "Come back here."

Slowly, as though being dragged, the pair trudged back. She took them aside one at a time, but as she hoped, they denied knowing anything, and without pressing them, she let them go.

That charade over, she called Garroway to give him an edited-for-humans outline of the case.

"Kerr wasn't kidding about this being grim," he said when she finished.

Allison frowned. "When did you talk to *him*?"

"A few minutes ago when he called about getting a warrant for the victim's apartment. I'm surprise you didn't call yourself instead of having him ask for you."

Was that what he claimed. She frowned at the phone. Detective Kerr had more initiative than she wanted to see! "What worries me most about this case is what the media will do with it."

"Shit, yes. I think I'll have the Public Affairs office withhold any mention of cannibalism and the extent of mutilation." He paused. "Or have you had some of the press up there?"

"That's where we're lucky. They won't realize until too late there's a newsworthy body in the North Quay." Disconnecting, she stepped into the building and moved to a far corner where she could make her next call without being overheard. Then she punched in the number for her grandmother's studio at home. As not only household alpha but the Dryden clan chief, Honora had to be told about the hunter.

"We have a problem, Baba," she said when Honora picked up, and quickly gave her the story. "Does that description fit any outsiders you know of?" Newcomers in the area usually hunted up Honora as soon as possible in order to establish contact with the local clan. No one wanted isolation in a sea of humans.

Honora's voice came back calm but thoughtful. "Not off-hand. But if she came in with a household, I may have met only the alpha. And of course if we're dealing with a rogue, she'll be avoiding us. Another possibility, if this is a juvenile, is that she's experiencing her first Shifts somehow without adult supervision to restrain her and properly channel her hunting drive. I'll spread the word to all the alphas that anyone know-ing outsiders needs to contact you right away. In the mean-time, let me check my files and call you back with everything I have." Honora sighed. "This would happen now. I estimate we have until Thursday before everyone starts heading for the Gathering...possibly including our outsider. So you don't have much time to find her."

Not even until Thursday, Allison reflected. She dropped the phone back in her pocket, knots chasing through her gut. More than the clan leaving town, they had a moon waxing toward full on Sunday. If this hunter let it control her, her hunting drive would intensify every night. She could be counted on to kill again...and again. They had no grace time at all.

BloodWalk
ISBN 0-9658345-0-6 $14.00

Garreth Mikaelian, a dedicated police officer, runs into more than he counted on when he investigates a very peculiar murder. It leads him to Lane Barber—young, beautiful, hypnotic, and a vampire.

Now Garreth is a vampire also, but the books on the legends and lore of vampirism don't seem to help. How can he keep his job, his friends, and his humanity while battling another vampire in this new life?

How can he avoid being the hunted while hunting Lane Barber?

Now back in print are Lee Killough's *Blood Hunt* and *Bloodlinks*. Together for the first time in one volume:

BloodWalk

Bridling Chaos
ISBN 0-9658345-3-0 $19.00

The blonde chick and the bald dude are back... fighting crime and each other in the twenty-first century.

When detective sergeant Janna Brill's partner emigrated to a colony world, she expected a new partner. But not "Mama" Maxwell, the flamboyant oddball whose disregard for the rulebook has sent him up and down in rank more times than a yo-yo. A partner like this could ruin her career...or get her killed...as they investigate a trio of baffling cases.

In *The Doppelgänger Gambit* there is an apparent suicide that Mama believes is murder. The problem is that the chief suspect has an ironclad alibi. The giant computer that keeps track of all citizens hour-by-hour provides this suspect with that alibi. To nail the man, Mama would have to prove the computer wrong—and knock out the keystone of law and order for an entire country.

In *Spider Play* a vandalized hearse and corpse lead Janna and Mama on a twisted trail from a gang war on Earth...to a citadel of technology in space...to a heart-stopping race from a corporate army all too ready to kill to protect its secrets.

Finally in *Dragon's Teeth* thefts and murders are committed by a gang that penetrates and escapes at will through what should be impregnable security surrounding political fund-raisers. There are lots of witnesses—even videotape. There are lots of suspects—diplomats, drag queens, spies, scientists, artists, even robots. There are lots of clues—and they prove the crimes were impossible to commit...

For the first time published together in one volume are all three Janna Brill and Mama Maxwell science fiction mysteries—*The Doppelgänger Gambit*, *Spider Play*, and *Dragon's Teeth*.

Bridling Chaos

Come check out our web site for details on these Meisha Merlin authors!

Kevin J. Anderson

Robert Asprin

Robin Wayne Bailey

Edo van Belkom

Janet Berliner

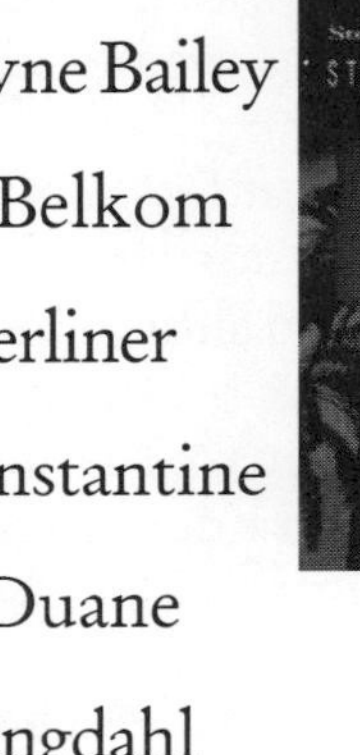

Storm Constantine

Diane Duane

Sylvia Engdahl

Jim Grimsley

George Guthridge

Keith Hartman

Beth Hilgartner

P. C. Hodgell

Tanya Huff

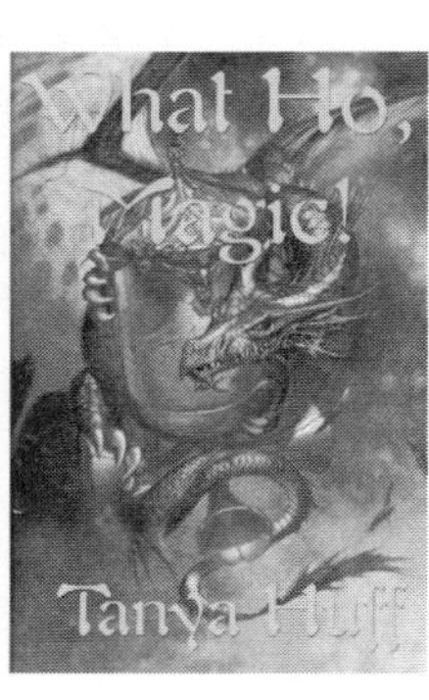

Janet Kagan

Caitlin R. Kiernan

Lee Killough

George R. R. Martin

Lee Martindale

Jack McDevitt

Sharon Lee & Steve Miller

James A. Moore

Adam Niswander

Andre Norton

Jody Lynn Nye

Selina Rosen

Kristine Kathryn Rusch

Pamela Sargent

Michael Scott

William Mark Simmons

S. P. Somtow

Allen Steele

Mark Tiedeman

Freda Warrington

http://www.MeishaMerlin.com